'It's a long climb to Heaven,' Chrestomanci observed. 'Is there anything you'd like to know on the way?'

'Yes,' said Thasper. 'Did you say the gods are trying to kill me?'

'They are trying to eliminate the Sage of Dissolution, which they may not realize is the same thing. You see, you are the Sage.'

'But I'm not!' Thasper insisted. 'The Sage is a lot older than me, and he asks questions I never even thought of until I heard of him.'

'Ah, yes,' said Chrestomanci. 'I'm afraid there is an awful circularity to this. It's the fault of whoever tried to put you away as a small child. As far as I can work out, you stayed three years old for seven years – until you were making such a disturbance in our world that we had to find you and let you out. But in this world of Theare, highly organized and fixed as it is, the prophecy stated that you would begin preaching Dissolution at the age of twenty-three, or at least in this very year.'

DIANA WYNNE JONES
MINOR ARCANA

CASSELL PLC

VISTA

First published in Great Britain 1996
by Victor Gollancz

This Vista edition published 1998
Vista is an imprint of the Cassell Group
Wellington House, 125 Strand, London WC2R 0BB

Copyright © Diana Wynne Jones 1996

The right of Diana Wynne Jones to be identified as author
of this work has been asserted by her in accordance with
the Copyright, Designs and Patents Act, 1988.

A catalogue record for this book is
available from the British Library.

ISBN 0 575 60191 4

Printed and bound in Great Britain by
Cox & Wyman Ltd, Reading, Berks

98 99   10 9 8 7 6 5 4 3 2 1

Contents

Contents

Introduction

These stories were written at intervals over a long period, but it so happened that, with the exception of 'The True State of Affairs', each time I had written one of them, someone asked me for a story for a collection. I began to feel positively precognitive.

The trouble is that the collection didn't always match the story. 'The Sage of Theare' started because I remembered, or thought I remembered, a story by Borges being read on the radio, in which a scholar arduously tracked down a learned man but never quite found him. I have never actually found that story either. If it exists, it behaves like its own plot. But years after I thought I remembered hearing it, I started having dreams about it – strange circular dreams in a strange city where gods took a hand – and the dream person never found the wise man he was looking for. In order to exorcise the dreams, I wrote the story. I was writing Chrestomanci books at the time, so the story fairly naturally included Chrestomanci too. While I was finishing it, Susan Schwartz asked me for something for a collection called *Hecate's Cauldron* and, with some doubts, I sent it to her. She used it and, to my dismay, it stuck out like a sore thumb. All the other stories were very female. Chrestomanci strides among them like a grasshopper in a beehive. His effect on the gods in the story is rather the same too.

'The Master' was another dream, or maybe a nightmare, which I dreamed more than once and had again to exorcise by writing it down. I know it is really part of the complex of ideas out of which *Fire and Hemlock* got written, but I couldn't explain how. It is of course about precognition. At that time, I was quite worried about the way most of my books came true at me after I had written them, but I am glad to say that the events in 'The Master' have (so far) not happened to me.

One rainy afternoon quite a long time later, I sat down and wrote 'The Girl Who Loved the Sun'. I had been thinking about all those Greek stories where women get turned into plants and animals, and I kept wondering *how* and *why*: *how* it felt to the person it happened to and *why* they let it happen. It seemed to me that nothing that radical could happen to someone without their personal consent and I wondered *why* one might consent. When I had done the first draft, I had two phone-calls. The first was from my sister who wanted to tell me she had been writing poems about women who were turned into plants and animals and asking much the same questions as I had (my sister and I seem to share trains of thought quite often); and the second was someone wanting a story about unhappy love. I sent this story, as doubtfully as I had earlier sent 'The Sage of Theare', because I was not sure it quite counted. But they said it did. You must see what you think.

Much earlier than all of these, while I was thinking out the multiplicity of alternate worlds that occur in *The Lives of Christopher Chant*, I wrote 'Dragon Reserve, Home Eight' almost by way of clarifying things. At that time, though, I was thinking of the worlds as rather like a wad of different coloured paper handkerchiefs. If you were to take that wad and crumple it in one hand, each colour would be separate, but wrapped in with the others. And I was also thinking of an enchanter's gifts rather more as inborn psychic talents. As so often happens, when I came to write the actual book a good four years later, everything turned out differently, and probably no one would realize this story had anything to do with it unless I told them. Again, I had just done a rather rough and unsatisfactory first draft when Robin McKinley asked me for a fantasy story. I sent this one, but she refused it on the grounds that it was not fantasy. This struck me as fair and reasonable, even though I knew it was going to be fantasy later.

I asked myself for a story with 'What the Cat Told Me'. When I wrote it, I was suffering cat-deprivation. I was brought up with cats and didn't have one at that time (this was four years ago, just before someone suddenly arrived and organized me a cat, so this one came true in a way). I love the exacting self-centredness of cats. The story is about that. Then I was asked to compile a collection of Fantasy Stories and I put this one in among the original selection, which I knew was going to be far too long. I mean, what can one *leave out* of a fantasy collection? My idea was to leave my own story out. But when it came to cutting the list down to publishable size, the editors, to my great surprise, insisted that this one stayed in. I was glad. It was fun to write.

It was even more fun to write 'nad and Dan adn Quaffy'. This one is a loving send-up of a well-known author whose writing I admire and read so avidly that I'm sure I know where a lot of it comes from. The idea for it came to me as I typed *nad* for *and* for the hundredth time, changed it, found it was now *adn*, reached for my coffee in frustration and idly realized – among other things – that this other writer did this too. Typos are a great inspiration. Depending on which side you hit the wrong key, *coffee* can be either *xiddaw* or *voggrr*, both of which are obviously alien substances that induce a state of altered consciousness. And yet again, when I was halfway through it, giggling as I wrote, I was asked for a story about computers.

By complete contrast, 'The True State of Affairs' is one of the first adult stories I wrote. It has an oddly learned origin. I had been reading *The Kingis Quair*, which is a true story by King James I of Scotland, about the time he was in prison.

Staring out from his cell, he fell in love (courtly love) with a girl he only ever saw in the distance. Of course it all stopped when he was released. It occurred to me to wonder what the girl felt about it, so I wrote the story. In the mid-sixties I sent it to an agent. In the early seventies, puzzled to have heard nothing, I went to see the agent. She gave it back to me untouched, explaining that she had not bothered to read it because no one wanted to read this fantasy sort of stuff. She thought I should give up writing. She did her honest best to discourage me. I am really no credit to her at all. When I took this story out of a drawer over a year ago, I was quite unrepentant, and I still think it well worth reading.

Diana Wynne Jones
Bristol, 1996.

The Sage of Theare

There was a world called Theare in which Heaven was very well organized. Everything was so precisely worked out that every god knew his or her exact duties, correct prayers, right times for business, utterly exact character and unmistakable place above or below other gods. This was the case from Great Zond, the King of the Gods, through every god, godlet, deity, minor deity and numen, down to the most immaterial nymph. Even the invisible dragons that lived in the rivers had their invisible lines of demarcation. The universe ran like clockwork. Mankind was not always so regular, but the gods were there to set him right. It had been like this for centuries.

So it was a breach in the very nature of things when, in the middle of the yearly Festival of Water, at which only watery deities were entitled to be present, Great Zond looked up to see Imperion, god of the sun, storming towards him down the halls of Heaven.

'Go away!' cried Zond, aghast.

But Imperion swept on, causing the watery deities gathered there to steam and hiss, and arrived in a wave of heat and warm water at the foot of Zond's high throne.

'Father!' Imperion cried urgently.

A high god like Imperion was entitled to call Zond Father. Zond did not recall whether or not he was actually Imperion's father. The origins of the gods were not quite so orderly as their present existence. But Zond knew that, son of his or not, Imperion had breached all the rules. 'Abase yourself,' Zond said sternly.

Imperion ignored this command too. Perhaps this was just as well, since the floor of Heaven was awash already, and steaming. Imperion kept his flaming gaze on Zond. 'Father! The Sage of Dissolution has been born!'

Zond shuddered in the clouds of hot vapour and tried to feel resigned. 'It is written,' he said, 'a Sage shall be born who shall question everything. His questions shall bring down the exquisite order of heaven and cast all the gods into disorder. It is also written—' Here Zond realized that Imperion had made him break the rules too. The correct procedure was for Zond to summon the god of prophecy and have that god consult the Book of Heaven. Then he realized that Imperion *was* the god of prophecy. It was one of his precisely allocated duties. Zond rounded on Imperion. 'What do you mean coming and telling me? You're god of prophecy! Go and look in the Book of Heaven!'

'I already have, Father,' said Imperion. 'I find I prophesied the coming of the Sage of Dissolution when the gods first began. It is written that the Sage shall be born and that I shall not know.'

'Then,' said Zond, scoring a point, 'how is it you're here telling me he *has* been born?'

'The mere fact,' Imperion said, 'that I can come here and interrupt the Water Festival shows that the Sage has been born. Our Dissolution has obviously begun.'

There was a splash of consternation among the watery gods. They were gathered down the hall as far as they could get from Imperion, but they had all heard. Zond tried to gather his wits. What with the steam raised by Imperion and the spume of dismay thrown out by the rest, the halls of Heaven were in a state nearer chaos than he had known for millennia. Any more of this, and there would be no need for the Sage to ask questions. 'Leave us,' Zond said to the watery gods. 'Events even beyond my control cause this Festival to be stopped. You will be informed later of any decision I make.' To Zond's dismay, the watery ones hesitated – further evidence of Dissolution. 'I promise,' he said.

The watery ones made up their minds. They left in waves, all except one. This one was Ock, god of all oceans. Ock was equal in status to Imperion and heat did not threaten him. He stayed where he was.

Zond was not pleased. Ock, it always seemed to him, was the least orderly of the gods. He did not know his place. He was as restless and unfathomable as mankind. But, with Dissolution already begun, what could Zond do? 'You have our permission to stay,' he said graciously to Ock, and to Imperion: 'Well, how did you know the Sage was born?'

'I was consulting the Book of Heaven on another matter,' said Imperion, 'and the page opened at my prophecy concerning the Sage of Dissolution. Since it said that I would not know the day and hour when the Sage was born, it followed that he has already been born, or I would not have known. The rest of the prophecy was commendably precise, however. Twenty years from now, he will start questioning Heaven. What shall we do to stop him?'

'I don't see what we can do,' Zond said hopelessly. 'A prophecy is a prophecy.'

'But we must do something!' blazed Imperion. 'I insist! I am a god of order, even more than you are. Think what would happen if the sun went inaccurate! This means more to me than anyone. I want the Sage of Dissolution found and killed before he can ask questions.'

Zond was shocked. 'I can't do that! If the prophecy says he has to ask questions, then he has to ask them.'

Here Ock approached. 'Every prophecy has a loophole,' he said.

'Of course,' snapped Imperion. 'I can see the loophole as well as you. I'm taking advantage of the disorder caused by the birth of the Sage to ask Great Zond to kill him and overthrow the prophecy. Thus restoring order.'

'Logic-chopping is not what I meant,' said Ock.

The two gods faced one another. Steam from Ock suffused Imperion and then rained back on Ock, as regularly as breathing. 'What did you mean, then?' said Imperion.

'The prophecy,' said Ock, 'does not appear to say which world the Sage will ask his questions in. There are many other worlds. Mankind calls them if-worlds, meaning that they were once the same world as Theare, but split off and went their own ways after each doubtful event in history. Each if-world has its own Heaven. There must be one world in which the gods are not as orderly as we are here. Let the Sage be put in that world. Let him ask his predestined questions there.'

'Good idea!' Zond clapped his hands in relief, causing untoward tempests in all Theare. 'Agreed, Imperion?'

'Yes,' said Imperion. He flamed with relief. And, being unguarded, he at once became prophetic. 'But I must warn you,' he said, 'that strange things happen when destiny is tampered with.'

'Strange things maybe, but never disorderly,' Zond asserted. He called the watery gods back and, with them, every god in Theare. He told them that an infant had just been born who was destined to spread Dissolution, and he ordered each one of them to search the ends of the earth for this child. ('The ends of the earth' was a legal formula. Zond did not believe that Theare was flat. But the expression had been unchanged for centuries, just like the rest of Heaven. It meant 'Look everywhere.')

The whole of Heaven looked high and low. Nymphs and godlets scanned mountains, caves and woods. Household gods peered into cradles. Watery gods searched beaches, banks and margins. The goddess of love went deeply into her records, to find who the Sage's parents might be. The invisible dragons swam to look inside barges and houseboats. Since there was a god for everything in Theare, nowhere was missed, nothing was omitted. Imperion searched harder than any, blazing into every nook and crevice on one side of the world, and exhorting the moon goddess to do the same on the other side.

And nobody found the Sage. There were one or two false alarms, such as when a household goddess reported an infant that never stopped crying. This baby, she said, was driving her up the wall and, if this was not Dissolution, she would like to know what was. There were also several reports of infants born with teeth, or six fingers, or suchlike strangeness. But, in each case, Zond was able to prove that the child had nothing to do with Dissolution. After a month, it became clear that the infant Sage was not going to be found.

Imperion was in despair, for, as he had told Zond, order meant more to him than to any other god. He became so worried that he was actually causing the sun to lose heat. At length, the goddess of love advised him to go off and relax with a mortal woman before he brought about Dissolution himself. Imperion saw she was right. He went down to visit the human woman he had loved for some years. It was established custom for gods to love mortals. Some visited their loves in all sorts of fanciful shapes, and some had many loves at once. But Imperion was both honest and faithful. He never visited Nestara as anything but a handsome man, and he loved her devotedly. Three years ago, she had borne him a son, whom Imperion loved almost as much as he loved Nestara. Before the Sage was born to trouble him, Imperion had been trying to bend the rules of Heaven a little, to get his son approved as a god too.

The child's name was Thasper. As Imperion descended to earth, he could see Thasper digging in some sand outside Nestara's house – a beautiful child, fair-haired and blue-eyed.

Imperion wondered fondly if Thasper was talking properly yet. Nestara had been worried about how slow he was learning to speak.

Imperion alighted beside his son. 'Hello, Thasper. What are you digging so busily?'

Instead of answering, Thasper raised his golden head and shouted. 'Mum!' he yelled. 'Why does it go bright when Dad comes?'

All Imperion's pleasure vanished. Of course no one could ask questions until he had learned to speak. But it would be too cruel if his own son turned out to be the Sage of Dissolution. 'Why shouldn't it go bright?' he asked defensively.

Thasper scowled up at him. 'I want to know. *Why* does it?'

'Perhaps because you feel happy to see me,' Imperion suggested.

'I'm not happy,' Thasper said. His lower lip came out. Tears filled his big blue eyes. 'Why does it go bright? I want to *know*. Mum! I'm not happy!'

Nestara came racing out of the house, almost too concerned to smile at Imperion. 'Thasper love, what's the matter?'

'I want to *know*!' wailed Thasper.

'What do you want to know? I've never known such an enquiring mind,' Nestara said proudly to Imperion, as she picked Thasper up. 'That's why he was so slow talking. He wouldn't speak until he'd found out how to ask questions. And if you don't give him an exact answer, he'll cry for hours.'

'When did he first start asking questions?' Imperion inquired tensely.

'About a month ago,' said Nestara.

This made Imperion truly miserable, but he concealed it. It was clear to him that Thasper was indeed the Sage of Dissolution and he was going to have to take him away to another world. He smiled and said, 'My love, I have wonder-

ful news for you. Thasper has been accepted as a god. Great
Zond himself will have him as cupbearer.'

'Oh not now!' cried Nestara. 'He's so little!'

She made numerous other objections too. But, in the end,
she let Imperion take Thasper. After all, what better future
could there be for a child? She put Thasper into Imperion's
arms with all sorts of anxious advice about what he ate and
when he went to bed. Imperion kissed her goodbye, heavy-
hearted. He was not a god of deception. He knew he dared not
see her again for fear he told her the truth.

Then, with Thasper in his arms, Imperion went up to the
middle-regions below Heaven, to look for another world.

Thasper looked down with interest at the great blue curve
of the world. 'Why—?' he began.

Imperion hastily enclosed him in a sphere of forgetfulness.
He could not afford to let Thasper ask things here. Questions
that spread Dissolution on earth would have an even more
powerful effect in the middle-region. The sphere was a silver
globe, neither transparent nor opaque. In it, Thasper would
stay seemingly asleep, not moving and not growing, until the
sphere was opened. With the child thus safe, Imperion hung
the sphere from one shoulder and stepped into the next-door
world.

He went from world to world. He was pleased to find there
were an almost infinite number of them, for the choice proved
supremely difficult. Some worlds were so disorderly that he
shrank from leaving Thasper in them. In some, the gods
resented Imperion's intrusion and shouted at him to be off. In
others, it was mankind that was resentful. One world he came
to was so rational that, to his horror, he found the gods were
dead. There were many others he thought might do, until he
let the spirit of prophecy blow through him, and in each case
this told him that harm would come to Thasper here. But at
last he found a good world. It seemed calm and elegant. The

few gods there seemed civilized but casual. Indeed, Imperion was a little puzzled to find that these gods seemed to share quite a lot of their power with mankind. But mankind did not seem to abuse this power, and the spirit of prophecy assured him that, if he left Thasper here inside his sphere of forgetfulness, it would be opened by someone who would treat the boy well.

Imperion put the sphere down in a wood and sped back to Theare, heartily relieved. There, he reported what he had done to Zond, and all Heaven rejoiced. Imperion made sure that Nestara married a very rich man who gave her not only wealth and happiness but plenty of children to replace Thasper. Then, a little sadly, he went back to the ordered life of Heaven. The exquisite organization of Theare went on untroubled by Dissolution.

Seven years passed.

All that while, Thasper knew nothing and remained three years old. Then one day, the sphere of forgetfulness fell in two halves and he blinked in sunlight somewhat less golden than he had known.

'So that's what was causing all the disturbance,' a tall man murmured.

'Poor little soul!' said a lady.

There was a wood around Thasper, and people standing in it looking at him, but, as far as Thasper knew, nothing had happened since he soared to the middle-region with his father. He went on with the question he had been in the middle of asking. 'Why is the world round?' he said.

'Interesting question,' said the tall man. 'The answer usually given is because the corners wore off spinning around the sun. But it could be designed to make us end where we began.'

'Sir, you'll muddle him, talking like that,' said another lady. 'He's only little.'

'No, he's interested,' said another man. 'Look at him.'

Thasper was indeed interested. He approved of the tall man. He was a little puzzled about where he had come from, but he supposed the tall man must have been put there because he answered questions better than Imperion. He wondered where Imperion had got to. 'Why aren't you my Dad?' he asked the tall man.

'Another most penetrating question,' said the tall man. 'Because, as far as we can find out, your father lives in another world. Tell me your name.'

This was another point in the tall man's favour. Thasper never answered questions: he only asked them. But this was a command. The tall man understood Thasper. 'Thasper,' Thasper answered obediently.

'He's sweet!' said the first lady. 'I want to adopt him.' To which the other ladies gathered around most heartily agreed.

'Impossible,' said the tall man. His tone was mild as milk and rock firm. The ladies were reduced to begging to be able to look after Thasper for a day, then. An hour. 'No,' the tall man said mildly. 'He must go back at once.' At which all the ladies cried out that Thasper might be in great danger in his own home. The tall man said, 'I shall take care of that, of course.' Then he stretched out a hand and pulled Thasper up. 'Come along, Thasper.'

As soon as Thasper was out of it, the two halves of the sphere vanished. One of the ladies took his other hand and he was led away, first on a jiggly ride, which he much enjoyed, and then into a huge house, where there was a very perplexing room. In this room, Thasper sat in a five-pointed star and pictures kept appearing around him. People kept shaking their heads. 'No, not that world either.' The tall man answered all Thasper's questions, and Thasper was too interested even to be annoyed when they would not allow him anything to eat.

'Why not?' he said.

'Because, just by being here, you are causing the world to jolt about,' the tall man explained. 'If you put food inside you, food is a heavy part of this world, and it might jolt you to pieces.'

Soon after that, a new picture appeared. Everyone said 'Ah!' and the tall man said, 'So it's Theare!' He looked at Thasper in a surprised way. 'You must have struck someone as disorderly,' he said. Then he looked at the picture again, in a lazy, careful kind of way. 'No disorder,' he said. 'No danger. Come with me.'

He took Thasper's hand again and led him into the picture. As he did so, Thasper's hair turned much darker. 'A simple precaution,' the tall man murmured, a little apologetically, but Thasper did not even notice. He was not aware what colour his hair had been to start with, and besides, he was taken up with surprise at how fast they were going. They whizzed into a city, and stopped abruptly. It was a good house, just on the edge of a poorer district. 'Here is someone who will do,' the tall man said, and he knocked at the door.

A sad-looking lady opened the door.

'I beg your pardon, madam,' said the tall man. 'Have you by any chance lost a small boy?'

'Yes,' said the lady. 'But this isn't—' She blinked, 'Yes it *is*!' she cried out. 'Oh Thasper! How could you run off like that? Thank you so much, sir.' But the tall man had gone.

The lady's name was Alina Altun, and she was so convinced that she was Thasper's mother that Thasper was soon convinced too. He settled in happily with her and her husband, who was a doctor, hard-working but not very rich. Thasper soon forgot the tall man, Imperion and Nestara. Sometimes it did puzzle him – and his new mother too – that when she showed him off to her friends she always felt bound to say, 'This is Badien, but we always call him Thasper.'

Thanks to the tall man, none of them ever knew that the real Badien had wandered away the day Thasper came and fell in the river, where an invisible dragon ate him.

If Thasper had remembered the tall man, he might also have wondered why his arrival seemed to start Dr Altun on the road to prosperity. The people in the poorer district nearby suddenly discovered what a good doctor Dr Altun was, and how little he charged. Alina was shortly able to afford to send Thasper to a very good school, where Thasper often exasperated his teachers by his many questions. He had, as his new mother often proudly said, a most enquiring mind. Although he learned quicker than most the Ten First Lessons and the Nine Graces of Childhood, his teachers were nevertheless often annoyed enough to snap, 'Oh, go and ask an invisible dragon!' which is what people in Theare often said when they thought they were being pestered.

Thasper did, with difficulty, gradually cure himself of his habit of never answering questions. But he always preferred asking to answering. At home, he asked questions all the time: 'Why does the kitchen god go and report to Heaven once a year? Is it so I can steal biscuits? Why are invisible dragons? Is there a god for everything? Why is there a god for everything? If the gods make people ill, how can Dad cure them? Why must I have a baby brother or sister?'

Alina Altun was a good mother. She most diligently answered all these questions, including the last. She told Thasper how babies were made, ending her account with, 'Then, if the gods bless my womb, a baby will come.' She was a devout person.

'I don't want you to be blessed!' Thasper said, resorting to a statement, which he only did when he was strongly moved.

He seemed to have no choice in the matter. By the time he was ten years old, the gods had thought fit to bless him with two brothers and two sisters. In Thasper's opinion, they were, as blessings, very low grade. They were just too young to be any use. 'Why can't they be the same age as me?' he demanded, many times. He began to bear the gods a small but definite grudge about this.

Dr Altun continued to prosper and his earnings more than kept pace with his family. Alina employed a nursemaid, a cook and a number of rather impermanent houseboys. It was one of these houseboys who, when Thasper was eleven, shyly presented Thasper with a folded square of paper. Wondering, Thasper unfolded it. It gave him a curious feeling to touch, as if the paper was vibrating a little in his fingers. It also gave out a very strong warning that he was not to mention it to anybody. It said:

> Dear Thasper,
>   Your situation is an odd one. Make sure that
> you call me at the moment when you come face to
> face with yourself. I shall be watching and I will
> come at once.
>   Yrs,
>   Chrestomanci

Since Thasper by now had not the slightest recollection of his early life, this letter puzzled him extremely. He knew he was not supposed to tell anyone about it, but he also knew that this did not include the houseboy. With the letter in his hand, he hurried after the houseboy to the kitchen.

He was stopped at the head of the kitchen stairs by a tremendous smashing of china from below. This was followed immediately by the cook's voice raised in nonstop abuse. Thasper knew it was no good trying to go into the kitchen. The houseboy – who went by the odd name of Cat – was in the process of getting fired, like all the other houseboys before him. He had better go and wait for Cat outside the back door. Thasper looked at the letter in his hand. As he did so, his fingers tingled. The letter vanished.

'It's gone!' he exclaimed, showing by this statement how astonished he was. He never could account for what he did next. Instead of going to wait for the houseboy, he ran to the living-room, intending to tell his mother about it, in spite of the warning. 'Do you know what?' he began. He had invented this meaningless question so that he could tell people things and still make it into an enquiry. 'Do you know what?' Alina looked up. Thasper, though he fully intended to tell her about the mysterious letter, found himself saying, 'The cook's just sacked the new houseboy.'

'Oh bother!' said Alina. 'I shall have to find another one now.'

Annoyed with himself, Thasper tried to tell her again. 'Do you know what? I'm surprised the cook doesn't sack the kitchen god too.'

'Hush dear. Don't talk about the gods that way!' said the devout lady.

By this time, the houseboy had left and Thasper lost the urge to tell anyone about the letter. It remained with him as his own personal exciting secret. He thought of it as The Letter From A Person Unknown. He sometimes whispered the strange name of The Person Unknown to himself when no one could hear. But nothing ever happened, even when he said the name out loud. He gave up doing that after a while. He had other things to think about. He became fascinated by Rules, Laws and Systems.

Rules and Systems were an important part of the life of mankind in Theare. It stood to reason, with Heaven so well organized. People codified all behaviour into things like the Seven Subtle Politenesses, or the Hundred Roads to Godliness. Thasper had been taught these things from the time he was three years old. He was accustomed to hearing Alina argue the niceties of the Seventy-Two Household Laws with her friends. Now Thasper suddenly discovered for himself that all Rules made a magnificent framework for one's mind to clamber about in. He made lists of rules, and refinements on rules, and possible ways of doing the opposite of what the rules said while still keeping the rules. He invented new codes of rules. He filled books and made charts. He invented games with huge and complicated rules, and played them with his friends. Onlookers found these games both rough and muddled, but Thasper and his friends revelled in them. The best moment in any game was when somebody stopped playing and shouted, 'I've thought of a new rule!'

This obsession with rules lasted until Thasper was fifteen. He was walking home from school one day, thinking over a list of rules for Twenty Fashionable Hairstyles. From this, it will be seen that Thasper was noticing girls, though none of the girls had so far seemed to notice him. And he was thinking which girl should wear which hairstyle, when his attention was caught by words chalked on a wall:

> IF RULES MAKE A FRAMEWORK FOR THE MIND TO
> CLIMB ABOUT IN, WHY SHOULD THE MIND NOT
> CLIMB RIGHT OUT? SAYS THE SAGE OF DISSOLUTION.

That same day, there was consternation again in Heaven. Zond summoned all the high gods to his throne. 'The Sage of Dissolution has started to preach,' he announced direfully. 'Imperion, I thought you got rid of him.'

'I thought I did,' Imperion said. He was even more appalled than Zond. If the Sage had started to preach, it meant that Imperion had got rid of Thasper and deprived himself of Nestara quite unnecessarily. 'I must have been mistaken,' he admitted.

Here Ock spoke up, steaming gently. 'Father Zond,' he said, 'may I respectfully suggest that you deal with the Sage yourself, so that there will be no mistake this time?'

'That was just what I was about to suggest,' Zond said gratefully. 'Are you all agreed?'

All the gods agreed. They were too used to order to do otherwise.

As for Thasper, he was staring at the chalked words, shivering to the soles of his sandals. What was this? Who was using his own private thoughts about rules? Who was this Sage of Dissolution? Thasper was ashamed. He, who was so good at asking questions, had never thought of asking this one. Why should one's mind not climb right out of the rules, after all?

He went home and asked his parents about the Sage of Dissolution. He fully expected them to know. He was quite agitated when they did not. But they had a neighbour, who sent Thasper to another neighbour, who had a friend, who, when Thasper finally found his house, said he had heard that the Sage was a clever young man who made a living by mocking the gods.

The next day, someone had washed the words off. But the day after that, a badly printed poster appeared on the same wall.

THE SAGE OF DISSOLUTION ASKS BY WHOSE ORDER IS ORDER ANYWAY?? COME TO SMALL UNCTION SUBLIME CONCERT HALL TONITE 6:30.

At 6:20, Thasper was having supper. At 6:24, he made up his mind and left the table. At 6:32 he arrived panting at Small Unction Hall. It proved to be a small shabby building quite near where he lived. Nobody was there. As far as Thasper could gather from the grumpy caretaker, the meeting had been the night before. Thasper turned away, deeply disappointed. Who ordered the order was a question he now longed to know the answer to. It was deep. He had a notion that the man who called himself the Sage of Dissolution was truly brilliant.

By way of feeding his own disappointment, he went to school the next day by a route which took him past the Small Unction Concert Hall. It had burnt down in the night. There were only blackened brick walls left. When he got to school, a number of people were talking about it. They said it had burst into flames just before 7:00 the night before.

'Did you know,' Thasper said, 'that the Sage of Dissolution was there the day before yesterday?'

That was how he discovered he was not the only one interested in the Sage. Half his class were admirers of Dissolution. That, too, was when the girls deigned to notice him. 'He's amazing about the gods,' one girl told him. 'No one ever asked questions like that before.' Most of the class, however, girls and boys alike, only knew a little more than Thasper, and most of what they knew was second-hand. But a boy showed him a carefully cut-out newspaper article in which a well-known scholar discussed what he called 'The so-called Doctrine of Dissolution.' It said, long-windedly, that the Sage and his followers were rude to the gods and against all the rules. It did not tell Thasper much, but it was something. He saw, rather ruefully, that his obsession with rules had been quite wrong-headed and had, into the bargain, caused him to fall behind the rest of his class in learning of this wonderful new Doctrine. He became a Disciple of Dissolution on the spot. He joined the rest of his class in finding out all they could about the Sage. He went round with them, writing up on walls

DISSOLUTION RULES OK.

For a long while after that, the only thing any of Thasper's class could learn of the Sage were scraps of questions chalked on walls and quickly rubbed out.

WHAT NEED OF PRAYER? WHY SHOULD THERE BE A
HUNDRED ROADS TO GODLINESS, NOT MORE OR LESS?
DO WE CLIMB ANYWHERE ON THE STEPS TO HEAVEN?
WHAT IS PERFECTION: A PROCESS OR A STATE? WHEN WE
CLIMB TO PERFECTION IS THIS A MATTER FOR THE GODS?

Thasper obsessively wrote all these sayings down. He was
obsessed again, he admitted, but this time it was in a new way.
He was thinking, thinking. At first, he thought simply of
clever questions to ask the Sage. He strained to find questions
no one had asked before. But in the process, his mind seemed
to loosen, and shortly he was thinking of how the Sage might
answer his questions. He considered order and rules and
Heaven, and it came to him that there was a reason behind all
the brilliant questions the Sage asked. He felt light-headed
with thinking.

The reason behind the Sage's questions came to him the
morning he was shaving for the first time. He thought, *The
gods need human beings in order to be gods!* Blinded with this
revelation, Thasper stared into the mirror at his own face half
covered with white foam. Without humans believing in them,
gods were nothing! The order of Heaven, the rules and codes
of earth, were all only there because of people! It was
transcendent. As Thasper stared, the letter from the Unknown
came into his mind. 'Is this being face to face with myself?' he
said. But he was not sure. And he became sure that when that
time came, he would not have to wonder.

Then it came to him that the Unknown Chrestomanci was
almost certainly the Sage himself. He was thrilled. The Sage
was taking a special mysterious interest in one teenage boy,
Thasper Altun. The vanishing letter exactly fitted the elusive
Sage.

The Sage continued elusive. The next firm news of him was
a newspaper report of the Celestial Gallery being struck by
lightning. The roof of the building collapsed, said the report,

'only seconds after the young man known as the Sage of Dissolution had delivered another of his anguished and self-doubting homilies and left the building with his disciples.'

'He's not self-doubting,' Thasper said to himself. 'He knows about the gods. If *I* know, then *he* certainly does.'

He and his classmates went on a pilgrimage to the ruined gallery. It was a better building than Small Unction Hall. It seemed the Sage was going up in the world.

Then there was enormous excitement. One of the girls found a small advertisement in a paper. The Sage was to deliver another lecture, in the huge Kingdom of Splendour Hall. He had gone up in the world again. Thasper and his friends dressed in their best and went there in a body. But it seemed as if the time for the lecture had been printed wrong. The lecture was just over. People were streaming away from the Hall, looking disappointed.

Thasper and his friends were still in the street when the Hall blew up. They were lucky not to be hurt. The Police said it was a bomb. Thasper and his friends helped drag injured people clear of the blazing Hall. It was exciting, but it was not the Sage.

By now, Thasper knew he would never be happy until he had found the Sage. He told himself that he had to know if the reason behind the Sage's questions was the one he thought. But it was more than that. Thasper was convinced that his fate was linked to the Sage's. He was certain the Sage *wanted* Thasper to find him.

But there was now a strong rumour in school and around town that the Sage had had enough of lectures and bomb attacks. He had retired to write a book. It was to be called *Questions of Dissolution*. Rumour also had it that the Sage was in lodgings somewhere near the Road of the Four Lions.

Thasper went to the Road of the Four Lions. There he was shameless. He knocked on doors and questioned passers-by.

He was told several times to go and ask an invisible dragon, but he took no notice. He went on asking until someone told him that Mrs Tunap at No. 403 might know. Thasper knocked at No. 403, with his heart thumping.

Mrs Tunap was a rather prim lady in a green turban. 'I'm afraid not, dear,' she said. 'I'm new here.' But before Thasper's heart could sink too far, she added, 'But the people before me had a lodger. A very quiet gentleman. He left just before I came.'

'Did he leave an address?' Thasper asked, holding his breath.

Mrs Tunap consulted an old envelope pinned to the wall in her hall. 'It says here, "Lodger gone to Golden Heart Square", dear.'

But in Golden Heart Square, a young gentleman who might have been the Sage had only looked at a room and gone. After that, Thasper had to go home. The Altuns were not used to teenagers and they worried about Thasper suddenly wanting to be out every evening.

Oddly enough, No. 403 Road of the Four Lions burnt down that night.

Thasper saw clearly that assassins were after the Sage as well as he was. He became more obsessed with finding him than ever. He knew he could rescue the Sage if he caught him before the assassins did. He did not blame the Sage for moving about all the time.

Move about the Sage certainly did. Rumour had him next in Partridge Pleasaunce Street. When Thasper tracked him there, he found the Sage had moved to Fauntel Square. From Fauntel Square, the Sage seemed to move to Strong Wind Boulevard, and then to a poorer house in Station Street. There were many places after that. By this time, Thasper had developed a nose, a sixth sense, for where the Sage might be.

A word, a mere hint about a quiet lodger, and Thasper was off, knocking on doors, questioning people, being told to ask an invisible dragon, and bewildering his parents by the way he kept rushing off every evening. But, no matter how quickly Thasper acted on the latest hint, the Sage had always just left. And Thasper, in most cases, was only just ahead of the assassins. Houses caught fire or blew up, sometimes when he was still in the same street.

At last he was down to a very poor hint, which might or might not lead to New Unicorn Street. Thasper went there, wishing he did not have to spend all day at school. The Sage could move about as he pleased, and Thasper was tied down all day. No wonder he kept missing him. But he had high hopes of New Unicorn Street. It was the poor kind of place that the Sage had been favouring lately.

Alas for his hopes. The fat woman who opened the door laughed rudely in Thasper's face. 'Don't bother me, son! Go and ask an invisible dragon!' And she slammed the door again.

Thasper stood in the street, keenly humiliated. And not even a hint of where to look next. Awful suspicions rose in his mind: he was making a fool of himself; he had set himself a wild goose chase; the Sage did not exist. In order not to think of these things, he gave way to anger. 'All right!' he shouted at the shut door. 'I *will* ask an invisible dragon! So there!' And, carried by his anger, he ran down to the river and out across the nearest bridge.

He stopped in the middle of the bridge, leaning on the parapet, and knew he was making an utter fool of himself. There were no such things as invisible dragons. He was sure of that. But he was still in the grip of his obsession, and this was something he had set himself to do now. Even so, if there had been anyone about near the bridge, Thasper would have gone away. But it was deserted. Feeling an utter fool, he made the prayer-sign to Ock, Ruler of Oceans – for Ock was the god in charge of all things to do with water – but he made the sign secretly, down under the parapet, so there was no chance of anyone seeing. Then he said, almost in a whisper, 'Is there an invisible dragon here? I've got something to ask you.'

Drops of water whirled over him. Something wetly fanned his face. He heard the something whirring. He turned his face that way and saw three blots of wet in a line along the parapet, each about two feet apart and each the size of two of his hands spread out together. Odder still, water was dripping out of nowhere all along the parapet, for a distance about twice as long as Thasper was tall.

Thasper laughed uneasily. 'I'm imagining a dragon,' he said. 'If there was a dragon, those splotches would be the places where its body rests. Water dragons have no feet. And the length of the wetness suggests I must be imagining it about eleven feet long.'

'I am fourteen feet long,' said a voice out of nowhere. It was rather too near Thasper's face for comfort and blew fog at him. He drew back. 'Make haste, child-of-a-god,' said the voice. 'What did you want to ask me?'

'I–I–I—' stammered Thasper. It was not just that he was scared. This was a body-blow. It messed up utterly his notions about gods needing men to believe in them. But he pulled himself together. His voice only cracked a little as he said, 'I'm looking for the Sage of Dissolution. Do you know where he is?'

The dragon laughed. It was a peculiar noise, like one of those water-warblers people make bird noises with. 'I'm afraid I can't tell you precisely where the Sage is,' the voice out of nowhere said. 'You have to find him for yourself. Think about it, child-of-a-god. You must have noticed there's a pattern.'

'Too right, there's a pattern!' Thasper said. 'Everywhere he goes, I just miss him, and then the place catches fire!'

'That too,' said the dragon. 'But there's a pattern to his lodgings too. Look for it. That's all I can tell you, child-of-a-god. Any other questions?'

'No – for a wonder,' Thasper said. 'Thanks very much.'

'You're welcome,' said the invisible dragon. 'People are always telling one another to ask us, and hardly anyone does. I'll see you again.' Watery air whirled in Thasper's face. He leaned over the parapet and saw one prolonged clean splash in the river, and silver bubbles coming up. Then nothing. He was surprised to find his legs were shaking.

He steadied his knees and tramped home. He went to his room and, before he did anything else, he acted on a superstitious impulse he had not thought he had in him, and took down the household god Alina insisted he keep in a niche over his bed. He put it carefully outside in the passage. Then he got out a map of the town and some red stickers and plotted out all the places where he had just missed the Sage. The result had him dancing with excitement. The dragon was right. There was a pattern. The Sage had started in good lodgings at the better end of town. Then he had gradually moved to poorer places, but he had moved in a curve, down to the station and back towards the better part again. Now, the Altuns' house was just on the edge of the poorer part. The Sage was *coming this way*! New Unicorn Street had not been so far away. The next place should be nearer still. Thasper had only to look for a house on fire.

It was getting dark by then. Thasper threw his curtains back and leaned out of his window to look at the poorer streets. And there it was! There was a red and orange flicker to the left – in Harvest Moon Street, by the look of it. Thasper laughed aloud. He was actually grateful to the assassins!

He raced downstairs and out of the house. The anxious

questions of parents and the yells of brothers and sisters
followed him, but he slammed the door on them. Two
minutes' running brought him to the scene of the fire. The
street was a mad flicker of dark figures. People were piling
furniture in the road. Some more people were helping a dazed
woman in a crooked brown turban into a singed armchair.

'Didn't you have a lodger as well?' someone asked her
anxiously.

The woman kept trying to straighten her turban. It was all
she could really think of. 'He didn't stay,' she said. 'I think he
may be down at the Half Moon now.'

Thasper waited for no more. He went pelting down the
street.

The Half Moon was an inn on the corner of the same road.
Most of the people who usually drank there must have been
up the street, helping rescue furniture, but there was a dim
light inside, enough to show a white notice in the window.
ROOMS, it said.

Thasper burst inside. The barman was on a stool by the
window craning to watch the house burn. He did not look at
Thasper. 'Where's your lodger?' gasped Thasper. 'I've got a
message. Urgent.'

The barman did not turn round. 'Upstairs, first on the left,'
he said. 'The roof's caught. They'll have to act quick to save
the house on either side.'

Thasper heard him say this as he bounded upstairs. He
turned left. He gave the briefest of knocks on the door there,
flung it open and rushed in.

The room was empty. The light was on and it showed a stark
bed, a stained table with an empty mug and some sheets of
paper on it, and a fireplace with a mirror over it. Beside the
fireplace, another door was just swinging shut. Obviously
somebody had just that moment gone through it. Thasper

bounded towards that door. But he was checked, for just a second, by seeing himself in the mirror over the fireplace. He had not meant to pause. But some trick of the mirror, which was old and brown and speckled, made his reflection look for a moment a great deal older. He looked easily over twenty. He looked—

He remembered the Letter from the Unknown. This was the time. He knew it was. He was about to meet the Sage. He had only to call him. Thasper went towards the still gently swinging door. He hesitated. The Letter had said call at once. Knowing the Sage was just beyond the door, Thasper pushed it open a fraction and held it so with his fingers. He was full of doubts. He thought, Do I really believe the gods need people? Am I so sure? What shall I say to the Sage after all? He let the door slip shut again.

'Chrestomanci,' he said, miserably.

There was a *whoosh* of displaced air behind him. It buffeted Thasper half around. He stared. A tall man was standing by the stark bed. He was a most extraordinary figure in a long black robe, with what seemed to be yellow comets embroidered on it. The inside of the robe, swirling in the air, showed yellow, with black comets on it. The tall man had a very smooth dark head, very bright dark eyes and, on his feet, what seemed to be red bedroom slippers.

'Thank goodness,' said this outlandish person. 'For a moment, I was afraid you would go through that door.'

The voice brought memory back to Thasper. 'You brought me home through a picture when I was little,' he said. 'Are you Chrestomanci?'

'Yes,' said the tall outlandish man. 'And you are Thasper. And now we must both leave before this building catches fire.'

He took hold of Thasper's arm and towed him to the door which led to the stairs. As soon as he pushed the door open, thick smoke rolled in, filled with harsh crackling. It was clear that the inn was on fire already. Chrestomanci clapped the door shut again. The smoke set both of them coughing, Chrestomanci so violently that Thasper was afraid he would choke. He pulled both of them back into the middle of the room. By now, smoke was twining up between the bare boards of the floor, causing Chrestomanci to cough again.

'This would happen just as I had gone to bed with flu,' he said, when he could speak. 'Such is life. These orderly gods of yours leave us no choice.' He crossed the smoking floor and pushed open the door by the fireplace.

It opened on to blank space. Thasper gave a yelp of horror.

'Precisely,' coughed Chrestomanci. 'You were intended to crash to your death.'

'Can't we jump to the ground?' Thasper suggested.

Chrestomanci shook his smooth head. 'Not after they've done this to it. No. We'll have to carry the fight to them and go and visit the gods instead. Will you be kind enough to lend me your turban before we go?' Thasper stared at this odd request. 'I would like to use it as a belt,' Chrestomanci croaked. 'The way to Heaven may be a little cold, and I only have pyjamas under my dressing-gown.'

The striped undergarments Chrestomanci was wearing did look a little thin. Thasper slowly unwound his turban. To go before gods bareheaded was probably no worse than going in nightclothes, he supposed. Besides, he did not believe there were any gods. He handed the turban over. Chrestomanci tied the length of pale blue cloth around his black and yellow gown and seemed to feel more comfortable. 'Now hang on to me,' he said, 'and you'll be all right.' He took Thasper's arm again and walked up into the sky, dragging Thasper with him.

For a while, Thasper was too stunned to speak. He could only marvel at the way they were treading up the sky as if there were invisible stairs in it. Chrestomanci was doing it in the most matter of fact way, coughing from time to time and shivering a little, but keeping very tight hold of Thasper nevertheless. In no time, the town was a clutter of prettily lit dolls' houses below, with two red blots where two of them were burning. The stars were unwinding about them, above and below, as if they had already climbed above some of them.

'It's a long climb to Heaven,' Chrestomanci observed. 'Is there anything you'd like to know on the way?'

'Yes,' said Thasper. 'Did you say the gods are trying to kill me?'

'They are trying to eliminate the Sage of Dissolution,' said Chrestomanci, 'which they may not realize is the same thing. You see, you are the Sage.'

'But I'm not!' Thasper insisted. 'The Sage is a lot older than me, and he asks questions I never even thought of until I heard of him.'

'Ah yes,' said Chrestomanci. 'I'm afraid there is an awful circularity to this. It's the fault of whoever tried to put you away as a small child. As far as I can work out, you stayed three years old for seven years – until you were making such a disturbance in our world that we had to find you and let you out. But in this world of Theare, highly organized and fixed as it is, the prophecy stated that you would begin preaching Dissolution at the age of twenty-three, or at least in this very year. Therefore the preaching had to begin this year. You did not need to appear. Did you ever speak to anyone who had actually heard the Sage preach?'

'No,' said Thasper. 'Come to think of it.'

'Nobody did,' said Chrestomanci. 'You started in a small way anyway. First you wrote a book, which no one paid much heed to—'

'No, that's wrong,' objected Thasper. 'He – I – er, the Sage was writing a book *after* the preaching.'

'But don't you see,' said Chrestomanci, 'because you were back in Theare by then, the facts had to try to catch you up.

They did this by running backwards, until it was possible for you to arrive where you were supposed to be. Which was in that room in the inn there, at the start of your career. I suppose you are just old enough to start by now. And I suspect our celestial friends up here tumbled to this belatedly and tried to finish you off. It wouldn't have done them any good, as I shall shortly tell them.' He began coughing again. They had climbed to where it was bitterly cold.

By this time, the world was a dark arch below them. Thasper could see the blush of the sun, beginning to show underneath the world. They climbed on. The light grew. The sun appeared, a huge brightness in the distance underneath. A dim memory came again to Thasper. He struggled to believe that none of this was true, and he did not succeed.

'How do you know all this?' he asked bluntly.

'Have you heard of a god called Ock?' Chrestomanci coughed. 'He came to talk to me when you should have been the age you are now. He was worried—' He coughed again. 'I shall have to save the rest of my breath for Heaven.'

They climbed on, and the stars swam around them, until the stuff they were climbing changed and became solider. Soon they were climbing a dark ramp, which flushed pearly as they went upwards. Here, Chrestomanci let go of Thasper's arm and blew his nose on a gold-edged handkerchief with an air of relief. The pearl of the ramp grew to silver and the silver to dazzling white. At length, they were walking on level whiteness, through hall after hall.

The gods were gathered to meet them. None of them looked cordial.

'I fear we are not properly dressed,' Chrestomanci murmured.

Thasper looked at the gods, and then at Chrestomanci, and squirmed with embarrassment. Fanciful and queer as Chrestomanci's garb was, it was still most obviously nightwear. The things on his feet were fur bedroom slippers. And there, looking like a piece of blue string around Chrestomanci's waist, was the turban Thasper should have been wearing. The gods were magnificent, in golden trousers and jewelled turbans, and got more so as they approached the greater gods. Thasper's eye was caught by a god in shining cloth of gold, who surprised him by beaming a friendly, almost anxious look at him. Opposite him was a huge liquid-looking figure draped in pearls and diamonds. This god swiftly, but quite definitely, winked. Thasper was too awed to react, but Chrestomanci calmly winked back.

At the end of the halls, upon a massive throne, towered the mighty figure of Great Zond, clothed in white and purple, with a crown on his head. Chrestomanci looked up at Zond and thoughtfully blew his nose. It was hardly respectful.

'For what reason do two mortals trespass in our halls?' Zond thundered coldly.

Chrestomanci sneezed. 'Because of your own folly,' he said. 'You gods of Theare have had everything so well worked out for so long that you can't see beyond your own routine.'

'I shall blast you for that,' Zond announced.

'Not if any of you wish to survive,' Chrestomanci said.

There was a long murmur of protest from the other gods. They wished to survive. They were trying to work out what Chrestomanci meant. Zond saw it as a threat to his authority and thought he had better be cautious. 'Proceed,' he said.

'One of your most efficient features,' Chrestomanci said, 'is that your prophecies always come true. So why, when a prophecy is unpleasant to you, do you think you can alter it? That, my good gods, is rank folly. Besides, no one can halt his own Dissolution, least of all you gods of Theare. But you forgot. You forgot you had deprived both yourselves and mankind of any kind of free will, by organizing yourselves so precisely. You pushed Thasper, the Sage of Dissolution, into my world, forgetting that there is still chance in my world. By chance, Thasper was discovered after only seven years. Lucky for Theare that he was. I shudder to think what might have happened if Thasper had remained three years old for all his allotted lifetime.'

'That was my fault!' cried Imperion. 'I take the blame.' He turned to Thasper. 'Forgive me,' he said. 'You are my own son.'

Was this, Thasper wondered, what Alina meant by the gods blessing her womb? He had not thought it was more than a figure of speech. He looked at Imperion, blinking a little in the god's dazzle. He was not wholly impressed. A fine god, and an honest one, but Thasper could see he had a limited outlook. 'Of course I forgive you,' he said politely.

'It is also lucky,' Chrestomanci said, 'that none of you succeeded in killing the Sage. Thasper is a god's son. That means there can only ever be one of him, and because of your prophecy he has to be alive to preach Dissolution. You could have destroyed Theare. As it is, you have caused it to blur into a mass of cracks. Theare is too well organized to divide into two alternative worlds, like my world would. Instead, events have had to happen which could not have happened. Theare has cracked and warped, and you have all but brought about your own Dissolution.'

'What can we do?' Zond said, aghast.

'There's only one thing you can do,' Chrestomanci told him. 'Let Thasper be. Let him preach Dissolution and stop trying to blow him up. That will bring about free will and a free future. Then either Theare will heal, or it will split, cleanly and painlessly, into two healthy new worlds.'

'So we bring about our own downfall?' Zond asked mournfully.

'It was always inevitable,' said Chrestomanci.

Zond sighed. 'Very well. Thasper, son of Imperion, I

reluctantly give you my blessing to go forth and preach Dissolution. Go in peace.'

Thasper bowed. Then he stood there silent a long time. He did not notice Imperion and Ock both trying to attract his attention. The newspaper report had talked of the Sage as full of anguish and self-doubt. Now he knew why. He looked at Chrestomanci, who was blowing his nose again. 'How can I preach Dissolution?' he said. 'How can I not believe in the gods when I have seen them for myself?'

'That's a question you certainly should be asking,' Chrestomanci croaked. 'Go down to Theare and ask it.' Thasper nodded and turned to go. Chrestomanci leaned towards him and said, from behind his handkerchief. 'Ask yourself this too: Can the gods catch flu? I think I may have given it to all of them. Find out and let me know, there's a good chap.'

The Master

This is the trouble with being a newly qualified vet. The call came at 5:50 a.m. I thought it was a man's voice, though it was high for a man, and I didn't quite catch the name – Harry Sanovit? Harrison Ovett? Anyway, he said it was urgent.

Accordingly, I found myself on the edge of a plain, facing a dark fir forest. It was about midmorning. The fir trees stood dark and evenly spaced, exhaling their crackling gummy scent, with vistas of trodden-looking pine needles beneath them. A wolfwood, I thought. I was sure that thought was right. The spacing of the trees was so regular that it suggested an artificial pinewood in the zoo, and there was a kind of humming, far down at the edges of the senses, as if machinery was at work sustaining a man-made environment here. The division between trees and plain was so sharp that I had some doubts that I would be able to enter the wood.

But I stepped inside with no difficulty. Under the trees it was cooler, more strongly scented, and full of an odd kind of depression, which made me sure that there was some sort of danger here. I walked on the carpet of needles cautiously, relaxed but intensely afraid. There seemed to be some kind of path winding between the straight boles and I followed it into the heart of the wood. After a few turns, flies buzzed around something just off the path. *Danger!* pricked out all over my skin like sweat, but I went and looked all the same.

It was a young woman about my own age. From the flies and the freshness, I would have said she had been killed only hours ago. Her throat had been torn out. The expression on her half-averted face was of sheer terror. She had glorious red hair and was wearing what looked, improbably, to be evening dress.

I backed away, swallowing. As I backed, something came up beside me. I whirled around with a croak of terror.

'No need to fear,' he said. 'I am only the fool.'

He was very tall and thin and ungainly. His feet were in big, laced boots, jigging a silent, ingratiating dance on the pine needles, and the rest of his clothes were a dull brown and close-fitting. His huge hands came out to me placatingly. 'I am Egbert,' he said. 'You may call me Eggs. You will take no harm if you stay with me.' His eyes slid off mine apologetically, round and blue-grey. He grinned all over his small, inane face. Under his close crop of straw-fair hair, his face was indeed that of a near-idiot. He did not seem to notice the woman's corpse at all, even though he seemed to know I was full of horror.

'What's going on here?' I asked him helplessly. 'I'm a vet, not a – not a – mortician. What animal needs me?'

He smiled seraphically at nothing over my left shoulder. 'I am only Eggs, Lady. I don't not know nothing. What you need to do is call the Master. Then you will know.'

'So where is the Master?' I said.

He looked baffled by this question. 'Hereabouts,' he suggested. He gave another beguiling smile, over my right shoulder this time, panting slightly. 'He will come if you call him right. Will I show you the house, Lady? There are rare sights there.'

'Yes, if you like,' I said. Anything to get away from whatever had killed that girl. Besides, I trusted him somehow. When he had said I would take no harm if I was with him it been said in a way I believed.

He turned and cavorted up the path ahead of me, skipping soundlessly on his great feet, waving great, gangling arms, clumsily tripping over a tree root and, even more clumsily, just saving himself. He held his head on one side and hummed as he went, happy and harmless. That is to say, harmless to me so far. Though he walked like a great, hopping puppet, those huge hands were certainly strong enough to rip a throat out.

'Who killed that girl?' I asked him. 'Was it the Master?'

His head snapped around, swayingly, and he stared at me, appalled, balancing on the path as though it were a tightrope. 'Oh, no, Lady. The Master wouldn't not do that!' He turned sadly, almost tearfully, away.

'I'm sorry,' I said.

His head bent, acknowledging that he had heard, but he continued to walk the tightrope of the path without answering, and I followed. As I did, I was aware that there was something moving among the trees to either side of us. Something softly kept pace with us there, and, I was sure, something also followed along the path behind. I did not try to see what it was. I was quite as much angry with myself as I was scared. I had let my shock at seeing that corpse get the better of my judgement. I saw I must wait to find out how the red-headed girl had got herself killed. Caution! I said to myself. Caution! This path was a tightrope indeed.

'Has the Master got a name?' I asked.

That puzzled Eggs. He stood balancing on the path to think. After a moment he nodded doubtfully, shot me a shy smile over his shoulder, and walked on. No attempt to ask my name, I noticed. As if I was the only other person there and 'Lady' should be enough. Which meant that the presences among the trees and behind on the path were possibly not human.

Around the next bend, I found myself facing the veranda of a chalet-like building. It looked a little as if it were made of wood, but it was no substance that I knew. Eggs tripped on the step and floundered towards the door at the back of the veranda. Before I could make more than a move to help him, he had saved himself and his great hands were groping with an incomprehensible lock on the door. The humming was more evident here. I had been hoping that what I had heard at the edge of the wood had been the flies on the corpse. It was not. Though the sound was still not much more than a vibration at the edge of the mind, I knew I had been right in my first idea. Something artificial was being maintained here, and whatever was maintaining it seemed to be under this house.

In this house, I thought, as Eggs got the door open and floundered inside ahead of me. The room we entered was full of – well, devices. The nearest thing was a great cauldron, softly bubbling for no reason I could see, and giving out a gauzy violet light. The other things were arranged in ranks beyond, bewilderingly. In one place something grotesque stormed green inside a design painted on the floor; here a copper bowl smoked; there a single candle sat like something holy on a white stone; a knife suspended in air dripped gently into a jar of rainbow glass. Much of it was glass, twinkling, gleaming, chiming, under the light from the low ceiling that seemed to come from nowhere. There were no windows.

'Good heavens!' I said, disguising my dismay as amazement. 'What are all these?'

Eggs grinned. 'I know some. Pretty, aren't they?' He roved, surging about, touching the edge of a pattern here, passing his huge hand through a flame or a column of smoke there, causing a shower of fleeting white stars, solemn gong notes, and a rich smell of incense. 'Pretty, aren't they?' he kept repeating, and, '*Very* pretty!' as an entire fluted glass structure began to ripple and change shape at the end of the room. As it changed, the humming which was everywhere in the room changed, too. It became a purring chime, and I felt an indescribable pulling-feeling from the roots of my hair and under my skin, almost as if the glass thing were trying to change me as it changed itself.

'I should come away from that if I were you,' I said as firmly and calmly as I could manage.

Eggs turned and came floundering towards me, grinning eagerly. To my relief, the sound from the glass modulated to a new kind of humming. But my relief vanished when Eggs said, 'Petra knew all, before Annie tore her throat out. Do you know as much as Petra? You are clever, Lady, as well as beautiful.' His eyes slid across me, respectfully. Then he turned and hung, lurching, over the cauldron with the gauzy violet light. 'Petra took pretty dresses from here,' he said. 'Would you like for me to get you a pretty dress?'

'Not at the moment, thank you,' I said, trying to sound kind. As I said, Eggs was not necessarily harmless. 'Show me the rest of the house,' I said, to distract him.

He fell over his feet to oblige. 'Come. See here.' He led me to the side of the devices, where there was a clear passage and some doors. At the back of the room was another door, which slid open by itself as we came near. Eggs giggled proudly at that, as if it were his doing. Beyond was evidently a living room. The floor here was soft, carpetlike, and blue. Darker blue blocks hung about, mysteriously half a metre or so in the air. Four of them were a metre or so square. The fifth was two metres each way. They had the look of a suite of chairs and a sofa to me. A squiggly mural-thing occupied one wall and the entire end wall was window, which seemed to lead to another veranda, beyond which I could see a garden of some kind. 'The room is pretty, isn't it?' Eggs asked anxiously. 'I like the room.'

I assured him I liked the room. This relieved him. He stumbled around a floating blue block, which was barely disturbed by his falling against it, and pressed a plate in the wall beyond. The long glass of the window slid back, leaving the room open to the veranda. He turned to me, beaming.

'Clever,' I said, and made another cautious attempt to find out more. 'Did Petra show you how to open that, or was it the Master?'

He was puzzled again. 'I don't not know,' he said, worried about it.

I gave up and suggested we go into the garden. He was pleased. We went over the veranda and down steps into a rose garden. It was an oblong shape, carved out from among the fir trees, about fifteen metres from the house to the bushy hedge at the far end. And it was as strange as everything else. The square of sky overhead was subtly the wrong colour, as if you were seeing it through sunglasses. It made the colour of the roses rich and too dark. I walked through it with a certainty that it was being maintained – or created – by one of the devices in that windowless room.

The roses were all standards, each planted in a little circular bed. The head of each was about level with my head. No petals fell on the gravel-seeming paths. I kept exclaiming, because these were the most perfect roses I ever saw, whether full bloom, bud, or overblown. When I saw an orange rose – the colour I love most – I put my hand up cautiously to make sure that it was real. It was. While my fingers lingered on it I happened to glance at Eggs, towering over me. It was just a flick of the eyes, which I don't think he saw. He was standing there, smiling as always, staring at me intently. There was, I swear, another shape to his face and it was not the shape of an idiot. But it was not the shape of a normal man, either. It was an intent, *hunting* face.

Next moment he was surging inanely forward. 'I will pick you a rose, Lady.' He reached out and stumbled as he reached. His hand caught a thorn in a tumble of petals. He snatched it back with a yelp. 'Oh!' he said. 'It hurts!' He lifted his hand

and stared at it. Blood was running down the length of his little finger.

'Suck it,' I said. 'Is the thorn still in it?'

'I don't know,' Eggs said helplessly. Several drops of blood had fallen among the fallen petals before he took my advice and sucked the cut, noisily. As he did so, his other hand came forward to bar my way. 'Stay by me, Lady,' he said warningly.

I had already stopped dead. Whether they had been there all along or had been summoned, materialized, by the scent of blood, I still do not know, but they were there now, against the hedge at the end of the garden, all staring at me. Three Alsatian dogs, I told myself foolishly and knew it was nonsense as I thought it. Three of them. Three wolves. Each of them must have been, in bulk if not in height, at least as big as I was.

They were dark in the curious darkness of that garden. Their eyes were the easiest to see, light wolf-green. All of them staring at me, staring earnestly, hungrily. The smaller two were crouched in front. One of those was brindled and larger and rangier than his browner companion. And these two were only small by comparison with the great black she-wolf standing behind with slaver running from her open jaws. She was poised either to pounce or to run away. I have never seen anything more feral than that black she-wolf. But they were all feral, stiff-legged, terrified, half in mind to tear my throat out, and yet they were held there for some reason, simply staring. All three were soundlessly snarling, even before I spoke.

My horror – caught from the wolves to some extent – was beyond thought and out into a dreamlike state, where I simply knew that Eggs was right when he said I would be safe with him, and so I said what the dream seemed to require. 'Eggs,' I said, 'tell me their names.'

Eggs was quite unperturbed. His hand left his mouth and pointed at the brindled wolf in front. 'That one is Hugh, Lady. Theo is the one beside him. She standing at the back is Annie.'

So now I knew what had torn red-headed Petra's throat out. And what kind of a woman was she, I wondered, who must have had Eggs as servant and a roomful of strange devices, and on top of this gave three wild beasts these silly names? My main thought was that I did not want my throat torn out, too. And I had been called here as a vet after all. It took quite an effort to look those three creatures over professionally, but I did so. Ribs showed under the curly brownish coat of Theo. Hugh's haunches stuck out like knives. As for Annie standing behind, her belly clung upwards almost to her backbone. 'When did they last eat?' I said.

Eggs smiled at me. 'There is food in the forest for them, Lady.'

I stared at him, but he seemed to have no idea what he was saying. It was to the wolves' credit that they did not seem to regard dead Petra as food, but from the look of them it would not be long before they did so. 'Eggs,' I said, 'these three are starving. You and I must go back into the house and find food for them.'

Eggs seemed much struck by this idea. 'Clever,' he said. 'I am only the fool, Lady.' And as I turned, gently, not to alarm the wolves, he stretched out his hands placatingly – at least, it looked placating, but it was quite near to an attempt to take hold of me, a sketch of it, as it were. That alarmed me, but I dared not show it here. The wolves' ears pricked a little as we moved off up the garden, but they did not move, to my great relief.

Back through the house Eggs led me in his lurching, puppet's gait, around the edges of the room with the devices, where the humming filled the air and still seemed to drag at me in a way I did not care for at all, to another brightly lit, windowless room on the other side. It was a kitchen-place, furnished in what seemed to be glass. Here Eggs cannoned into a glass table and stopped short, looking at me expectantly. I gazed around at glass-fronted apparatus, some of it full of crockery, some of it clearly food stores, with food heaped behind the glass, and some of it quite mysterious to me. I made for the glass cupboard full of various joints of meat. I could see they were fresh, although the thing was clearly not a refrigerator. 'How do you open this?' I asked.

Eggs looked down at his great hands, planted in encircling vapour on top of the glass table. 'I don't not know, Lady.'

I could have shaken him. Instead I clawed at the edges of the cupboard. Nothing happened. There it was, warmish, piled with a good fifty kilograms of meat, while three starving wolves prowled outside, and nothing I could do seemed to have any effect on the smooth edge of the glass front. At length I pried my fingernails under the top edge and pulled, thinking it moved slightly.

Eggs's huge hand knocked against mine, nudging me awkwardly away. 'No, no, Lady. That way you'll get hurt. It is under stass-spell, see.' For a moment he fumbled doubtfully at the top rim of the glass door, but, when I made a movement to come back and help, his hands suddenly moved, smoothly and surely. The thing clicked. The glass slid open downwards and the smell of meat rolled out into the kitchen.

So you *do* know how to do it! I thought. And I *knew* you did! There was some hint he had given me, I knew, as I reached for the nearest joint, which I could not quite see now.

'No, *no*, Lady!' This time Eggs pushed me aside hard. He was really distressed. 'Never put hand into stass-spell. It will die on you. You do this.' He took up a long, shiny pair of tongs which I had not noticed because they were nested into the top of the cupboard, and grasped the nearest joint with them. 'This, Lady?'

'And two more,' I said. 'And when did you last eat, Eggs?' He shrugged and looked at me, baffled. 'Then get out those two steaks, too,' I said. Eggs seemed quite puzzled, but he fetched out the meat. 'Now we must find water for them as well,' I said.

'But there is juice here in this corner!' Eggs objected. 'See.' He went to one of the mysterious fixtures and shortly came back with a sort of cardboard cup swaying in one hand, which he handed me to taste, staring eagerly while I did. 'Good?' he asked.

It was some form of alcohol. 'Very good,' I said, 'but not for wolves.' It took me half an hour of patient work to persuade Eggs to fetch out a large lightweight bowl and then to manipulate a queer faucet to fill it with water. He could not see the point of it at all. I was precious near to hitting him before long. I was quite glad when he stayed behind in the kitchen to shut the cabinets and finish his cup of 'juice'.

The wolves had advanced down the garden. I could see their pricked ears and their eyes above the veranda boards, but they did not move when I stepped out on to the veranda. I had to make myself move with a calmness and slowness I was far from feeling. Deliberately, I dropped each joint, one by one, with a sticky thump on to the strange surface. From the size and the coarse grain of the meat, it seemed to be venison – at least, I hoped it was. Then I carefully lowered the bowl to stand at the far end of the veranda, looking all the time through my hair at the wolves. They did not move, but the open jaws of the big wolf, Annie, were dripping.

The bowl down, I backed away into the living room, where I just had to sit down on the nearest blue block. My knees gave.

They did not move for long seconds. Then all three disappeared below the veranda and I thought they must have slunk away. But the two smaller ones reappeared, suddenly, silently, as if they had materialized, at the end of the veranda beside the bowl. Tails trailing, shaking all over, they crept towards it. Both stuck their muzzles in and drank avidly. I could hear their frantic lapping. And when they raised their heads, which they both did shortly, neatly and disdainfully, I realized that one of the joints of meat had gone. The great wolf, Annie, had been and gone.

Her speed must have reassured Theo and Hugh. Both sniffed the air, then turned and trotted towards the remaining joints. Each nosed a joint. Each picked it up neatly in his jaws. Theo seemed about to jump down into the garden with his. But Hugh, to my astonishment, came straight towards the open window, evidently intending to eat on the carpet as dogs do.

He never got a chance. Theo dropped his joint and sprang at him with a snarl. There was the heavy squeak of clawed paws. Hugh sprang around, hackles rising the length of his lean, sloping back, and snarled back without dropping his portion. It was, he seemed to be saying, his own business where he went to eat. Theo, crouching, advancing on him with lowered head and white teeth showing, was clearly denying him this right. I braced myself for the fight. But at that moment, Annie reappeared, silent as ever, head and great forepaws on the edge of the veranda, and stood there, poised. Theo and Hugh vanished like smoke, running long and low to either side. Both took their food with them, to my relief. Annie dropped out of sight again. Presently there were faint, very faint, sounds of eating from below.

I went back to the glassy kitchen, where I spent the next few hours getting Eggs to eat, too. He did not seem to regard anything in the kitchen as edible. It took me a good hour to persuade him to open a vegetable cabinet and quite as long to persuade him to show me how to cook the food. If I became insistent, he said, 'I don't not know, Lady,' lost interest, and shuffled off to the windowless room to play with the pretty

lights. That alarmed me. Every time I fetched him back, the
humming chime from the glass apparatus seemed to drag at
me more intensely. I tried pleading. 'Eggs, I'm going to cut
these yams, but I can't find a knife somehow.' That worked
better. Eggs would come over obligingly and find me a thing
like a prong and then wander off to his 'juice' again. There
were times when I thought we were going to have to eat
everything raw.

But it got done in the end. Eggs showed me how to ignite a
terrifying heat source that was totally invisible and I fried the
food on it in a glass skillet. Most of the vegetables were quite
strange to me, but at least the steak was recognizable. We
were just sitting down on glass stools to eat it at the glass table,
when a door I had not realized was there slid aside beside me.
The garden was beyond. The long snout of Hugh poked
through the gap. The pale eyes met mine and the wet nose
quivered wistfully.

'What do you want?' I said, and I knew I had jerked with
fear. It was obvious what Hugh wanted. The garden must
have filled with the smell of cooking. But I had not realized
that the wolves could get into the kitchen when they
pleased. Trying to seem calm, I tossed Hugh some fat I'd
trimmed off the steaks. He caught it neatly and, to my
intense relief, backed out of the door, which closed behind
him.

I was almost too shaken to eat after that, but Eggs ate his
share with obvious pleasure, though he kept glancing at me as
if he was afraid I would think he was making a pig of himself.
It was both touching and irritating. But the food – and the
'juice' – did him good. His face became pinker and he did not
jig so much. I began to risk a few cautious questions. 'Eggs, did
Petra live in this house or just work here?'

He looked baffled. 'I don't know.'

'But she used the wolves to help her in her work, didn't

she?' It seemed clear to me that they *must* have been laboratory animals in some way.

Eggs shifted on his stool. 'I don't not know,' he said unhappily.

'And did the Master help in the work, too?' I persisted.

But this was too much for Eggs. He sprang up in agitation, and, before I could stop him, he swept everything off the table into a large receptacle near the door. 'I can't say!' I heard him say above the crash of breaking crockery.

After that he would listen to nothing I said. His one idea was that we must go to the living room. 'To sit elegantly, Lady,' he explained. 'And I will bring the sweet foods and the juice to enjoy ourselves with there.'

There seemed no stopping him. He surged out of the kitchen with an armload of peculiar receptacles and a round jug of 'juice' balanced between those and his chin, weaving this way and that among the devices in the windowless room. These flared and flickered and the unsupported knife danced in the air as I pursued him. I felt as much as saw the fluted glass structure changing shape again. The sound of it dragged at the very roots of me.

'Eggs,' I said desperately. 'How do I call the Master? Please.'

'I can't say,' he said, reeling on into the living room.

Some enlightenment came to me. Eggs meant exactly what he said. I had noticed that when he said 'I don't *not* know,' this did not mean that he did not know: it usually seemed to be something he could not explain. Now I saw that when he said 'I can't say,' he meant that he was, for some reason, unable to tell me about the Master. So, I thought, struggling on against the drag of the chiming apparatus, this means I must use a little cunning to get him to tell me.

In the living room Eggs was laying out dishes of sweets and little balls of cheese near the centre of the large blue sofa-like block. I sat down – at one end of it. Eggs promptly came and sat beside me, grinning and breathing 'juice' fumes. I got up and moved to the other end of the sofa. Eggs took the hint. He stayed where he was, sighing, and poured himself another papery cup of his 'juice'.

'Eggs,' I began. Then I noticed that the wolf, Hugh, was crouched on the veranda facing into the room, with his brindled nose on his paws and his sharp haunches outlined against the sunset roses. Beyond him were the backs of the two others, apparently asleep. Well, wolves always leave at least one of their pack on guard when they sleep. I told myself that Hugh had drawn sentry duty and went back to thinking how I could induce Eggs to tell me how to get hold of this Master. By this time I felt I would go mad unless someone explained this situation to me.

'Eggs,' I began again, 'when I ask you how I fetch the Master, you tell me you can't say, isn't that right?' He nodded eagerly, obligingly, and offered me a sweet. I took it. I was doing well so far. 'That means that something's stopping you telling me, doesn't it?' That lost him. His eyes slid from mine. I looked where his eyes went and found that Hugh had been moving, in the unnoticed silent way a wild creature can. He was now crouched right inside the room. The light feral eyes were fixed on me. Help! I thought. But I had to go on with what I was saying before Eggs's crazed mind lost it. 'So I'm going to take it that when you say "I can't say," you mean "Yes," Eggs. It's going to be like a game.'

Eggs's face lit up. 'I like games, Lady!'

'Good,' I said. 'The game is called Calling-the-Master. Now I know you can't tell me direct how to call him, but the rule is that you're allowed to give me hints.'

That was a mistake. 'And what is the hint, Lady?' Eggs asked, in the greatest delight. 'Tell me and I will give it.'

'Oh – I – er—' I said. And I felt something cold gently touch

my hand. I looked down to find Hugh standing by my knees.
Beyond him, Theo was standing up, bristling. 'What do you
want now?' I said to Hugh. His eyes slid across the plates of
sweets and he sighed, like a dog. 'Not sweets,' I said firmly.
Hugh understood. He laid his long head on my knee,
yearningly.

This produced a snarl from Theo out on the veranda. It
sounded like pure jealousy.

'You can come in, too, if you want, Theo,' I said hastily.
Theo gave no sign of understanding, but when I next looked
he was half across the threshold. He was crouched, not lying.
His hackles were up and his eyes glared at Hugh. Hugh's eyes
moved to see where he was, but he did not raise his chin from
my knee.

All this so unnerved me that I tried to explain what a hint
was by telling Eggs a story. I should have known better. 'In
this story,' I said, absently stroking Hugh's head as if he were
my dog. Theo instantly rose to his feet with the lips of his
muzzle drawn back and his ears up. I removed my hand – but
quick! 'In this story,' I said. Theo lay down again, but now it
was me he was glaring at. 'A lady was left three boxes by her
father, one box gold, one silver, and one lead. In one of the
boxes there was a picture of her. Her father's orders were that
the man who guessed which of the three boxes her picture
was in could marry her—'

Eggs bounced up with a triumphant laugh. 'I know! It was
in the lead box! Lead protects. I can marry her!' He rolled
about in delight. 'Are you that lady?' he asked eagerly.

I suppressed a strong need to run about screaming. I was
sure that if I did, either Theo or Annie would go for me. I was
not sure about Hugh. He seemed to have been a house pet.
'Right,' I said. 'It *was* in the lead box, Eggs. This *other* lady
knew that, but the men who wanted to marry her had to
guess. All of them guessed wrong, until one day a beautiful

man came along whom this *other* lady wanted to marry. So what did she do?'

'Told him,' said Eggs.

'No, she was forbidden to do that,' I said. *God give me patience!* 'Just like you. She had to give the man hints instead. Just like you. Before he came to choose the box, she got people to sing him a song and – remember, it was the *lead* box – every line in that song rhymed with "lead". A rhyme is a word that sounds the same,' I added hurriedly, seeing bewilderment cloud Eggs's face. 'You know – "said" and "bled" and "red" all rhyme with "lead".'

'Said, bled, red,' Eggs repeated, quite lost.

'Dead, head,' I said. Hugh's cold nose nudged my hand again. Wolves are not usually scavengers, unless in dire need, but I thought cheese would not hurt him. I passed him a round to keep him quiet.

Theo sprang up savagely and came half across the room. At the same instant, Eggs grasped what a rhyme was. 'Fed, instead, bed, wed!' he shouted, rolling about with glee. I stared into Theo's grey-green glare and at his pleated lip showing the fangs beneath it, and prayed to heaven. Very slowly and carefully, I rolled a piece of cheese off the sofa towards him. Theo swung away from it and stalked back to the window. 'My hint is bedspread, Lady!' Eggs shouted.

Hugh, meanwhile, calmly took his cheese as deftly and gently as any hunting dog and sprang up on to the sofa beside me, where he stood with his head down, chewing with small bites to make the cheese last. 'Now you've done it, Hugh!' I said, looking nervously at Theo's raked-up back and at the sharp outline of Annie beyond him.

'Thread, head, watershed, bread!' bawled Eggs. I realized he was drunk. His face was flushed and his eyes glittered. He had been putting back quantities of 'juice' ever since he first showed me the kitchen. 'Do I get to marry you now, Lady?' he asked soulfully.

Before I could think what to reply, Hugh moved across like lightning and bit Eggs on his nearest large folded knee. He jumped clear even quicker, as Eggs surged to his feet, and streaked off to join Theo on the veranda. I heard Theo snap at him.

Eggs took an uncertain step that way, then put his hand to his face. 'What is this?' he said. 'This room is chasing its tail.' It was clear the 'juice' had caught up with him.

'I think you're drunk,' I said.

'Drink,' said Eggs. 'I must get a drink from the faucet. I am dying. It is worse than being remade.' And he went blundering and crashing off into the windowless room.

I jumped up and went after him, sure that he would do untold damage bumping into cauldron or candle. But he wove his way through the medley of displays as only a drunk man can, avoiding each one by a miracle, and reached the kitchen when I was only halfway through the room. The hum of the crystal apparatus held me back. It dragged at my very skin. I had still only reached the cauldron when there was an appalling splintering crash from the kitchen, followed by a hoarse male scream.

I do not remember how I got to the kitchen. I only remember standing in the doorway, looking at Eggs kneeling in the remains of the glass table. He was clutching at his left arm with his right hand. Blood was pulsing steadily between his long fingers and making a pool on the glass-littered floor. The face he turned to me was so white that he looked as if he were wearing greasepaint. 'What will you do, Lady?' he said.

Do? I thought. I'm a vet. I can't be expected to deal with humans! 'For goodness' sake, Eggs,' I snapped at him. 'Stop this messing about and get me the Master! Now. This instant!'

I think he said, 'And I thought you'd never tell me!' But his voice was so far from human by then it was hard to be sure. His body boiled about on the floor, surging and seething and changing colour. In next to a second the thing on the floor was a huge grey wolf, with its back arched and its jaws wide in agony, pumping blood from a severed artery in its left foreleg.

At least I knew what to do with that. But before I could move, the door to the outside slid open to let in the great head and shoulders of Annie. I backed away. The look in those light, blazing eyes said: 'You are not taking my mate like *she* did.'

*

Here the chiming got into my head and proved to be the ringing of the telephone. My bedside clock said 5:55 a.m. I was quite glad to be rid of that dream as I fumbled the telephone up in the dark. 'Yes?' I said, hoping I sounded as sleepy as I felt.

The voice was a light, high one, possibly a man's. 'You won't know me,' it said. 'My name is Harrison Ovett and I'm in charge of an experimental project involving wild animals. We have a bit of an emergency on here. One of the wolves seems to be in quite a bad way. I'm sorry to call you at such an hour, but—'

'It's my job,' I said, too sleepy to be more than proud of the professional touch. 'Where are you? How do I get to your project?'

I think he hesitated slightly. 'It's a bit complicated to explain,' he said. 'Suppose I come and pick you up? I'll be outside in twenty minutes.'

'Right,' I said. And it was not until I put the phone down that I remembered my dream. The name was the same, I swear. I would equally swear to the voice. This is why I have spent the last twenty minutes feverishly dictating this account

of my dream. If I get back safely I'll erase it. But if I don't –
well, I am not sure what anyone can do if Annie's torn my
throat out, but at least someone will know what became of
me. Besides, they say forewarned is forearmed. I have some
idea what to expect.

The Girl Who Loved the Sun

There was a girl called Phega who became a tree. Stories from the ancient times when Phega lived would have it that when women turned into trees it was always under duress, because a god was pursuing them, but Phega turned into a tree voluntarily. She did it from the moment she entered her teens. It was not easy and it took a deal of practice, but she kept at it. She would go into the fields beyond the manor house where she lived and there she would put down roots, spread her arms and say, 'For you I shall spread out my arms.' Then she would become a tree.

She did this because she was in love with the sun. The people who looked after her when she was a child told her that the sun loved the trees above all other living things. Phega concluded that this must be so from the way most trees shed their leaves in winter when the sun was unable to attend to them very much. As Phega could not remember a time when the sun had not been more to her than mother, father or life itself, it followed that she had to become a tree.

At first she was not a very good tree. The trunk of her tended to bulge at hips and breast and was usually an improbable brown colour. The largest number of branches she could achieve was four or five at the most. These stood out at unconvincing angles and grew large pallid leaves in a variety of shapes. She strove with these defects valiantly, but for a long time it always seemed that when she got her trunk to look more natural, her branches were fewer and more misshapen, and when she grew halfway decent branches, either her trunk relapsed or her leaves were too large or too yellow.

'Oh, sun,' she sighed, 'do help me to be more pleasing to you.' Yet it seemed unlikely that the sun was even attending to her. 'But he will!' Phega said and, driven by hope and yearning, she continued to stand in the field, striving to spread out more plausible branches. Whatever shape they were, she could still revel in the sun's impartial warmth on them and in the searching strength of her roots reaching into the earth. Whether the sun was attending or not, she knew the deep peace of a tree's long, wordless thoughts. The rain was pure delight to her, instead of the necessary evil it was to other people, and the dew was a marvel.

The following spring, to her delight, she achieved a reasonable shape, with a narrow, lissom trunk and a cloud of spread branches, not unlike a fruiting tree. 'Look at me, sun,' she said. 'Is this the kind of tree you like?'

The sun glanced down at her. She stood at that instant between hope and despair. It seemed that he attended to the wordless words.

But the sun passed on beaming, not unkindly, to glance at the real apple trees that stood on the slope of the hill.

'I need to be different in some way,' Phega said to herself.

She became a girl again and studied the apple trees. She watched them put out big pale buds and saw how the sun drew those buds open to become leaves and white flowers. Choking with the hurt of rejection, she saw the sun dwelling lovingly on those flowers, which made her think at first that flowers were what she needed. Then she saw that the sun drew those flowers on, quite ruthlessly, until they died, and that what came after were green blobs that turned into apples.

'Now I know what I need,' she said.

It took a deal of hard work, but the following spring she was able to say, 'Look at me, sun. For you I shall hold out my arms budded with growing things,' and spread branches full of white blossom that she was prepared to force on into fruit.

This time, however, the sun's gaze fell on her only in the way it fell on all living things. She was very dejected. Her yearning for the sun to love her grew worse.

'I still need to be different in some way,' she said.

That year she studied the sun's ways and likings as she had never studied them before. In between she was a tree. Her yearning for the sun had grown so great that when she was in human form, it was as if she were less than half alive. Her parents and other human company were shadowy to her. Only when she was a tree with her arms spread to the sunlight did she feel she was truly in existence.

As that year took its course she noticed that the place the sun first touched unfailingly in the morning was the top of the hill beyond the apple trees. And it was the place where he lingered last at sunset. Phega saw this must be the place the sun loved best. So, though it was twice as far from the manor, Phega went daily to the top of that hill and took root there. This meant that she had an hour more of the sun's warm company to spread her boughs into, but the situation was not otherwise as good as the fields. The top of the hill was very dry. When she put down roots, the soil was thin and tasted peculiar. And there was always a wind up there. Phega found she grew bent over and rather stunted.

'But what more can I do?' she said to the sun. 'For you I shall spread out my arms, budded with growing things, and root within the ground you warm, accepting what that brings.'

The sun gave no sign of having heard, although he continued to linger on the top of the hill at the beginning and end of each day. Phega would walk home in the twilight considering how she might grow roots that were adapted to the thin soil and pondering ways and means to strengthen her trunk against the wind. She walked slightly bent over and her skin was pale and withered.

Up till now Phega's parents had indulged her and not interfered. Her mother said, 'She's very young.' Her father agreed and said, 'She'll get over this obsession with rooting herself in time.' But when they saw her looking pale and withered and walking with a stoop, they felt the time had come to intervene. They said to one another, 'She's old enough to marry now and she's ruining her looks.'

The next day they stopped Phega before she left the manor on her way to the hill. 'You must give up this pining and rooting,' her mother said to her. 'No girl ever found a husband by being out in all weathers like this.'

And her father said, 'I don't know what you're after with this tree nonsense. I mean, we can all see you're very good at it, but it hasn't got much bearing on the rest of life, has it? You're our only child, Phega. You have the future of the manor to consider. I want you married to the kind of man I can trust to look after the place when I'm gone. That's not the kind of man who's going to want to marry a tree.'

Phega burst into tears and fled away across the fields and up the hill.

'Oh, dear!' her father said guiltily. 'Did I go too far?'

'Not at all,' said her mother. 'I would have said it if you hadn't. We must start looking for a husband for her. Find the right man and this nonsense will slide out of her head from the moment she claps eyes on him.'

It happened that Phega's father had to go away on business anyway. He agreed to extend his journey and look for a suitable husband for Phega while he was away. His wife gave him a good deal of advice on the subject, ending with a very strong directive not to tell any prospective suitor that Phega had this odd habit of becoming a tree – at least not until the young man was safely proved to be interested in marriage anyway. And as soon as her husband was away from the manor, she called two servants she could trust and told them to follow Phega and watch how she turned into a tree. 'For it must be a process we can put a stop to somehow,' she said, 'and if you can find out how we can stop her for good, so much the better.'

Phega, meanwhile, rooted herself breathlessly into the shallow soil at the top of the hill. 'Help me,' she called out to the sun. 'They're talking of marrying me and the only one I love is you!'

The sun pushed aside an intervening cloud and considered her with astonishment. 'Is this why you so continually turn into a tree?' he said.

Phega was too desperate to consider the wonder of actually, at last, talking to the sun. She said, 'All I do, I do in the remote, tiny hope of pleasing you and causing you to love me as I love you.'

'I had no idea,' said the sun and he added, not unkindly, 'but I do love everything according to its nature, and your nature is human. I might admire you for so skilfully becoming a tree, but that is, when all is said and done, only an imitation of a tree. It follows that I love you better as a human.' He beamed and was clearly about to pass on.

Phega threw herself down on the ground, half woman and half tree, and wept bitterly, thrashing her branches and rolling back and forth. 'But I love you,' she cried out. 'You are the light of the world and I love you. I *have* to be a tree because then I have no heart to ache for you, and even as a tree I ache at night because you aren't there. Tell me what I can do to make you love me.'

The sun paused. 'I do not understand your passion,' he said. 'I have no wish to hurt you, but this is the truth: I cannot love you as an imitation of a tree.'

A small hope came to Phega. She raised the branches of her

head. 'Could you love me if I stopped pretending to be a tree?'

'Naturally,' said the sun, thinking this would appease her. 'I would love you according to your nature, human woman.'

'Then I make a bargain with you,' said Phega. 'I will stop pretending and you will love me.'

'If that is what you want,' said the sun and went on his way.

Phega shook her head free of branches and her feet from the ground and sat up, brooding, with her chin on her hands. That was how her mother's servants found her and watched her warily from among the apple trees. She sat there for hours. She had bargained with the sun as a person might bargain for their very life, out of the desperation of her love, and she needed to work out a plan to back her bargain with. It gave her slight shame that she was trying to trap such a being as the sun, but she knew that was not going to stop her. She was beyond shame.

'There is no point imitating something that already exists,' she said to herself, 'because that is pretending to be that thing. I will have to be some kind that is totally new.'

Phega came down from the hill and studied trees again. Because of the hope her bargain had given her, she studied in a new way, with passion and depth, all the time her father was away. She ranged far afield to the forests in the valleys beyond the manor, where she spent days among the trees, standing still as a tree, but in human shape – which puzzled her mother's servants exceedingly – listening to the creak of their growth and every rustle of every leaf, until she knew them as trees knew other trees and comprehended the abiding restless stillness of them. The entire shape of a tree against the sky became open to her and she came to know all their properties. Trees had power. Willows had pithy centres and grew fast; they caused sleep. Elder was pithy too; it could give powerful protection, but had a touchy nature and should be treated politely. But the oak and the ash, the giant trees that held their branches closest to the sun's love, had the greatest power of all. Oak was constancy and ash was change. Phega studied these two longest and most respectfully.

'I need the properties of both these,' she said.

She carried away branches of leafing twigs to study as she walked home, noting the join of twig to twig and the way the leaves were fastened on. Evergreens impressed her by the way they kept leaves for the sun even in winter, but she was soon sure they did it out of primitive parsimony. Oaks, on the other hand, had their leaves tightly knotted on by reason of their strength.

'I shall need the same kind of strength,' Phega said.

As autumn drew on, the fruiting trees preoccupied her, since it was clear that it was growth and fruition the sun seemed most to love. They all, she saw, partook of the natures of both oaks and elders, even hawthorn, rowan and hazel. Indeed many of them were related to the lowlier bushes and fruiting plants; but the giant trees that the sun most loved were more exclusive in their pedigrees.

'Then I shall be like the oak,' Phega said, 'but bear better fruit.'

Winter approached and trees were felled for firewood. Phega was there, where the foresters were working, anxiously inspecting the rings of the sawn trunk and interrogating the very sawdust. This mystified the servants who were following her. They asked the foresters if they had any idea what Phega was doing.

The foresters shook their heads and said, 'She is not quite sane, but we know she is very wise.'

The servants had to be content with this. At least after that they had an easier time, for Phega was mostly at home in the manor examining the texture of the logs for the fires. She studied the bark on the outside and then the longwise grains and the roundwise rings of the interior, and she came to an important conclusion: an animal stopped growing when it had attained a certain shape, but a tree did not.

'I see now,' she said, 'that I have by no means finished growing.' And she was very impatient because winter had put a stop to all growth, so that she had to wait for spring to study its nature.

In the middle of winter her father came home. He had found the perfect husband for Phega and was anxious to tell Phega and her mother all about the man. This man was a younger son of a powerful family, he said, and he had been a soldier for some years, during which time he had distinguished himself considerably and gained a name for sense and steadiness. Now he was looking for a wife to marry and settle down with. Though he was not rich, he was not poor either and he was on good terms with the wealthier members of his family. It was, said Phega's father, a most desirable match.

Phega barely listened to all this. She went away to look at the latest load of logs before her father had finished speaking. 'He may not ever come here,' she said to herself, 'and if he does, he will see I am not interested and go away again.'

'Did I say something wrong?' her father asked her mother. 'I had hoped to show her that the man has advantages that far outweigh the fact that he is not in his first youth.'

'No – it's just the way she is,' said Phega's mother. 'Have you invited the man here?'

'Yes, he is coming in the spring,' her father said. 'His name is Evor. Phega will like him.'

Phega's mother was not entirely sure of this. She called the servants she had set to follow Phega to her privately and asked them what they had found out. 'Nothing,' they said. 'We think she has given up turning into a tree. She has never so much as put forth a root while we are watching her.'

'I hope you are right,' said Phega's mother. 'But I want you to go on watching her, even more carefully than before. It is now extremely important that we know how to stop her becoming a tree if she ever threatens to do so.'

The servants sighed, knowing they were in for another dull and difficult time. And they were not mistaken because, as soon as the first snowdrops appeared, Phega was out in the countryside studying the way things grew. As far as the servants were concerned, she would do nothing but sit or stand for hours watching a bud, or a tree, or a nest of mice or birds. As far as Phega was concerned, it was a long fascination as she divined how cells multiplied again and again and at length discovered that, while animals took food from solid things, plants took their main food from the sun himself. 'I think that may be the secret at last,' she said.

This puzzled the servants, but they reported it to Phega's mother all the same. Her answer was, 'I *thought* so. Be ready to bring her home the instant she shows a root or a shoot.'

The servants promised to do this, but Phega was not ready yet. She was busy watching the whole course of spring growth transform the forest. So it happened that Evor arrived to meet his prospective bride and Phega was not there. She had not even noticed that everyone in the manor was preparing a feast in Evor's honour. Her parents sent messengers to the forest to fetch her, while Evor first kicked his heels for several hours in the hall and finally, to their embarrassment, grew impatient and went out into the yard. There he wondered whether to order his horse and leave.

'I conclude from this delay,' he said to himself, 'that the girl is not willing – and one thing I do not want is a wife I have to force.' Nevertheless, he did not order his horse. Though Phega's parents had been at pains to keep from him any suggestion that Phega was not as other girls were, he had been unable to avoid hearing rumours on the way. For by this time Phega's fame was considerable. The first gossip he heard, when he was furthest away, was that his prospective bride was a witch. This he had taken for envious persons' way of describing wisdom and pressed on. As he came nearer, rumour had it that she was very wise, and he felt justified – though the latest rumour he had heard, when he was no more than ten miles from the manor, was that Phega was at least a trifle mad. But each rumour came accompanied by statements about Phega's appearance which were enough to make him tell himself that it was too late to turn back anyway. This kept him loitering in the yard. He wanted to set eyes on her himself.

He was still waiting when Phega arrived, walking in through the gate quickly but rather pensively. It was a grey day, with the sun hidden, and she was sad. 'But,' she told herself, 'I may as well see this suitor and tell him there was no point in his coming and get it over with.' She knew her parents were responsible and did not blame the man at all.

Evor looked at her as she came and knew that rumour had understated her looks. The time Phega had spent studying had improved her health and brought her from girl to young woman. She was beautiful. Evor saw that her hair was the colour of beer when you hold a glass of it to the light. She was wearing a dress of smooth silver-grey material which showed that her body under it when she moved was smooth-muscled and sturdy – and he liked sturdy women. Her overgarment was a curious light, bright green and floated away from her arms, revealing them to be very round and white. When he looked at her face, which was both round and long, he saw beauty there, but he also saw that she was very wise. Her eyes were grey. He saw a wildness there contained by the deep calm of long, long thought and a capacity to drink in knowledge. He was awed. He was lost.

Phega, for her part, tore her thoughts from many hours of standing longing among the great trees and saw a wiry man of slightly over middle height, who had a bold face with a keen stare to it. She saw he was not young. There was grey to his beard – which always grew more sparsely than he would have liked, though he had combed it carefully for the occasion – and some grey in his hair too. She noticed his hair particularly because he had come to the manor in light armour, to show his status as a soldier and a commander, but he was carrying his helmet politely in the crook of his arm. His intention was to show himself as a polished man of the world. But Phega saw him as iron-coloured all over. He made her think of an axe, except that he seemed to have such a lot of hair. She feared he was brutal.

Evor said, 'My lady!' and added as a very awkward after-thought, 'I came to marry you.' As soon as he had said this, it struck him as so wrong and presumptuous a thing to say to a woman like this one, that he hung his head and stared at her feet, which were bare and, though beautiful, stained green with the grass she had walked through. The sight gave him courage. He thought that those feet were human after all, so it followed that the rest of her was, and he looked up at her eyes again. 'What a thing to say!' he said.

He smiled in a flustered way. Phega saw that he was somewhat snaggle-toothed, not to speak of highly diffident in spite of his grey and military appearance, and possibly in awe of her. She could not see how he could be in awe of her, but his uneven teeth made him a person to her. Of a sudden, he was not just the man her parents had procured for her to marry, but another person like her, with feelings like Phega had herself. 'Good gods!' she thought, in considerable surprise. 'This is a person I could maybe love after all, if it were not for the sun.' And she told him politely that he was very welcome.

They went indoors together and presently sat down to the feast. There Evor got over his awe a little, enough to attempt to talk to Phega. And Phega, knowing he had feelings to be hurt, answered the questions he asked and asked things in return.

The result was that before long, to the extreme delight of Phega's parents, they were talking of his time at war and of her knowledge, and laughing together as if they were friends – old friends. Evor's wonder and joy grew. Long before the feast was over, he knew he could never love any other woman now. The effect of Phega on him was like a physical tie, half glorious, half painful, that bound him to respond to every tiny movement of her hand and every flicker of her lashes.

Phega found – and her surprise increased – that she was comfortable with Evor. But however amicably they talked, it was still as if she was only half alive in the sun's absence – though it was an easy half life – and, as the evening wore on, she felt increasingly confined and trapped. At first she assumed that this feeling was simply due to her having spent so much of the past year out of doors. She was so used to having nothing but the sky with the sun in it over her head that she often did find the manor roof confining. But now it was like a cage over her head. And she realized that her growing liking for Evor was causing it.

'If I don't take care,' she said to herself, 'I shall forget the bargain I made with the sun and drift into this human contract. It is almost too late already. I must act at once.'

Thinking this, she said her goodnights and went away to sleep.

Evor remained, talking jubilantly with Phega's parents. 'When I first saw her,' he said, 'I thought things were hopeless. But now I think I have a chance. I think she likes me.'

Phega's father agreed, but Phega's mother said, 'I'm sure she *likes* you all right, but – I caught a look in her eye – this may not be enough to make her marry you.'

Saying this, Phega's mother touched on something Evor had sensed and feared himself. His jubilation turned ashy – indeed he felt as if the whole world had been taken by drought: there was no moisture or virtue in it anywhere from pole to pole. 'What more can I do?' he said, low and slow.

'Let me tell you something,' said Phega's mother.

'Yes,' Phega's father broke in eagerly. 'Our daughter has a strange habit of—'

'She is,' Phega's mother interrupted swiftly, 'under an enchantment which we are helpless to break. Only a man who truly loves her can break it.'

Hope rose in Evor, as violent as Phega's hope when she bargained with the sun. 'Tell me what to do,' he said.

Phega's mother considered all the reports her servants had brought her. So far as she knew, Phega had never once turned into a tree all the time her father was away. It was possible she had lost the art. This meant that, with luck, Evor need never know the exact nature of her daughter's eccentricity. 'Sometime soon,' she said, 'probably at dawn, my daughter will be compelled by the enchantment to leave the manor. She will go to the forest or the hill. She may be compelled to murmur words to herself. You must follow her when she goes and, as soon as you see her standing still, you must take her in your arms and kiss her. In this way you will break the spell and she will become your faithful wife ever after.' And, Phega's mother told herself, this was very likely what would happen. 'For,' she thought, 'as soon as he kisses her, my daughter will discover that there are certain pleasures to be had from behaving naturally. Then we can all be comfortable again.'

'I shall do exactly what you say,' said Evor, and he was so uplifted with hope and gratitude that his face was nearly handsome.

All that night he kept watch. He could not have slept anyway. Love roared in his ears and longing choked him. He went over and over the things Phega had said and each individual beauty of her face and body as she said these things, and when, in the dawn, he saw her stealing through the hall to the door, there was a moment when he could not move. She was even more lovely than he remembered.

Phega softly unbarred the door and crossed the yard to unbar the gate. Evor pulled himself together and followed. They walked out across the fields in the white time before sunrise, Phega pacing very upright, with her eyes on the sky where the sun would appear, and Evor stealing after. He softly took off his armour piece by piece as he followed her and laid it down carefully in case it should clatter and alarm her.

Up the hill Phega went where she stood like one entranced, watching the gold rim of the sun come up. And such was Evor's awe that he loitered a little in the apple trees, admiring her as she stood.

'Now,' Phega said, 'I have come to fulfil my bargain, Sun, since I fear this is the last time I shall truly want to.' What she did then, she had given much thought to. It was not the way she had been accustomed to turn into a tree before. It was far more thorough. For she put down careful roots, driving each of her toes downwards and outwards and then forcing them into a network of fleshy cables to make the most of the thin soil at the top of the hill. 'Here,' she said, 'I root within the soil you warm.'

Evor saw the ground rise and writhe and low branches grow from her insteps to bury themselves also. 'Oh, no!' he cried out. 'Your feet were beautiful as they were!' And he began to climb the hill towards her.

Phega frowned, concentrating on the intricacy of feathery rootlets. 'But they were not the way I wanted them,' she said and she wondered vaguely why he was there. But by then she was putting forth her greatest effort, which left her little attention to spare. Slowly, once her roots were established, she began to coat them with bark before insects could damage them. At the same time, she set to work on her trunk, growing swiftly, grain by growing grain. 'Increased by yearly rings,' she murmured.

As Evor advanced, he saw her body elongate, coating itself with matte pewter-coloured bark as it grew, until he could barely pick out the outline of limbs and muscles inside it. It was like watching a death. 'Don't!' he said. 'Why are you *doing* this? You were lovely before!'

'I was like all human women,' Phega answered, resting before her next great effort. 'But when I am finished I shall be a wholly new kind of tree.' Having said that, she turned her attention to the next stage, which she was expecting to enjoy. Now she stretched up her arms, and the hair of her head, yearning into the warmth of the climbing sun, and made it all into limblike boughs which she coated like the rest of her, carefully, with dark silver bark. 'For you I shall hold out my arms,' she said.

Evor saw her, tree-shaped and twice as tall as himself, and cried out, 'Stop!' He was afraid to touch her in this condition. He knelt at her roots in despair.

'I can't stop now,' Phega told him gently. She was gathering herself for her final effort and her mind was on that, though the tears she heard breaking his voice did trouble her a little. She put that trouble out of her head. This was the difficult part. She had already elongated every large artery of her body, to pass through her roots and up her trunk and into her boughs. Now she concentrated on lifting her veins, and every nerve with them, without disturbing the rest, out to the ends of her branches, out and up, up and out, into a mass of living twigs, fine-growing and close as her own hair. It was impossible. It hurt – she had not thought it would hurt so much – but she was lifting, tearing her veins, thrusting her nerve ends with them, first into the innumerable fine twigs, then into even further particles to make long sharp buds.

Evor looked up as he crouched and saw the great tree

surging and thrashing above him. He was appalled at the effort. In the face of this gigantic undertaking he knew he was lost and forgotten and, besides, it was presumptuous to interfere with such willing agony. He saw her strive and strive again to force those sharp buds open. 'If you must be a tree,' he shouted above the din of her lashing branches, 'take me with you somehow, at least!'

'Why should you want that?' Phega asked with wooden lips that had not yet quite closed, just where her main boughs parted.

Evor at last dared to clasp the trunk with its vestigial limbs showing. He shed tears on the grey bark. 'Because I love you. I want to be with you.'

Trying to see him forced her buds to unfurl, because that was where her senses now were. They spread with myriad shrill agonies, like teeth cutting, and she thought it had killed her, even while she was forcing further nerves and veins to the undersides of all her pale viridian leaves. When it was done, she was all alive and raw in the small hairs on the undersides of those leaves and in the symmetrical ribs of vein on the shiny upper sides, but she could sense Evor crouching at her roots now. She was grateful to him for forcing her to the necessary pain. Her agony responded to his. He was a friend. He had talked of love, and she understood that. She retained just enough of the strength it had taken to change to alter him too to some extent, though not enough to bring him beyond the animal kingdom. The last of her strength was reserved for putting forth small pear-shaped fruit covered with wiry hairs, each containing four triangular nuts. Then, before the wooden gap that was her mouth had entirely closed, she murmured, 'Budding with growing things.'

She rested for a while, letting the sun harden her leaves to a dark shiny green and ripen her fruit a little. Then she cried wordlessly to the sun, 'Look! Remember our bargain. I am an entirely new kind of tree – as strong as an oak, but I bear fruit that everything can eat. Love me. Love me now!' Proudly she shed some of her three-cornered nuts on to the hilltop.

'I see you,' said the sun. 'This is a lovely tree, but I am not sure what you expect me to do with you.'

'Love me!' she cried.

'I do,' said the sun. 'There is no change in me. The only difference is that I now feed you more directly than I feed that animal at your feet. It is the way I feed all trees. There is nothing else I can do.'

Phega knew the sun was right and that her bargain had been her own illusion. It was very bitter to her; but she had made a change that was too radical to undo now and, besides, she was discovering that trees do not feel things very urgently. She settled back for a long low-key sort of contentment, rustling her leaves about to make the best of the sun's heat on them. It was like a sigh.

After a while, a certain activity among her roots aroused a mild arboreal curiosity in her. With senses that were rapidly atrophying, she perceived a middle-sized iron-grey animal with a sparse bristly coat which was diligently applying its long snout to the task of eating her three-cornered nuts. The animal was decidedly snaggle-toothed. It was lean and had a sharp corner to the centre of its back, as if that was all that remained of a wiry man's military bearing. It seemed to sense her attention, for it began to rub itself affectionately against her grey trunk – which still showed vestiges of rounded legs within it.

Ah well, thought the tree, and considerately let fall another shower of beech mast for it.

That was long ago. They say that Phega still stands on the hill. She is one of the beech trees that stand on the hill that always holds the last rays of the sun, but so many of the trees in that wood are so old that there is no way to tell which one she is. All the trees show vestiges of limbs in their trunks and all are given at times to inexplicable thrashings in their boughs, as if in memory of the agony of Phega's transformation. In the autumn their leaves turn the colour of Phega's hair and often fall only in spring, as though they cling harder than most leaves in honour of the sun.

There is nothing to eat their nuts now. The wild boar vanished from there centuries ago, though the name stayed. The maps usually call the place Boar's Hill.

Dragon Reserve, Home Eight

Where to begin? Neal and I had had a joke for years about a little green van coming to carry me off – this was when I said anything more than usually mad – and now it was actually happening. Mother and I stood at my bedroom window watching the van bouncing up the track between the dun green hills, and neither of us smiled. It wasn't a farm van, and most of our neighbours visit on horseback anyway. Before long, we could see it was dark green with a silver dragon insigne on the side.

'It *is* the Dragonate,' Mother said. 'Siglin, there's nothing I can do.' It astonished me to hear her say that. Mother only comes up to my shoulder, but she held her land and our household, servants, Neal and me, and all three of her husbands, in a hand like iron, *and* she drove out to plough or harvest if one of my fathers was ill. 'They said the dragons would take you,' she said. 'I should have seen. You think Orm informed on you?'

'I know he did,' I said. 'It was my fault for going into the Reserve.'

'I'll blood an axe on him,' Mother said, 'one of these days. But I can't do it over this. The neighbours would say he was quite right.' The van was turning between the stone walls of the farmyard now. Chickens were squirting and flapping out of its way and our sheepdog pups were barking their heads off. I could see Neal up on the wash-house roof watching yearningly. It's a good place to watch from because you can hide behind the chimney. Mother saw Neal too. 'Siglin,' she said, 'don't let on Neal knows about you.'

'No,' I said. 'Nor you either.'

'Say as little as you can, and wear the old blue dress – it makes you look younger,' Mother said, turning towards the door. 'You might just get off. Or they might just have come about something else,' she added. The van was stopping outside the front door now, right underneath my window. 'I'd best go and greet them,' Mother said, and hurried downstairs.

While I was forcing my head through the blue dress, I heard heavy boots on the steps and a crashing knock at the door. I shoved my arms into the sleeves, in too much of a hurry even to feel indignant about the dress. It makes me look about twelve and I am nearly grown up! At least, I was fourteen quite a few weeks ago now. But Mother was right. If I looked too immature to have awakened, they might not question me too hard. I hurried to the head of the stairs while I tied my hair with a childish blue ribbon. I knew they had come for me, but I had to *see*.

They were already inside when I got there, a whole line of tall men tramping down the stone hallway in the half-dark, and Mother was standing by the closed front door as if they had swept her aside. What a lot of them, just for me! I thought. I got a weak, sour feeling and could hardly move for horror. The man at the front of the line kept opening the doors all down the hallway, calm as you please, until he came to the main parlour at the end. 'This room will do nicely,' he said. 'Out you get, you.' And my oldest father, Timas, came shuffling hurriedly out in his slippers, clutching a pile of accounts and looking scared and worried. I saw Mother fold her arms. She always does when she is angry.

Another of them turned to Mother. 'We'll speak to you first,' he said, 'and your daughter after that. Then we want the rest of the household. Don't any of you try to leave.' And they went into the parlour with Mother and shut the door.

They hadn't even bothered to guard the doors. They just assumed we would obey them. I was shaking as I walked back to my room, but it was not terror any more. It was rage. I mean – we have all been brought up to honour the Dragonate. They are the cream of the men of the Ten Worlds. They are supposed to be gallant and kind and dedicated and devote their lives to keeping us safe from Thrallers, not to speak of maintaining justice, law and order all over the Ten Worlds. Dragonate men swear that Oath of Alienation, which means they can never have homes or families like ordinary people. Up to then, I'd felt sorry for them for that. They give up so much. But now I saw they felt it gave them the right to behave as if the rest of us were not real people. To walk in as if they owned our house. To order Timas out of his own parlour. Oh, I was angry!

I don't know how long Mother was in the parlour. I was so angry it felt like seconds until I heard flying feet and Neal hurried into my room. 'They want you now.'

I stood up and took some of my anger out on poor Neal. I said, 'Do you still want to join the Dragonate? Swear that stupid Oath? Behave like you own the Ten Worlds?'

It was mean. Neal looked at the floor. 'They said straight away,' he said. Of course he wanted to join. Every boy does, particularly on Sveridge, where women own most of the land. I swept down the stairs, angrier than ever. All the doors in the hallway were open and our people were standing in them, staring. The two housemen were at the dining-room door, the cattlewomen and two farmhands were looking out of the kitchen, and the stableboy and the second shepherd were craning out of the pantry. I thought, They still will be my people some day! I refuse to be frightened! My fathers were in the doorway of the bookroom. Donal and Yan were in work-clothes and had obviously rushed in without taking their boots off. I gave them what I hoped was a smile, but only

Timas smiled back. They all know! I thought as I opened the parlour door.

There were only five of them, sitting facing me across our best table. Five was enough. All of them stood up as I came in. The room seemed full of towering green uniforms. It was not at all like I expected. For one thing, the media always shows the Dragonate as fair and dashing and handsome, and none of these were. For another, the media had led me to expect uniforms with big silver panels. These were all plain green, and four of them had little silver stripes on one shoulder.

'Are you Sigrid's daughter, Siglin?' asked the one who had opened all the doors. He was a bleached, pious type like my father Donal and his hair was dust-colour.

'Yes,' I said rudely. 'Who are you? Those aren't Dragonate uniforms.'

'Camerati, lady,' said one who was brown all over with wriggly hair. He was young, younger than my father Yan, and he smiled cheerfully, like Yan does. But he made my stomach go cold. Camerati are the crack force, cream of the Dragonate. They say a man has to be a genius even to be considered for it.

'Then what are you doing here?' I said. 'And why are you all standing up?'

The one in the middle, obviously the chief one, said, 'We always stand up when a lady enters the room. And we are here because we were on a tour of inspection at Holmstad anyway, and there was a Slaver scare on this morning. So we offered to take on civic duties for the regular Dragonate. Now if that answers your questions, let me introduce us all.' He smiled too, which twisted his white, crumpled face like a demon mask. 'I am Lewin, and I'm Updriten here. On your far left is Driten Palino, our recorder.' This was the pious type, who nodded. 'Next to him is Driten Renick of Law Wing.' Renick was elderly and iron-grey, with one of those necks that look like a chicken's leg. He just stared. 'Underdriten Terens is on my left, my aide and witness.' That was brown-and-wriggly. 'And beyond him is Cadet Alectis, who is travelling with us to Home Nine.'

Alectis looked a complete baby, only a year older than me, with pink cheeks and sandy hair. He and Terens both bowed and smiled so politely that I nearly smiled back. Then I realized that they were treating me as if I was a visitor. In my own home! I bowed freezingly, the way Mother usually does to Orm.

'Please sit down, Siglin,' Lewin said politely.

I nearly didn't, because that might keep them standing up too. But they were all so tall I'd already got a crick in my neck. So I sat grandly on the chair they'd put ready facing the table. 'Thank you,' I said. 'You are a very kind host, Updriten Lewin.' To my great joy, Alectis went bright red at that, but the other four simply sat down too. Pious Palino took up a memo block and poised his fingers over its keys. This seemed to be in case the recorder in front of Lewin went wrong. Lewin set that going. Wriggly Terens leaned over and passed me another little square box.

'Keep this in your hand,' he said, 'or your answers may not come out clearly.'

I caught the words *lie detector* from his wriggly head as clearly as if he had said them aloud. I don't think I showed how very scared I was, but my hand made the box wet almost straight away.

'Court is open,' Lewin said to the recorder. 'Presiding Updriten Lewin.' He gave a string of numbers and then said, 'First hearing starts on charges against Siglin, of Upland Holding, Wormstow, North Sveridge on Home Eight, accused of being heg and heg concealing its nature. Questions begin. Siglin, are you clear what being heg is?' He crumpled one eyebrow upwards at me.

'No,' I said. After all, no one has told me in so many words. It's just a thing people whisper and shudder at.

'Then you'd better understand this,' Lewin said. He really was the ugliest and most outlandish of the five. Dragonate men are never posted to the world of their birth, and I thought Lewin must come from one a long way off. His hair was black, so black it had blue lights, but, instead of being dark all over to match it, like wriggly Terens, he was a lot whiter than me and his eyes were a most piercing blue – almost the colour they make the sky on the media. 'If the charges are proved,' he said, 'you face death by beheading, since that is the only form of execution a heg cannot survive. Renick—'

Elderly Renick swept sourly in before Lewin had finished speaking. 'The law defines a heg as one with human form who is not human. Medical evidence of brain pattern or nerve and muscle deviations is required prior to execution, but for a first hearing it is enough to establish that the subject can perform one or more of the following: mind-reading, kindling fire or moving objects at a distance, healing or killing by the use of the mind alone, surviving shooting, drowning or suffocation, or enslaving or otherwise afflicting the mind of a beast or human.'

He had the kind of voice that bores you anyway. I thought, Great gods! I don't think I can do half those things! Maybe I looked blank. Palino stopped clicking his memo block to say, 'It's very important to understand why these creatures must be stamped out. They can make people into puppets in just the same way that the Slavers can. Foul.' Actually, I think he was explaining to Alectis. Alectis nodded humbly. Palino said, definitely to me, 'Slavers do it with those V-shaped collars. You must have seen them on the media. Quite foul.'

'We call them Thrallers,' I said. Foul or not, I thought, I'm the only one of me I've got! I can't help being made the way I am.

Lewin flapped his hand to shut Palino up and Renick went on again. 'A heg is required by law to give itself up for execution. Any normal person who knowingly conceals a heg is likewise liable for execution.' Now I knew why Mother had told me to keep Neal out of it.

Then it seemed to be Palino's turn. He said, 'Personal details follow. How old are you – er – Sigrun?'

'Sig*lin*,' I said. 'Fourteen last month.'

Renick stretched out his chicken neck. 'In this court's opinion, subject is old enough to have awakened as heg.' He looked at Terens.

Terens said, 'I witness. Girls awaken early, don't they?'

Palino, tapping away, said, 'Mother, Sigrid, also of Upland Holding.'

At which Lewin leaned forward. 'Cleared by this court,' he said. I was relieved to hear that. Mother is clever. She hadn't let them know she knew.

Palino said, 'And your father is—?'

'Timas, Donal and Yan,' I said. I had to bite the inside of my cheek not to laugh at how annoyed he was by that.

'Great Tew, girl!' he said. 'A person can't have three fathers!'

'Hold it, Palino,' said Lewin. 'You're up against local customs here. Men outnumber women three to one on Home Eight.'

'In Home Eight law, a woman's child is the child of all her husbands equally,' Renick put in. 'No more anomalous than the status of the Ahrings on Seven really.'

'Then tell me how I rephrase my question,' Palino said waspishly, 'in the light of the primitive customs on Home Eight.'

I said, 'There's no such place as Home Eight. This world is called Sveridge.' Primitive indeed!

Palino gave me a pale glare. I gave him one back. Lewin cut

in, smooth and humorous. 'You're up against primitive Dragonate customs here, Siglin. We refer to all the worlds by numbers, from Albion, Home One, to Yurov, Home Ten, and the worlds of the Outer Manifold are Cath One, Two, Three and Four to us. Have you really no idea which of your mother's husbands is actually your father?'

After that they all began asking me. Being heg is inherited, and I knew they were trying to find out if any of my fathers was heg too. At length even Alectis joined in, clearing his throat and going very red because he was only a Cadet. 'I know we're not supposed to know,' he said, 'but I bet you've tried to guess. I did. I found out in the end.'

That told me he was Sveridge too. And he suddenly wasn't a genius in the Camerati any more, but just a boy. 'Then I bet you wished you hadn't!' I said. 'My friend Inga at Hillfoot found out, and hers turned out to be the one she's always hated.'

'Well,' said Alectis, redder still. 'Er – it wasn't the one I'd hoped—'

'That's why I've never asked,' I said. And that was true. I'd always hoped it was Timas till now. Donal is so moral, and Yan is fun, but he's under Donal's thumb even more than he's under Mother's. But I didn't want my dear old Timas in trouble.

'Well, a cell-test should settle it,' Lewin said. 'Memo for that, Palino. Terens, remind me to ask how the regular Dragonate usually deal with it. Now – Siglin, this charge was laid against you by a man known as Orm the Worm Warden. Do you know this man?'

'Don't I just!' I said. 'He's been coming here and looking through our windows and giggling ever since I can remember! He lives on the Worm Reserve in a shack. Mother says he's a bit wrong in the head, but no one's locked him up because he's so good at managing dragons.'

There! I thought. That'll show them you can't trust a word
Orm says! But they just nodded. Terens murmured to Alectis,
'Sveridge worm, *Draco draco*, was adopted as the symbol of the
Dragonate—'

'We *have* all heard of dragons,' Palino said to him nastily.

Lewin cut in again. I suppose it was his job as presiding
Updriten. 'Siglin. Orm, in his deposition, refers to an incident
in the Worm Reserve last Friday. We want you to tell us what
happened then, if anything.'

Grim's teeth! I thought. I'd hoped they'd just ask me questions. You can nearly always get round questions without
lying. And I'd no idea what Orm had said. 'I don't usually go to
the Dragon Reserve,' I said, 'because of being Mother's heir.
When I was born, the Fortune Teller said the dragons would
take me.' I saw Renick and Palino exchange looks of contempt
at our primitive customs. But Mother had in a good Teller, and
I believe it enough to keep away from the Reserve.

'So why did you go last Friday?' said Lewin.

'Neal dared me to,' I said. I couldn't say anything else with a
lie detector in my hands. Neal gets on with Orm, and he goes
to the Reserve a lot. Up to Friday, he thought I was being silly
refusing to go. But the real trouble was that Neal had been
there all along, riding Barra beside me on Nellie, and now
Lewin had made me mention Neal, I couldn't think how to
pretend he hadn't been there. 'I rode up behind Wormhill,' I
said, 'and then over the Saddle until we could see the sea. That
means you're in the Reserve.'

'Isn't the Reserve fenced off at all?' Renick asked dis-
approvingly.

'No,' I said. 'Worms – dragons – can fly, so what's the point?
They stay in because the shepherds bombard them if they
don't, and we all give them so many sheep every month.' And
Orm makes them stay in, bad cess to him! 'Anyway,' I said, 'I
was riding down a kyle – that's what we call those narrow

stony valleys – when my horse reared and threw me. Next
thing I knew—'

'Question,' said Palino. 'Where was your brother at this
point?'

He *would* spot that! I thought. 'Some way behind,' I said. Six
feet, in fact. Barra is used to dragons and just stood stock still.
'This dragon shuffled head down with its great snout across
the kyle,' I said. 'I sat on the ground with its great amused eye
staring at me and listening to Nellie clattering away up the
kyle. It was a youngish one, sort of brown-green, which is
why I hadn't seen it. They can keep awfully still when they
want to. And I said a rude word to it.

' "That's no way to speak to a dragon!" Orm said. He was
sitting on a rock on the other side of the kyle, quite close,
laughing at me.' I wondered whether to fill the gap in my story
where Neal was by telling them that Orm always used to be
my idea of Jack Frost when I was little. He used to call at
Uplands for milk then, to feed dragon fledglings on, but he
was so rude to Mother that he goes to Inga's place now. Orm is
long and skinny and brown, with a great white bush of hair
and beard, and he smells rather. But they must have smelt
him in Holmstad, so I said, 'I was scared, because the dragon
was so near I could feel the heat off it. And then Orm said,
"You have to speak politely to this dragon. He's my particular
friend. You give me a nice kiss, and he'll let you go." '

I think Lewin murmured something like, 'Ah, I thought it
might be that!' but it may just have been in his mind. I don't
know because I was in real trouble then, trying to pick my way
through without mentioning Neal. The little box got so wet it
nearly slipped out of my hand. I said, 'Every time I tried to get
up, Orm beckoned, and the dragon pushed me down with its
snout with a gamesome look in its eye. And Orm cackled with
laughter. They were both really having fun.' This was true,
but the dragon also pushed between me and Neal and

mantled its wings when Neal tried to help. And Neal said some
pretty awful things to Orm. Orm giggled and insulted Neal
back. He called Neal a booby who couldn't stand up for
himself against women. 'Then,' I said, 'then Orm said I was
the image of Mother at the same age – which isn't true: I'm
bigger all over – and he said, "Come on, kiss and be friends!"
Then he skipped down from his rock and took hold of my
arm—'

I had to stop and swallow there. The really awful thing was
that, as soon as Orm had hold of me, I got a strong picture from
his mind: Orm kissing a pretty lady smaller than me, with
another dragon, an older, blacker one, looking on from the
background. And I recognized the lady as Mother, and I was
absolutely disgusted.

'So I hit Orm and got up and ran away,' I said. 'And Orm
shouted to me all the time I was running up the kyle and
catching Nellie, but I took no notice.'

'Question,' said Renick. 'What action did the dragon take?'

'They – they always chase you if you run, I'd heard,' Alectis
said shyly.

'And this one appears to have been trained to Orm's
command,' Palino said.

'It didn't chase me,' I said. 'It stayed with Orm.' The reason
was that neither of them could move. I still don't know what I
did – I had a picture of myself leaning back inside my own
head and swinging mighty blows, the way you do with a
pickaxe – and Neal says the dragon went over like a cartload of
potatoes and Orm fell flat on his back. But Orm could speak
and he screamed after us that I'd killed the worm and I'd pay
for it. But I was screaming too, at Neal, to keep away from me
because I was heg. That was the thing that horrified me most.
Before that I'd tried not to think I was. After all, for all I knew,
everyone can read minds and get a book from the bookcase
without getting up from their chair. And Neal told me to pull

myself together and think what we were going to tell Mother. We decided to say that we'd met a dragon in the Reserve and I'd killed it and found out I was heg. I made Neal promise not to mention Orm. I couldn't bear even to think of Orm. And Mother was wonderfully understanding, and I really didn't realize that I'd put her in danger as well as Neal.

Lewin looked down at the recorder. 'Dragons are a preserved species,' he said. 'Orm claims that you caused grievous bodily harm to a dragon in his care. What have you to say to that?'

'How could I?' I said. Oh I was scared. 'It was nearly as big as a house.'

Renick was on to that at once. 'Query,' he said. 'Prevarication?'

'Obviously,' said Palino, clicking away at his block.

'We haven't looked at that dragon yet,' Terens said.

'We'll do that on our way back,' Lewin said, sighing rather. 'Siglin, I regret to say there is enough mismatch between your account and Orm's, and enough odd activity on that brainmeasure you hold in your hand, to warrant my taking you to Holmstad Command Centre for further examination. Be good enough to go with Terens and Alectis to the van and wait there while we complete our inquiries here.'

I stood up. Everything seemed to drain out of me. I could lam them like I lammed that dragon, I thought. But Holmstad would only send a troop out to see why they hadn't come back. And I put my oldest dress on for nothing! I thought as I walked down the hallway with Terens and Alectis. The doors were all closed. Everyone had guessed. The van smelt of clean plastic and it was very warm and light because the roof was one big window. I sat between Terens and Alectis on the back seat. They pulled straps round us all – safety straps, but they made me feel a true prisoner.

After a while, Terens said, 'You could sue Orm if the

evidence doesn't hold up, you know.' I think he was trying to be kind, but I couldn't answer.

After another while, Alectis said, 'With respect, Driten, I think suspects should be told the truth about the so-called lie detector.'

'Alectis, I didn't hear you say that,' Terens said. He pretended to look out of the window, but he must have known I knew he had deliberately thought *lie detector* at me as he passed me the thing. They're told to. Dragonate think of everything. I sat and thought I'd never hated anything so much as I hated our kind, self-sacrificing Dragonate, and I tried to take a last look at the stony yard, tipped sideways on the hill, with our square stone house at the top of it. But it wouldn't register somehow.

Then the front door opened and the other three came out, bringing Neal with them. Behind them, the hall was full of our people, with Mother in front, just staring. I just stared too, while Palino opened the van door and shoved Neal into the seat beside me. 'Your brother has admitted being present at the incident,' he said as he strapped himself in beside Neal. I could tell he was pleased.

By this time, Lewin and Renick had strapped themselves into the front seat. Lewin drove away without a word. Neal looked back at the house. I couldn't. 'Neal—?' I whispered.

'Just like you said,' Neal said, loudly and defiantly. 'Behaving as if they own the Ten Worlds. I wouldn't join now if they begged me to!' Why did I have to go and say that to him? 'Why did *you* join?' Neal said rudely to Alectis.

'Six brothers,' Alectis said, staring ahead.

The other four all started talking at once. Lewin asked Renick the quickest way to the Reserve by road and Renick said it was down through Wormstow. 'I hope the dragons eat you!' Neal said. This was while Palino was leaning across us to say to Terens, 'Where's our next inspection after this hole?'

And Terens said, 'We go straight on to Arkloren on Nine. Alectis will get to see some other parts of the Manifold shortly.' Behaving as if we didn't exist. Neal shrugged and shut up.

The Dragonate van was much smoother and faster than a farm van. We barely bounced over the stony track that loops down to Hillfoot, and it seemed no time before we were speeding down the better road, with the rounded yellowish Upland Hills peeling past on either side. I love my hills, covered with yellow ling that only grows here on Sveridge, and the soft light of the sun through our white and grey clouds. Renick, still making conversation, said he was surprised to find the hills so old and worn down. 'I thought Eight was a close parallel with Seven!' he said.

Lewin answered in a boring voice, 'I wouldn't know. I haven't seen Seven since I was a Cadet.'

'Oh, the mountains are much higher and greener there,' Renick said. 'I was posted in Camberia for years. Lovely spot.'

Lewin just grunted. Quite a wave of homesickness filled the van. I could feel Renick thinking of Seven and Alectis not wanting to go to Nine. Terens was remembering boating on Romaine when he was Neal's age. Lewin was thinking of Seven, in spite of the grunt. We were coming over Jiot Fell already then, with the Giant Stones standing on top of the world against the sky. A few more turns in the road would bring us out above Wormstow where Neal and I went – used to go – to school. What about me? I was thinking. I'm homesick for life. And Neal. Poor Mother.

Then the air suddenly filled with noise, like the most gigantic sheet being torn.

Lewin said, 'What the—?' and we all stared upwards. A great silvery shape screamed overhead. And another of a fatter shape, more blue than silver, screamed after it, both of them only just inside the clouds. Alectis put up an astonished pointing arm. 'Thraller! The one behind's a Slaver!'

'What's it doing *here*?' said Terens. 'Someone must have slipped up.'

'Ours was a stratoship!' said Palino. 'What's going on?'

A huge ball of fire rolled into being on the horizon, above the Giant Stones. I felt Lewin slam on the brakes. 'We got him!' one of them cried out.

'The Slaver got ours,' Lewin said. The brakes were still yelling like a she-worm when the blast hit.

I lose the next bit. I start remembering again a few seconds later, sitting up straight with a bruised lip, finding the van round sideways a long way on down the road. In front of me, Renick's straps had broken. He was lying kind of folded against the windscreen. I saw Lewin pull himself upright and pull at Renick. And stop pulling quickly. My ears had gone deaf, because I could only hear Lewin as if he was very far off. '—hurt in the back?'

Palino looked along the four of us and shouted, 'Fine! Is Renick—?'

'Dead,' Lewin shouted back. 'Neck broken.' He was jiggling furiously at buttons in the controls. My ears started to work again and I heard him say, 'Holmstad's not answering. Nor's Ranefell. I'm going back to Holmstad. Fast.'

We set off again with a roar. The van seemed to have lost its silencer and it rattled all over, but it went. And how it went. We must have done nearly a hundred down Jiot, squealing on the bends. In barely minutes, we could see Wormstow spread out below, old grey houses and new white ones, and all those imported trees that make the town so pretty. The clouds over the houses seemed to darken and go dense.

'Uh-oh!' said Terens.

The van jolted to another yelling stop. It was not the clouds. Something big and dark was coming down through the clouds, slowly descending over Wormstow. Something enormous. 'What *is* that?' Neal and Alectis said together.

'Hedgehog,' said Terens.

'A slaveship,' Palino explained, sort of mincing the word out to make it mean more. 'Are – are we out of range here?'

'I most thoroughly hope so,' Lewin said. 'There's not much we can do with hand weapons.'

We sat and stared as the thing came down. The lower it got, the more Renick's bent-up shape was in my way. I kept wishing Lewin would do something about him, but nobody seemed to be able to think of anything but that huge descending ship. I saw why they call them hedgehogs. It was rounded above and flat beneath, with bits and pieces sticking out all over like bristles. Hideous somehow. And it came and hung squatting over the roofs of the houses below. There it let out a ramp like a long black tongue, right down into the Market Square. Then another into High Street, between the rows of trees, breaking a tree as it passed.

As soon as the ramps touched ground, Lewin started the van and drove down towards Wormstow.

'No, stop!' I said, even though I knew he couldn't. The compulsion those Slavers put out is really strong. Some of it shouts inside your head, like your own conscience through an amplifier, and some of it is gentle and creeping and insidious, like Mother telling you gently to come along now and be sensible. I found I was thinking, Oh well, I'm sure Lewin's right. Tears rolled down Alectis's face, and Neal was sniffing. We had to go to the ship, which was now hanging a little above us. I could see people hurrying out of houses and racing to crowd up the ramp in the Market Square. People I knew. So it must be all right, I thought. The van was having to weave past loose horses that people had been riding or driving. That was how I got a glimpse of the other ramp, through trees and the legs of a horse. Soldiers were pouring down it, running

like a muddy river, in waves. Each wave had a little group of
kings, walking behind it, directing the soldiers. They had
shining crowns and shining Vs on their chests and walked
mighty, like gods.

That brought me to my senses. 'Lewin,' I said. 'Those are
Thrallers and you're *not* to do what they say, do you hear?'
Lewin just drove round a driverless cart, towards the Market
Square. He was going to be driving up that ramp in a second. I
was so frightened then that I lammed Lewin – not like I
lammed the dragon, but in a different way. Again it's hard to
describe, except that this time I was giving orders. Lewin was
to obey *me*, not the Thrallers, and my orders were to drive
away *at once*. When nothing seemed to happen, I got so scared
that I seemed to be filling the whole van with my orders.

'Thank you,' Lewin said, in a croaking sort of voice. He
jerked the van round into Worm Parade and roared down it,
away from the ship and the terrible ramps. The swerve sent
the van door open with a slam and, to my relief, the body of
poor Renick tumbled out into the road.

But everyone else screamed out, 'No! What are you doing?'
and clutched their heads. The compulsion was far, far worse if
you disobeyed. I felt as if layers of my brain were being peeled
off with hot pincers. Neal was crying, like Alectis. Terens was
moaning. It hurt so much that I filled the van frantically with
more and more orders. Lewin made grinding sounds deep in
his throat, and kept on driving away, with the door flapping
and banging.

Palino took his straps undone and yelled. 'You're going the
wrong way, you damn cariarder!' I couldn't stop him at all. He
started to climb into the front seat to take the controls away
from Lewin. Alectis and Neal both rose up too and shoved him
off Lewin. So Palino gave that up and scrambled for the open
flapping door instead. Nobody could do a thing. He just
jumped out and went rolling in the road. I didn't see what he

did then, because I was too busy giving orders, but Neal says he simply scrambled up and staggered back towards the ship and the ramp.

We drove for another horrible half-mile, and then we must have got out of range. Everything suddenly went easy. It was like when somebody lets go the other end of a rope you're both pulling, and you go over backwards. Wham. And I felt too dim and stunned to move.

'Thank the gods!' I heard Terens more or less howl.

'It's Siglin you should be thanking,' Lewin said. 'Alectis, climb over to the front and shut that door. Then try and raise Holmstad again.'

Neal says the door was too battered to shut. Alectis had to hold it with one hand while he worked the broadcaster with the other. I heard him saying that Holmstad still didn't answer through the roaring and rattling the van made when Lewin put on speed up the long looping gradient of Wormjiot. We hadn't nearly got up to the Saddle, when Terens said, 'It's going! Aren't they quick!' I looked back, still feeling dim and horrible, in time to see the squatting hedgehog rise up inside the clouds again.

'Now you can thank the gods,' Lewin said. 'They didn't think we were worth chasing. Try medium wave, Alectis.' There is an outcrop of ragged rock near the head of Wormjiot. Lewin drove off the road and stopped behind it while Alectis fiddled with knobs.

Instead of getting dance music and cookery hints, Alectis got a voice that fizzed and crackled. 'This is Dragonate Fanejiot, Sveridge South, with an emergency message for all Dragonate units still in action. You are required to make your way to Fanejiot and report there soonest.' It said that about seven times, then it said, 'We can now confirm earlier reports that Home Nine is in Slaver hands. Here is a list of bases on Home Eight that have been taken by Slavers.' It was a long list.

Holmstad came quite early on it, and Ranefell about ten names after that.

Lewin reached across and turned it off. 'Did someone say we slipped up?' he said. 'That was an understatement.'

'Fanejiot is two thousand flaming miles from here!' Terens said. 'With an ocean and who knows how many Slavers in between!'

'Well put,' said Lewin. 'Did Palino's memo block go to the Slavers with him?'

It was lying on the back seat beside Neal. Neal tried to pretend it wasn't, but Alectis turned round and grabbed it as Neal tried to shove it on the floor. I was lying back in my straps, feeling grey and thinking, We could get away now. I'd better lam them all again. But all I did was lie there and watch Neal and Alectis having an angry tug-of-war. Then watch Lewin turn round and pluck the block away from the pair of them.

'Don't be a fool,' he said to Neal. 'I've already erased the recorder. And if I hadn't had Renick and Palino breathing righteously down our necks, I'd never have recorded anything. It goes against the grain to take in children.'

Lewin pressed the *erase* on the memo block and it gave out a satisfied sort of gobble. Neither of the other two said anything, but I could feel Alectis thinking how much he had always hated Palino. Terens was looking down at Wormstow through a fieldglass and trying not to remember a boy in Cadets with him who had turned heg and given himself up. I felt I wanted to say thank you. But I was too shy to do anything but sit up and look at Wormstow too, between the jags of the rock. Even without a fieldglass, I could see the place throbbing like a broken anthill with all the Slaver troops.

'Getting ready to move out and mop up the countryside,' Terens said.

'Yes, and that's where most people live,' Lewin said. 'Farms and holdings in the hills. What's the quickest way to the Dragon Reserve?'

'There's a track on the right round the next bend,' said Neal. 'Why?'

'Because it's the safest place I can think of,' Lewin said.

Neal and I looked at one another. You didn't need to be heg to tell that Neal was thinking, just as I was, that this was a bit much. They were supposed to help all those people in the holdings. Instead, they thought of the safest place and ran there! So neither of us said that the track was only a bridle path, and we didn't try to warn them not to take the van into the Reserve. We just sat there while Lewin drove it uphill, and then lumping and bumping and rattling up the path. The path gave out in the marshy patch below the Saddle, but Lewin kept grinding and roaring on, throwing up peat in squirts, until we tipped downhill again and bounced down a yellow fellside. We were in the Reserve by then. The ling was growing in lurid green patches, black at the roots, where dragons had burnt it in the mating season. They fight a lot then.

We got some way into the Reserve. The van gave out clanging sounds and smelt bad, but Lewin kept it going by driving on the most level parts. We were in a wide stony scoop, with yellow hills all round, when the smell got worse and the van just stopped. Alectis let go of the door. 'Worms – dragons,' he said, 'don't like machines, I've heard.'

'Now he tells us!' said Terens, and we all got out. We all looked as if we had been in an accident – I mean, I know we had in a way, but we looked worse than I'd expected: sort of ragged and pale and shivery. Lewin turned his foot on a stone, which made him clutch his chest and swear. Neither of the other two even asked if he was all right. That is the Dragonate way. They just set out walking. Neal and I went with them, thinking of the best place to dodge off up a kyle, so that we could run home and try and warn Mother about the Slavers.

'Where that bog turns into a stream – I'll say when,' Neal was whispering, when a dragon came over the hill into the valley and made straight for us.

'Stand still!' said Alectis. Lewin and Terens each had a gun in their hand without seeming to have moved. Alectis didn't, and he was white.

'They only eat moving prey,' Neal said, because he was sorry for him. 'Make sure not to panic and run and you're fine.'

I was sorry for Alectis too, so I added, 'It's probably only after the van. They love metal.'

Lewin crumpled his face at me and said 'Ah!' for some reason.

The dragon came quite slowly, helping itself with its spread wings and hanging its head rather. It was a bad colour, sort of creamy through the brown-green. I thought it might be one of the sick ones that turn man-eater, and I tried to brace myself and stop feeling so tired and shaky so that I could lam it. But Neal said, 'That's Orm's dragon! You didn't kill it after all!'

It *was* Orm's dragon. By this time, it was near enough for me to see the heat off it quivering in the air, and I recognized the gamesome, shrewd look in its eye. But since it had every reason to hate me, that didn't make me feel much better. It came straight for me too. We all stood like statues. And it came right up to me and bent its neck, and laid its huge brown head on the ling in front of my feet, where it puffed out a sigh that made Lewin cough and gasp another swearword. It had felt me coming, the dragon said, and it was here to say sorry. It hadn't meant to upset me. It had thought it was a game.

That made me feel terrible. 'I'm sorry too,' I said. 'I lost my head. I didn't mean to hurt you. That was Orm's fault.'

Orm was only playing too, the dragon said. Orm called him Huffle, and I could too if I liked. Was he forgiven? He was ashamed.

'Of course I forgive you, Huffle,' I said. 'Do you forgive me?'

Yes. Huffle lifted his head up and went a proper colour at once. Dragons are like people that way.

'Ask him to fetch Orm here,' Lewin said urgently.

I didn't want to see Orm, and Lewin was a coward. 'Ask him yourself,' I said. 'He understands.'

'Yes, but I don't think he'd do it for me,' Lewin said.

'Then, will you fetch Orm for Lewin?' I asked Huffle.

He gave me a cheeky look. Maybe. Presently. He sauntered away past Terens, who moved his head back from Huffle's rattling right wing, looking as if he thought his last hour had come, and went to have a look at the van. He put out a great clawed foot, in a thoughtful sort of way, and tore the loose door off it. Then he tucked the door under his right front foreleg and departed, deliberately slowly, on three legs, helping himself with his wings, so that rocks rattled and flapped all along the valley.

Alectis sat down rather suddenly. But Lewin made him leap up again and help Terens get the broadcaster out of the van before any more dragons found it. They never did get it out. They were still working and waggling at it to get it loose, and Lewin was standing over Neal and me, so that we couldn't sneak off, when we heard that humming kind of whistle that you get from a dragon in flight. We whirled round. This dragon was a big black one, coasting low over the hill opposite and gliding down the valley. They don't often fly high. It came to ground with that grinding of stones and leathery slap of wings closing that always tells you a dragon is landing. It arched its black neck and looked at us disdainfully.

Orm was sitting on its back looking equally disdainful. It was one of those times when Orm looks grave and grand. He sat very upright, with his hair and beard combed straight by the wind of flying, and his big pale eyes hardly looked mad at all. Neal was the only one of us he deigned to notice. 'Good afternoon, Neal Sigridsson,' he said. 'You keep bad company. Dragonate are not human.'

Neal was very angry with Orm. He put my heart in my mouth by saying, quite calmly, 'Then in that case, I'm the only human here.' With that dragon standing glaring! I've been brought up to despise boys, but I think that is a mistake.

To my relief, Orm just grinned. 'That's the way, boy,' he said. 'Not a booby after all, are you?'

Then Lewin took my breath away by going right up to the dragon. He had his gun, of course, but that wouldn't have been much use against a dragon. He went so near that the dragon had to turn its head out of his way. 'We've dropped the charges,' he said. 'And you should never have brought them.'

Orm looked down at him. 'You,' he said, 'know a thing or two.'

'I know dragons don't willingly attack humans,' Lewin said. 'I always read up on a case before I hear it.' At this, Orm put on his crazy look and made his mad cackle. 'Stop that!' said Lewin. 'The Slavers have invaded. Wormstow's full of Slaver troops and we need your help. I want to get everyone from the outlying farms into the Reserve and persuade the dragons to protect them. Can you help us do that?'

That took my breath away again, and Neal's too. We did a quick goggle at one another. Perhaps the Dragonate was like it was supposed to be after all!

Orm said, 'Then we'd better get busy,' and slid down from the dragon. He still towered over Lewin. Orm is huge. As soon as he was down, the black dragon lumbered across to the van and started taking it to bits. That brought other dragons coasting whistling in from all sides of the valley, to crunch to earth and hurry to the van too. In seconds, it was surrounded in black and green-brown shapes the size of haybarns. And Orm talked, at the top of his voice, through the sound of metal tearing, and big claws screaming on iron, and wings clapping, and angry grunts when two dragons happened to get hold of the same piece of van. Orm always talks a lot. But this time, he was being particularly garrulous, to give the dragons time to lumber away with their pieces of van, hide them and come back. 'They won't even do what Orm says until they've got their metal,' I whispered to Terens, who got rather impatient with Orm.

Orm said the best place to put people was the high valley at the centre of the Reserve. 'There's an old she-drake with a litter just hatched,' he said. 'No one will get past her when she's feared for her young. I'll speak to her. But the rest are to promise me she's not disturbed.' As for telling everyone at the farms where to come, Orm said the dragons could do that, providing Lewin could think of a way of sending a message by them. 'You see, most folk can't hear a dragon when it speaks,' he said. 'And some who can hear—' with a nasty look at me '—speak back to wound.' He was still very angry with me. I kept on the other side of Terens and Alectis when the dragons all came swooping back.

Terens set the memo block to *repeat* and tapped out an official message from Lewin. Then he tore off page after page with the same thing on it. Orm handed each page to a dragon, saying things like, 'Take this to the fat cow up at Hillfoot.' Or, 'Drop this on young vinegar lady at Crowtop – hard.' Or, 'This is for Dopey at High Jiot, but don't give it her, give it to her youngest husband or they'll never get moving.'

Some of the things he said made me laugh a lot. But it was only when Alectis asked what was so funny and Neal kicked my ankle, that I realized I was the only one who could hear the things Orm said. Each dragon, as it got its page, ran down the valley and took off, showering us with stones from the jump they gave to get higher in the air than usual. Their wings boom when they fly high. Orm took off on the black dragon last of all, saying he would go and warn the she-drake.

Lewin crumpled his face ruefully at the few bits of van remaining, and we set off to walk to the valley ourselves. It was a long way. Over ling slopes and up among boulders in the kyles we trudged, looking up nervously every so often when fat bluish Slaver fliers screamed through the clouds overhead. After a while, our dragons began booming overhead too, seawards to roost. Terens counted them and said every one we had sent seemed to have come back now. He said he wished he had wings. It was sunset by the time we reached the valley. By that time, Lewin was bent over, holding his chest and swearing every other step. But everyone was still pretending, in that stupid Dragonate way, that he was all right. We came up on the cliffs, where the kyle winds down to the she-drake's valley, and there was the sunset lighting the sea and the towers of rock out there, and the waves crashing round the rocks, where the young dragons were flying to roost – and Lewin actually pretended to admire the view. 'I knew a place like this on Seven,' he said. 'Except there were trees instead of dragons. I can't get used to the way Eight doesn't have trees.'

He was going to sit down to rest, I think, but Orm came up the kyle just then. Huffle was hulking behind him. 'So you got here at last!' Orm said in his rudest way.

'We have,' said Lewin. 'Now would you mind telling me what you were playing at bringing those charges against Siglin?'

'You should be glad I did. You'd all be in a slaveship now if I hadn't,' Orm said.

'But you weren't to know that, were you?' Terens said.

'Not to speak of risking being charged yourself,' added Lewin.

Orm leant on his hand against Huffle, like you might against a wall. 'She half killed this dragon!' he said. 'That's why! All I did was ask her for a kiss and she screams and lays into poor Huffle. My own daughter, and she tries to kill a dragon! And I thought, Right, my lady, then you're no daughter of mine any more! And I flew Huffle's mother straight into Holmstad and laid charges. I was that angry! My own father tended dragons, and his mother before him. And my daughter tried to kill one! You wonder I was angry?'

'Nobody *told* me!' I said. I had that draining-away feeling again. I was quite glad when Terens took hold of my elbow and said something like, 'Steady, steady!'

'Are you telling the truth?' Neal said.

'I'm sure he is,' Lewin said. 'Your sister has his eyes.'

'Ask Timas,' said Orm. 'He married your mother the year after I did. He can take being bossed about. I can't. I went back to my dragons. But I suppose there's a record of that?' he said challengingly to Lewin.

'And the divorce,' said Lewin. 'Terens looked it up for me. But I expect the Slavers have destroyed it by now.'

'And she never told you?' Orm said to me. He wagged his shaggy eyebrows at me almost forgivingly. 'I'll have a bone to pick with her over that,' he said.

Mother arrived just as we'd all got down into the valley. She looked very indomitable, as she always does on horseback, and all our people were with her, down to both our shepherds. They had carts of clothes and blankets and food. Mother knew the valley as well as Orm did. She used to meet Orm there when she was a girl. She set out for the Reserve as soon as she heard the broadcast about the invasion, and the dragon we sent her met them on the way. That's Mother for you. The rest of the neighbours didn't get there for some hours after that.

I didn't think Mother's face – or Timas's – could hold such a mixture of feelings as they did when they saw Neal and me and the Dragonate men all with Orm. When Orm saw Mother, he folded his arms and grinned. Huffle rested his huge chin on Orm's shoulder, looking interested.

'Here she comes,' Orm said to Huffle. 'Oh, I do love a good quarrel!'

They had one. It was one of the loudest I'd ever heard. Terens took Neal and me away to help look after Lewin. He turned out to have broken some ribs when the blast hit the van, but he wouldn't let anyone look even until I ordered him to. After that, Neal, Alectis and I sat under our haycart and talked, mostly about the irony of Fate. You see, Neal has always secretly wished Fate had given him Orm as a father, and I'm the one that's got Orm. Neal's father is Timas. Alectis says he can see the likeness. We'd both gladly swap. Then Alectis confessed that he'd been hating the Dragonate so much that he was thinking of running away – which is a serious crime. But now the Slavers have come, and there doesn't seem to be much of a Dragonate any more, he feels quite different. He admires Lewin.

Lewin consented to rest while Terens and Mother organized everyone into a makeshift camp in the valley, but he was up and about again the next day, because he said the Slavers were bound to come the day after, when they found the holdings were deserted. The big black she-drake sat in her cave at the head of the kyle, with her infants between her forefeet, watching groups of people rushing round to do what Lewin said, and didn't seem to mind at all. Huffle said she'd been bored and bad-tempered up to then. We made life interesting. Actually that she-drake reminds me of Mother. Both of them made me give them a faithful report of the battle.

I don't think the Slavers knew about the dragons. They just knew that there was a concentration of people in here, and they came straight across the Reserve to get us. As soon as the dragons told Orm they were coming, Lewin had us all out hiding in the hills in their path, except for Mother and Timas and Inga's mother and a few more who had shotguns. They had to stay and guard the little kids in the camp. The rest of us had any weapon we could find. Neal and Alectis had bows and arrows. Inga had her airgun. Donal and most of the farmers had scythes. The shepherds all had their slingshots. I was in the front with Lewin, because I was supposed to stop the effect of the Slavers' collars. Orm was there too, although nobody had ever admitted in so many words that Orm might be heg. All Orm did was to ask the dragons to keep back, because we didn't want *them* enslaved by those collars.

And there they came, a huddle of sheep-like troops, and then another huddle, each one being driven by a cluster of kingly Slavers, with crowns and winking V-shaped collars. And there again we all got that horrible guilty compulsion to come and give ourselves up. But I don't think those collars have any effect on dragons. Half of us were standing up to walk into the Slavers' arms, and I was ordering them as hard as I could not to, when the dragons smelt those golden crowns and collars. There was no holding them. They just whirred down over our heads and took those Slavers to pieces for the metal. Lewin said, 'Ah!' and crumpled his face in a grin like a fiend's. He'd thought the dragons might do that. I think he may really be a genius, like they say Camerati are. But I was so sick at that, and then again at the sight of nice people like Alectis and Yan killing the sheeplike troops, that I'm not going to talk about it any more. Terens says I'm

not to go when the Slavers come next. Apparently I broadcast the way I was feeling, just like the Slavers do, and even
the dragons felt queasy. The she-drake snorted at that.
Mother says, 'Nonsense. Take travel pills and behave as my
daughter should.'

Anyway, we have found out how to beat the Slavers. We
have no idea what is going on in the other of the Ten Worlds,
or even in the rest of Sveridge, but there are fifty more
Worm Reserves around the world, and Lewin says there
must be stray Dragonate units too who might think of using
dragons against Slavers. We want to move out and take over
some of the farms again soon. The dragons are having far too
much fun with the sheep. They keep flying over with woolly
bundles dangling from their claws, watched by a gloomy
crowd of everyone's shepherds. 'Green dot,' the shepherds
say. 'The brutes are raiding Hightop now.' They are very
annoyed with Orm, because Orm just gives his mad cackle
and lets the dragons go on.

Orm isn't mad at all. He's afraid of people knowing he's
heg – he still won't admit he is. I think that's why he left
Mother and Mother doesn't admit she was ever married to
him. Not that Mother minds. I get the feeling she and Orm
understand one another rather well. But Mother married
Donal, you see, after Timas. Donal, and Yan too, have both
told me that the fact that I'm heg makes no difference to
them – but you should see the way they both look at me! I'm
not fooled. I don't blame Orm for being scared stiff Donal
would find out he was heg. But I'm not sure I shall ever like
Orm, all the same.

I am putting all this down on what is left of Palino's memo
block. Lewin wanted me to, in case there is still some History
yet to come. He has made his official version on the recorder.
I'm leaning the block on Huffle's forefoot. Huffle is my friend
now. Leaning on a dragon is the best way to keep warm on a

chilly evening like this, when you're forced to camp out in the Reserve. Huffle is letting Lewin lean on him too, beyond Neal, because Lewin's ribs still pain him. There is a lot of leaning-space along the side of a dragon. Orm has just stepped across Huffle's tail, into the light, chortling and rubbing his hands in his most irritating way.

'Your mother's on the warpath,' he says. 'Oh, I do love a good quarrel!'

And here comes Mother, ominously upright, and with her arms folded. It's not Orm she wants. It's Lewin. 'Listen, you,' she says. 'What the dickens is the Dragonate thinking of, beheading hegs all these years? They can't help what they are. And they're the only people who can stand up to the Thrallers.'

Orm is cheated of his quarrel. Lewin looked up, crumpled into the most friendly smile. 'I do so agree with you,' he said. 'I've just said so in my report. And I'd have got your daughter off somehow, you know.'

Orm is cackling like the she-drake's young ones. Mother's mouth is open and I really think that, for once in her life, she has no idea what to say.

What the Cat Told Me

I am a cat. I am a cat like anything. Keep stroking me. I came in here because I knew you were good at stroking. But put your knees together so I can sit properly, front paws under. That's better. Now keep stroking, don't forget to rub my ears, and I will purr and tell.

I am going to tell you how I came to be so very old. When I was a kitten, humans dressed differently and they had great stamping horses to pull their cars and buses. The Old Man in the house where I lived used to light a hissing gas on the wall when it got dark. He wore a long black coat. The Boy who was nice to me wore shabby breeches that only came to his knees, and he mostly went without shoes, just like me. We slept in a cupboard under the stairs, Boy and I. We kept one another warm. We kept one another fed, too, later on. The Old Man did not like cats or boys. He only kept us because we were useful.

I was more useful than Boy. I had to sit in a five-pointed star. The Boy would help Old Man mix things that smoked and made me sneeze. I had to sneeze three times. After that things happened. Sometimes big purple cloud things came and sat beside me in the star. Fur stood up on me and I spat, but the things only went away when Old Man hit the star with his stick and told them *'Begone!'* in a loud voice. At other times the things that came were small, real things you could hit with your paw: boxes, or strings of shiny stones no one could eat, or bright rings that fell *tink* beside me out of nowhere. I did not mind those things. The things I really hated were the third kind. Those came inside me and used my mouth to speak. They were nasty things with hateful thoughts, and they made *me* hateful. And my mouth does not like to speak. It ached afterwards and my tongue and throat were so sore that I could not wash the hatefulness off me for hours.

I so hated those inside-speaking things that I used to run away and hide when I saw Old Man drawing the star on the cellar floor. I am good at hiding. Sometimes it took Boy half the day to find me. Then Old Man would shout and curse and hit Boy, and call him a fool. Boy cried at night in the cupboard afterwards. I did not like that, so after a while I scratched Old Man instead. I knew none of it was Boy's fault. Boy made Old Man give me nice things to eat after I had sat in the star. He said it was the only way to get me to sit there.

Boy was clever, you see. Old Man thought he was a fool, but Boy told me – at night in the cupboard – that he only pretended to be stupid. Boy was an orphan like me. Old Man had bought him for a shilling from a baby-farmer ages before I was even a kitten, because his hair was orange, like the ginger patches on me, and that is supposed to be a good colour for magic. Old Man paid a whole farthing for me, for much the same reason, because I am brindled. And Boy had been with Old Man ever since, learning things. It was not only magic that Boy learnt. Old Man was away quite a lot when Boy was small. Boy used to read Old Man's books in the room upstairs, and the newspapers, and anything else he could find. He told me he wanted to learn magic in order to escape from Old Man, and he learnt the other things so that he could manage in the wide world when he did escape; but he had been a prisoner in the house for years now and, although he knew a great deal, he still could not break the spell Old Man had put on him to keep him inside the house. 'And I really hate him,' Boy said to me, 'because of the cat before you. I want to stop him doing any more magic before I leave.'

And I said –

What was that? How could Boy and I talk together? Do you think I am a stupid cat, or something? I am nearly as clever as Boy. How do you think I am telling you all this? Let me roll over. My stomach needs rubbing. Oh, you rub well! I really like you. Well – No, let me sit up again now – I think the talking must be something to do with those inside-speaking things. When I was a kitten, I could understand what people said of course, but I couldn't do it back, not at first, until I had been lived in and been spoken through by quite a lot of Things. Boy thought they stretched my mind. And I was clever to start with, not like the cat before me.

Old Man killed the cat before me somehow. Boy would not tell me how. It was a stupid cat, he said, but he loved it. After he told me that, I would not go near Boy for a whole day. It was not just that I was nervous about being killed too. How *could* he love any cat that wasn't *me*? Boy caught me a pigeon off the roof, but I still wouldn't speak to him. So he stole me a saucer of milk and swore he would make sure Old Man didn't kill me too. He liked me a lot better than the other cat, he said, because I was clever. Anyway, Old Man killed the other cat doing magic he would not be able to work again without a certain special powder. Besides, the other cat was black and did not look as interesting as me.

After Boy had told me a lot of things like this, I put my nose to his nose and we were friends again. We made a conspiracy – that was what Boy called it – and swore to defeat Old Man and escape somehow. But we could not find out how to do it. We thought and thought. In the end I stopped growing because of the strain and worry. Boy said no, it was because I was full grown.

I said, 'Why, in that case, are *you* still growing? You're already more than ten times my size. You're nearly as big as Old Man!'

'I know,' said Boy. 'You're an elegant little cat. I don't think I shall be elegant until I'm six feet tall, and maybe not even then. I'm so clumsy. *And* so hungry!'

Poor Boy. He did grow so, around then. He did not seem to know his own size from one day to the next. When he rolled over in the cupboard he either squashed me or he burst out into the hallway. I had to scratch him quite hard, several nights, or he would have smothered me. And he kept knocking things over when he was awake. He spilt the milk jug – which I didn't mind at all – and he kicked Old Man's magic tripod by accident and smashed six jars of smelly stuff. Old Man cursed and called Boy a fool, worse than ever. And I think Boy really was stupid then, because he was so hungry. Old Man was too mean to give him more to eat. Boy ate my food, so I was hungry too. He said he couldn't help it.

I went on the roof and caught pigeons. Boy roasted them over the gaslight at night when Old Man was asleep. Delicious. But the bones made me sick in the corner. We hid the feathers in the cupboard and, after I had caught a great many pigeons, night after night, the cupboard began to get warm. Boy began to get his mind back. But he still grew and he was still hungry. By the time I had stopped growing for a year, Boy was so big his breeches went right up his legs and his legs went all hairy. Old Man couldn't hit him any more then, because Boy just put out a long, long arm and held Old Man off.

'I need more clothes,' he told Old Man.

Old Man grumbled and protested, but at last he said, 'Oh, all right, you damn scarecrow. I'll see what I can do.' He went unwillingly down into the cellar and heaved up one of the flagstones there. He wouldn't let me look in the hole, but

I know that what was under that flagstone was Old Man's collection of all the rings and shiny stones that came from nowhere when I sat in the five-pointed star. I saw Old Man take some chinking things out. Then he slammed down the stone and went away upstairs, not noticing that one shiny thing had spilled out and gone rolling across the floor. It was a little golden ball. It was fun. I chased it for hours. I patted it and it rolled, and I pounced, and it ran away all round the cellar. Then it spoiled the fun by rolling down a crack between two flagstones and getting lost. Then I found I was shut in the cellar and had to make a great noise to be let out.

That reminds me – does your house have balls in it? Then buy me one tomorrow. Until then, a piece of paper on some string will do.

Where was I? Oh yes. Someone came and let me out, smelling of mildew. I nearly didn't know Boy at first. He had a red coat and white breeches and long black boots on, all rather too big for him. He said it was an old soldier's uniform Old Man had picked up cheap, and how did I get shut in the cellar?

I sat round his neck and told him about the flagstone where Old Man kept his shinies. Boy was *very* interested. 'That would buy an awful lot of food,' he said. He was still hungry. 'We'll take it with us when we escape. Let's try escaping next time he works magic.'

So that night we made a proper plan at last. We decided to summon a Good Spirit, instead of the hateful things Old Man always fetched. 'There must be *some* good ones,' Boy said. But since we didn't know enough to summon a good one on our own, we had to make Old Man do it for us somehow.

We did it the very next day. I played up wonderfully. As soon as Old Man started to draw on the cellar floor, I ran away, so that Old Man would not suspect us. I dug my claws hard into Boy's coat when he caught me, so that Old Man could hardly pull me loose. And I scratched Old Man, very badly, so that there was blood, when he put me inside the five-pointed star. Then I sat there, humped and sulky, and it was Boy's turn.

Boy did rather well too. At first he was just the usual kind of clumsy, and kicked some black powder into some red powder while they were putting it out in heaps, and the cellar filled with white soot. It was hard not to sneeze too soon, but I managed not to. I managed to hold the sneeze off until Old Man had done swearing at Boy and begun on the next bit, the mumbling. Then I sneezed – once. Boy promptly fell against the tripod, which dripped hot stuff on the spilt powder. The cellar filled with big purple bubbles. They drifted and shone and bobbed most enticingly. I would have loved to chase them, but I knew I mustn't, or we would spoil what we were doing. Old Man couldn't leave off his mumbling, because that would spoil the spell, but he glared at Boy through the bubbles. I sneezed again – two – to distract him. Old Man raised his stick and began on the chanting bit. And Boy pretended to trip and, as he did, he threw a fistful of powder he had ready into the gaslight.

Whup! it went.

Old Man jumped and glared, and went on grimly chanting – he had to, you see, because you can't stop magic once you have started – and all the bubbles drifted to the floor and burst. *Smicker, smicker,* very softly. As each one burst, there was a little tiny pink animal on the floor, running about and calling 'Oink, oink, oink!' in small squeaky voices. That nearly distracted me, as well as Old Man. I stared out at them with longing. I would have given *worlds* to jump out of the star and chase those beasties. They looked so beautifully *eatable*. But I knew I mustn't try to come out of the star yet, so I shut my eyes and yawned to hold in the third sneeze and thought hard, hard, hard of a Good Thing. *Let a Good Thing come!* I thought. I thought as hard as you do when you see a saucer of milk held in the air above you, and you want them to put it on the floor – quick. Then I gave my third sneeze.

That reminds me. Milk? Yes, please, or I won't be able to tell you any more.

Thank you. Keep your knee steady. You may stroke me if you wish. Where was I?

Right. When I opened my eyes all the delicious beauties had vanished and the light burnt sort of dingily. Old Man was beating Boy over the head with a stick. He could do that for once, because Boy was crouched by the wall laughing until his face ran tears. 'Pigs!' he said. 'Tiny little pigs! Oh, oh, oh!'

'I'll pig *you*!' Old Man screamed. 'You spoilt my spell! Look at the pentangle – there's nothing there at all!'

But there was. I could feel the new Thing inside me. It wasn't hateful at all, but it felt lost, and a bit feeble. It was too scared to say or do anything, or even let me move, until Old Man crossly broke the pentangle and stumped away upstairs.

Boy stood rubbing his head. 'Pity it didn't work, Brindle,' he said. 'But wasn't it worth it, just for those pigs!'

'Master,' the Good Thing said with my mouth. 'Master, how can I serve you, bound as I am?'

Boy stared, and his face went odd colours. I always wonder how you humans manage that. 'Good Lord!' he said. 'Did we do it after all? Or is it a demon?'

'I don't think I'm a demon,' Good Thing said doubtfully. 'I may be some kind of spirit. I'm not sure.'

'Can't you get out of me?' I said to it in my head.

'No. Our Master would not be able to hear me if I did,' it told me.

'Bother you then!' I said, and started to wash.

'You can serve me anyway, whatever you are,' Boy said to Good Thing. 'Get me some food.'

'Yes, Master,' it made me say, and obeyed at once. I had just reached that stage of washing where you have one foot high in the air. I fell over. It was most annoying. Next minute, I was rolling about in a huge warm room full of people cooking things. A kitchen, Boy said it was later. It smelt marvellous . . . I hardly minded at all when Good Thing made me leap up and snatch a roast leg of mutton from the nearest table. But I did mind – a lot – when two men in white hats rushed at me shouting, '*Damn cat!*'

Good Thing didn't know what to do about that at all, and it nearly got us caught. 'Let *me* handle this!' I spat at it, and it did. I told you, it was a bit feeble. I dived under a big dresser where people couldn't reach me and crouched there right at the back by the wall. It was a pity I had to leave the meat behind. It smelt wonderful. But I had to leave it, or they'd have gone on chasing me. 'Now,' I said, when my coat had settled flat again, 'you tell me what you want me to take and I'll take it properly this time.'

Good Thing agreed that might work better. We waited until they'd all gone back to cooking and then slunk softly out into the room again. And Good Thing had been thinking all this time. It made me a sort of invisible sack. It was most peculiar. No one could see the sack, not even me, and it didn't get in my way at all. I just knew it was behind me, filling up with the food I stole. Good Thing made me take stuff I'd never have dreamed of eating myself, like cinnamon jelly and – yuk! – cucumber, as well as good honest meat and venison pie and other reasonable things.

Then we were suddenly back in the cellar, where Boy was glumly clearing up. When he saw the food spilling out on to the floor, his face lit up. Good Thing had been right. He loved the jelly and even ate cucumber. For once in his life he really had enough to eat. I helped him eat the venison pie and we both had strawberries and cream to finish with. I love those.

Which reminds me – Oh. Strawberries are out of season? Never mind. I'll stay with you until they come back in. Rub my stomach again.

I was heavy and kind of round after that meal. Good Thing complained rather. 'Well, get out of me then and it won't bother you,' I said. I wanted to sleep.

'In a minute,' it said. 'Master, the cat tells me you want to escape, but I'm afraid I can't help you there.'

Boy woke up in dismay. He was dropping off to sleep on the floor, being so full. 'Why *not*?'

'Two reasons,' Good Thing said apologetically. 'First, there is a very strong spell on you, which confines you to this house, and it is beyond my power to break it. Second, there is an equally strong spell on me. You and the cat broke part of it, the part which confined me to a small golden ball, but I am still forced to stay in the house where the golden ball is. The only other place I can go is the house I – came from.'

'Damn!' said Boy. 'I did hope—'

'The spell that confines the cat is nothing like so strong,' Good Thing said. 'I could raise that for you.'

'That's something at least! Do that,' said Boy. He was a generous Boy. 'And if you two could keep on fetching food, so that I can put my mind to something besides how hungry I am, then I might think of a way to break the spell on you and me.'

I was a little annoyed. It seemed that we had got Good Thing just because the golden ball had escaped from Old Man, and not because of Boy's cleverness or my powers of thought. But though I knew the ball was down a crack just inside the place where Old Man usually drew his pentangle, I didn't mention it to Boy in case his feelings were hurt too.

We had great good times for quite a long while after that, Boy, Good Thing and I, and Old Man never suspected at all. He was away a lot round then anyway. While he was away, there were always a jug of milk and a loaf that appeared magically every four days, but Boy and I would have half-starved on that without Good Thing. Good Thing took me to the kitchen-place every day at suppertime and we came back with every kind of food in the invisible sack. When Good Thing was not around – it quite often went away in the night and left me in peace – I went out across the roofs. I led a lovely extra life on top of the town. I met other cats by moonlight, but they were never as clever as me. I found out all sorts of things and came and told them to Boy. He was always very wistful about not being able to go out himself, but he listened to everything. He was like that. He was my friend. And he was a great comfort to me when I had my first kittens. I didn't know what was happening to me. Boy guessed and he told me. Then he told me that we must hide the kittens or Old Man would know I had been able to go out. We were very secret and hid them in our cupboard in a nest of pigeon feathers.

I am good at having kittens. I'll show you presently. I always have three, one tabby, one ginger and one mixed like me. I had three kittens then, and Old Man never knew, even though they were quite noisy sometimes, specially after I taught them how to play with Good Thing.

When Good Thing came out of me, I could see it quite well, though Boy never could. It was quite big outside me, up to Boy's shoulder, and frail and wafty, and it could float about at great speed. It enjoyed playing. I used to hunt it all round the house and leap on it, pretending to tear it to bits – and of course it would waft away between my paws. Boy used to guess where Good Thing was from my behaviour and laugh at me hunting it. He laughed even more when my kittens were old enough to play hunting Good Thing too.

By this time, Boy was a fine strong Boy, full of thoughts, and his soldier clothes were getting too short and tight. He

asked Good Thing to get him some more clothes next time
Old Man was away. So Good Thing and I went to another
part of the mansion where the kitchen was. Boy said 'house'
was the wrong word for that place. He was right. It was big
and grand. This time when we got there, we went sneaking
at a run up a great stair covered with red carpet – or I went
sneaking with Good Thing inside me – and along more
carpet to a large room with curtains all round the walls. The
curtains had pictures that Good Thing said were lords and
ladies hunting animals with birds and horses. I never knew
that *birds* were any help to people.

There was a space between the curtains and the walls, and
Good Thing sent me sneaking through that space, around
the room. There were people in the room. I peeped at them
through a crack in the curtains.

There was a very fine Man there, almost as tall and fine as
my Boy, but much older. With him were two of the ones in
white hats from the kitchen. They held their hats in their
hands, sorrowfully. With them was a Woman in long
clothes, looking cross as Old Man.

'Yes indeed, sir, I saw this cat for myself, sir,' the Woman
said. 'It stole a cake under my very eyes, sir.'

'I swear to you, sir,' one of the white hats said, 'it appears
every evening and vanishes like magic with every kind of
food.'

'It *is* magic, that's why,' said the other white hat.

'Then we had better take steps to see where it comes from,'
the fine Man said. 'If I give you this—'

Good Thing wouldn't let me stay to hear more. We ran on.
'Oh dear!' Good Thing said in my head as we ran. 'We'll have
to be very careful after this!' We came to a room that was
white and gold, with mirrors. Good Thing wouldn't let me
watch myself in the mirrors. The white and gold walls were
all cupboards filled with clothes hanging or lying inside. We

stuffed the invisible sack as full as it would hold with clothes
from the cupboards, so that we would not need to go back.
For once it felt heavy. I was glad to get back to Boy waiting in
Old Man's bookroom.

'Great Scot!' said Boy as the fine coats, good boots, silk
shirts, cravats and smooth trousers tumbled out on to the
floor. 'I can't wear these! These are fit for a king! The Old
Man would be bound to notice.' But he could not resist
trying some of them on, all the same. Good Thing told me he
looked good. I thought Boy looked far finer than the Man
they belonged to.

After this, Boy became very curious about the mansion
where the clothes and the food came from. He made me
describe everything. Then he asked Good Thing, 'Are there
books in this mansion too?'

'And pictures and jewels,' Good Thing said through me.
'What does Master wish me to fetch? There is a golden harp,
a musical box like a bird, a—'

'Just books,' said Boy. 'I need to learn. I'm still so
ignorant.'

Good Thing always obeyed Boy. The next night, instead of
going to the kitchen, Good Thing took me to a vast room
with a round ceiling held up by freckled pillars, where the
walls were lined with books in shelves. Good Thing had one
of its helpless turns there. 'Which do you think our Master
wants?' it asked me feebly.

'*I* don't know,' I said. 'I'm only a cat. Let's just take all we
can carry. I want to get back to my kittens.'

So we took everything out of one shelf, and it was not
right. Boy said he did not need twenty-four copies of the
Bible: one was enough. The same went for Shakespeare. And
he could not read Greek, he said. I spat. But we gathered up
all the books except two and went back.

We had just spilt all the books on to the floor of the room

with the freckled pillars, when the big door burst open. The Man came striding in, with a crowd of others. 'There's the cat now!' they all cried out.

Good Thing had me snatch another book at random, and we went.

'And I daren't go back for a while, Master,' Good Thing said to Boy.

I saw to my kittens, then I went out hunting. I fed Boy for the next few days – when he remembered to eat, that was. I stole a leg of lamb from an inn, a string of sausages from the butcher down the road, and a loaf and some buns from the baker. The kittens ate most of it. Boy was reading. He sat in his fine clothes and he read, the Bible first, then Shakespeare, and then the book of history Good Thing had me snatch. He said he was educating himself. It was as if he was asleep. When Old Man suddenly came back, I had to dig all my claws into Boy to make him notice.

Old Man looked grumpily round everywhere to make sure everything was in order. He was always suspicious. I was scared. I made Good Thing stay with the kittens in the cupboard and hid the remains of the sausages in there with them. Boy was all dreamy, but he sat on the book of history to hide it. Old Man looked at him, hard. I was scared again. Surely Old Man would notice that Boy's red coat was of fine warm cloth and that there was a silk shirt underneath? But Old Man said, 'Stupid as ever, I see,' and grumped out of the house again.

Talking of sausages, when do you eat? Soon? Good. Now, go on stroking.

The next day, Old Man was still away. Boy said, 'Those were wonderful books. I must have *more*. I wish I didn't have to trust a cat and a spirit to steal them. Isn't there *any* way I can go and choose books for myself?'

Good Thing drifted about the house, thinking. At last it got into me and said, 'There is no way I can take you to the mansion bodily, Master. But if you can go into a trance, I can take you there in spirit. Would that do?'

'Perfectly!' said Boy.

'Oh no,' I said. 'If you do, I'm coming too. I don't trust you on your own with my Boy, Good Thing. You might go feeble and lose him.'

'I will *not*!' said Good Thing. 'But you may come if you wish. And we will wait till the middle of the night, please. We don't want you to be seen again.'

Around midnight Boy cheerfully went into a trance. Usually he hated it when Old Man made him do it. And we went to the mansion again, all three of us. It was very odd. I could see Boy there the way I could see Good Thing, like a big, flimsy cloud. As soon as we were there, Boy was so astonished by the grandeur of it that he insisted on drifting all round it, upstairs and down, to see as much as he could. I was scared. Not everyone was asleep. There were gaslights or candles burning in most of the corridors, and someone could easily have seen me. But I stuck close to Boy because I was afraid Good Thing would lose him.

It was not easy to stay close. They could go through doors without opening them. When they went through one door upstairs, I had to jump up and work the handle in order to follow Boy inside. It was a pretty room. The quilt on the bed was a cat's dream of comfort. I jumped up and paddled on it, while Boy and Good Thing hovered to look at the person asleep there. She was lit up by the nightlight beside the bed.

'What a *lovely* girl!' I felt Boy think. 'She must be a princess.'

She sat up at that. I think it was because of me treading on her stomach. I went tumbling way backwards, which annoyed me a good deal. She stared. I glowered and wondered whether to spit. 'Oh!' she said. 'You're that magic cat my father wants to catch. Come here, puss. I promise I won't let him hurt you.' She held out her hand. She was nice. She knew how to stroke a cat, just like you do. I let her stroke me and talk to me, and I was just curling up to enjoy a rest on her beautiful quilt when a huge Woman sprang up from a bed on the other side of the room.

'Were you calling, my lady?' she asked. Then she saw me. She screamed. She ran to a rope hanging in one corner and heaved at it, screaming, *'That cat's back!'*

'Run!' Good Thing said to me. 'I'll look after Boy.'

So I ran. I have never run like that in my life, before or since. It felt as if everyone in the mansion was after me. Luckily for me, I knew my way round quite well by then. I ran upstairs and I ran down, and people clattered after me, shouting. I dived under someone's hand and dodged through a crooked cupboard place, and at last I found myself behind the curtains in the Man's room. He ran in and out. Other people ran in and out, but the Princess really had done something to help me somehow and not one of them thought of looking behind those curtains.

After a bit I heard the Princess in that room too. 'But it's a *nice* cat, Father – really sweet. I can't think why you're making all this fuss about it!' Then there was a sort of grating sound. I smelt the smallest whiff of fresh air. Bless her, she had opened the Man's window for me.

I got out of it as soon as the room was empty. I climbed down on to grass. I ran again. I knew just the way I should go. Cats do, you know, particularly when they have kittens waiting for them. I was dead tired when I got to Old Man's house. It was right on the other side of town. As I scrambled through the skylight in the roof, I was almost too tired to move. But I was dead worried about my kittens and about Boy too. It was morning by then.

My kittens were fine, but Boy was still lying on the floor of the bookroom in a trance, cold as ice. And as if that were not enough, keys grated in the locks and Old Man came back. All I could think to do was to lie round Boy's neck to warm him.

Old Man came and kicked Boy. 'Lazy lump!' he said. 'Anyone would think you were in a trance!' I couldn't think what to do. I got up and hurried about, mewing for milk, to distract Old Man. He wasn't distracted. Looking gleefully at Boy, he carefully put a jar of black powder away in his cupboard and locked it. Then he sat down and looked at one of his books, not bothering with me at all. He kept looking across at Boy.

My kittens distracted Old Man by having a fight in the cupboard about the last of the sausages. Old Man heard it and leapt up. 'Scrambling and squeaking!' he said. 'Mice! Could even be rats by the noise. Damn cat! Don't you ever do your job?' He hit at me with his stick.

I tried to run. Oh, I was tired! I made for the stairs, to take us both away from Boy and my kittens, and Old Man caught me by my tail halfway up. I was that tired . . . I was forced to bite him quite hard and scratch his face. He dropped me with a thump, so he probably did not hear the even louder thump from the bookroom. I did. I ran back there.

Boy was sitting up, shivering. There was a pile of books beside him.

'Good Thing!' I said. 'That was stupid!'

'Sorry,' said Good Thing. 'He would insist on bringing them.' The books vanished into the invisible sack just as Old Man stormed in.

He ranted and grumbled at Boy for laziness and for feeding me so that I didn't catch mice, and he made Boy set mousetraps. Then he stormed off to the cellar.

'Why didn't you come back sooner?' I said to Boy.

'It was too marvellous being somewhere that wasn't this house,' Boy said. He was all dreamy with it. He didn't even read his new books. He paced about. So did I. I realized that my kittens were not safe from Old Man. And if he found them, he would realize that I could get out of the house. Maybe he would kill me like the cat before. I was scared. I wished Boy would be scared too. I wished Good Thing would show some sense. But Good Thing was only thinking of pleasing Boy.

'Don't let him go into a trance again,' I said. 'Old Man will know.'

'But I *have* to!' Boy shouted. 'I'm *sick* of this house!' Then he calmed down and thought. 'I know,' he said to Good Thing. 'Fetch the Princess here.'

Good Thing got into me and bleated that this wasn't wise, now Old Man was back. I said so too. But Boy wouldn't listen. He had to have Princess. Or else he would go into a trance and see her that way. I understood then. Boy wanted kittens. Very little will stop boys or cats when they do.

So we gave in. When Old Man was asleep and snoring, Boy dressed himself in the middle of the night in the Man's finest clothes and looked fine as fine. He even washed in horrible cold water, in spite of all I said. Then Good Thing went to the mansion.

Instants later, the Princess was lying asleep on the floor of the bookroom. 'Oh,' Boy said sorrowfully. 'What a shame to wake her!' But he woke her up all the same.

She rubbed her eyes and stared at him. 'Who are you, sir?'

Boy said, 'Oh, Princess—'

She said, 'I think you've made a mistake, sir. I'm not a princess. Are you a prince?'

Boy explained who he was and all about himself, and she explained that her father was a rich magician. She was a disappointment to him, she said, because she could hardly do any magic and was not very clever. But Boy still called her Princess. She said she would call him Orange because of his hair. She may not have been clever, but she was nice. I sat on her knee and purred. She stroked me and talked to Boy for the whole night, until it began to get light. They did nothing but talk. I said to Good Thing that it was a funny way to have kittens. Good Thing was not happy. Princess did not understand about Good Thing. Boy gave up trying to explain. Good Thing drifted about sulking.

When it was really light, Princess said she must go back. Boy agreed, but they put it off and kept talking. That was when I had my good idea. I went to the cupboard and fetched out my kittens, one by one, and I put them into Princess's lap.

'Oh!' she said. 'What beauties!'

'Tell her she's to keep them and look after them,' I said to Boy.

He told her, and she said, 'Brindle can't *mean* it! It seems such a sacrifice. Tell her it's sweet of her, but I *can't*.'

'Make her take them,' I said. 'Tell her they're a present from you, if it makes her happier. Tell her they're a sign that she'll see you again. Tell her *anything* but make her take them!'

So Boy told her and Princess agreed. She gathered the tabby and the ginger and the mixed kitten into her hands and Good Thing took her and the kittens away. We stood staring at the place where she had been, Boy and I. Things felt empty, but I was pleased. My kittens were safe from Old Man, and Princess had kittens now, which ought to have pleased Boy, even if they were mine and not his. I did not understand why he looked so sad.

Old Man was standing in the doorway behind us. We had not heard him getting up. He glared at the fine way Boy was dressed. 'How did you come by those clothes?'

'I did a spell,' Boy said airily. Well, it was true in a way. Boy's mood changed when he realized how clever we had been. He said, 'And Brindle got rid of the mice,' and laughed.

Old Man was always annoyed when Boy laughed. 'Funny, is it?' he snarled. 'For that, you can go down to the cellar, you and your finery, and stay there till I tell you to come out.' And he put one of his spells on Boy, so that Boy had to go. Old Man locked the cellar door on him. Then he turned back, rubbing his hands and laughing too. 'Last laugh's mine!' he said. 'I *thought* he knew more than he let on, but there's no harm done. I've still got him!' He went and looked in almanacs and horoscopes and chuckled more. Boy was eighteen that day. Old Man began looking up spells, lots of them, from the bad black books that even he rarely touched.

'Brindle,' said Good Thing. 'I am afraid. Do one thing for me.'

'Leave a cat in peace!' I said. 'I need to sleep.'

Good Thing said, 'Boy will soon be dead and I will be shut out for ever unless you help.'

'But my kittens are safe,' I said, and I curled up in the cupboard.

'They will not be safe,' said Good Thing, 'unless you do this for me.'

'Do what for you?' I said. I was scared again, but I stretched as if I didn't care. I do *not* like to be bullied. You should remember that.

'Go to the cellar in my invisible sack and tell Boy where the golden ball is,' Good Thing said. 'Tell him to fetch it out of the floor and give it to you.'

I stretched again and strolled past Old Man. His face was scratched all over, I was glad to see, but he was collecting things to work spells with now. I strolled quite fast to the cellar door. There Good Thing scooped me up, and went inside, in near-dark. Boy was sitting against the wall.

'Nice of you to come,' he said. 'Will Good Thing fetch Princess again tonight?' He did not think there was any danger. He was used to Old Man behaving like this. But I thought of my kittens. I showed him the place where the golden ball had got lost down the crack. I could see it shining down there. It took me ages to persuade Boy to dig it out, and even then he only worked at it idly, thinking of Princess. He could only get at it with one little finger, which made it almost too difficult for him to bother.

I heard Old Man coming downstairs. I am ashamed to say that I bit Boy, quite hard, on the thumb of the hand he was digging with. He went '*Ow!*' and jerked and the ball flew rolling into a corner. I raced after it.

'Put it in your mouth. Hide it!' said Good Thing.

I did. It was hard not to swallow it. Then when I didn't swallow, it was hard not to spit it out. Cats are made to do one or the other. I had to pretend it was a piece of meat I was taking to my kittens. I sat in the corner, in the dark, while Old Man came in and locked the door and lit the tripod lamp.

'If you need Brindle,' Boy said, sulkily sucking his hand, '*you* can look for her. She bit me.'

'This doesn't need a cat,' Old Man said. Boy and I were both astonished. 'It just needs *you*,' he told Boy. 'This is the life-transfer spell I was trying on the black cat. This time, I know how to get it right.'

'But you said you couldn't do it without a special powder!' Boy said.

Old Man giggled. 'What do you think I've been away looking for all this year?' he asked. 'I've got a whole jar of it! With it, I shall put myself into your body and you into my body, and then I shall kill this old body off. I won't need it or you after that. I shall be young and handsome and I shall live for years. Stand up. Get into the pentangle.'

'Blowed if I shall!' said Boy.

But Old Man did spells and made him. It took a long time, because Boy resisted even harder than I usually did, and shouted spells back. In the end, Old Man cast a spell that made Boy stand still and drew the five-pointed star round him, not in the usual place.

'I shall kill my old body with you inside it rather slowly for that,' he said to Boy. Then he drew another star, a short way off. 'This is for my bride,' he said, giggling again. 'I took her into my power ten years ago, and by now she'll be a lovely young woman.' Then he drew a third star, overlapping Boy's, for himself, and stood in it chuckling. 'Let it start!' he cried out, and threw the strong, smelly black powder on the tripod. Everything went green-dark. When the green went, Princess was standing in the empty star.

'Oh, it's *you*!' she and Boy both said.

'Ahah!' said Old Man. 'Hee-hee! So you and she know one another, do you? How you did it, boy, I won't enquire, but it makes things much easier for me.' He began on his chanting.

'Give the golden ball to Princess,' Good Thing said to me. 'Hurry. Make Boy tell her to swallow it.'

I ran across to Princess and spat the golden ball into her star. She pulled her skirt back from it.

'Brindle wants you to swallow it,' Boy said. 'I think it's important.'

People are peculiar. Princess must have known it was very important, but she said faintly. 'I can't! Not something that's been in a cat's *mouth*!'

Old Man saw the golden ball. He glared, still chanting, and raised his stick. The ball floated up and came towards him. Princess gave a last despairing snatch and caught it, just in time. She put it in her mouth.

'Ah! Back again!' said Good Thing.

Princess swallowed. She changed. She had been nice

before, but sort of stupid. Now she was nice and as clever as
Boy. 'You toad!' she said to Old Man. 'That was part of my
soul! You took it, didn't you?'

Old Man raised his stick again. Princess held up both
hands. Magic raged, strong enough to make my fur stand up,
and Old Man did not seem to be able to do much at first. It
was interesting. Princess had magic too, only I think it had all
gone into Good Thing. But not quite enough. She started to
lose. 'Help me!' she said to Boy.

Boy started to say a spell, but, at that moment, the door of
the cellar burst open, and half the wall fell in with it. The
Man rushed in with a crowd of others.

'Father!' said Princess. 'Thank goodness!'

'Are you all right?' said the Man. 'We traced you through
those kittens. What are you trying to do here, Old Man? The
life-transfer, is it? Well that's enough of *that*!' The Man made
signs that stood my coat up on end again.

Old Man screamed. I could tell he was dying. The spell had
somehow turned back on him. He was withering and shrink-
ing and getting older and older. Boy jumped out of his star
and ran to Princess. They both looked very happy. Old Man
snarled at them, but he could do nothing but round on me.
Everyone does that. They all kick the cat when they can't
kick a person. 'So you had *kittens*!' he screamed. 'This is all
your fault, cat! For that, you shall have kittens to drown for
the next thousand years!'

'I soften that curse!' the Man shouted.

Then everything went away and I was not in the town I
knew any more. I have been wandering about, all these
years, ever since. Old Man's curse means that I am good at
having kittens. It is not a bad curse, because the Man has
softened it. Old Man meant my kittens to be drowned every
time. But instead, if I can find an understanding person – like
you – who will listen to my story, then my kittens will have

good homes, and so will I for a time. You won't mind. They'll be beautiful kittens. They always are. You'll see very soon now. After supper.

nad and Dan adn Quaffy

S he had struggled rather as a writer until she got her word processor. Or not exactly *struggled*, she thought, frowning at her screen and flipping the cursor back to correct *adn* to *and*. For some reason, she always garbled the word *and* – it was always *adn* or *nad*; *dna* or *nda* were less frequent, but all of them appeared far oftener than the right way. She had only started to make this mistake after she gave up her typewriter and she felt it was a small price to pay.

For years she had written what seemed to her the most stirring sort of novels, about lonely aliens among humans, or lonely humans among aliens, or sometimes both kinds lonely in an unkind world – all without ever quite hitting the response from readers she felt she was worth. Then came her divorce, which left her with custody of her son Daniel, then thirteen. That probably provided an impetus of some sort in itself, for Danny was probably the most critical boy alive.

'Mum!' he would say. 'I wish you'd give *up* that lonely-heart alien stuff! Can't you write about something decent for a change?' Or, staring at her best efforts at cookery, he said, 'I can't be expected to eat *this*!' After which, he had taken over cooking himself: they now lived on chilli con carne and stir-fry. For, as Danny said, 'A man can't be expected to learn more than one dish a year.' At the moment, being nearly fifteen, Danny was teaching himself curry. Their nice Highgate house reeked of burnt garam masala most of the time.

But the real impetus had come when she found Danny in her workroom sternly plaiting the letters of her old typewriter into metal braid. 'I've had this old thing!' he said, when she tore him away with fury and cursings. 'So have you. It's out of the ark. Now you'll have to get a word processor.'

'But I don't know how to work the things!' she had wailed.

'That doesn't matter. I do. I'll work it for you,' he replied inexorably. 'And I'll tell you what one to buy too, or you'll only waste money.'

He did so. The components were duly delivered and installed, and Daniel proceeded to instruct his mother in how to work as much of them as – as he rather blightingly said – her feeble brain would hold. 'There,' he said. 'Now write something worth reading for a change.' And he left her sitting in front of it all.

When she thought about it, she was rather ashamed of the fact that her knowledge of the thing had not progressed one whit beyond those first instructions Danny had given her. She had to call on her son to work the print-out, to recall most of the files and to get her out of any but the most simple difficulty. On several occasions – as when Danny had been on a school trip to Paris or away with his school cricket team – she had had to tell her publisher all manner of lies to account for the fact that there would be no copy of anything until Danny got back. But the advantages far outweighed these difficulties – or at least she knew they did *now*.

That first day had been a nightmare. She had felt lost and foolish and weak. She had begun – not having anything else in mind – on another instalment of lonely aliens. And everything kept going wrong. She had to call Danny in ten times in the first hour, and then ten times after lunch, and then again when, for some reason, the machine produced what she had written of Chapter I as a list, one word to a line. Even Danny took most of the rest of the day to sort out what she had done to get that. After that, he hovered over her solicitously, bringing her mugs of black coffee, until, some-where around nine in the evening, she realized she was in double bondage, first to a machine and then to her own son.

'Go away!' she told him. 'Out of my sight! I'm going to learn to do this for myself or die in the attempt!'

Danny gave her bared teeth a startled look, and fled.

By this time she had been sitting in front of board and screen for nearly ten hours. It seemed to her that her threat to die in the attempt was no idle one. She felt like death. Her back ached and so did her head. Her eyes felt like running blisters. She had cramp in both hands and one foot asleep. In addition, her mouth was foul with too much coffee and Danny's chilli con carne. The little green letters on the screen kept retreating behind the glass to the distant end of a long, long tunnel. 'I *will* do this!' she told herself fiercely. 'I am an intelligent adult – probably even a genius – and I will *not* be dominated by a mere machine!'

And she typed all over again:

Chapter One

The Captain had been at board and screen ever since jump – a total of ten hours. Her hands shook with weariness, making it an effort to hold them steady on her switches. Her head was muzzy, her mouth foul with nutrient concentrates. But since the mutiny, it was sit double watches or fail to bring the starship *Candida* safely through the intricate system of Meld . . .

At this point, she began to get a strange sense of power. She *was* dominating this damned machine, even though she was doing it only by exploiting her own sensations. Also, she was becoming interested in what might be going to happen to the starship *Candida* – not to speak of the reasons that had led up to the mutiny aboard her. She continued writing furiously until long after midnight. When she stopped at last, she had to pry her legs loose from her chair.

'*That's* more like it, Mum!' Danny said the next morning, reading it as it came from the printer.

He was, as usual, right. *Starship Candida* was the book that made the name of F. C. Stone. It won prizes. It sold in resorts and newsagents all over the world. It was – reviewers said – equally remarkable for its insight into the Captain's character as for the intricate personal relationships leading to the mutiny. Much was spoken about the tender and peculiar relationships between the sexes. This last made F. C. Stone grin rather. All she had done was to revenge herself on Danny by reversing the way things were between them. In the book, the Captain was all-powerful and dominating and complained a lot about the food. The Mate had a hypnotically induced mindset that caused him to bleat for assistance at the first sign of trouble.

Her next book, *The Mutineers*, was an even greater success. For this one, F. C. Stone extended the intricate personal relationships to the wider field of galactic politics. She discovered she revelled in politics. Provided she was making up the politics herself, there seemed no limit to how intricate she could make them.

Since then she had, well, *not* stuck to a formula – she was much more artfully various than that – but, as she said and Danny agreed, there was no point in leaving a winning game. Though she did not go back to starship *Candida*, she stayed with that universe and its intricate politics. There were aliens in it too, which she always enjoyed. And she kept mostly out in space, so that she could continue to describe pilots astronauting at the controls of a word processor. Sooner or later in most of her books, someone, human or alien, would have sat long hours before the screen, until, dazed with staring, aching in the back, itching in the nose –

for the burning of Asian spices in the kitchen tended to give
her hay fever – and with cramped hands, this pilot would
be forced to manoeuvre arduously through jump. This part
always, or nearly always, got written when F. C. Stone was
unable to resist staying up late to finish the chapter.

Danny continued to monitor his mother. He was proud of
what he had made her do. In holidays and round the edges
of school, he hung over her shoulder and brought her
continual mugs of strong black coffee. This beverage began
to appear in the books too. The mutineer humans drank
gav, while their law-abiding enemies quaffed *chvi*. Spacer
aliens staggered from their nav-couches to gulp down *kivay*;
and the mystics of Meld used *xfy* to induce an altered state
of consciousness – although this was not generally spotted
as being the same substance. And it was all immensely
popular.

It was all due to the word processor, she thought, giving
the nearest component a friendly pat as she leant towards
the screen again. The latest mug of cooling *kivay* sat beside
her. Her nose was, as usual, tickled by burnt ginger or
something. Her back was beginning to ache – or, more
truthfully, her behind was. She ought to get a more comfortable chair, but she was too fond of this old one. Anyway, the
latest book was the thing. For this one, she had at last gone
back to starship *Candida*. There had been a lot of pressure
from her fans. And her publisher thought there was enough
material in their suggestions, combined with F. C. Stone's
own ideas, to make a trilogy. So she had decided to start in
the way she knew would get her going. She typed:

> Jump. Time nad the world stretched dna went out.
> Back. The Captain had sat at her boards for four
> objective days – four subjective minutes or four
> subjective centuries. Her head ached, gums adn all.

She cursed. Hands trembling on controls, she struggled to get her fix on this system's star.

Now what had some vastly learned reader suggested about this system's star? It had some kind of variability, but that was all she could remember. Damn. All her notes for it were in that file Danny had set up for her. He was at school. But he had written down for her how to recall it. She fumbled around for his piece of paper – it had worked halfway under a black box whose name and function she never could learn – and took a swig of lukewarm *xfy* while she studied what to do. It looked quite simple. She took another sip of *gav*. Store the new book. Careful not to cancel this morning's work. There. Screen blank. Now type in this lot, followed by *Candida 2*. Then—

A clear childish voice spoke. 'This is Candida Two, Candy,' it said. 'Candida One, I need your confirmation.'

It was no voice F. C. Stone knew and it seemed to come from the screen. Her eyes turned to the mug of *kivay*. Perhaps she was in a state of altered consciousness.

'Candida One!' the voice said impatiently. 'Confirm that you are conscious. I will wait ten seconds and then begin life-saving procedures. Ten, nine, eight . . .'

This sounded serious. Coffee poisoning, thought F. C. Stone. I shall change to carrot juice or cocoa.

'. . . seven, six, five,' counted the childish voice, 'four, three . . .'

I'd better say something, thought F. C. Stone. How absurd. Weakly she said, 'Do stop counting. It makes me nervous.'

'*Are* you Candida One?' demanded the voice. 'The voice-pattern does not quite tally. Please say something else for comparison with my records.'

Why should I? thought F. C. Stone. But it was fairly clear that if she stayed silent the voice would start counting again and then, presumably, flood the room with the antidote for *xfy*.

No, no, this was ridiculous. There was no way a word processor could flood anyone's system with anything. Come to that, there was no way it could speak either – or was there? She must ask Danny. She was just letting her awe of the machine, and her basic ignorance, get on top of her. Let us be rational here, she thought. If she was not suffering from *gav* poisoning, or if, alternatively, the smell of charred turmeric at present flooding the house did not prove to have hallucinogenic properties, then she had worked too long and hard imagining things and was now unable to tell fantasy from reality ... unless ... – what a *wonderful* thought! – Danny had, either for a joke or by accident, connected one of the black boxes to the radio and she was at this moment receiving its *Play for the Day*.

Her hand shot out to the radio beside her, which she kept for aural wallpaper during the duller part of her narratives, and switched it on. Click. *'During this period Beethoven was having to contend with his increasing deafness ...'*

The childish voice cut in across this lecture. 'This voice is not correct,' it pronounced, putting paid to that theory. 'It is the voice of a male. Males are forbidden access to any of my functions beyond basic navigational aids. Candida One, unless you reply confirming that you are present and conscious, I shall flood this ship with sedative gas ten seconds from now.'

Then perhaps Danny has put a cassette in the radio as a joke, thought F. C. Stone. She turned off the radio and, for good measure, shook it. No, no cassette in there.

And the childish voice was at its counting again '... six, five, four ...'

Finding that her mouth was hanging open, F. C. Stone used it. 'I know this is a practical joke,' she said. 'I don't

know what it is you've done, Danny, but my God, I'll skin
you when I get my hands on you!'

The countdown stopped. 'Voice-patterns are beginning to
match,' came the pronouncement, 'though I do not understand your statement. Are you quite well, Candy?'

Fortified by the knowledge that this had to be a joke of
Danny's, F. C. Stone snapped, 'Yes, of course I am!' Very few
people knew that the C. in F. C. Stone stood for Candida, and
even fewer knew that she had, in her childhood, most
shamingly been known as Candy. But Danny of course knew
both these facts. 'Stop this silly joke, Danny, and let me get
back to work.'

'Apologies,' spoke the childish voice, 'but who is Danny?
There are only two humans on this ship. Is that statement
addressed to the male servant beside you? He asks me to
remind you that his name is Adny.'

The joke was getting worse. Danny was having fun with
her typos now. F. C. Stone was not sure she would ever
forgive him for that. 'And I suppose you're going to tell me
we've just emerged in the Dna System and will be coming in
to ladn at Nad,' she said bitterly.

'Of course,' said the voice.

F. C. Stone spent a moment in angry thought. Danny had
to be using a program of some kind. She ought first to test
this theory and then, if it was correct, find some way to
disrupt the program and get some peace. 'Give me your
name,' she said, 'with visual confirmation.'

'If you like,' the voice responded. Had it sounded puzzled?
Then Danny had thought of this. 'I am Candida Two. I am
your conscious-class computer modelled on your own brain.'
It sounded quite prideful, saying this. But, thought F. C.
Stone, a small boy co-opted by a grand fifteen-year-old like
Danny *would* sound prideful. 'We are aboard the astroship
Partlett M32/A401.'

Motorways, thought F. C. Stone, but where did he get the name?

'Visual,' said the voice. Blocks of words jumped into the screen. They seemed to be in Russian? Greek? capitals.

It had to be a computer game of some kind, F. C. Stone thought. Now what would Danny least expect her to do? Easy. She plunged to the wall and turned the electricity off. Danny would not believe she would do that. He would think she was too much afraid of losing this morning's work – and maybe she would, but she could do it over again. As the blocks of print faded from the screen, she stumped off to the kitchen and made herself a cup of *xfi* – no, COFFEE! – and prowled around in there amid the smell of cauterized ginger while she drank it, with some vague idea of letting the system cool off thoroughly. She had a vague notion that this rendered a lost program even more lost. As far as she was concerned, this joke of Danny's couldn't be lost enough.

The trouble was that she was accustomed so to prowl whenever she was stuck in a sentence. As her annoyance faded, habit simply took over. Halfway through the mug of *quaffy*, she was already wondering whether to call the taste in the Captain's mouth merely *foul*, or to use something more specific like *chicken shit*. Five minutes later, F. C. Stone mechanically made herself a second mug of *chofiy* – almost as mechanically noting that this seemed to be a wholly new word for the stuff and absently constructing a new kind of alien to drink it – and carried it through to her workroom to resume her day's stint. With her mind by then wholly upon the new solar system just entered by the starship *Candida* – there was no need to do whatever-it-was the learned fan wanted: after all, neither of them had *been* there and *she* was writing this book, not him – she switched the electricity back on and sat down.

Neat blocks of Graeco-Cyrillic script jumped to her screen.

'Candy!' said the childish voice. 'Why don't you answer? I repeat. We are well inside the Dna System and coming up to jump.'

F. C. Stone was startled enough to swallow a mouthful of scalding *c'phee* and barely notice what it was called. 'Nonsense, Danny,' she said, somewhat hoarsely. 'Everyone knows you don't jump inside a solar system.'

The script on the screen blinked a little. 'His name is Adny,' the voice said, sounding a little helpless. 'If you do not remember that, nor that micro-jumps are possible, then I see I must attend to what he has been telling me. Candy, it is possible that you have been overtaken by senility—'

'*Senility!*' howled F. C. Stone. Many murderous fates for Danny crowded through her mind.

'—and your male has been imploring me to ask you to authorize his use of functions Five through Nine to preserve this ship. Will you so authorize? Some action is urgent.'

A certain curiosity emerged through F. C. Stone's anger. How far was Danny prepared to take his joke? How many possibilities had he allowed for? 'I authorize,' she said carefully, 'his use of functions Five through *Eight* only.' And let's see if he planned for that! she thought.

It seemed he had. A symbol of some kind now filled the screen, a complex curlicue the like of which F. C. Stone had never seen, or imagined her equipment capable of producing. A wholly new voice spoke, male and vibrant. 'I thank you,' it said. 'Function Eight will serve for now. This justifies my faith in you, Candida Three. I am now able to bypass the computer and talk to you direct. Please do not turn your power-source off again. We must talk.'

It was a golden voice, the voice, perhaps, of an actor, a voice that made F. C. Stone want to curl up and purr and maybe put her hair straight, even while she was deciding there was no way Danny could have made his rough and squawky baritone sound like this. Gods! He must have hired someone! She gave that boy far too much money. She took another swig of *ogvai* while she noted that the voice was definitely in some way connected to the symbol on the screen. The curlicue jumped and wavered in time to its words.

'What do you mean by calling me Candida Three?' she asked coldly.

'Because you are the exact analogue of my mistress, Candida One,' the golden voice replied. 'Her ship's computer is known as Candida Two. It therefore followed that when I had searched the universes and discovered you, I came to think of you as Candida Three. I have been studying you – most respectfully, of course – through this machine you use and the thoughts you set down on it, for two years now, and—'

'And Daniel has been reading other books besides mine,' F. C. Stone interrupted. 'Unfaithful brat!'

'I beg your pardon?' The symbol on the screen gave an agitated jump.

Score one to me! F. C. Stone thought. 'My son,' she said. 'And we're talking parallel universes here, I take it?'

'We are.' The golden voice sounded both cautious and bemused. 'Forgive me if I don't quite follow you. You take the same sudden leaps of mind as my mistress, though I have come to believe that your mind is far more open than hers. She was born to a high place in the Matriarchy and is now one of the most powerful members of the High Coven—'

'Coven!' said F. C. Stone. 'Whose book is this out of?'

There was a pause. The curlicue gave several agitated jumps. Then the golden voice said, 'Look, please let me explain. I'm delaying jump as long as I can, but there really is only a very narrow window before I have to go or abort.'

He sounded very pleading. Or perhaps *beguiling* was a

better word, F. C. Stone thought, for that kind of voice. 'All right,' she said. 'Get on with the program. But just tell me first what you mean when you say *mistress*, Danny.'

'Adny,' he said. 'My name is Adny.'

'Adny, then,' said F. C. Stone. '*Mistress* has two meanings.'

'Why, I suppose I mean both,' he answered. 'I was sold to Candy as a child, the way all men are in this universe. Men have almost no rights in the Matriarchy and the Matriarchy is the chief power in our galaxy. I have been luckier than most, being sold to a mistress who is an adept of the High Coven. I have learnt from her—'

F. C. Stone gave a slight exasperated sigh. For a moment there, she had been uneasy. It had all seemed far more like a conversation than any program Danny could produce. But his actor-friend seemed to have got back to his lines now. She shot forth another question. 'So where is your mistress now?'

'Beside me, unconscious,' was the reply.

'Senile?' said F. C. Stone.

'Believe me, they are liable to it,' he said. 'The forces they handle do seem to damage them, and it does seem to overtake them oftenest when they're out in space. But—' she could hear the smile in his voice '—I must confess that I was responsible for this one. It took me years of study before I could outwit her, but I did it.'

'Congratulations, Adny,' said F. C. Stone. 'What do you want me to do about it? You're asking me to help you in your male backlash, is that it?'

'Yes, but you need do almost nothing,' he replied. 'Since you are the counterpart of Candida One, the computer is accepting you already. If you wish to help me, all I need is your voice authorizing Candida Two to allow me functions Nine and Ten. I can then tap my mistress's full power and navigate the ship to my rendezvous, whereupon I will cut this connection and cease interrupting you in your work.'

'*What!*' said F. C. Stone. 'You mean I don't get to navigate a word processor?'

'I don't understand,' said Adny.

'Then you'd better!' said F. C. Stone. She was surprised at how strongly she felt. 'Listen, Danny or Adny, or whoever you are! My whole career, my entire *success* as a writer, has been founded on the fact that I *enjoy*, more than anything else, sitting in front of this screen and pretending it's the controls of a starship. I enjoy the dazed feeling, I like the exhaustion, I don't mind getting cramp, and I even like drinking myself sick on *ogvai*! The only reason I haven't turned the machine off again is the chance that you're going to let me do it for real – or what feels like for real, I don't care which – and I'm not going to let that chance slip. You let me pilot my WP and I'll even authorize you to function Eleven afterwards, if there is such a thing. Is that clear?'

'It is very clear, Great Lady,' he said. There was that in his tone that suggested he was very used to yielding to demanding women, but could there have been triumph in it too?

F. C. Stone was not sure of that tone, but she did not let it worry her. 'Right,' she said. 'Brief me.'

'Very well,' he said, 'though it may not be like you expect. We are about to make a micro-jump which, in the normal way, would bring us out above the spaceport, but in this case is designed to bring us directly above the city of Nad and, hopefully, inside the Coven's defences there. Other ships of my conspiracy should be materializing too, hopefully at the same moment, so the jump must be made with utmost accuracy. I can broadcast you a simulacrum of *Partlett*'s controls, scaled down to correspond to your own keyboard. But you must depress the keys in exactly the order in which I highlight them. Can you do this?'

'Yes,' said F. C. Stone. 'But stop saying *hopefully* or I shan't grant you any functions at all. The word shouldn't be used like that and I detest sloppy English!'

'Yours to command,' Adny said. She could hear the smile in his voice again. 'Here are your controls.'

The curlicue faded from the screen, to be replaced by a diagrammatic image of F. C. Stone's own keyboard. It was quite recognizable, except, to her dismay, an attempt had been made to repeat it three times over. The two outer representations of it were warped and blurred. 'Gods!' said F. C. Stone. 'How do I use this? There isn't room for it all.'

'Hit HELP before you use the extra keys on the right and CAP before you use the ones on the left,' Adny's voice reassured her. 'Ready?'

She was. She took a hasty sip of cooling *qavv* to steady herself and hovered over her keyboard, prepared to enjoy herself as never before.

It was actually a bit of a let-down. Keys on her screen shone brighter green. Obedient to them, F. C. Stone found herself typing CAP A, d, HELP N and then HELP N, a, D. Some part of her mind suggested that this still looked like Danny's joke, while another part, more serious, suggested it might be overwork and perhaps she should see a doctor. But she refused to let either of these thoughts distract her and typed CAP D, n, HELP A in high excitement.

As she did so, she heard the computer's childish voice again. 'Ready for jump. Candida One, are you sure of this? Your co-ordinates put us right on top of Nad, in considerable danger from our own defences.'

'Reassure her,' Adny's voice said urgently.

Without having to think, F. C. Stone said soothingly, 'It's all right, Candida Two. We have to test those defences. Nad is under orders not to hurt us.' And she thought, As to the manner born! I'd have made a good Matriarch!

'Understood,' said the childish voice. 'Jump as given, on

the count of zero. Five, four, three' – F. C. Stone braced herself – 'two, one, zero.'

Did she feel a slight lurch? Was there a mild ripple of giddiness? She was almost sure not. A quick look round the workroom assured her that all was as usual.

'Jumping,' said Candida Two. 'There will be an interval of five subjective minutes.'

'Why?' said F. C. Stone, like a disappointed child.

Adny's voice cut in hastily. 'Standard for a microjump. Don't make her suspicious!'

'But I don't *feel* anything!' F. C. Stone complained in a whisper.

The keyboards vanished from the screen. 'Nobody does,' said Adny. 'Computer's out of the circuit now. You can speak freely. There is no particular sensation connected with jump, though disorientation does occur if you try to move about.'

'Damn!' said F. C. Stone. 'I shall have to revise all my books!' An acute need to visit the toilet down the passage came upon her. She picked up her mug of *chphy* reflexively, thought better of that, and put it down again. Her mind dwelt on that toilet, its bowl stained from Danny's attempt, some years ago, to concoct an elixir of life, and its chain replaced by a string of cow bells. To take her mind off it, she said, 'Tell me what you mean to do when you and the other ships come out over Nad. Does this start a revolution?'

'It's rather more complicated than that,' said Adny. 'Out of the twelve Male Lodges, there are only six prepared to rebel. Two of the remaining six are neutral traditionally and supported in this by the Minor Covens; but the Minor Covens are disaffected enough to ally with the Danai, who are a helium life-form and present a danger to all of us. The four loyal Lodges are supposed to align with the Old Coven and on the whole they do, except for the Fifth Lodge, which has thrown in with the Midmost Coven, who are against

everyone else. Their situation is complicated by their concessions to the Traders, who are largely independent, save for
overtures they seem to have made to the Anders. The Anders
– another life-form – have said they are *our* allies, but this
flirting with the Traders makes us suspicious. So we decided
on a bold ploy to test—'

'Stop!' said F. C. Stone. Much as she loved writing this
kind of stuff, hearing someone talk like it made her head
reel. 'You mean, you've gone to all this trouble just for a test
run?'

'It's more complicated than—' began Adny.

'No, I don't want to know!' said F. C. Stone. 'Just tell me
what happens if you fail.'

'We can't fail,' he replied. 'If we do, the High Coven will
crush the lot of us.'

'Me too?' F. C. Stone enquired anxiously.

'Possibly,' said Adny. 'They may not realize how I did this,
but if they do, you can probably stop them by destroying
your machine.'

'Never!' said F. C. Stone. 'I'd rather suffer – or, better still,
win!'

A bell rang. The keyboard reappeared, elongated and bent,
in her screen. 'Emerged over Nad,' the computer said.
'Candy! What is this? I count sixteen other ships emerged,
two Trader, four Ander and the rest appear to be Matriarch.
We jump back.'

'Give me functions Nine and Ten!' Adny snapped.

'I authorize Adny—' said F. C. Stone.

'Oh, Candy!' the computer said reproachfully. 'Why are
you so good to that little creep? He's only a man.'

'I authorize Adny in functions Nine and Ten,' F. C. Stone
almost shrieked. It was the only way she could think of to
stop the most unpleasant sensations which were suddenly
manifesting, mostly in her head and stomach. It was as if surf

were breaking through her in bubbles of pain. A tearing feeling across her shoulders made her think she was germinating claws there. And psychic attack or not, she knew she just had to get to that toilet.

'Acknowledged,' the computer said glumly.

She leapt from her chair and ran. Behind her she heard claps of sound and booms that seemed to compress the air around her. Through them she heard Adny's voice issuing orders, but that was shortly overlaid by a high-pitched whistling, drilling through her ears even through the firmly shut toilet door.

But in the loo, adjusting her dress, a certain sanity was restored to F. C. Stone. She looked at her own face in the mirror. It was encouragingly square and solid and as usual – give or take a sort of wildness about the eyes – and it topped the usual rather overweight body in its usual comfortably shapeless sweater. She raked her fingers through the greying frizz of her hair, thinking as she did so that she would make a very poor showing beside Adny of the golden voice. The action brought away two handfuls of loose hair. As always, she was shedding hair after a heavy session at the word processor – a fact she was accustomed to transfer to her aliens, who frequently shed feathers or fur during jump. Things were quite normal. She had simply been overworking and let Danny's joke get to her.

Or perhaps it was charred chilli powder, she thought as she marched out into the passage again. Possibly due to its hallucinogenic nature, that damnable whistling was still going on, pure torture to her ears. From the midst of it, she could hear Adny's voice. 'Nad Coven, do we have your surrender, or do we attack again?'

I've had enough! thought F. C. Stone. She marched to her desk, where the screen was showing Adny's curlicue, pulsing to the beat of the beastly shrilling. 'Stop this noise!' she commanded. 'And give me a picture of *Partlett*'s flight deck.' If you *can*, she thought, feeling for the moment every inch the Captain of the starship *Candida*.

The whistling died to an almost bearable level. 'I need function Eleven to give you vision,' Adny said – irritably? – casually? – or was it *too* casually? He was certainly over-casual when he added, 'It does exist, you know.'

Give him what he wants and get rid of him, thought F. C. Stone. 'I authorize function Eleven then,' she said.

'*Oh!*' said the computer, like a hurt child.

And there was a picture on the screen, greenish and jumping and sleeting green lines, but fairly clear for all that. *Partlett*'s controls, F. C. Stone noted absently, had fewer screens than she expected – far fewer than she put in her books – but far more ranks of square buttons and, far, far too many dials for comfort, all of them with a shabby, used look. But she was looking mostly at the woman who seemed to be asleep in the padded swivel seat in front of the controls. Mother-naked, F. C. Stone was slightly shocked to see, and not a mark or a wrinkle on her slender body, nor on her thin and piquant face. Abruptly F. C. Stone remembered being quite proud of her looks when she was seventeen, and this woman was herself at seventeen, only beyond even her most idealized memories. Immense regret suffused F. C. Stone.

The whistling, blessedly, stopped. 'Candy is really the same age as you,' Adny observed.

Her attention turned to him. His seat was humbler, a padded swivel stool. Sitting on it was a small man with a long, nervy face – the type of man who usually has tufts of hair growing in his ears and below his eyes, as if to make up for the fact that such men's hair always tends to be thin and fluffy on top. Adny's hair was noticeably thin on top, but he had smoothed and curled it to disguise the fact, and it was obvious that he had plucked and shaved all other hair from his wrinkled little body – F. C. Stone had no doubt of this, since he was naked too. The contrast between his appearance and his voice was, to say the least of it, startling.

Adny saw her look and grinned rather ruefully as he leant forward to hold a paper cup under some kind of tap below the control panel. She realized he could see her too. The contrast between herself and the sleeping beauty beside him made her feel almost as rueful as he looked. 'Can you give me a picture of Nad and any damage there?' she asked, still clinging to her role as Captain. It seemed the only way to keep any dignity.

'Certainly,' he said, running his finger down a row of the square buttons.

She found herself apparently staring down at a small town of old houses built up against the side of a hot stony hill – red roofs, box-like white houses, courtyards shaded with trees. It was quite like a town in Spain or Italy, except that the shapes of the walls and the slant of the roofs was subtly different and wrong. It was the very smallness of the difference between this and towns she knew which, oddly enough, convinced F. C. Stone for once and for all that this place was no fake. She really was looking at a real town in a real world somewhere else entirely. There was a smoking, slaggy crater near the market square, and another downhill below the town. That had destroyed a road. She had glimpses of the other spaceships, drifting about looking rather like hot air balloons.

'Why is it such a small place?' she said.

'Because Nad is only a small outpost of the Matriarchy,' Adny replied in his golden voice. The picture flipped back to show he had turned to face her on his stool, sipping steaming liquid from his paper cup. No doubt it was *kfa* or even *quphy*. He smiled through its steam in a way that must have beguiled the poor sleeping beauty repeatedly, and she found she was wishing he had turned out to be an alien instead. 'I owe you great thanks on behalf of the Second Male Lodge,' he said. 'We now have the Nadlings where we want them. And since you have given me full control of this ship and access to all my ex-mistress's power, I can move on to the central worlds in strength and use her as a hostage there.'

Hitler and Napoleon were both small men, F. C. Stone thought, with golden voices. It gave her a slight, cold *frisson* to think what she might have loosed on the unfortunate Matriarchy. 'You gave me the impression that this *was* the central world,' said F. C. Stone.

'Not in so many words,' said Adny. 'You don't think I'd be fool enough to move against the strength of the Matriarchy without getting hold of a conscious-class computer first, do you?'

F. C. Stone wished to say that, Yes, she did. People took that sort of desperate risk in her books all the time. It depressed her to find him such a cautious rebel. *And* he had cheated her, as well as his sleeping beauty – and no doubt he was all set to turn the whole works into a Patriarchy. It was a total waste of a morning.

Or was it? she wondered. A matriarchy where men were sold as slaves was right up her street. There was certainly a book in there. Perhaps she should simply be grateful and hope that Adny did not get too far.

'Tell me,' she said, at which he looked up warily from his cup, 'what is that stuff you're drinking? *Goffa*? *Xvay*?'

She was glad to see she had surprised him. 'Only coffee,' he said.

The True State of Affairs

I am still not sure how I come to be locked up here, but things are coming clearer. I shall find out in the end. Meanwhile, at the risk of sending myself mad by handling reality, I have screwed out of the jailor two sheets of brownish paper, curling at the edges, ink, and a bundle of long white feathers – most of which I have frayed and crumpled trying to turn them into pens. But this one, though it scratches like the devil, seems to be working. I suspect the penknife he gave me is blunt. You do not give prisoners sharp weapons. I have tried honing it on a corner of the wall, but it bit the stone to pieces and remained itself obdurately blunt.

Lord, it's good to talk, even manually, my own dialect again! Use a word like *obdurate* here and they stare. Their talk is only faintly dusted with Latin – and I notice, looking back over this while I sharpened my feather again, that I have caught it too. I did not come round to a really wholehearted Roman word until the last sentence.

I thought I would describe my prison and perhaps what I can gather of this castle – or *stronghold* as they call it here – but paper is so short that all I will say is that the walls are very thick, of very cold stone, and this window small and high. The light is going too. What comes in here is orange already. I shall not have time to write much more. Fancy a prisoner crying for *time* – but this is how the urge to write gets you. Since it is winter, I am wrapped in the cloak and a blanket from my bed, and still cold. I shall have to go and be brisk in the courtyard shortly. They light a fire in the mornings these days, but I can

never make the fuel last all day. Anyway, I shall go and look
at the tree before the light goes and then, perhaps, try a little
carefully muted charm on the jailor and hope crystallized
fruit might be the outcome – I crave for sugar so here. You
see how adjusted I am to the life. And only a month ago I
was a free woman and thought myself unhappy.

He did not give me anything sweet, the swine. It was one of
his bad days and his corns were killing him. He told me all
about his daughter's ingratitude again.

My name is Emily, and I am twenty-seven years old. I was
brought up in Kent, where my father had his parish. Poor
Father died five years ago, and Mother died last summer.

There, I feel better for having written that down. I believe
who I am again. Here, they seem to think my name is Edna
(a name I hate), and I am not sure that they know who Edna
is any more than I do. They seem to think I am from the
North. The man I call Smooth-one asked me several times if I
came from the North, and I conclude that was because my
accent is so different from this dialect of theirs.

I blame my troubles on their dialect – and on that bitch
Hilda. If I had only understood more than a fraction of what
was going on, I like to think nothing would have induced me
to change into her clothes, even soaking wet as I was. But
there they all were, milling about in those extraordinary
garments, speaking with their strange intonation, using
words I am only now beginning to grasp the meaning of, and
plainly so little concerned with me or my troubles that I
couldn't help returning the compliment and feeling unconcerned with theirs. I blame myself there. If I had only known
how important it was going to be, I think I might have

understood a great deal more. But it would have meant listening with stiff attention, like you do to a language you only half know, and they were all taking so little notice of me that their conversations, if they started in my neighbourhood, frequently ended on the other side of the room. And meanwhile another conversation would start up near me and drown the first.

Of course, I was intrigued by the atmosphere of desolation and panic. I still am. They were like refugees, all of them. There was a feeling of *sauve qui peut*. But I still don't think that explains why the peacock young man departed in such a hurry with most of the men and left the women to look after themselves. He seemed so fond of that Hilda. And he looked nice, in a self-centred patrician way. And she – well, I should say she was one of those who can't be fond of anybody. The tall, flat-breasted, mauve-handed kind. No strong feelings, and sex scares them silly. I suppose she was pretty, but it seemed out of character the way she let him trail his little finger lustfully about the palm of her hand whenever he spoke to her. It can't have been the custom. Nobody else does it, not even Edwin, thank the Lord. No, I can't make it out. Nor do I want to. I dislike the woman too much, particularly now I see how she conned me into dressing up in her clothes and posing as her, even to the extent of clumping about in those wooden patten-things to make me look the right height, and the scarf – to keep the cold out, I trustfully thought. I'm not usually that much of a fool, and I remember it did strike me as a little too good to be true when they suddenly became so kind and concerned – Hilda and that fat maid of hers – but I had been ignored for so long, and I was so wet and exhausted, that I was pathetically grateful to be noticed at last.

That's right, Emily. Make excuses to yourself. You were dumb. And I didn't even see the point when Red-face comes bursting in and grabs me and not Hilda. I think light dawned a little when they pulled me out of the coach – or Black Maria, or whatever it was – and into the stone bowels of this stronghold, where the tall, smooth type was waiting: they were obviously so disconcerted when they saw me clearly. My word, they are an unpleasant pair, those two. Smooth-one is worse, although it was Red-face who hit me. Up till then, I had been all taken up with this ridiculous paranoid fancy that the whole odd business had been laid on just for my benefit. It keeps recurring. That's one of my reasons for writing this. I have a dread that I am mad, and that outside this stronghold England is going on just as usual. Inside, they are humouring me. I have to keep telling myself that I was never important enough to be humoured to that extent. Then, say I, perhaps I made it all up for myself? If so, I did a pretty thorough job. And you don't make up people like Smooth-one.

When I saw Smooth-one sauntering up to Red-face, I took a nasty knock up against reality. It was just like stubbing your toe. He was factual and horrible from the wriggly red hairs in his sideburns to the dust on the toes of his boots. And I was only a tiresome sort of Thing to him. You don't make up people who are never going to be bothered to find you interesting. At least, I never have. Smooth-one, I am sure, whatever political thing is going on around here, had me shut up in these rooms primarily as one might chuck an unwanted letter in a drawer. He couldn't care less – except that I had turned out to be the wrong woman, and that irritated him. But he was angry with Red-face, not with me. He certainly could not be bothered to listen to my faint-hearted protest that I was a foreigner and scarcely knew Hilda.

That makes me very resentful. If there's one thing I mind more than having been fooled by Hilda, it's not being important to these people. It reminds me of the way you feel in hospital, when you are there with some minor complaint and all the staff are only interested in the woman in the next bed who has something really bad and complicated. You almost feel it would be worth being very ill just to be noticed. I almost feel I would rather be Hilda than a nobody they think is called Edna. And coming here was oddly like being entered into hospital. There was the same kind of waiting about on the margins of the system, while the jailor pottered up and the soldiers discussed my case with him. I remember he said: 'Lady or not?' and both the soldiers shrugged. Then he jangled keys and opened these rooms up, and I was installed officially as an inmate, high up somewhere in this stronghold, for no reason that seems to me adequate.

Yes. Having written this, as well as considered it for a month, I see it must be so. This is a genuine citadel, not a madhouse. Edwin is a genuine jailor. I am a genuine prisoner, and it is still exceedingly cold. Of my borrowed finery, I retain Hilda's dress and the little underneath it. It is of fine, white wool, down to my feet, beautifully and curiously embroidered with spreading designs of blue, whose intricacies I now feel I know by heart. I could draw them without looking. But it has a devilishly low neck, no doubt becoming, but in no way seasonable. And, after a month, it has a grubby, wilted look. Perhaps I have too. We are both gathering dust in our drawer here. I see no end to the process.

When I got this paper, I had a fancy that I would write great things and spend my pens discovering truths. I would love to. I have a feeling that truths are gathering at the back of my head, ready to burst through. But they will not burst. The dreary trivia of prison are too much for them. I am bound to the minute perpetually, and, besides, I am not one of those who finds it easy to think in grand abstractions, and

I find it even more difficult to set them down clearly. So perhaps, sadly, since I am nearly at the end of my paper, I had better simply describe these rooms which I wandered at first in such a tense and weary way. The living-room opens on to a courtyard with a shallow coping, high on the roof. I went out there as if it were freedom, but I could only see steep angles and corners of roofs and towers. There is no way out from it. It is like an island. And on its right side I looked over the coping and saw a deep, deep well of a drop between towers – a drop of a hundred feet and more down to a minute, dank courtyard surrounded by blank walls and a few blanker windows. I had a headache and it made me dizzy to look. I had to go inside. The aerial isolation of my quarters is almost inexpressible. It depressed me then (and does still) so that I went straight to the square dusty bed in the next room and lay restlessly down on it. I can almost laugh now at the way I considered that when they came to let me out they could easily wake me up. And I actually fell asleep thinking it. That was just one piece of my early folly.

Thank God – theirs or mine, whichever is this benevolent – Edwin now thinks I must really be a lady after all. I hope he tells someone. It was the writing that did it. He came in with supper soon after I had finished, whereupon I defensively took up my two sheets. He, cocking his dirty old head on one side, said:

'My word, there's a fine heap of scribbles. Is all that paper full?'

I said it was, and, suspecting that he could not read, or barely so, I boldly held them out for him to see. He looked at it up and down and sideways, like a bird sighting a worm, and, with a marked increase of respectfulness, said he wished he knew his letters.

So I was right. He can't read. As long as I keep it from
Wolfram, I can write what I like, thank God. Maybe I shall
keep handy a sheet of scribbles that don't matter to me to
show Wolfram if he asks – for Edwin is such an old gossip
that he is bound to mention it. He regards it as so phenom-
enal that a woman can write where he cannot. And from this
he has concluded I am a lady born: not that he has said so,
but it's obvious from his manner. And to mark his respect he
has brought me a whole sheaf of slightly better paper and
more feathers, and sharpened my penknife for me. When I
need ink, I must ask. Well, well. No doubt, silly old man, he
thinks he will get handsomely tipped for this in the end, by
my grateful noble relatives, but I think, too, that he has a
genuine respect for birth. Maybe they all have here. Look at
the lengths those people went to to preserve that bitch Hilda.
And to think I have spent a whole month trying to convince
Edwin by other means.

It soon became my main object. Not just vulgar snobbery
either. Even in my first week, when I was not bothering to
think what impression I produced, so sure was I that my
imprisonment must be only temporary, I was having to fend
Edwin off with the utmost loftiness. He is a lewd old man,
and sly and cowardly about it. He never dares come out with
a direct proposal, but his hints and innuendoes are legion –
even the ones I can understand, and I am sure there are
many I don't.

The trouble was that I was too polite to start with. I was
too shattered to be otherwise than mild, and I naturally tend
to smile and be conciliatory if I can. And besides, I had a
feeling that my relationship with this jailor was to be so short
as to be unimportant. So things got off on the wrong foot.
But he did not start really bobbing and leering until the
second day, when the weather first turned cold and he had
his teenage aide, Hobby, who seems half daft, haul up a

bundle of logs for a fire. As my hair was still soaking, I took it
down and tried to dry it by the fire. Unfortunately, I was not
yet familiar with the routine. He came in on his round half
an hour after. Of course, I jumped up nervously. I was
jumping up all the time that week, expecting God knows
what, but hoping it was release. I wore out with it and went
thin. Hilda's dress now hangs rather loose. And you should
have seen the man's face. Lechery incarnate.

'Oh-ho!' says he. 'There's a long lock to lengthen a man's
limb!' He has a maddening habit of alliteration.

'My hair was wet,' I said uppishly. 'I need to dry it before I
catch my death.'

Death, of course, is a reference to orgasm in their parlance
– I should have guessed, since it was once in ours too – and
for a while things got really awkward. In the end I barricaded
myself into the bedroom and waited for him to leave. He did
leave in the end, for he has his pretence of being over-
burdened with work to keep up, but not for a long time. And
until now he was not really convinced he was mistaken in
me. I have concluded that letting one's hair down here
means just what it implies with us. Perhaps that was why
Hilda's crew accorded me so little consideration.

One's relationship with one's jailor is an odd thing. One is
at once a nuisance to him and of abiding interest. This one, at
least, hangs about and questions my every action. And I am
totally, if rebelliously, dependent on him for everything,
including tastes of the outside world. We resent one another
enormously. I have built a character for myself, for his
benefit, of lofty eccentricity. I pretend I don't care about
anything. That maddens him. For his one desire, apart from
lechery, is gossip. Nothing makes him talk more freely than
my indifference. All I have learnt, I learnt this way. And
then, if I feed into my indifference a few smiles, a little
subterranean coaxing compliment, I can usually get material

objects out of him too. That was how I got my first supply of
paper. The truth is, of course, that he has nothing to do but
wait on me. He has built a character too for me, of the poor
overworked turnkey, and talks of his rounds and his prisoners
and his poor feet endlessly. But I am now fairly convinced that
I am his sole charge – though I dare not let him know it: our
precarious amity would be over. Since the only other prisoner
I know of is certainly in other, more competent hands, I
am sure I am his only one. And he loves and hates me
accordingly.

I shall have to thank the gods again that I stopped there and
constructed a page of dire scribbles, snatches of verse, a speech
from *Hamlet*, details of prison routine, and other random
things. Wolfram slunk in, saying he heard I was writing, and
held out his long cold hand for a sample. So I gave him the
prepared sheet, thanking my stars, and he looked it over, a
little laboriously. Wolfram is certainly literate, but I think my
English and my rather personal calligraphy bothered him
rather. It was clear he could not make much of most of it.

'I see you're a maker,' he said, pointing to one of the
snatches of verse.

It did happen to be part of a poem I had written a while
back; so I said yes, I was – *maker* to them is *poet* – a trifle piqued
that he had not credited me with 'To be or not to be,' but no
doubt that was above his head. I used to think Wolfram had
intelligence, but now I think he is simply devious.

He said, with a rather obvious deviousness: 'Freda the
Maker was the daughter of a thrall, Edna.' How I hate the
name Edna.

I repressed an urge to point to a place where I had written
'My name is Emily and I do not want to die' and answered:
'Maybe. But I'm not.'

Perhaps I should have said my father was a priest. Edwin implies that priests have high status here, particularly Woden's. But then not all of them are noble, I think, and I am determined to cling to the highest rank they will concede me. Hilda can do that for me at least. (They have still not caught her, by the way, so Edwin says. Red-face must be mad.)

My name is Emily Emily Emily. Let no one forget.

Wolfram went on, in a bored sort of way, to the usual interrogation. To which I said the usual things, and he slunk away again. I have not quite worked out who or what Wolfram is. He is plainly Edwin's superior, even though he is more like Uriah Heep than any living man I know, and I suspect that he must be some kind of steward or seneschal here and hoping to rise in the world. He has time. He seems younger than I am. But he tells me first one thing then another, so it's anyone's guess. He's illegitimate, I suspect, and sore about it. Though, to judge from Edwin's remarks, it's no disgrace if only you happen to be the right man's bastard. Wolfram perhaps had the wrong father. But he is educated after a fashion, and dresses in a scruffy version of the peacock-man's style.

When he first appeared, he frightened me a lot. He did the pompous legal bit, said he had come to ask me some questions for my own good. Luckily, by then I had come to myself a little – enough at least to realize that when people say it's for your own good in prison they tend to mean the opposite. Anyway, Wolfram sits himself down at this table with pen and paper and makes me sit facing him. I thought it best to seem docile, so I gave him answers. That is, I said No to everything except the question: *Are you a lady born?* to which I said Yes, firmly and at once. This is what makes me suspect Wolfram to be a bastard: he does not believe me. He probably knows all there is to know about social climbing.

As to my other answers, I have no idea whether he believes me or not, and I am not sure he cares – except that Smooth-one may have offered him some kind of reward for finding out about me. It is clear I puzzle them. But I now have a feeling that, provided I remain a mystery and claim high rank, they may not dare to harm me. From what Edwin says, their position is not so secure that they can risk offending any more nobility. The actual questions still mean little to me and meant next to nothing at first.

Did I go between Holland and Hathriver? Did I carry messages to the Lowlands? Do I know where Hugh is? Or Hilda? Did Hugh give me Hilda's clothes? Was I in Mark to find Asgrim? Has anyone sent me a message since I was here? (How, I ask you?) Has Asgrim ever sent me a message? With a message? Am I a thrall? Am I a lady? In either case, was my father for Hathriver or the Lowlands? Did I go between the North and Hathriver? Was the message I carried from Asgrim? Or to Asgrim? Was I for Asgrim or Hugh?

Was I the Queen of the Fairies? as I said to Wolfram on his third or fourth visit. He went a dull, pimply red and stopped asking me for a week, but he did remark that I should be kept prisoner until my answers were more satisfactory. This, in a way, set my mind at rest. I no longer jump up expecting to be let out every hour. I am simply, quietly and drearily, miserable.

I have thought about escaping. There is no hope of doing it by climbing. I could not drop forty feet to the nearest roof below the courtyard. I *could* let myself down by bedclothes

from the yard, if they could be made long enough, but that
nearest roof is in front of one of the few inhabited rooms in
the place. There is a crowd of soldiers or something down
there, who lean out on fine nights and call rude remarks up
at me if I am out. I don't fancy getting into their clutches. Or I
could clobber Edwin, which I would love to do if I had a
weapon. All I have, though, is blocks of wood for the fire,
which they saw too small to be much good – no doubt
having thought of that. And I suspect that Edwin would take
a deal of clobbering, and my arms are not strong. Oh God! I
do curse myself for being so ineffectual, but I cannot see
myself physically escaping; and I know that the longer I stay
here the more timorous I get. My only hope is to discover
enough of the names and policies of this country to be able to
give Wolfram a convincing and blameless account of how I
came to be in Hilda's shoes (or rather, pattens: I have burnt
the things long ago and continue to shiver). This was another
of my motives for writing. I thought I could set down what I
know and maybe, in the setting down, hit upon my story.

To continue then. In the first week I learnt little, since I
had not established a *modus vivendi* with Edwin then and was
not thinking it necessary. In the second week I had Wolfram's various questions for a guide, but they meant next to
nothing to me. I set about leading Edwin on to talk – but
what with his perfidious daughter, his corns and his imaginary duties, he filled hours of loitering, stinking and grinning
and rattling his keys, without letting much out to the
purpose. But things are gradually emerging, sideways, in
parenthesis and by implication. The York and Lancaster of
this country are Mark and Hathriver, and Mark seems to be
in the ascendant, viewed from here. I have learnt that Red-
face and Smooth-one constitute Mark, and that Mark is, in
fact, the place I am now in. The stronghold is in the town,
and they are both called Mark, I think. But just as I had

decided that of course my father was a nobleman who
supported Mark, I began to gather that the situation was not
that simple. Hathriver and Mark have another rival called
Holland – or the Lowlands – and I *think* that may be Hilda's
party. And I shall not join her, or let my father join. Then
there is the North, which is another thing again, and as I am
thought to be of that party, perhaps I had better stay that
way. The only trouble is that Edwin knows next to nothing
about us. He regards us as barbarians, but does not quite like
to say so. And since he supposes me to know more than he
does, he tends to defer to me. He says things like: 'But you
know all about that, better than poor me'. Edwin is always
'poor me,' the old hypocrite. But I think from the sound of it
that the North is sitting on the fence and claiming neutrality
– in which case they have no business to be locking me up
like this. Now I think of it, I see I had better throw in a little
indignation over that into my next round of answers to
Wolfram's questions.

But this is mere playing about. I am a supporter of
Hathriver and shall ever be – and please I pray all the gods in
the pantheon, do not let Wolfram see this. Keep it from his
slimy fingers. Keep it from his restless eyes. And let me not
blush again in front of Edwin, not for all the reverence of all
the nations. I'm not even sure that I really want to escape.

What a fool I am to write a thing like that just as the light
goes and I have to stop. There it sat, clean in the middle of a
page at the end of a block of writing, staring at anyone who
cared to look. In future, since I know I must write such
things, I swear to embed them deep in a page of writing, and
not put them down till I can. My heart is still in my mouth at
how Wolfram came in after supper and asked for my paper,
saying calmly he must check that there were still the same

number of pages. When I asked him indignantly why, he said
that there had been messages going out and I need not think I
was going to get away with it. And he took the bundle, written
and unwritten, up in his long cold fingers and carried it under
the lamp to count. I sat and tried to look negligent. I have
never felt so horrified in my life. My hands went all wet and
stiff, and my chest hammers even now when I write of it. I
could almost have hoped a sheet was missing – more than
almost: I prayed it would be and I would get the blame. My
man has been up to something, and God help him if they catch
him at it. I wish I knew what it was. I might invent something.
Oh *why* is it so hard to get news? They won't show *him* any
kindness. What with this, and fearing every minute that
Wolfram would uncover my last page and read the last
paragraph, with his own name and that other to catch his eye,
I could scarcely breathe. If he had asked me to stand, my knees
would have given way. And look at me. Here I go in my folly
writing all about it. Fill the page, idiot. Hurry on.

Perhaps I need not have worried about him reading it. My
writing is quirky. And that lamp is so dim that I can hardly see
block capitals by it. I think the other is far worse. Who could I
send messages to? But he must have hundreds. Dear God, not
a sign. I've been out twice to the courtyard, and nothing, and
no one. What are they doing over there?

I feel sick. It's the usual time, and still nothing. And the
horrible hurting things that Edwin says he has seen men do to
men here. Oh terrible. Terrible. I shall go and have one more
look, and if there is still nothing, I shall write down all about it,
though I did not intend to. I meant only to refer to it, to keep
myself in secret. But I have to do something positive, and this
is all I can think of. Then if Wolfram reads it perhaps they'll kill
me too.

No. Nothing. Very well.

Almost at the end of my second week, I discovered the tree. If I stood in the yard, against the wall of my living-room, between the door and the coping that looks over that horrible well of a drop, I could see through a gap between two large blocks of masonry. And there was that little graceful tree, busily shedding yellow leaves across another courtyard like mine but deeper, with higher walls. The tree was not in the courtyard. I could not make out where it grew from. But I thought rather wistfully that anybody in that courtyard would be able to see that tree all the time. There was nobody in the courtyard. There had not been since I arrived, but there was a dim light most evenings in the block of building that abutted on it. I was busy establishing my aloof and indifferent character with Edwin at the time, so I did not ask about the light. But I was so enchanted to see that tree that I broke out of character and asked him how in the world it grew there.

It was one of his brutal evenings. He farted a lot and spat rather. 'Curiosity killed the cat,' he said.

'You mean you don't know,' I said, and I remember I was huddling a blanket round me. Hilda's dress is made for summer, and the evenings were chilly then and have grown no warmer since.

'I know everything about this stronghold,' Edwin retorted. 'But if I don't please to tell you, I don't please. That there tree' – I nearly laughed – 'took root from a bird-dropping in my father's time, on the roof of the head turnkey's house. My father was head turnkey then. And there's nobody knows what it feeds on. Apple-tree, it is. Good pippins.' Then he belched.

'Is the roof stone, or tile, or thatched?' I asked.

'Maybe a bit of thatch,' he conceded. 'But that's no food for apples, is it?'

'I don't know,' I said distantly, and he went on to how much better things were in his father's day. Peace and plenty, if you were to believe him, unlike the troubled times now. Nobody thought of being king then. No need for a king. The country was an alliance of free men, all equal, and thralls knew their place. This alliance of free men, I gather, was in fact an oligarchy of twelve major patricians and twenty-three minor ones. Below them is a sketchy middle class, a large yeomanry (to which Edwin claims to belong), and what sounds like a very large number of serfs or thralls, who actually belong to the great estates (like the Russian muzhiks) and have few or no rights. If ever a country was ripe for revolution, I would have thought this one was. But its culture seems largely pre-industrial, so, instead of revolution, there is this struggle for supremacy amongst the great – which I have got caught up in – a struggle which, according to Edwin's ideas, Mark is winning. Though this may be a partial view.

I wanted to go out that night and see the tree again, but Edwin locks the outer door on his after-supper round and I had to wait till morning. Then I went and looked at it repeatedly. And while I was watching it part with leaf after golden leaf, a man came out into the courtyard beneath it. It was the first time I had seen anyone there, so I watched him with interest, and wrapped my arms across my chest to keep out some of the sneaking breeze. He was better clad than I, in dark grey stuff that looked thick. I watched him walk slowly across the courtyard – until I could see him nearly full length – and turn his face up at the sky and the tree, with a curious look of release. Poor man. I knew so well what that tree felt like to see. And presently a gust in the breeze loosed a flutter of round yellow leaves, and blew them over him. I could hear the rattle of them from here. He put out his hand and caught one. He did it in such a deft, matter-of-fact way that you would never have guessed how difficult it is to catch a gusting leaf, nor, perhaps, what a precious thing it was to catch. He had it in his hand for quite a while, looking at it, without apparent intensity. Then he put it in his pocket. I didn't grudge him his leaf, but I envied him his chance to catch it. After that, he moved about the court for some minutes, neither slowly, nor in the brisk way you do when you're consciously taking exercise. Just savouring it, I think. I remember seeing his head and shoulders move along by the wall, until he disappeared behind the building, and then seeing him reappear full length on the further side of the court, look up at the tree, and move out of sight again. Two other watchful people were in view some of the time, guards plainly, and they never let him get more than about twenty feet away from either of them. What impressed me with this man was the way he kept his dignity and his privacy in spite of them. You felt a personality, uninvaded and strong, even from my distance. Then they seemed to tell him to come in: that was enough, now. It seemed to me that he stood very still for a moment, as if he were coping with a strong impulse to protest – nor do I blame him – before he went quietly towards where the door must be, hidden from where I was. But, on the way, he looked up and saw me. Our eyes met, and we knew what we were both feeling like. He did not stare, nor look hurriedly away either. He just moved his head calmly round, so I am sure the guards never noticed him see me. I was the one who stared, and I went on staring for half an hour at the yard and at the windows, in hopes of seeing him again.

I must remember to ease out of Edwin whether they believe here too that you get one happy day if you catch a falling leaf.

He was there again the next day, for slightly longer. He has been there every day since, at the same time, for half an hour or so, until yesterday. And I am there too, walking up and down the narrow part of this court where I can see a narrow slice of his. That second day, he was on the lookout for me, I know he was, but he was very cunning about it. He strolled around, aimlessly it seemed, into the right quarter of his yard, and there he walked in a sort of half-moon course, so that he was facing my way more than any other. I never caught him actually staring, until they told him to come in. Then he looked at me, just as he did the first time, and looked hard, as if he had been waiting to say something with that look. But looks are not that expressive, from that distance, with guards standing by, and I ran in here in a state of doubt and hectic gladness. I went straight to the bedroom and saw myself as whole as possible in the blotchy mirror there. I was flushed, but too thin, and my face is long and on the hollow side these days. Nevertheless, I have good bones and may have looked all right from a distance. But my hair and eyebrows, being fair, may not show up. Could he see my eyes, which are my best part? I could get an idea of his. Indeed, when I saw him a second time, I thought I had seldom seen a more comely man. He is tall and his hair is dark. His shoulders are broad, and the rest of him shapely. I like the way he walks – with a sort of characteristic swing of the shoulders I would know among thousands. It is strange how people's personalities show, even from this distance. This, I know, is a good man and a strong man. Whatever they have him here for, it must be because of his connection with Hathriver and not for anything wrong that he did.

After this, I could not wait to wring something out of Edwin about him. That afternoon I said, not as if I cared: 'I didn't know there was a prisoner over the way there. Is he one of yours?' I was fairly sure, even then, that Edwin had only me, but I had to humour him or get nothing.

'Ooh,' he says. 'That one. Have they let him out? I heard he was being kept indoors until Yule or after. No,' he said. 'Not one of mine. I don't go over that way, you know. Too much for my poor feet, what with all I have to do here. And I wouldn't do it, what's more, if they asked me. You know it takes six of them to watch him. He's dangerous.'

He didn't look dangerous to me, and I pitied him heartily if he had six men constantly about him. How could he call his soul his own? Yet he plainly does, to his credit. I asked why he should be so dangerous.

Edwin rolled up his eyes and, showing me both yellow eyeballs, gave out a rapid set of hints which passed quite above my head. But some of it certainly referred to people killed by my man. 'Mind you,' said Edwin, putting his leery eyes back in their natural place, 'it's political, really, why they have him here. Political. His side can't get along so well without him, you see, and they were lucky enough to grab him when they did. Lucky losers make winners worse, if you know what I mean.' I did not. I said he didn't know what he was talking about, but that offended him. I had still not learnt to judge my tone with Edwin then. 'I know,' he retorted, 'and much more could I mathel if I were asked.' And, not intending to be asked, he went away.

I wish I had a better ear for speech. I see I am not rendering Edwin's peculiar dialect as it really is at all. I keep replacing his words and phrases by what I understand them to mean in my English. He would never use a word like *political*. The words are *menward* and *landminding*. But when I think of what he says, I think of it in translation, as it were.

I had to get to work on Edwin more tactfully thereafter. But before I had much time to do so, the weather turned bitterly cold. That had me in trouble, because I had been forced to wash through some of my underclothes and try to dry them by the fire. They were still not dry that frosty morning. I had to ask Edwin if he could by any means procure me some more clothes. He refused. It was not his job, he said, but if I had any money he could send out for some for me. He knew I had no money, the old swine. I have not even got the brooch that Red-face snatched off me, or I would have bartered that. Crystallized fruit was one thing, clothing quite another. And I had to go out to see my man, even if I froze. So I took the blanket off the bed again, wrapped myself in that and went.

We both of us had to keep moving that day. It was so frosty, and the wind howled and hummed across the roofs, bringing little stutters of dry snow with it. My man had a thick green cloak that fell in great folds from his shoulders when the wind left it alone, but I could tell he was as cold as I was by the way he gripped it round him and stamped his feet. Your circulation slows badly if you live in confinement. I could see he was pale with it. The guards hated the cold and, for once, kept huddled under the wall with their backs to the weather, so that he could look at me most of the time. We circled, watching one another, as if we were at a minuet, or some other dance, distant and courtly, far off and frustrating. Its absurdity bothered us both. He stopped still, with a kind of military stamp, in the middle of his space, and stood laughing over at me about it. The wind, I remember, was whipping his hair forward and across his face. And I laughed back, not only because it was funny, but because I was delighted to find he had a sense of humour. And, still laughing, he shivered, gestured 'This is no good' and took to walking again.

Then I tried sitting on the coping of my court to stop my part of the minuet, but it was far too cold there. The wind took my blanket, and I very nearly lost it down the drop; and it took my hair too and blew it out of its pins. Between hair and blanket and the sudden freezing suffusion of wind on my body, I hardly knew what to do for a moment. When I looked at him again, with the blanket safe at least, he was turning his mouth down, shaking his head and smiling, as much as to say: 'Don't sit there any more, or you'll lose what little you have.' And I nodded and smiled and got up again. While I did so, they told him to come in – it was a shorter time than usual, but they had had enough – and they damn near caught him smiling at me. He thought they had, and, as he went, he shot me a look so alarmed that it really upset me.

'Why *shouldn't* he look at me, if he wants to?' I said, right aloud, as I came in. I talk to myself a great deal. You do, if you have only yourself to talk to. They were not letting him do anything, as far as I could see. He was checked at every turn. But above all, I suppose, they were determined that he should not communicate with a soul – though what they think they have to fear from me still defeats me.

But it is quite clear that communication is at the root of it. And he is out to do it if he can. He must have succeeded in some degree, or Wolfram would not have counted my paper so busily. And I know by now that they have taken some kind of vengeance on him. I have been out almost between every sentence, but there is no sign of him today either. Dear gods, mine and his, let it be no worse than close confinement again. I would gladly give up seeing him if it could be no worse. Confinement is bad enough. The weather is mild at the moment and the sun almost warm, and though the tree has no leaves left, it is still beautiful.

I know he is very cunning, but the odds are so great. No. Enough of that. I shall tell about the day after that, which was frostier than the first. Edwin and Hobby come tramping in, Edwin to lock and unlock and to give me my can of milk and my bread, Hobby (who must have given his name to the hob-nail, I think) to pound about striking sparks from the floor, clearing up, lighting the fire and hauling me in an iron jug of water. He tramples in and out, while Edwin stands officiously at the door. On his third entrance, Hobby brought in an armful of something red.

'This came for you,' says Edwin, who never lets Hobby speak for himself if he can avoid it.

Now that was really interesting. Something *came*. Perhaps Hilda had remembered my existence. I stood up eagerly.

Edwin chuckled. 'Brought you to your feet, didn't it?' he said nastily.

All I could do was to look haughty and ask what it was. Hobby put the bundle in my arms and, unwrapping it, I found it was this beautiful red cloak. It has a loose hood, three brass clasps in the shape of lions' heads down the front and, inside, it is lined with soft brown fur – I don't know from what animal. It is full long for me. On a man it would be calf-length, but it is so warm that I never bother that it trails. 'Whoever sent this?' I said, too pleased to be haughty.

It was immediately apparent that Edwin had no idea and was not going to tell me. He rubbed his nose theatrically, and looked both wise and stupid. 'Ah-ha! Wouldn't you like to know? One who knows your needs. You tell me.'

I was shaking the thing out and stroking it, and at that second unluckily turned the hood the wrong way out. A yellow leaf from the apple tree fluttered and fell on the floor. I don't think Edwin saw its significance for a moment, but he continued to chuckle and press me to name the man who sent it. And the sight of that leaf struck me with such gratitude and such terror, and such secret joy and determination to conceal it, that I blushed. I know I have never blushed so in my life before. I could feel my eyes and my neck hot with it.

Edwin pointed at me and cackled his head off. 'Ah-ha! Who's the fancyman?'

I told him that I had not the faintest idea, but of course he did not believe me and of course he told Wolfram. Wolfram adds 'Who sent you the cloak?' to his list of questions when he remembers. I say stoutly that I don't know. I have searched the thing from hem to hem in hopes of a message, but there is nothing except the leaf. I see now that he dared not risk more. He must have taken risks enough as it was, and I still don't see how he did it. I hope it was not *his* leaf, but I fear it must have been. It is a little dry and crumpled, as if it has been in a pocket. I know he can get more. They pile up in the courtyard there in drifts, but this one he caught. It seems more generous to send the leaf even than the cloak.

Well, I have put on the cloak and gone for a last stroll in the evening, which looks very orange and heavy. The soldiers below laughed and jeered as usual and called up to me to come down and keep them warm in bed, and more besides, and I took no notice. There is still no sign of my man. The lamp is not lit in the window, either. Have they taken him away? Or have they moved him to a dungeon, or worse? Oh this is terrible. I am hard put to it not to cry, though Edwin will be in in a minute. Perhaps in a year or so I shall learn fortitude.

Thank God, he was there this morning. I wish I could say none the worse. But he was very pale, and moving in a slow, cautious way – I could see it was all he could do not to limp. What have those fiends done to him? I want to do it to them, many times over, and invent more besides. Your imagination is a horrible thing. It feeds on vagueness. If only I knew what they did, it would seem less terrible. At least, I hope it would. I feel pain all over when I think of the way he laboured carefully about that yard. And he did not dare look at me, it was plain. It was very obvious he was deliberately *not* looking my way. And that gave me my hint. I strolled about, trying to look careless, and half the time I could hardly see him for the most painful tears. The sky, sympathetic for once, kept sending gentle big drops of rain that were almost warm, from somewhere south. Lord, how I hope they are not going to break his spirit and violate his personality. That I could not bear to see. I keep thinking, when I see him, 'Else a great Prince in prison lies,' though I do not know what else *from*. Nor do I know if he is a great prince, though it is clear he is, or was, someone important. Until this morning, he certainly bore himself like someone important. If he must send messages, let him not be *caught*.

I have been at Edwin to know a little more. All I know so far can be contained in the one word *Hathriver*. My man was a major figure in that party, so much I know. And I have not learnt much more, and I have been sickened by Edwin's cackles and belching talk of 'punishment'. I said carelessly that I supposed the message must have been traced now, since Wolfram only found it necessary to count my paper once.

'The message is known of,' said Edwin, 'but not traced. There's paper missing, and they've been at him to find where it's gone. You might as well try opening an oyster with your bare hands. He won't say. So they dealt out a little punishment instead, as you might call it. But they daren't mark him too bad, more's the pity. It might be they have to send him back whole and sound, one of these days, you see. Or if Regan and Wrinkle get taken in Widburn this week, the other side gets its own back the same way, doesn't it?'

'Oh goodness,' says I, wearily, keeping an eye on the bobbing float, 'do you mean to say they're still fighting? How dreary.'

'Up and down,' says Edwin. 'Up and down. Lowlands is on the walk again, and a deal of them got killed down there a week ago. And Hathriver is massing, but no one knows for sure if it's in Widburn or Gardale. You in the North still bide your time, don't you? But there's messages there, like the ones you carried.'

Rather rashly, I opened my mouth to deny that, and then, because he had seen me draw breath, I had to say: 'I daresay the time isn't ripe.' I catch Edwin's habit of wise saws and empty proverbs.

'No, nor will it be,' says he, pointing his biggest key in the direction of my man, 'while he sits there. He was to be king, that one. But now we're a body without a head until Wrinkle gets crowned.'

I think the name *Wrinkle*, or whatever, is Smooth-one's. I can't work out how to spell it from Edwin's pronunciation. Sometimes it seems even to have an aspirate and be *Hrinkle*, and, for a long time, I thought it was *Uncle* and saw Smooth-one as a kind of Big Brother – a role to which he is not unfitted. Red-face is either *Regin* or *Regan*. The pronunciation is exactly between the two. And, while I am at it, I will make a prophecy that Uncle will rid himself of Regan when he gets to be king, or whatever power he can scramble into.

But Edwin, leaving and waving his ridiculous keys about, sent a parting shot at my man which I find more interesting than anything else. 'This will teach him,' he says, 'to try freeing the thralls. This is a judgement on him for meddling with the order of things. And now, having tasted it, they're shouting night and day to have nature stood on its head and themselves free men like their betters.'

So there *is* likely to be revolution. And my man appears to have started it by trying to free the thralls. I wish I knew more. It seems an enlightened step. But I hope he hasn't bitten off more than he can chew. Born slaves can be very crude. One remembers the bloody passages of the Peasants' Revolt, not to speak of Russia and Spartacus. He and his fellow patricians could well share the fate of the aristocrats in the French Revolution. And this, I see, assumes that he will be released from here, as Edwin hinted. Oh I shall be lonely if they release him. Yet I hope they do. It's not right that a great Prince in prison lies – great Prince indeed if he was going to be king. But I won't have it that he is a bloodthirsty seizer of power, or cold politician, as Uncle evidently is. He is not. You can see it in his bearing. If he was to be king, either he has a claim, or he is convinced the country needs a supreme head. By the sound of it, they're so busy fighting among themselves that they'd be wide open to a foreign attack.

Why do I write my pages so full? I'm going to have to be very cunning now in order to find a scrap of paper that won't be missed. I shall not have much time for this writing. I have been hard at work all day filling my remaining sheets for Wolfram's benefit – a thing I should have done before, if I had not been more lucky than prudent. I have produced a mass of doodles and weird speculations, and followed this up by describing a bicycle. You cannot imagine how hard it is to describe a bicycle. If he reads it, Wolfram might well think I am mad. But if my man can do this for me, I feel I should take some risks too. And when I think what he did, it seems

too great a length to go to. I hope the result is as precious to
him as it is to me.

The message had not gone at all, you see. It came to me
today. Hobby brought it, of all people. While he was lighting
the fire this morning and Edwin had gone hobbling through
to unlock the outside door, Hobby calmly fetches this piece
of paper out of his great boot and hands it to me. Then he
goes on stacking up the kindling, just as if nothing had
happened. I know I stared at him. I couldn't behave with
Hobby's nonchalance, not if my life depended on it, though I
am going to have to try. It was only a tiny, folded scrap of
paper – they must have gone over his things with a tooth-
comb to find it missing – and I pushed it down the front of
Hilda's dress, most clumsily. What with haste, cold and
excitement, I know I went pale – anyway, my impressions of
things were all thin, grey and ringing. It seemed as if the only
real things in the place were the softish and grubby corners
of that paper against my left breast, and this mauve-faced,
sniffing youth imperturbably scratching flint and dropping
sparks on his tinder, showing me the while the great studded
soles of his boots. I had to hold on to the table to keep steady.

'You're pale today,' says Edwin, stomping back in. 'What's
the matter with you?'

'I don't feel terribly well,' I answered truthfully enough.
To my annoyance and extreme terror, the wretched man
came up close and examined me, blowing his cabbage-
flavoured breath over me in waves. And the most grotesque
and upsetting thing was that he seemed genuinely concerned. He put out his filthy old hand and pulled down the
skin below each of my eyes with his thumb.

'I've seen many go this way in prison,' says he. 'You need
good red meat and parsley, or the sickness will get you. I'll
speak to Wolfram.'

It was all I could do not to cackle with insane laughter. Red meat! Parsley! Try as I would, the laughter came out as a slight whimper and, I think purely because of his concern, tears came into my eyes.

He patted my shoulder. 'There, there,' he said, and I know it was with real kindness. 'I'll see to it. Prison's no place for a lady, when all's said and done.' Then he shuffled out, pushing Hobby in front of him.

I knew I would have a clear hour then. I determined to wash, do my hair and eat breakfast before I luxuriated in that note. So I said to myself. And before their footsteps were beyond my hearing, I was crouching in front of the fire tremulously unfolding the paper. The note was very short and evidently written in a hurry. He can hardly have seconds together to call his own. And I shall commit the folly of transcribing it (though I burnt the original), simply because I know I shall do it sometime, so why not now? It said: 'What is your name? This now I can only think of you as My Lady. If you can answer, smile at me when you come out into your yard this morning.' He did not sign it. Perhaps he did not dare. Perhaps he thinks I know who he is. I shall ask him his name when I tell him mine. Oh, has anyone ever been so glad to receive a soiled scrap of paper as I am to have this? I wish I had dared keep it. The writing, though hurried, is strong and slanting, evidently educated, habitual writing – the script of one who knows his own mind and has an eye for appearances: it is, despite its haste, handsomely done, in straight lines well disposed on the paper. Calligraphy is different here, though. They do not join their letters to speak of – only the 't' by its cross-stroke to the next letter.

Glad as I am, he should not have risked it. It is so evident they hurt him. He was still trying not to limp this morning, though not so markedly, and he is paler than I have seen him. But I came to the parapet at once and smiled, and I could see he was overjoyed. He did not do more than glance up at me, under his eyebrows; but then he turned away and looked up at the sky and the tree and practically laughed. I could have laughed too. To have given someone so much pleasure. I could see he thinks himself amply rewarded for his pain and his cunning – what a terrible thing it is that so much trouble should produce so little, and that little seem so poignantly valuable. Seeing him this morning was the most intensely splendid thing. I have worked out what he must have done. He hid the paper first, waited for the inevitable discovery and its outcome, and, as soon as that was over and suspicion in another direction (watching ways out of the stronghold), he sent me the message. It amazes me how much he must want to know my name, and the determination with which he set about finding out without injuring me.

I am going to try to be as cunning. I have finished six sheets of wild scraps of writing for Wolfram's benefit and got to the end of my present supply of paper. And the ink too. I have to tip the well on its side to get any. Now I must pray that the next supply of paper is slightly different, and get my penknife sharpened too.

I thought I would not get this paper and he would not get his answer after all. I nearly went mad. But I'm glad I hit Wolfram. I wish I'd hit Edwin too.

Wolfram came in while I was out in the courtyard looking over at my man's dark window, waiting to see them light the lamp there and wondering what he was thinking. When I came in again, my lamp was lit, and there was Wolfram, to my horror, reading my prepared pages and scanning these private ones too. I just had to hope that my calligraphy is too foreign for him – I still don't know how much he managed to read, and I am simply praying that he did not light on anything important. The idiocy of writing all this is unspeakable. It's lunacy. I don't know why I go on. Perhaps I am a little mad, like Wolfram thinks.

Wolfram put down my pages rather hurriedly and looked at me very carefully when I came in – and no doubt I did look a little wild, with sheer horror. He said: 'They tell me you aren't feeling well.'

'No,' I said. 'I'm not.'

'What do you feel?' he said.

'Terrible,' I said, and raked round my body for symptoms. 'Cold, weak, trembling, you know.' All of which was true, what with my terror and the fire being out. I rubbed one of my chilblains and hoped those symptoms would be adequate.

'Does your head pain you at all?' he said.

I said: 'No. I feel lightheaded,' as I did, after the agitations of that day. At which he looked very dubious. Edwin came in just then, and they both stood studying me most dubiously. They both looked so solemn that I could have shrieked with hysterical laughter, but it was so alarming too that I felt I could not bear any more. I made for a chair and sat down on it with something of a flop, wondering whatever they would do with me.

Edwin said: 'Well?'

Wolfram said: 'Not too good, is it? Hear this.' And he took up one of my papers and began to read it out. I was so horrified that I had to lean my face on the back of the chair. I scarcely understood what he was reading, until I heard him say haltingly: '"I would like a penny-farthing, even though I could never get into its saddle. They are a good six feet high, and you sometimes go right over the top."' Then I realized that it was part of my essay on bicycles – those sheets are a

set of such observations, sometimes vaguely Pascal, sometimes plain childish. 'And hear this,' said Wolfram. '"Privacy
is to be had in the mind and nowhere else. But to chart your
private landscape is to change it to a public motorway. I shall
keep something clear of autobahns."'

My hand was under my mouth, and I made it all wet by
smiling. I had to stay with my head down until I could
control that smile. The Lord knows what possessed me to put
down such things! When I was no longer smiling, I turned
and found them both staring at me. Edwin, very pompously,
came and took my pulse, which I know from the way my
heart was going must have seemed very abnormal. He shook
his head at Wolfram.

Wolfram came and stood over me. 'You're not well,' he
said. 'It's plain from this writing that you are not yourself.
You will have to rest. I shall tell Edwin not to give you any
more pens and paper for the time being.'

This was awful. It took away the very thing I had been
depending on. It was so horrible that I don't remember much
of what I did next. All I know is that somehow I was over the
other side of the room, where Wolfram must have retreated
from me, hammering at him with both fists and shrieking: 'I
must have paper! I need pens! I shall go mad if I don't have
them. Really mad! I don't need to rest. All I do here is rest.
Let me have paper, you swine!' Wolfram was weakly holding
up his arms to his face, too taken aback to do anything. And I
went on hammering at him, hoping it would kill him.

Edwin came up behind saying things like, 'Steady, steady.
There's enough of that, now.' And he grabbed me very
expertly – do all prisoners get like this? – and hauled me
away back to a chair. When he dumped me on it, I burst into
tears, and howled like a baby with my fists in my eyes.
Edwin, I remember, stood by with one hand heavily on my
shoulder to keep me in place. And I think he thought

Wolfram had mismanaged things, because he said, with much less respect than he usually uses to Wolfram: 'Don't you know how to humour them? Here's I been humouring all this time, and you go and do this.' I keep wondering how he thinks he has been humouring me, the old hypocrite.

Wolfram was very sulky and dusting himself as if I'd sullied him. 'Violent bitch!' he said, and some more on those lines. Maybe Edwin glared at him – Edwin has a line in malevolent glares that takes some equalling – for he said in the end: 'Oh very well. Do what you like. I agree about the fuel and you can bring up some wine, but don't blame me if she scratches your eyes out one day.' And then he took himself off, very hastily, shuddering a little.

I must remember to write Rational Prose for Wolfram in future. Thank the Lord I wrote his papers more clearly than my own, or he might have picked on something much more vital.

Edwin stood over me until I managed to stop crying. Then he told me rather roughly to get to bed and stay there. I went. I was exhausted anyway and I did not dare disobey for fear they put me in whatever they use for a strait-jacket here. But, after a while, I heard the knobby trampling of young Hobby's boots, going in and out. Then Edwin knocked on the door and shouted: 'Best come out and eat supper while it's hot.' So I put on the cloak and dragged myself out – I felt as if I had fought several rounds against a heavyweight boxer – and there, of all the wonders, was a fire blazing again, food on the table considerably more appetizing than any they had ever given me before, and, best of all, a pile of fresh paper, a bundle of quills and a supply of ink. Hobby was busy sharpening the penknife, presenting to me nothing but a head of uncombed hair, and Edwin was looking smug and

modest in a dour kind of way. At the sight, particularly of the
paper, I started to cry again.

'What's wrong?' said Edwin. 'Not to your liking?'

I had to nod feverishly, to reassure him. The last thing I
wanted to do was to make him angry. 'Oh yes. It's all
marvellous.' At which I howled in earnest and seemed
unable to stop. I must have been overwrought, I suppose.
Anyway, Edwin called it that, and seemed not displeased,
and made me sit down and drink some wine. Then he sent
Hobby away, but insisted on standing over me himself to see
to it that I ate. I had not the slightest desire to eat. I only
wanted to be at this paper. As I packed in mouthful after
unwanted mouthful, I continually found myself looking at it,
longingly, and then being afraid that Edwin had seen my
unusual eagerness. Perhaps he did, but he seems to put it
down to my derangement – there is no doubt, I'm afraid,
that he thinks me, to say the least of it, unbalanced. Perhaps I
am, a little, though not as he imagines. At least I have the
credit of being a mad *lady*, rather than a simple mad*woman*. A
month ago I should not have been treated so well.

He went at last, and took the supper. But the fire and the
lamp continued to burn. Vowing not to sit up beyond the
time the fire died – they will notice if the lamp is unusually
low in oil – I set to work with the penknife to saw a strip an
inch wide off the bottom of each sheet of paper. I am lucky. It
is different paper, better quality too: the pens do not catch in
it as they did in the other. So there is no reason why it should
not be a different shape from the second supply (which is,
anyway, different from the first). But the fact that it is a
better quality makes it that much harder to saw through. The
penknife is blunt as a stick now. I did not dare risk spoiling a
sheet, since, though I could have burnt it, I am fairly sure
they know how many sheets they gave me, and an absent
one would be missed when Wolfram chooses to count them

again. And a jagged sheet would show as badly. So it meant doing each one individually, and getting them straight first go. Lord, it took hours! And I got so tired that the last one I did in the night is wobbly from sheer weariness. I had to get up as soon as it was light and, wrapped in cloak and blanket and crouching on the floor in the whistling draught whose source I can't trace, finish the job then. I could not cut them on the table, since the cuts would show in the wood. Some show in the stone of the floor still, although I have rubbed dirt in and shuffled my feet on the spot for hours now. Mark is built of soft limestone – or my part is.

But at last I had a sheaf of thin strips of paper, just right to fold and push down inside a hobnailed boot. I hid all but one in various places around the rooms – some in the under-struts of the table, some in several parts of the bed (which never gets clean sheets, but perhaps might some day), and some in cracks in the stonework. The best place is one of the chairs, which is rickety and starting apart. I have packed it stable again with paper, and dirtied the edges so they will not show. When I came to write the note, I was shaking so with tension and exhaustion that I could hardly write for a while. I had to start a sheet of Rational Prose for Wolfram to steady my hand, but I did not dare be too long at it, because the sun was well up by then and I knew they would be in any minute with fuel and food. And, apart from anything else, this is the one time of day when I am certain to see Hobby. I hardly knew what to write, now it came to the point. I had to dash something down without thinking in the end. Hurriedly, but as clearly as I could write, I scribbled: 'My name is Emily. I am from England. What is your name? Do take care in future – I hate them to hurt you.' Then I heard them coming upstairs, and I had barely time to get the ink dry before I had to fold the paper and tuck it out of sight down my dress.

Oh, I thought Edwin would never give me a chance to pass it to Hobby. Usually, Edwin clumps about, leaving Hobby with me to light the fire. But that day he would have to hang about, surveying me musingly. I think I looked ill. I certainly do now. He must have been afraid of losing his prisoner irretrievably, I imagine, but I was far too impatient and agitated to see why he was staying. It seemed to me he knew all about my note and was hoping I would give myself away. When you have a secret, you cannot believe that the rest of the world does not know all about it. In the end, I said rather desperately that I thought I would go back to bed.

'Aye,' he said. 'Do that.' And he watched me off into the bedroom before he clumped away to unlock the yard door.

With my heart absolutely hammering, I stole out again and up to Hobby. He, to my everlasting relief, looked up with a bit of a grin as I came creeping into the room again, clearly expecting me, and held out his hand for the paper, in his nonchalant way, even before I had got it out of my dress.

'When can you get it to him?' I whispered, and, Lord, it sounded loud.

'Midday,' he replied, quite casually, and much louder. He obviously knows just how much is audible. Hobby is an old campaigner, clearly. Interesting. I wish I knew more about our Hobby. He cannot be more than sixteen, but he has the lined, knowing face of a middle-aged man, poor kid. He stuffed the note in his boot, carelessly it seemed, yet there was a delicacy about the way he did it, not to crumple the paper, that suggested that mine was by no means only the second note to go into that great space beside his skinny ankle. I saw him do it, then I fled as quietly as my draperies would permit, back to bed. And I was glad to be there. It was a hideous effort to get out again for breakfast, as Edwin decreed I should. He says I shall get weak in bed. He may be right.

I have spent today between bed and here. It is a choice between freezing at rest or sitting strenuously upright and warm. Today there is the sharpest frost yet. But I had to go out into the yard this morning, all the same. I did not want my man to think the message had been discovered – and I know what I went through when he was not there. I would not have anyone go through that without a reason.

He was better today. He swung round the space with his earlier air entirely and, since the guards were sheltering again, we could look at one another most of the time. I admire the shape of his chin when he puts his head up to look over at me. But then his whole head is comely. I believe he must have thought I was unwell, just like Edwin, because he looked with a little jerk of the head when he first saw me. Then he smiled. He has a curious, growing, lingering smile that seems to come by stages, until his whole body has it, not merely his face. I wish I smiled that way. I smile quick and glad – and I know he cannot see my dimple from there. And to see him there, and well again, seemed to be all I could ask.

But at midday I could hardly contain myself. I could not believe Hobby could escape the surveillance of six guards – I have never seen more than two at once, but they are seldom the same two. And I cursed the vagueness that hangs over all the doings and arrangements over there. I could imagine what it might be like, but I will not let myself – I don't know why. Yet I have a clear picture in my head of what his prison is. It is bound to be wrong, so I won't dwell on it. I would much rather have it vague.

Hobby came in with more fuel this afternoon. I am to be kept warm now. And, when Edwin's back was turned, he gave me a little nod. So he did it, bless him. I have been writing at this ever since. Oh I am glad, but I feel hectic and foolish too. My note seems pitiful. Whatever possessed me to say I was from England? I can't imagine it will mean a thing to him. And the foolish fussy way I told him to take care. I almost wish I'd never sent it. I wonder if he felt the same after going to such lengths to send me his. And the fool I am! I tell him to take care, then ask him his name, so that he has to go through it all again to get more paper. Insensate ass you are, Emily. Let him ignore me. I'd rather not know his name, not at that price.

No strength to write today

Nor today

Better today. But ye gods! I've been here three months now! This is the third time I have had all the embarrassment of explaining to Edwin that I need the wad of flannel he provides. This time, there were no innuendoes about staunching, thank God! Either my rank is supposed to put me above such talk, or he has grown tired of it. But the amazing thing is the way I lost count. Perhaps it was wilful. I was determined not to make a set of notches anywhere, nor to date this writing. But I am still incredulous at the way I have been blithely writing 'A month ago' when it was two months or more when Hilda the bitch hustled me into this. It must be December now – though I don't think they name the months as we do. Edwin has been talking of Yule, which they have instead of Christmas, being heathens, I suppose. Yule is close, it seems. There is a bitter frost still, and Wolfram has allowed Hobby to put a brazier in my bedroom. I have been in there most of this last week, unwell, though what illness it was I have no idea. Edwin calls it 'Jail fever' and claims he saw it coming on. I think it was distress over that message. And it was foolish, I know, to go outside with whatever it was, but I could not let him think anything had happened to me. Then, the second day I went, Edwin came in unexpectedly and caught me out there, and that was the end of that for the time being. My man – I should not still call him that – saw Edwin before I did and walked out of sight at once, with a cool I hope I equalled. Because I realized from that there was something wrong and went right on to the far end of the courtyard before I turned round to see. I think Edwin thought I was going to jump off, because he was after me quicker than I have ever seen him move before. He dragged me in, and he has kept the door locked until today, when I have given him my solemn oath that I do not intend to make away with myself. A very solemn oath, on his gods and mine, which I suppose I shall have to keep.

Dear, I feel weak and weary. I shall have to write the rest tomorrow.

Oh, much better today, and a third note, very concerned. This I must answer and give to Hobby tomorrow. I'll do it last thing at night, as a grand luxury. Hobby brought the second note the morning I fell ill and thrust it at me while he was removing the primitive bucket-closet from my bedroom. I could hardly believe he could have gone through that again so soon. That was why I went out that morning, and he was there, unharmed. He must have done as I did and secreted a supply of paper. This was just such a scrap of paper as the first. It said: 'My name is Asgrim and I shall take care, now I have a reason for it. Why have they shut you up here if you are not from this land?'

I did not find that note easy to answer. It was rather a shock to find his name was the one most prominent among Wolfram's questions, and equally perturbing to find him puzzled about why I am here. Somehow, I had a notion that he would know why. I had to flog myself into action to reply, no doubt because I was ill, but also because his question rent me apart with uncertainties and self-distrust. I said in the end: 'I don't know why I am here, but I hope to find out.' Then I paused for a long time, knowing this was too curt to send on its own, but not having the face to reply in kind to his 'now I have a reason for it.' I should have done. I could have done. There are so many things I almost said, and I didn't dare. This is a great Prince, after all. And men seem to find that kind of thing easier to say than women. I don't know why. At last, when Hobby was actually clumping upstairs, I dashed down: 'I am everlastingly grateful for the cloak' and left it at that. And having left it, was sorry.

The effort of composing that exhausted me. I could do nothing else. But all the time I was ill, the worst part by far was the trouble raised by his name and his question. His name *is* Hathriver. I don't know why I had not realized before who he must be. But now I know, it has all fallen together in my head, Wolfram's hints and questions and Edwin's jumbled monologues, and I see that he is indeed a great man. It is not merely that he heads a faction. He was the inspiration of a movement, and he gave it his character. Without him, it must be less than nothing. Hrinkle and Regan, though not yet secure, are virtually now only mopping up the remaining opposition. And it is hideously clear that as soon as they *are* secure, Asgrim and Hathriver will be quietly done away with. I have begun to pray for guerrilla warfare and the uprising of thralls. Let us have some stiff-necked opposition from minor patricians. I hope even Hilda prospers, so long as the mopping-up can be prolonged. I wish I knew how he came to be reduced to this hopeless incarceration. It seems such cruel luck. And here he is wasting his energies sneaking notes to someone like me. It is too bad.

I have found myself dwelling on my own pointless existence. It made last week horrible. Round and round. On and on. When I saw his question written, I saw, like the sun coming blazing through clouds, that I need not really be here at all. It was simple timorous inadequacy that caused me not to explain, if not to Smooth-one, at least to Wolfram, clearly and strenuously, who I am and what had happened. If I had done that straight away, I should not be here now. But I let people push me about, and then I got involved in this ridiculous attempt to pretend to high birth. Me! Fancy! I never knew I was a snob before. Now I am too deep in for any explanation. They suspect me of God knows what. And if I did explain, my account of why I held my tongue for so long is going to seem more than inadequate: it is going to sound like lies. And I know perfectly well that it *is* my duty to explain – I am wasting the time and energy of Edwin, Hobby and Wolfram, using fuel and food, and quite simply continuing an imposture. All my reasons why I should *not* explain are the dreariest rationalisations of the fact that, if I went from here, I should not be able to see a sliver of a courtyard and a man walking in it.

Was anything more gross? Nothing, perhaps, except the lies I told Wolfram while I was lying in bed. He came, reluctantly, but fancying, I am sure, that he might get his answers if he bullied me when I was down. I had been dreading this. I knew he would come. He does not consider me as anything more than an animate object. But when he came it was unexpectedly easy. I gave exactly the same answers, without turning a hair, even to the question Had I ever had a message from Asgrim? It has become simply mechanical reaction. And I even felt it was funny that I should have become guilty after the event, as it were. Wolfram kicked a chair in his frustration and slid away. He has not been back since.

I regard myself as a confirmed sinner and hardened imposter. I believe one should be open with oneself. Things have come to a pretty pass if one has to deceive oneself as well as other people. One should be one's own last stronghold of truth. Odd, though, that I couldn't drag the truth out of myself unaided. It took the integrity of that man over there to do it.

This third note says: 'Did your jailor see me? Or are you ill? I would give much to see you safe and well.' I have rather clung to that last sentence today after Edwin's depressing interlude. Asgrim has been anxious and he has missed me. He may even have gone through all the hell of vague horrors that I did after he stole the paper. And, since he cannot have an unlimited quantity of paper secreted, he must want to know what has happened quite badly, or he would not have sent. I wonder why he couldn't ask Hobby. Or did he simply want another word from me? Anyway, I gave him that word, this morning, by Hobby, the product of much pen-spoiling last night. You can't chew a quill, naturally, so I find I draw them back and forth between my fingers when I am stuck for words, until they look mangy and go floppy. I wrote: 'I have been ill, but, as you saw yesterday, I am better now. I was refused pen and paper, and that made me ill, since I was afraid I would not be able to answer you.'

Now, I think that was over-effusive, rash and forward. He might well be glad that a hundred-foot drop separates us, if I am going to be that emotional. Not emotional in words, I know, I know, but by implication. To show that I was so set on replying to him. That was the rash thing. But then I didn't know what I know now. Even so, I should have recollected that he was a great Prince and not shown myself so fawningly eager to oblige him.

I had better have this out with myself. My habit of running
several days' writing into one section is designed to confuse
my sense of time and confound Wolfram, not to bury the
truth from myself. The truth of the matter is that I wish I had
not sent that last note. It is all Edwin's fault for deciding I
need cheering up.

Edwin came in early yesterday afternoon, quite out of
routine, and instead of hanging about jangling his keys like
he usually does, he draws up a chair to the fire, sits his
unhygienic person on it, and squanders half my remaining
wood on getting a good blaze. Then, rubbing his hands and
smiling, he said I looked peaky and down in the mouth and
he was going to cheer me up with a little cosy chat.

I said, as kindly as I could – I could see he meant well –
that it was very good of him, and gave an internal, imaginary
scream at the thought of hearing about his daughter's
ingratitude again. The truly dreadful thing about being in
prison is that people can come and talk at you and you can
do nothing to stop them. And, feeling I needed something to
help me through Elsie and her sins, I suggested we both
drank some wine. I have a thick green bottle of wine, which I
have hardly touched till now.

'I never say no to wine,' says Edwin. I rather thought he
didn't. So I poured it out, and I remember leaning patiently
(but I hope politely) back in the chair, sipping and enjoying
the fire, while Edwin got his monologue launched. 'Yule's
nearly here,' he said. 'Folks will be seeing their folks soon. I'll
be having Elsie and her man with me, more fool I.' Upon
which, I waited for the history of what Elsie had had from
Edwin and not given back, and how her man had backed her
up; but I think Edwin suddenly realized that I was not likely
to see any of my folks that Yule and was moved by a sort of
craggy tact to dismiss Elsie from his discourse for once.
Anyway, with one of his liquid coughs, he veered off from

Elsie and on to Yule, and the arrangements for Yule in the stronghold. There is to be junketing below, it seems. Wolfram is not invited to it, poor creature. But the soldiers were none of them allowed leave, this year, to their disgust, and are determined to be as lively as they can in spite of it. (To my mind, they are quite lively enough anyway. There are drunken songs roared out every evening.) I gather Edwin hopes to get drunk in their company, whatever Elsie has to say about it. But he was sorry, he said, for the guard over the way. They were not allowed a moment's relaxation.

And so he got on to Asgrim. He never mentions him by name. I did wonder why, but now I have come to suspect that it is a backhanded mark of respect. Edwin regards a man's name as a potent part of him, and saying it seems to him something like an invocation. Asgrim, even shut up and guarded unceasingly, is still a very powerful enemy. To say his name would be to Edwin as strongly unlucky as quoting *Macbeth* in a theatre. So he says 'over the way' and 'that one', and jerks his thumb to make his meaning clear.

Well, 'over the way' having money, it seems, is to keep Yule in style. This is good. It adds an air of comfort to my vague imaginings of privation over there. I hope he has been allowed to make his prison generally cheerful. While I was taking this in, I found Edwin rambling off upon the privileges and duties of rank, which, he seems to think, are to make oneself as showy as possible in order to bring richness and ceremonial to the eye of those less privileged. Right, in a way, I suppose. Mankind seems to need objects of admiration. We treat millionaires and filmstars with indulgence for giving us glamour, distantly. But he was on the wrong tack for Asgrim. Even Wolfram is showier than Asgrim. So I was forced to give Edwin a few covert nudges to bring him back to 'over the way' again. And he came back on the same subject in a new place, never noticing my hints or his inconsistencies at all.

'Funny to think he was to have married the Lady Hilda this Yule, if all had gone well with him,' he said.

'*Was* he to?' I said, with inane brightness. '*Do* tell.' And my heart went thump down. Edwin went droning on, and I really believe I never said another word until he got up to go. And, having written it, I don't want to add another written word either.

No, I have to go on. I can't sleep, so I am ruining my eyes trying to write by lamplight. If I make myself ill again I don't care. Perhaps it is not so bad after all. From Edwin's sketchy and jumbled droning, I think Asgrim was negotiating to marry Hilda, but, whether because he was imprisoned or for some other reason, things never reached the point of a firm contract. What does that matter? It simply shows that the life of the great ones is another matter from mine – or Edwin's. I do wish it hadn't been Hilda of all people, but what is more fitting, now I think about it? The wretched woman is extremely good-looking (though she'd be a yammering ninny in bed) and no doubt a great lady. The alliance would bring her party alongside Hathriver, I suppose, and more power to his elbow. Very fitting match, very fitting, very necessary. Oh damn it.

Why carry on like this over a thoughtfully sent cloak and three little letters? Emily, you are a presumptuous fool. Remember by rights it should have been Hilda in this place anyway. And that, now I think, was a little fiendish of Regan and Uncle – Uncle thought of it, I bet. To have your betrothed – or nearly betrothed – flaunted at you, so near and yet so far, across a hundred-foot drop. That is really twisting the knife. I'm glad it was a perfect stranger instead, heartily glad. I have done some good.

It only remains to get myself into some kind of order. I

have been trying to do so by going back over the wording of the three notes, disregarding the emotion I packed round them. I am afraid there is still something. There is 'My Lady' and 'now I have a reason'. But, hell, Emily, get shut up in prison for months and then see a pretty girl over the way. Most men would feel a twinge. And the third note, which I had the effrontery to call concerned, is coolness itself really – the query of a decent man who thought he might just inadvertently have caused trouble for a friend.

And I have gone over his bearing, particularly when I saw him the morning Edwin unlocked the door again. He jumped when he saw me. It was clear he had not expected to see me. But he didn't smile – though I did, the fool – until just before he went in. But then it was mild weather again and the guards were very observant. Oh it is impossible to tell what he thought. How can you tell from this distance anyway? The fire is dead. I shall have to go to bed or freeze.

And now I *am* mad. Really crazy. I am trying to make myself regret what I did and I can't. I am in a frenzy of hope and feel as if I have staked my last halfpenny.

You can get into this odd state. You can do a thing when you thought nothing could be further from your intentions. You mean to do nothing, and yet, before you have caught yourself, the strip of paper is in your hand, the thing is written, and you are handing it to Hobby. Hobby looked rather surprised too. And so cunning had my worse nature been, that it was only written just before Edwin and Hobby came in, and my better, prudent nature had no say in the matter at all. Nor has it still. And I shall have to wait till tomorrow morning to know. Twenty-two great hours. I blame the frost. I woke early, aching with cold, and got up in dreary agitation to watch a smoky sun up over the roofs, setting them glittering because of the ice on them. My worse nature had plenty of time to work on me.

I just hope my note doesn't strike Asgrim as blatantly as I intended it. 'I must tell you,' wrote this crazy fool, 'that I am not a lady by birth. I know you are a great man, and I know, too, that Hilda should have been in this prison in my place.' Get the implications of that one! The man would be a fool not to. And he is certainly no fool. What I shall get back – if I get anything – will be a cold 'Lady, I think you must still be unwell.' Oh why did I *do* it?

Asgrim has not had the note yet – if, that is, Hobby gets it to him at midday as he did the others – so, when I saw him just now, he was risking a little cordiality. My note about my illness didn't offend him. But what will he think about this next one, hard on its heels? The guards were stamping their feet and blowing their fingers, which preoccupied them. Asgrim smiled over at me and seemed to have his hands tucked under his arms. I saw that, because he slipped a little on the frosty floor of the yard, and threw out an arm involuntarily, and it was all tangled in his cloak. At which he grinned over at me— 'Don't think I'm always this ridiculous: it's just the cold.' I was sliding up and down with my hands on the coping, and I tried to smile back. It was a nervous baring of teeth. In spite of the cold, I stayed still and looked at him carefully – as I shall never dare come out and see him again. He still has his air of integrity. His face is full of private thoughts and decided notions, and, I suppose, personal dignity. I can see only too well how that dignity could become hauteur towards someone who had angered him. No, I shan't come and look at him tomorrow. He will not want anything to do with me. And he went in with a cheerful nod to me, not knowing what I have done.

Oh now this is too much. Much more than I deserve. This is evil paid with good, seven times over. Hobby brought me *two* slips of paper with the afternoon fuel, and I have never been so happy in my life. The first was the note: 'What has Hilda or your birth to do with it? I am head over ears in love with you. Tell me how I came to anger you.' The other is a poem:

> Unbounded truth is not a thing
> Cramped to time and bound in place.
> It strangely changes space,
> Enlarging laws to loyalty
> And making words reality,
> And stones words or nothing.
> The boundaries containing me
> Are wider than the world, by grace
> Of truth, which is another thing.

God, I am so happy I have been singing ever since Edwin left after cheering me up about his daughter. I have my reply all ready. It goes: 'You have made me very happy indeed. I was not angry. My jailor had told me you were betrothed to Hilda.' That, I hope, should make him something like as happy as he has made me – but when I think over my other answers, they are all so cautious and formal that no one would think I was a feeling being. What makes me so unable to come out into the open? He has. I must learn to go straighter for this truth he so values. Of course 'truth' has many meanings. I hope he intends them all. In future I shall try not to be devious about it. Fear makes me devious – as it may most women, I think.

The answer went this morning, but I wonder if Asgrim has been able to attend to it. I had no idea he was a widower, none at all. But then I know so little about him. Anyway, this morning I went out as usual, when the time came. Asgrim was out there already, and his son was with him.

The two were in the middle of the courtyard, visible to waist-level, laughing excitedly and taking some object continually one from another. First Asgrim would have it – 'I'm older than you: I know all about these things' – then the boy would wrest it back – 'Trust you to do it wrong. I'm the expert and it goes like this. Oh. No. It doesn't. Here, you try.' And Asgrim would have it back. And despite all their trying, the thing simply failed to work. It looked as if they were too glad to see one another to bend their minds to it properly. They were in continual fits of laughter. Asgrim was laughing when he saw me. He gave me a wonderfully happy smile from almost beneath his shoulder, while he bent over the object – which seemed to be all colours of the rainbow and no shape I had ever seen – and I could gladly have leaped the drop and joined them there, so splendid was it to see them happy. All I could do was laugh too. While I was laughing, Asgrim said something to the boy. I would take a bet it was: 'Don't look now, but that's the lady I told you about over there.'

The boy didn't look. He was far too busy doing something with string to the colourful object, but he gave a little nod, preoccupied. I would put him at twelve or thirteen, and a splendidly light-hearted, energetic, matter-of-fact, jolly, *boyish* boy he seems, in spite of being a prisoner. There are no doubts about him, no nonsense, no adolescence really yet – just a mite of a lordly air, which you would expect in the son of a patrician. He and Asgrim are not very much alike. It is odd how rarely children markedly resemble their parents. He has inherited his father's comely build. Though he is skinny with it, the broad shoulders are there. But his hair is several shades lighter – and remarkably fine, glossy hair it is – and his face a brown and snubby one, though good-looking enough in its way, because his eyes are strikingly large.

While they were tussling with their toy, I had a look to see how the guards were taking it. There were three – one extra for the boy, I suppose – sheltering under the opposite wall from the extremely brisk wind and looking a little less like zombies than usual. I almost suspected them of taking an interest in the toy, and – it's hard to express – but it looked as if the boy had stirred them up a bit. Anyway, Asgrim suddenly began walking away backwards with the object, and, when he had reached the wall, he threw it in the air. The boy was holding a string, and the thing proved to be a kite, of a size and complexity I had never seen before. And up it went, with that round and round plunging movement, struggling its way up over the roofs, long and colourful, in a way that lifted your heart to see. I could hear them cheering. I nearly cheered too. 'Oh, great!' I said. The guards were watching it too, as if they liked it. Asgrim seemed to be going to look at me to see what I thought. Then, somehow, he didn't. He looked firmly away. And before I could feel hurt, I found the reason in Edwin's liquid cough, just behind my left shoulder.

Well, there I was caught avidly intent on the courtyard opposite. There was no point in concealing it. 'There's a boy over there,' I said to Edwin. 'With a kite.' As if he had no eyes.

Edwin spat, and the wind caught his dottle of spit and splashed it on the roof. 'I know,' he said. 'I came up to get a sight of him. Fine lad, ain't he?'

'Yes,' I said. 'Who is he?'

'His son. Kiartan. They fetched him from Markwater for Yule, for a week, to show him he's in one piece. That's where they keep him – Markwater – under lock and key. And if he tries any tricks, Kiartan's a goner, see.' And, to make quite sure I saw, Edwin would have to draw his hand across his throat and deliver a croak with it.

Now this is too bad – though, I suppose, only to be expected when a man like Smooth-one has his hands on both. I can hardly bear to think of the strain it must put on Asgrim, and the need to be docile and cautious. And that child should be barging about the countryside letting off energy, not cooped up like this. The only good thing about it is that the boy does not look as if they are unkind to him – though you can see he is in a holiday mood just now. No doubt he's a little more sober alone. But I now value those messages even more highly, since Asgrim must have known the risk to Kiartan.

I think Kiartan must have noticed his father carefully not looking at me, and I think it is clear that the restraints he is under vex him more than somewhat. Quite as clearly, he plays on his childhood and considerable charm to break out of restraints whenever he can. If being a captive has taught him this, then it is another bad thing – though I can neither blame him nor grumble at the outcome. Kiartan took a look at Asgrim gazing unmeaningfully at the roofs, and his face bunched up a little, rebelliously. Then he took a look across at me – quite a long look, sideways, to see what I was like. He seemed to like what he saw. Most kids do like me, which was one reason why I gave up teaching: they mobbed and they clamoured, not unkindly but quite uncontrollably. Kiartan, in a cool way that makes me laugh to remember, then hitches the kite-string round his wrist and goes marching into a spot where I get the fullest view of him. Then, deliberately, with a vivid but slightly artificial smile, he waved his arm at me and yelled: 'Hallo!'

Asgrim was shattered, and extremely angry with him at first, I think. There was nothing I could do but wave back and shout 'Hallo!' too. Edwin also waved, chirpily, and called out: 'Hallo there, lad!' The old snob. He doesn't treat Hobby so kindly.

Asgrim looked rather nervously at the guards to see what they thought of this sociability, and they shrugged a little— 'Boys will be boys.' At that, I think the fun of it dawned on Asgrim. That smile of his grew on his face, and he came up beside his son and waved too, almost more defiantly than Kiartan. Then he and Kiartan looked at one another and found it ever so funny. They bent about, howling with laughter. I could not help laughing too. To think that communicating was that simple after all! They brought their kite down by laughing. It fell on a roof and dropped down the intervening pit, whence they had to haul it up, and, when it was up, the guards evidently decided they were enjoying themselves too much and marched them indoors. Both of them waved again as they went.

Edwin followed me indoors. Now the ice is broken and we are officially on speaking terms with 'over the way', he is much more communicative. I have the history of their capture. It is all that young devil Kiartan's fault, too. I might have guessed. Asgrim was not likely to have let himself be taken alone. He is far too canny. In fact, it seems that he is so cunning both in diplomacy and warfare, and so apt to turn up where he is least expected, that they call him 'the old Fox'. Edwin used this phrase, nervously, crossing his fingers against bad luck and looking over his shoulder in Asgrim's direction, as if it were used so often that it almost amounted to the man's name.

As for their capture, Edwin gave me a ravelled history of a set of battles between Asgrim's side and Hrinkle's – or they may have been mere skirmishes. He told me the place and outcome of each, but they meant nothing to me, until the last, which seems to have been in the neighbourhood of Hathriver itself. Asgrim won this encounter, this is the irony

of it. Regan and Rinkle were somehow penned against a hill
in a heap of wounded and forced to give in. It ought to have
been decisive. And it looks as if Asgrim thought it *was*
decisive, because he made certain conditions and then let
Regan and Wrinkle go. Edwin thinks this very stupid of him,
considering the outcome, but my reading of it is that Asgrim
was hoping to generate good will by his clemency. He had no
idea that Kiartan was there.

Kiartan, it seems, since the engagement was so near home,
had taken part in it too. Or at least gone to watch. No doubt
he thought it would be exciting, and he certainly got more
excitement than he could have bargained for. Edwin has it
that he took part in things to such purpose that he got hurt
and the man with him had to go and ask Asgrim to help him.
Whatever happened, it seems clear that Kiartan was sitting
on the hill above the battlefield, that Regin and Rinkle met
him when they trailed away from their defeat, and that
Asgrim found out belatedly that Kiartan was there. Uncle,
being a great opportunist, snapped Kiartan up on the spot.
Edwin has them parley amusingly, Kiartan unwisely and
indignantly protesting that his father was on the way to help
him, and Uncle remarking that this was a stroke of luck. And
he promptly set an ambush. Asgrim came tearing up the hill
a few minutes later, knowing that Kiartan was sitting in
Wrinkle's path, and fell into the ambush. Edwin tells me that
this outcome was a further stroke of luck for the Mark party.
In the normal way, Asgrim would have come with a band of
picked and trusted men – for whom the word seems to be
hearthmen – but he had been in too much of a hurry to collect
them. Those he had collected seem to have been raff and
scaff and they ran away, leaving both Asgrim and Kiartan in
Hrinkle's hands, and enabling Hrinkle to turn total defeat
into a resounding victory.

I can hardly imagine a more depressing reverse. If I had

been Asgrim I would have gone mad. I can't think how he manages to behave with such dignity – I suppose it's the last thing left.

It is astonishing that Asgrim has time to think of me too. I would quite forgive him for thinking of nothing but Kiartan – particularly as Kiartan is clearly living it up a little over there. I could hear his voice from time to time, even through these walls, as I was writing. And they were out there again just before nightfall. Kiartan was tearing round the yard shouting, behaving childishly for thirteen, screaming with that kind of raucous excitement which is not far off brute fury, and plainly so bottled up and sick of confinement that my heart ached for him. He has nothing to do but resort to childishness. I could see Asgrim knew it. He was watching very soberly from between two guards. They were not letting him take exercise – Oh dear no: routine did not permit it – although they stretched a point for Kiartan, I suspect because life would have become impossible in there if they hadn't.

Asgrim saw me come out to see what the noise was about and gave me a small friendly wave. It horrified me for a second, because I forgot we were now on speaking terms. But the guards have accepted the precedent, it seems, for they made no objection. I waved back, and to Kiartan too, who hurtled by, waving back almost viciously poor kid. No wonder they let him come out. Yet, somehow, amidst all the clamour over there, Asgrim has found time and application to send me another note – maybe the very disturbance makes it easier to do. It was a very, very small scrap of paper and it just said: 'You have made me rarely so happy.' A month ago – no, *no* – *three* months ago, that would have puzzled me, or I would have got it slightly wrong. Now I

know that 'rarely so' means 'intensely' or, anyway, something stronger than 'very'. Edwin's feet are always 'rarely so
painful' – and I used to think he was saying 'really so' for
weeks.

But I fear this might well be the last note I get. I have not
of course been able to put them all together, but I have a
feeling that if I were to do so they would amount to a
complete sheet of paper. I think he just hid a whole sheet
and took the consequences. He is too well observed to do as
I did. And the poem was wasteful – he wrote it out formally
and it took twice the usual quantity. If my foolish fishing
note is to be blamed for anything, it is for causing him to
squander nearly a third of a page on me at one go.

He's too good – rarely so good – and much quicker than I am
to spot where the advantage lies. It's Yule today, it seems.
Edwin claims that it is the shortest day in the year – with
what truth I am not sure: I have lost count thoroughly.
Anyway, it is dark and leaden, and dawn came late. Night is
coming already. I can hardly see to write. If I crane round by
the window, I can just see the tip of the orange sun, sinking.
The junketing below is already getting under way, by the
sound of it: there is a lot of crashing about and laughter,
which echoes rather heavily up here.

Edwin came in this morning unexpectedly – while I was
writing about poor Kiartan, in fact – quite pink with good
spirits, saying that Elsie and her man had come and would I
forgive him if he didn't come and cheer me up this afternoon. I said of course I would forgive him, although, in fact, I
have come to value these sessions for what I can learn of
Hathriver. Whereupon Edwin, overjoyed, apparently, by my
good nature (he seems to forget it was he who took it upon
himself to inaugurate these sessions), goes hopping briskly

out again and returns with a great bunch of holly and some ivy, which he says it is the custom to have.

I said it was the same in the North too, and thanked him several times. I don't think he realizes what it means to have living green leaves in one's hands again. I could have cried. I had forgotten how glossy and stiff holly can be, and how green its stems. The red of the berries is the clearest and sweetest colour. As for ivy – I had never considered before the delicate veined shape of its leaves, or how specially dissimilar it is from holly, both in its duller gloss and more supple texture. The two plants seem each to be from a different world – both different again from mine.

And while I was fingering them incredulously and sniffing their vegetable pungency, Edwin remarked that Well, he must be off, and it was nice to know that the strange people of the North had the same customs too. To which I replied – I don't know why, unless it was involuntary truthfulness – that we didn't keep Yule exactly. And he wondered loudly what on earth we did with ourselves instead. I was forced to prevarication, rather than embark on an exposition of Christianity – which I can't imagine Edwin ever taking in, not in a month of Sundays.

'We keep Hogmanay,' I said. 'When the days have just begun to lengthen.' He departed more than ever convinced that we were barbarians, and in such a bustle of good humour at his daughter's coming, that I am forced to conclude that Elsie, ungrateful or not, must be dear to him. Then I heard Kiartan over the way, and put down the sheaf of greenstuff and went out.

Kiartan appeared to have settled down a little today. When I came out, the two of them were walking in the yard, talking happily together, and Kiartan was only exhibiting the confinement of his energies in the odd reel and skip, or the occasional little clowning stagger, as I have seen boys do in

bus queues or other irksome situations. That child has the
most beautiful hair. It is very fine and straight and smooth
and, although neither dark nor fair, it has the quality of
catching light to itself, so that it shone even on a drear day
like today. It is a delight to look at. I think Asgrim finds it so
too. He looks at the boy with a kind of proud admiration, and
he several times seized some excuse or other to put his hand
on Kiartan's head. It was clear to me he was very happy this
morning. His whole walk was different and he smiled most
of the time. But, for all that, I get the impression that his
behaviour to his son is not simply unmitigated indulgence.

There was an occasion when Kiartan, in his clowning,
contrived to overbalance and, with much windmilling of his
arms, to stagger on to the feet of one of the guards – who
looked both peevish and long-suffering. Asgrim, though he
was still smiling, said something quiet and plainly a little
cutting. And Kiartan got up at once, looking a little soberly. I
have a feeling that the decrease in Kiartan's noise is Asgrim's
doing. He waited, I fancy, to see if Kiartan, having let off
steam, would then sober down of his own accord, and, from
last night's showing, Kiartan plainly did not. All the signs
were that he was working himself up to be uncontrollable.
Then I think Asgrim put his foot down. The guards must be
relieved. In an odd way, I think Kiartan is relieved too. I
think he has been with people who were only concerned to
keep him from escaping, who may have treated him not
unkindly but who have clearly no authority in their dealings
with him. His father has both authority and standards.
People of Kiartan's age need that – not that they admit it
readily. Kiartan made a face behind Asgrim's back – the
perfunctory, obligatory grimace of the boy rebuked.

It was about then that Asgrim saw I had come out. I was
leaning against the wall watching them, and Asgrim, noticing me, looked glad. It seemed unfeigned and incautious

gladness; for he pulled himself together at once and gave me
a formal little wave – with, I noticed, a quick look over at the
guards, who were just then watching Kiartan and, possibly,
controlling a snigger or so at the face he had made. Kiartan
saw me too and was shy. Having been hauled over the coals
for his vicious hilarity, he was not sure how to behave at all.
He waved, with a sort of flop of the hand, and looked at his
father for guidance.

And Asgrim took my breath away – and probably Kiartan's
and the guards' too – by walking as near as he could and still
see me and then shouting across to me: 'Happy Yule!' Even
bellowing, at that distance, he has a remarkably pleasant
voice. Some men bray shouting: Asgrim does not. It was a
very fine yell, glad and wholehearted, which put me in
mind of nothing so much as a day I once spent in Cambridge.
The students had some kind of event on, and I heard them
continually shouting light-hearted things to one another in
the streets. I suppose I mean that Asgrim has a young voice,
but that is not quite it. I mean to say more that he threw
himself into that shout, the way those students did. He made
damn sure I heard him.

I shouted back: 'Thank you. Happy Yule to you,' not at all
sure I made such good hearing. I shout high and windy. But I
was so pleased to hear him and so amused at the cheek of it,
that I think I sounded joyful too.

Then he shouted: 'How are you keeping the time?' and I
did not understand what he meant straight away. I had a
moment when I insanely wondered how he knew my watch
was with an English pawnbroker, and while I wondered, he
shouted again, amplifying: 'Have you any good things? Any
money?'

That embarrassed me a little, but I felt I must reply. So I
yelled: 'I'm all right. I've got some holly and some ivy.'

For some reason, this amused him vastly. He turned to

Kiartan, and Kiartan laughed heartily too. For the rest of the time they were out there they kept turning to me and laughing – not at all unkindly, but I felt foolish, because I still cannot see why my answer should have been so funny.

Well, it came to an end and they had to go as usual. I went in here, where it is very quiet and lonely, not really having much heart to go on writing. Most of the morning I wandered about sticking up holly and ivy over the fireplace and windows and trying to pretend it was Christmas – which it may be, for all I know – and while I was doing it I found myself smiling again and again at the way Asgrim had seized on the fact that we were officially acquainted and could exchange real, public words. And what better excuse than season's greetings, shouted to the other prisoner? Natural courtesy, of course. Not that one can go far at the top of one's voice, but it is better than nothing. It seemed to me, from the way he shouted the moment he saw me, that he had decided on it beforehand and was putting his plan into operation before anyone thought to stop him. And it worked. The guards had another established precedent on their hands before they got their breath back.

But I had not seen the full extent of the plan – for I am now sure this was what it was – until the afternoon, when Wolfram suddenly appeared, very sullen and disdainful (for Edwin, it seemed, was off duty entertaining the ungrateful Elsie), ushering Hobby (who is never off duty). And Hobby was doubled up under a great hamper, which he was carrying on his shoulders, and which he slung on the floor as if his knees had given beneath it.

'This is for you,' says Wolfram. 'From Asgrim.' And his manner went on to say 'And I can't *think* what possessed him,' as clearly as if he had spoken. 'You are to unpack it in my sight, if you please.'

I suppose it was inevitable that he would want to see what the hamper held, and it took the edge off my pleasure a little. But at least I did not blush. Wolfram was so fed up at having the bother of trudging up here with Hobby, that he reduced it all to an ordinary, tedious business, and no blushing matter. Edwin would have made such a to-do that he would have had me scarlet within seconds. All the same, it was irritating to have Wolfram there, sighing and sulking and picking his pimples all the time I was unpacking this fantastic cornucopia of good things. And it was almost as irritating to have poor Hobby kneel there and follow every item with his eyes like a hungry dog. I tried not to be annoyed. I am sure he had never seen such a spread, any more than I had. But I did so want to gloat in peace.

There is so much. Oranges, apples, several kinds of meat cured and seasoned in a way I have never come across before, jars of ginger, pots and boxes of crystallized fruit, things that seem to be flower-petals sugared, biscuits, short-bread, gingerbread, things like bakewell tarts full of almonds, raisins by the bunch, nuts, and a number of dark, wet fruit-cakes, so spicy and so full of black fruit that you would take them for Christmas pudding if they were not also most stickily iced. I have no idea what to call them, but they are delicious, utterly delicious. I have almost sated my craving for sugar on them. Then there are two stone-like bottles of dark sweet wine, rather musky stuff, a little like port. I think I got drunk on it last night. I have a headache today.

These things I pulled out, thing after thing, and Hobby's eyes went to and fro, to and fro, wider with every box and jar. There was also a note, pinned to a pudding-cloth, very formal, written slow, with flourishes: 'Lady, please to have these, with Yuletide's greetings. Asgrim.' I could see at once that this was official stuff, for public exhibition. I could not resist pushing it under Wolfram's nose and saying: 'There.

Now I shall have to say Yes next time you ask me if I ever had a message from Asgrim.' And he grinned feebly, as if he thought this in bad taste. Maybe it was.

Then, about the middle, I came upon a small spray of leaves, evergreen, a little like privet in shape but very pleasant to smell; and wrapped round the stalk was another note, with untidy flourishes, which said: 'Greetings from Kjarten.' And I thought: 'Bless me, I've been spelling his name wrong!' and was extremely touched. I felt, and still feel, that those leaves are significant in some way, but I cannot find out how. Edwin has a hangover today twenty times as bad as mine and is not in the mood to tell me anything – all he can do is snarl: I have hardly spoken two words to him. I asked Wolfram what leaves they were. But he said, with great superiority, that he could not say. Whereupon Hobby piped up, hoarsely, and said (I think): 'That's alvery, that is.' Which left me no wiser.

But poor Hobby. When the things were all piled on the table, he looked at them so wistfully as he took up the empty hamper that I felt the greediest monster in the world. And Hobby has done so much for me, after all. So I said: 'Hobby, would you like some of these things?' He just dropped the hamper and held out both hands cupped together, with the widest, daftest smile I have ever seen, even from him. I loaded his fists with as much as they would take – almost a little of everything, he spread his fingers so avidly wide. How he got downstairs with that lot and the hamper I shall never know, for Wolfram would not have lifted a finger if Hobby pitched down three flights and broke his neck. Wolfram is too clear about his superior status. But, in fact, Hobby struggled off alone, because I heard Kiartan (spelt wrong again) just then and went tearing out into the yard to wave and say Thank you. Wolfram sauntered after me to make sure that only the barest greetings were exchanged.

Kiarten was there alone at first, very excited because it was snowing a little – breathless, undecided snow, not likely to lie. 'Look, it's snowing!' he shouted.

'Yes, but it won't stay,' I shouted.

'Want to bet?' yells he.

And I was just going to call out to say to tell his father Thank you, when Asgrim himself came out and shouted: 'Did you get the things?'

To which I tried to put into a single yell how delighted I was and how grateful. Asgrim made a gesture, as much as to say 'It was nothing,' and was smiling, when Wolfram, to my fury and indignation, told me I must go inside. I certainly did not dare disobey. And my heart sank as I went, because it looks as if Wolfram has decided to nip our sociability in the bud. He was out there some minutes longer bawling at the guards, saying they were to take their prisoners in at once. I don't know how much authority he has over there. He plainly enjoys hectoring people. But it sounded, as far as I could hear, as if the guards objected to him bullying them like that and retorted that they would bring their charges in in their own good time. I get the feeling that people resent Wolfram. I do. Edwin treats him with veiled contempt too. But Wolfram, curse it, has authority over me. He has stopped me calling out twice now. He was up here this morning as well, needlessly, not even asking questions, just kicking about in the snow and shivering, simply, as far as I can see, to make sure that I did not even say 'Good morning.' Oh how I hate Wolfram. If he comes this afternoon as well I shall hit him again.

Kjarten has won his half-made bet. It snowed in the night, not heavily, but enough to lime the roofs and crust the walls and make the whole stronghold light and ethereal. It is damp snow, crystalline already, and will be gone tomorrow. But just now it is splendid when the sun fires it up. Kjarten threw snowballs at Asgrim and, after being hit on the back of the neck, Asgrim retaliated, swingeingly, with one that burst all over Kjarten. After that, there was no stopping them for ten minutes or more. I can see the places all along the wall where they have scooped up the snow in great hasty handfuls. It does not make up for not seeing them now and not having spoken to them then. It looks too forlorn out there. Both of them looked dubiously at Wolfram kicking about behind me and said nothing either. They waved, but did not like to seem too cordial. Damn Wolfram. If

Oh dear. I mustn't let Wolfram see this. I have been writing Rational Prose to show him, if, as I suspect he will, he needs an excuse for his repeated presence here. He came this afternoon as well, and it is clear that Kjarten was the reason.

And this morning too. Poor Wolfram. But let's get it down. Wolfram is one of those people born without attractions of any kind. He is a damp and slinking soul in a damp and slinking body, a pointed nose, pimples, and unhealthy, shabby-looking hair. Though he is perhaps not so badly built, he is marred by a native gracelessness – he walks shambling and his shoulders droop – which must have left him friend-less and unadmired from his cradle up. In fact, I would be surprised if anyone but his mother ever loved him – I hope she did, or does. And if you get born this way (and a bastard as well, as I suspect), you enter irrevocably a miserable downward spiral. Nobody loves you: your response is to love nobody and to treat everybody like dirt. But you must have something, if only status, and you are prepared to crawl for that. You crawl, knowing people despise you and expecting to be slapped in the face. And so hideously do you crawl that of course your face is slapped. Whereupon you hate and despise everybody all the more. Wolfram is well on down this way. And he has no real intelligence or strength of mind to see how he is going and to halt his progress. He is unnecessarily arrogant and needlessly humble, and disliked by everyone. He is clever enough to know how people hate him, but who is not? One is tender as a snail about people's opinion of one. Wolfram is tender all over. He may even imagine slights and derision where none exist.

I knew all this without seeing that Wolfram might want the glamour of love at least as much as any other human being. And no girl would look at him – if he ever dared try, which is doubtful. But boys have a different view of young men. Wolfram had discovered this, I know, or he would not have taken so ill my remark about the Queen of the Fairies. And he is lonely and discontented, left out of the merrymaking and forced to do Edwin's work, when he follows me out into the courtyard and there is Kjarten, in all the glamour of gaiety, shouting excitedly about the snow. I don't know whether Wolfram had seen Kjarten before this, or whether he simply discovered what a good view of him could be had from here, but it is clear that, somehow, Kjarten burst upon him and overwhelmed him. He just cannot stop himself climbing these stairs twice a day and fastening his eyes on Kjarten.

I don't know quite when I realized what was the matter with Wolfram. I was furious when he appeared yesterday afternoon, slyly behind me, just after I had gone out into the dwindling, crystalline snow. I knew he was there by the restrained way Asgrim joined Kjarten at the wall and helped him build a squashy kind of snowman on the parapet. When I turned round, there was Wolfram kicking up wads of snow with his heel, looking sulky and noncommittal, and I meditated all sorts of impossible revenges.

Then there was quite a long dreary interval, during which I walked about, feeling as if Wolfram's presence had made everything commonplace, boring and nerve-racking. They were very subdued over the way too. But Kjarten is not the boy to stay subdued for long, particularly if it is the restraints of imprisonment that subdue him. He threw half the snowman pettishly at Asgrim and knocked the rest off the wall down into the drop. And then he recovered his good humour and they began snowballing again. By that time, in some way, I knew quite why poor Wolfram was staring so avidly at Kjarten's smooth, lucent head as it bobbed about and ducked and dodged. And I did not take it kindly at all. I was jealous as hell.

I said to Wolfram: 'Wouldn't you like to snowball too?'

He, watching away, shrugged his shoulders and remarked – not with his usual loftiness: rather wistfully – that it looked like fun. Whereupon, I did something I find it hard to forgive myself for. I scooped up a great stinging double handful of snow, said: 'There you are, then,' and threw it, hard.

It hit Wolfram all over the face and neck. It was the way he took it that makes me feel so bad. He shook his head and gasped, and then, quite meekly, put his fingers down inside his collar to fetch out the snow that had gone inside. And he said not a word. He just shot a funny furtive look over at the other courtyard to see if Kjarten had noticed his disgrace. Luckily, they were too busy there to attend to Wolfram. I could have kicked myself. That meekness and silence of Wolfram's brought before me, as nothing else could, Wolfram as a schoolboy, humiliated like this a hundred times a day. When it happens that often, you don't protest. You just wait for them to stop. And my snowball must have taken him right back to those days. I am sure of it.

I said I was sorry, very sorry, and asked him if I could help get the snow out. I said, untruthfully, that I had meant to miss him, and many more fine, apologetic things beside.

Wolfram said, Yes, please would I get it out. So I felt obliged to try. And I was so ashamed of my meanness, that I tried to propel him back out of sight of the other court, so that Asgrim would not see what I had done, but Wolfram, of course, would not budge. He stood there with his eyes fixed on Kjarten, while I fished and fumbled inside his greasy collar feeling more ashamed every second. It took some time, for you know how warmed snow clings to fabric and melts as you pull it. I know they saw. Wolfram said Thank you, nicely but absent-mindedly, when I had done, and made me feel worse than ever. And after they had gone in, each with a cautious wave our way, Wolfram sighed heavily – as heavily as I did – and slouched inside after me, where he felt obliged to put me through another interrogation for form's sake. His heart was in it even less than usual.

Luckily I left off there and made Rational Prose for the rest of the day, though there has been a hurry of happenings I wanted to get down. Wolfram has been up here each time Asgrim and Kjarten were out, and, on the last occasion, Edwin came out with a broom, ostensibly to sweep the snow off the courtyard, but actually to have a look at them too. Wolfram collected himself before Edwin as he does not bother to before me – he thinks I don't count, for some reason – and when they had gone in demanded to see the words I had made. 'Made' is like 'made up' here. I see I have used it without meaning to at the top of this paragraph. I am getting to talk and write as they do. Anyway, luckily I had three pages on the customs of the country, which he scanned negligently. I suspect he did not attend to a word, as I am sure most of it is inaccurate.

Wolfram is really crazy about Kjarten. He twitches when he sees him, and colours up. Then he bends forward, as if the sight of the laughing patrician child over there hurts him physically. He is pale and looks as if he is not sleeping. When he looks at Asgrim, which he does sooner or later, it is with patent envy. He can't bear the affection between them. It excludes him so. And I can hardly bear the sight of Wolfram so nakedly yearning, exposing his feelings like this. It's shaming. But Wolfram doesn't care. I would think he could hardly help himself if he was not so much more careful in front of Edwin. Of course, Edwin is a wicked old gossip, but I suspect there is more to it than that. I have an idea that homosexuality is regarded with abhorrence in this country. It may even be a crime here. And if that is so, I can understand Wolfram's caution. I do pity him. Terribly. He is eaten and aching with passion. And to feel criminal on top of that is too much. I suppose there is enough of a parallel between us for me to know how he feels.

It snowed heavily when I was positive it would thaw, and the snow comes down my chimney and makes the fire fizz. The odd thing about being in a foreign country is that you misinterpret the weather signs. I could have sworn it was only transient, this snow. Yet here is everything crusted a foot thick, and a drift at the end of my yard like a frozen sea-breaker. My feet get soaked when I go out, and I have to hold Hilda's dress right up at my knees. Never has the cloak been more welcome. Edwin says it nearly always snows like this around Yule. We in the North, he thinks, have it most of the year round. I said we did not – I hope accurately. Edwin is very grumpy. He hates snow, and Elsie was ungrateful again in some way I have not gathered. He takes it out on Hobby, whom he curses continuously. This morning, greatly daring, I told him to stop. I said Hobby had not caused the weather and it was not fair to rail at him. Edwin retorted there were plenty of reasons to rail at Hobby, snow or no snow, and threw a log at Hobby's head, which missed and brought a great fall of soot down the chimney that poor Hobby had to clear up. I shall keep my mouth shut in future. Hobby brought me another poem today – or the second verse of the same one – and I am far too grateful to want to add to his troubles. I gave him the last of my apples to make it up to him.

Kjarten has obviously made it easier for Asgrim to get hold of paper. What I have is half of a drawing which has been crumpled up and thrown in the fire. Asgrim must have filched it from the flames and hidden it. It is all singed, not only round the edges, but along several of the creases. But it must count as used, not missing. I am thankful, though I have an image of Kjarten confined and bored, scribbling sheaves of such drawings and throwing them wholesale among the burning logs, and Asgrim secretly in agony at not being able to collect them all. Or could it be they did it in collusion? It would make life more interesting to Kjarten if they did, and they are plainly much in one another's confidence.

Anyway, this is a wobbly and grotesque figure of a man on a horse – except that the man looks as if he were sitting below the horse's backbone. Kjarten plainly saw its deficiencies as well as I did, for he wrote across it, very heavily and crossly, so that his pen splayed: 'Truly Badd.' And then threw it away, I suppose. The horse has eight legs. That I thought a deficiency too for a while, until I recollected that Woden's horse (which had a name that I forget) had eight legs. I think this is meant to be Woden. I wonder who it was in the other half of the picture. It is odd to think these people are heathens. Asgrim and Kjarten must be Woden's men. It is only fitting. Woden, I remember, was god of poets and the valiant in war, and also the most guileful of them all. He suits what I know of Asgrim.

This is what was written on Woden's singed back:

> This truth is mine in closer things
> And walks in sight across the way,
> Watching the dun leaf stray,
> Only for my eyes smiling.
> It moves in long hair trailing
> And locked in words it sings.
> This strange truth is everything
> That walks at hand, and every day
> Quickens with the face it brings.

Not, I think, as good as the first, if I could judge rationally, which I hardly can – I am too taken by the particulars. He must have seen me watch him catch that leaf, but how he could have seen I can't think. Some people do have a very wide angle of vision and see more from the corners of their eyes than most. I think Asgrim does. But this all goes to show how I prefer truth manifest in particulars. Abstractions are hard for me to deal with. Asgrim, perhaps, is the other way on and finds abstractions more congenial. Many men do. But it looks as if he has come to value particulars too, which is very pleasing. In an odd way, I feel as if I had taught him to, though he had it all to do himself.

This was in reply to a note of mine about Kjarten. I forgot to say. I was too preoccupied with what answer to make, and with keeping up the writing for Wolfram. I finished the wine last night, between the two things, and was good for little else. But it helped me write some kind of avowal, which I think I owed Asgrim. I said: 'The hamper was too good of you – a feast for the gods. But it is more than your goodness that binds me to you.' I hope that will do. I have a dread of being *forward*, and I know simply nothing of how a woman is supposed to behave to an admirer here. And I know I have an awful tendency to sound sentimental.

Anyway, this morning, rather amusingly, Asgrim and Kjarten found a way of communicating in spite of Wolfram – who was here, feverish and pitiful, worse than ever, prowling about where he could see Kjarten as usual. Not long after they came out, when Kjarten had done some racing about, some sliding, and a little slinging of snow so that it narrowly missed the guards – I feel I would like to know more of Kjarten's relationship with those guards. I think he manages to make their lives a misery without ever quite overstepping the bounds his father has laid down. Of course boys are good at this, but I suspect that prison has perfected his technique. You learn a tightrope kind of brinkmanship in these circumstances – witness myself and my writing. Anyway, as I was saying, after Kjarten had done all this, he came back to Asgrim and they both stood facing me. Then they began to sing, stamping their feet to the rhythm, what I think was a wassail-song. I could not catch most of the words, though they sang them very lustily, because they were both singing, not quite in unison, and the snow deadened the noise. But it sounded splendid. And it was a good idea.

As soon as they had stopped, I clapped, and Wolfram, coming up with his tongue out round his lips, said urgently: 'Make him sing again.'

So I shouted: 'Lovely! Please sing some more.'

They were delighted. After some argument and consultation, they sang again, several more songs, all jolly, and one so silly that Kjarten could hardly get the words out. Wolfram was enchanted. He tapped his foot and smiled yearningly, and I daresay I did too. I wished we could sing in reply, but I'm sure Wolfram has a voice like a crow, even if we knew the same songs.

It was not Wolfram but the guards who stopped these goings-on. One of them came up to Asgrim and said something, at which Asgrim shrugged and Kjarten looked plain mulish. But Asgrim took Kjarten by the elbow and led him aside, and, after a little sober talking, Kjarten shrugged too. The concert was over, it seemed, and they were to go in. Wolfram let out a little moan of dismay, followed by some obscene words for the guards, but what could we do over here? I rather hoped Wolfram might try hectoring them again, but he made no attempt to. Possibly there has been some complaint about last time, and he has been told exactly how far his authority goes, for he turned away looking so miserable that my heart really bled for him – far more than for myself. After all, Asgrim is here indefinitely, at least until the mopping up of the opposition is over (God! I hope it's going slowly. I must ask Edwin). But Kjarten was only here for Yule and his stay must almost be over. There can't be many more occasions on which Wolfram can hope to see him.

I have just seen the most unfortunate scene. One of the most embarrassing and hurtful ever. Wolfram didn't appear this afternoon, and I could scarcely believe my good luck. Then I went out, hearing Kjarten, and found that Wolfram had somehow managed to insinuate himself over there. I don't know how, but he did it. I suppose he has grown too desperate to be cautious. From the look of things, he had been there some time.

He came out into the yard with them, and it was clear at once that Asgrim and Kjarten had both already had more than enough of him. Asgrim was behaving politely enough, but you can tell when someone is irritated: it was in the set of his head, the careful way he moved, the sudden sharp gesture he could not quite suppress, and the way he kept almost but not quite turning his back on Wolfram. Kjarten was trying to ignore him, which was not easy, because

Wolfram stuck as close to him as a dog at heel. Kjarten kept
giving Asgrim a helpless, meaning look that said 'Send him
away!' even from where I was. And, of course, Asgrim was
quite unable to send Wolfram away. As I said, the worst
thing about being a prisoner is that you have to put up with
everyone who foists himself on you. I could see Asgrim
getting more and more irritated and doing his best not to
show it. Never have I watched two people show more clearly
that they did not want a third. And Wolfram did not budge.
He just hung about beside Kjarten.

Maybe those two were rude, but it is hard to blame them.
It turns out – though I did not know it then – that this was
Kjarten's last day here. And Wolfram is a wet blanket at the
best of times. I have to confess to the most awfully mixed
feelings, seeing Wolfram actually over there. I can sympa-
thize as long as he seems to have no hope of getting his
hands on Kjarten, but, my God, I saw him there with moral
outrage! I was still sorry for him, but I could have punched
his nose. It was not his physical intentions that troubled me:
it is just that Wolfram is such an unpleasant person. I can
understand how he got that way, but it does not alter the fact
that he is fixed as being a cold-blooded snob, a greedy social
climber, and one of those people who casts on life a sort of
moral greyness and boredom of the spirit. Seeing him over
there, I felt like I did one time when I was calling on my
godmother, and her lunatic old aunt saw me from her
window and looked at me like a lizard that had just swallowed a fly. I knew that I had – for a minute at least – been
incorporated into her deranged world, and the thought
sickened me. I did not want Kjarten incorporated into
Wolfram's sickening world.

I know Asgrim felt the same. His irritation increased
noticeably every time Wolfram fawned on Kjarten – and
Wolfram fawned more and more fervently: I could hardly

bear to watch him. From this distance you lost the real emotion in the exaggeration of Wolfram's oily cringing. It just looked dreadful. I thought: 'Oh, how *can* he? How can anyone?' And Kjarten kept giving out a great false smile that snapped back into a scowl whenever Wolfram took his eyes off him, and then looking nervously at Asgrim for support. And it went on like this until Asgrim lost his temper. Wolfram obviously said something particularly fulsome to or about Kjarten, and Asgrim, unable to answer civilly, simply turned away without saying anything and looked over at me for a second. An expressive look. It said: 'Christ, I can't stand much more of this creep!' And while his back was turned Wolfram took hold of both Kjarten's hands and looked at him adoringly, sentimentally, yearningly – 'Walk on me, kick me, I am yours' – and was still doing it when Asgrim turned back. At the sight, Asgrim lost his self-control and cracked out one short insult. One can guess what it was. I couldn't hear the words, but I heard the sort of crunch of fury to his voice. Wolfram practically threw Kjarten's hands from his and drew himself up a little, pretending to be astonished. It did not look very convincing, but I suppose it was his only defence. You could see he was saying: '*What* did you say? Did I hear you aright?' And Asgrim, instead of retracting it, stood there and said it again, possibly with embellishments.

I am afraid that was foolish of him. Wolfram at once put on a flaming great act of outraged innocence and hysterical righteousness. He raved and he gestured, and he flung about the yard apostrophizing the guards, calling on them to bear witness to what Asgrim had said – the wicked, wicked slander, when Wolfram himself had done nothing, but nothing, to deserve it. And the guards conceded that Asgrim had said it, humouringly and a little insolently: it was clear they quite agreed with Asgrim but dared not say so. And

Wolfram ranted on again. I could hear his voice yapping and neighing, and I could not pick out one word in seven. Asgrim stood there looking totally unrepentant. I remember I could not see Kjarten. He had retreated where the wall hid him. Then Wolfram screamed at the guards to get that man out of his sight, take him away, lock him up, or he would complain that they had failed in their duty. And some more on the same lines.

Now it is clear that Wolfram has a certain amount of pull somewhere. As soon as he talked of complaining, they looked worried and said things to one another and nodded. Then all three of them came up to Asgrim. I thought for a moment that Asgrim was going to refuse to go. He and the guards stood looking at one another until the tension was almost unbearable. Then, thank God, he gave in and walked inside without them having to lay a finger on him. I could see by his face as he went that he was furious – probably as much with himself as with Wolfram.

Wolfram, panting rather after his histrionics, turned to Kjarten, who reappeared where I could see him and actually looked over at me as if he were wondering whether to draw me into the scene or not. He decided not. It was the coolest decision: he could manage on his own. Once his father had gone, Kjarten was so different that he took my breath away. Indeed, this was what kept me there, anxious and fascinated. I know most kids tend to have something of a façade before their parents, but this boy might have been two separate people. He dropped the playful, boyish boy completely. Tête-à-tête with Wolfram, this was a competent youngster, quite aware of his value, quite at home in the situation, and not disposed to sell himself cheap – though not above letting Wolfram see what a prize he was missing. I could have smacked him for that. I find it hard to describe the subtle flirtatiousness Kjarten infused into his businesslike stance.

He stood there with his arms folded, giving poor Wolfram the come-hither and the go-hence so seamlessly and expertly blended that I doubt if Wolfram knew what to make of him from one moment to the next. Myself wheedling candy from Edwin is crude mummery beside Kjarten's performance. Kjarten's was professional expertise. Plainly he had been there before.

Wolfram gained quite a little in dignity once they were alone. He fawned less and was earnest. The lord knows what he said, but it was clear he made his proposal in form. Kjarten listened, smiled slightly, looked away, listened again, and said very little. After a while, it almost seemed he was willing. Wolfram thought he was. He smiled and gained steadily in confidence until, at length, almost happily, and very tenderly, he laid his hand on Kjarten's arm. Having brought him to this point, Kjarten shook the hand off without hesitation. Then he stuck his head up missishly and laughed in Wolfram's face. It was total derision. He made it quite clear that he had led Wolfram on in order simply to reject him. Words went with his derision – I expect: 'Who, you? Not bloody likely. I've bigger fish to fry.' And having said them, Kjarten strolled away, still laughing, out of my sight and indoors. The door banged – whether for Wolfram's benefit or Asgrim's I can't say – and that was that. Lord, that kid was cruel! He left Wolfram literally writhing, doubled up, moving and twisting about with the shame of it, in a way I hope never to see again. It was so awful, and so private, that I got myself quickly out of sight. I was sure he would not want to think anyone saw him like that.

I felt quite sick, and I was shaking all over. Cruelty is sickening. I suppose I should have been relieved that Kjarten knew enough to avoid contact with Wolfram's dreary soul, but I am afraid Wolfram is the one I am sorry for. Little swine. For two pins I'd tell his father – except I know it would hurt Asgrim acutely and read like pure malice on my part. I wonder if Kjarten gained his expertise in prison or before. There's no knowing of course. But I fear it was prison, somehow. I can see him growing up as unpleasant as Hrinkle and worse than Wolfram unless he can take himself in hand – and what boy can take himself in hand in prison? And the curious thing is that I am sure both the parts of Kjarten that I have seen are quite genuine: he is as truly a boyish boy as he is a practised catamite.

I went out again after ten minutes or so to see what Wolfram was doing. Honestly, I would not have been surprised to see him at the bottom of the drop – since, of course, in order to leave the yard he would have to go in through their prison and brave Kjarten's derision again (which would be derision none the less for being mute and concealed). But Wolfram was gone. He must have braved it. I suppose he would still rather be alive and climb the social ladder. If he gets high enough, after all, he can beckon Kjartens to him by the dozen. Perhaps I'm wasting my sympathy on Wolfram. But I think not. He had the most sincere passion for that boy and has just had it flung in his face.

And then, while I was starting to write this down, Edwin came in with a note – and a number of words about the trouble I caused him. All those stairs. His favourite diatribe, with his feet 'rarely so bad' and so on. Then he stayed to see what the note was about, the nosy old hypocrite. I nearly didn't tell him, because it does make some difference, at least to Asgrim's behaviour, to know that it was Kjarten's last day.

The note was from Kjarten himself – nothing from Asgrim: I suppose there was no defensible excuse for it – and it says:

> Lady, I give you greetings and say you farewell. I
> shall not wave to you again as I leave tomorrow

morning early. I meant to call across to you but
had no chance, what with things. It was good to
see you every day.
                    Your friend,
                        Kjarten.

And that seems to me really quite a nice letter. I
wonder if he wrote it off his own bat or whether Asgrim
suggested it. That 'what with things' rather suggests he
thought of it himself. It asks for complicity in me. Maybe he
was trying to placate me, get me not to think too ill of him
for what he knew I saw. Maybe he was afraid I'd tell his
father. Probably I shall never know. And when I look at it,
it does its job and I cannot think too badly of the kid. Artful
little devil.

'Oh,' says Edwin, 'leaving, is he? His week's up, then, and
they'll take him back to Markwater.' And he began telling me
what Markwater was like, until he remembered I was
supposed to have caused him trouble and went stamping
busily off on some imaginary errand.

We are back to our old routine today. No Kjarten shouting, no
Wolfram, and only one sight of Asgrim, muffled up against the
latest snow and sombrely pacing about. It is so quiet and so
intensely lonely that I feel as if I had a flat kind of echo in my
head – like the noise the soldiers make down there in the
snow. It is awful. I had not realized how much variety Kjarten
brought here with him. I have almost finished everything in
the hamper now. Only some staleish gingerbread remains,
and I do not like gingerbread much. And, by the looks of it,
they are not letting Asgrim out for a second airing now that he
is alone again. The afternoon outing must have been a
concession to Kjarten's energy. It is now past the usual time –

as far as I can tell – and no one has come out. Oh dreary, dreary. What a long time till tomorrow morning.

Edwin has been up, on one of his 'cheering up' sessions. He found me disconsolately taking down my greenery, which is hard and dry and a little dusty, and he seemed to think I did right. The festive season is officially over. Most of it I burnt, in a bright raucous flaring that made Edwin's boots steam and stink, but I kept the freshest sprig of holly, some ivy, and Kjarten's little spray of leaves. These smell better than ever now – something like bay. They look like miniature laurel. I asked Edwin about them.

'Oh-ho!' says he. 'Alvery. Who'd be giving you alvery, now?' I told him it was from Kjarten. Edwin exclaimed that it was bare-faced daring, and seemed amazed that I did not know why. 'You *must* know,' he said. 'You carried their letters and all. Did you never mark it? Never? They took it as their token, alvery meaning freedom, as is well known, and there isn't a thrall that doesn't carry a sprig yet somewhere about him.'

Alvery, it seems is the badge of Hathriver, but of more significance than the red or the white rose, which, in spite of being Yorkshire born, I always forget which went with which party – perhaps it is more like the Irish green. Anyway, you wear it to show yourself a radical. Edwin discoursed of it repetitively for a long time, and, in the course of it, I discovered why Asgrim and Kjarten were so amused by my other greenstuff. Holly is for Lowland, and ivy for Mark. Edwin declares – though I do not believe him for one moment – that he never goes outside the stronghold but with ivy wreathed round his hat. He never goes out of the stronghold anyway. So I see to some extent why the alvery was sent. I have put it carefully in my bedroom, near where I have hidden the scrappet from Asgrim saying he was 'rarely so happy'. This is the only note I have dared keep.

And my hard feelings against Kjarten are dissipated so far
that I have spent most of today thinking of him, wondering if
he made the journey to Markwater locked in such a merci-
lessly jolting conveyance as brought me here. I hope they
allowed him some freer form of travel.

This day I sent Asgrim another note, to say I missed Kjarten
too, acutely. I can see Asgrim is really lonely. He has not the
heart to shout things, though he called 'Good morning'. But
that was all. For the rest of the time he paced, like animals do
in the zoo, firmly and aimlessly, with a heavy swing round to
go the other way when he came to the wall. He looked
desolately caged, older, and rather worn out. I hope he will
recover – not to shout to me, but simply not to eat his heart
out like this. I am too sad for this. I shall spend the rest of the
day writing limericks.

No reply today. Asgrim still slow and sad, but waved to me
and seemed to try to be cheerful.

Nor today. So I have been sucking in hints from Edwin's talk
and thinking of alvery and Hobby. Fortunately, I have grown
used to concealing my interest in anything from Edwin,
because I should certainly otherwise have caused Hobby
some trouble by trying to find out more about him. He has
intrigued me ever since he brought the first note. And he
knew about alvery. He was quite scornful when Wolfram did
not – or pretended not to, I think. That might have been a
bad slip on Hobby's part, if he had shown his scorn in front of
someone less self-engrossed than Wolfram. But again he
seemed to know just how far he could go there. As I think I

said, Hobby is an old campaigner. He cannot, he just cannot, be as daft as he seems. He must, clearly, be a Hathriver man, but whether simple messenger, spy, or fifth columnist I have no way of finding out. Hobby is about as impenetrable as a youth could be. From what Edwin deigns to say of him, I take it Hobby is a native of Mark and – though this is pure conjecture – possibly a thrall by birth. I think his being a thrall would explain Edwin's way of treating him, and Wolfram's. Don't they have a sign to show they are thralls? Or does everybody just know? If I am right, then Hobby supports Hathriver naturally, for what I suppose you might call political reasons. Freedom is in it. And this troubles me. For I fear poor Hobby must think he is carrying me messages of state, full of important secrets bearing on his own poor future, whereas, in actual fact – Oh, I am a *fraud*. And I have really drifted. It is too late to explain now. Edwin takes it as a well known fact, these days, that I was at least a messenger of some standing, if not a Female Spy. This could just be Edwin's way of adding to his own importance, except that I think Wolfram thinks so too.

Wolfram, Edwin tells me, has taken to his bed. I am not surprised. He must be shattered. Edwin thinks, though, that Wolfram is simply sulking. Edwin never allows anyone to be ill except himself – he is always supposed to be on the brink of collapsing from overwork. No. That is not quite fair. He was very kind to me, in his way, when I was ill. And his 'cheering up' is supposed to be a continuation of the same kindness, though it gives him a solid hour a day of ardent gossip. And he gossips to me today that Wolfram is furious because he can't get satisfaction from Hrinkle (or Hrinkle's representative: this is not quite clear from the way Edwin puts it) over the way Asgrim insulted him. I gather Wolfram and the guards both had their say to whoever it was, and the guards, while not exactly defending Asgrim, contrived to suggest that it was their business and not Wolfram's. Wolfram, it seems, lost his cause, partly through his own hysterical exaggerations, and partly because Asgrim, it appears, is well known to have a really savage temper. I must say, from what I have seen I wouldn't have guessed it. But Edwin assures me he has. There have been occasions, almost legendary, when Asgrim has fallen into rages so terrible that strong men flew like chaff before him. So Edwin. I would be tempted to put this down to *saeva indignatio* – but then I don't know the facts. If he *has* this appalling temper, then I can only say he must have been exercising extraordinary restraint over the way there.

An answer today, thank the gods. The god on this one appears to be Thor. At least, he is very large and carries a hammer. Possibly he is attacking the World Serpent, but his adversary is in the half of the picture I have not got. Like Woden, he is angrily crossed out and a little charred. Asgrim has room to spread himself a little on the other side. 'Thank you,' he says. 'I am lonely now. But there is room for thought again. See this. Truth is made up of many small things, some good, some evil, and some merely in being. Would you say in your knowledge that the small things have more worth than the great thoughts we build out of them?'

Well, I have been all day thinking this over. I am divided between concern and pleasure. The pleasure not only that he wrote, but that he thought me worth consulting – and that I divined the way he was thinking from his verses. But concern. For one thing, it's a strange thing to write to a lady you say you love. For another, I keep fearing that Kjarten's short visit has unbalanced Asgrim and that he is now turning a treadmill of unreal ratiocination. Philosophy is fine, but I have a sneaking feeling it exists in a void. If he is in such a treadmill, I can't see that it is working anything except pointless further machinery. Dare I say this? Not, I think. Asgrim may be a person whose decisions really have to rest on some kind of philosophical groundwork. Though I fail to see what decision he can possibly arrive at from any conclusion of mine about truth, I shall try to come to one. Maybe at least I can stop the treadmill.

Perhaps if I write my thoughts down I will arrive somewhere. Asgrim, I can see, sets great store by what I have called abstractions – his 'great thoughts' – anyway, by the general ideas you have about life and which, once you have formed them, shape your future acts by a kind of driving splendour. They are your beliefs and make you tick. I think 'splendour' is an important word. For, to be worthwhile, and to feel yourself worthwhile, you must have a sense of splendour – of ultimate, forceful goodness – which serves you both as yardstick and mainspring. Asgrim, clearly, has had this sense. The adoption of alvery bears witness to it. And, possibly, being wealthy, gifted and powerful, he came by the notion of splendour rather easily and it seemed large and perspicuous to him. He acted by it. Even Edwin allows this. Then he was imprisoned. Almost everything he valued was removed or destroyed, and the ideas he had started were persecuted (Edwin tells me that any thrall found with alvery is to be executed, on Hrinkle's orders). He was forced to the small dreary round of prison life, where a detail like dirty drinking-water – as mine is today – assumes worldwide proportions: trivia are all you have. And yet, in order to sustain your identity and sanity, you are forced to find your sense of splendour even in these trivia. I found it when I saw Asgrim catch his leaf. Asgrim found it seeing me, I think, where some men might have called upon religion. But Asgrim is a heathen, so he calls his 'great thoughts' truth – and not, perhaps, now I think of it, so irreligiously, for

Woden, in a strange inhuman way, is an eternal seeker after truth of a kind. There is a trouble in this kind of truth, however. You are a subtle, civilized person, though in prison. The disparity between your 'great thoughts' and your daily trudging life strikes you with the flat, swingeing force of irony. They are miles apart; but, since they are both part of you, you must struggle to reconcile, if not to unite them; and you want a reason for it – not the simple, flat reason that both things are in your consciousness. What do you do? I think what Asgrim has asked me is what he shall do about this terrible disparity.

This is what I shall write, then – though it is a struggle to find words for it that are in his dialect as well as mine. 'Both have equal worth, I think. One cannot have great thoughts without the small things to shape them from; but, on their own, most small things are meaningless. They need to be fired up. Without greater thoughts, we would live only from moment to moment, not even truly in space and time, which is perhaps how animals live. Does this help your trouble?'

That took the whole of one side of one of my strips of paper, and half of the reverse. It was hard to fold without showing the writing. But it is done, and Hobby took it this morning. Asgrim, not yet having it, was pacing pensively, churning ratiocination in every line of him. I am afraid he will have bulged out into some new area of trouble before he gets my answer. But he smiled over at me as if he were trying to bring himself to order – a braced and businesslike smile, which went away quickly and left him looking weary.

You know, I think it was cruel of them to bring him Kjarten. Before Yule, Asgrim had found some sort of equilibrium. Now I can see it has gone. He is drearily fretting, pointlessly exacerbated and, I suspect, on rather worse terms with his guards than he was. Not that they were ever comradely. But there was a kind of acceptance on both sides.

Asgrim seemed to accept that they watched his every move: they, that Asgrim was their job of work. Now I can see them exchanging snappish remarks, that seem personal, with a real edge of malice to them. The swart, hefty one, in particular, seems to have his knife into Asgrim properly. And Asgrim does not spare him, either. There was a moment, just now, before they came in, when my heart was really in my mouth.

I have no idea what it was about, but the swart one began it – said something, obviously insolent, and looked at the sky with his tongue bulging his cheek, inviting annoyance. And Asgrim, who three weeks ago would have let it ride, showed his annoyance and snapped at him. Whereupon the swart one, having got his opening, lowers his jowl, glowers, and takes a couple of rolling contumacious steps in Asgrim's direction. And Asgrim, in his turn, does the unwisely provocative thing and turns his back and stalks away from him. At which, swart one started after him with his fists clumped, growling, and was only stopped by the other guard catching his elbow and placating him – and not with any words complimentary to Asgrim by the look of things. He looked nastily at Asgrim saying them, and Asgrim snarled something back over his shoulder plainly quite as uncomplimentary. There followed an uneasy stasis, with all three looking most unloving, broken by the second guard bowing deeply and derisively and, with a wave of his hand, inviting Asgrim to step indoors again. Asgrim took his time about it. He delayed, until the swart one was within an ace of taking him and pushing him in, and then he slipped in front of him, nodding gaily at me – almost in Kjarten's manner of ferocious vivacity – and sailed inside as if he did it of his own free will. They followed glaring.

I don't like it. They are all getting on one another's nerves almost unendurably – and it must lead you to hate one another, seven of you all cooped up together, and one at least of you resenting every minute of it. I hope Asgrim finds his equilibrium again. And I hope the guards recover too, before he has insulted them irremediably. The trouble must be confinement, and the weather: it snows perpetually, sleetily and depressingly, and if the guards have any time off duty they must have to spend it staring at the icy yards. It isn't weather to go out in. I had to spend half an hour warming my hands before I could write this.

There is one blessing to the weather, though – it's an ill wind. Edwin has just left after giving me a garrulous account of how slowly the mopping up is going. The roads to the Lowlands are all flooded and impassable, it seems, and Regan is sitting at the edge of the floods with a miserable army, waiting for winter to be over so that he can get at Hilda's party. Hilda's crew – which I now gather is really led by her brother Hugh – are snug in the town of Holland and sniping at Regan by boat from time to time. The mother of Hilda and Hugh, a woman of granite, has her own army and is on the march in spite of the weather, towards a place which was at one time a distant associate of Hathriver, but what her intention is Edwin doesn't know. He is chiefly taken up with the grim stamina of this warlike old lady. So am I. It is little short of incredible. She is fully sixty, it seems, and as bloodthirsty as Hrinkle.

Hrinkle is very bloodthirsty. He has a line in calculated cruelty which puts me in mind of Caesar docking the right hands of that tribe of offending Gauls, or William the Conqueror placidly burning the English crops to starve his conquest into submission. Hrinkle burnt in Hathriver last autumn, it seems, all the harvested grain and every piece of livestock he could lay hands on. Now, because the weather precludes fighting, he is emulating Caesar and having the ears off any man, free or thrall, found with alvery in his possession. There was a purge in Mark itself over Yule, I gather. Edwin was brutally jolly about it and seemed to think it very good statesmanship. I think it is sickening. I had to ask him to talk of something else (I have just been hiding my sprig somewhere safer). So Edwin goes on to a piece of mass murder in a place called Widburn, where support for Asgrim is very strong – or was, until Hrinkle took a member of each family (arbitrarily, men, women, or children) and cut the throat of each as a warning to the rest. We now hear nothing from Widburn, it seems.

While Edwin was telling me this, I was screaming inside that people surely wouldn't stand for it. They must rise and stop it. But now I see this is unlikely. Hrinkle has taken the most efficient steps to security. People may suffer furious sorrow, but without leaders they will not rise up. Be persistently cruel enough, and the populace, with shaken diligence, knuckles under. Most ordinary men are too committed to their work and their family to do otherwise. You need ideas – splendours – to fire you to uprising. Once the ideas are afoot, then the smallest transgression of justice on the ruler's part is seized on as if it were the direst cruelty. Without ideas, you cringe and accept major cruelty, let alone small transgressions. And it seems to me that the ideas have not had long enough to brew in. Asgrim has been at work only on half a generation, which is not enough to leaven the mass. The ideas are being tramped out and apathy is spreading over the country. Hrinkle knows his job. And since his job is merely the wielding of practical power, it cannot matter to him that he has tramped away vitality along with hope and opposition.

Vitality in a country is a strange matter. You have it, in a matter-of-fact way, in the Lowlands. They are getting on with the business of opposing these tyrants. From Edwin's remarks I get a clear sense of the quality of these Lowlanders. They are a dour, tough and unforthcoming people and stick to their cause like bulldogs. I can see Hilda's fat maid was a typical Lowlander, unfriendly, parochial, and faithful in her limited way. They will do. I suspect they will retain these qualities even when they are conquered. The hope and vitality in them is self-centred and does not lead to despair and apathy.

But I get no such feeling about places north and west of here, adherents of Hathriver. Edwin gives me quite heart-rending glimpses of privation and apathy. What these people once were is now only conjectural; but I get fleeting notions of mercurial ebullience. They sang in Hathriver. Widburn was festive. Gardale was the most beautiful of the valleys. None of this is very resonant as I write it down, but, as it drops from Edwin, it rings of people more gifted and joyous than those in the Lowlands, more outgoing, more open to ideas and much less stable. I think these people, being less obstinately self-satisfied than the Lowlands, are that much more vulnerable to Hrinkle's treatment. Take away hope, and they have no kind of vitality. From Edwin's sketchy account, I fear that if Asgrim were to be released tomorrow he would find himself helpless amidst his countrymen's dejection. I hope not. They have had a mere nine months of oppression, but that may be sufficient. By Edwin's account, there is plague there, as well as starvation, and I fear the worst. I see I must pin my hopes for long resistance and Asgrim's life on the unlovable dour Lowlands alone.

I have just been out to examine the weather. I have suddenly realized that the later it thaws, the longer the mopping up will take. It may be the middle of January now, which ought to mean another month of foul weather at least. But there are signs of amelioration. It is wet cold now, snowing slush almost. Oh God, in that case make it rain incessantly. Turn the Lowlands into an island and cut Mark off from Hathriver too, if that is possible.

My prayers answered today. It is pouring. Hobby was soaked when he came in this morning, and he did not bring a message, or not a written one. When he saw me look, when Edwin was out unlocking the doors, he said: 'The answer's Thank you. He's a bit beset this now.' Then he shut his mouth and sneezed through his nose over the kindling. I said he had caught a cold, surely; and he replied he was used to it. But he sniffled so and looked so mauve and wretched that I told Edwin he'd find himself without Hobby if he didn't make sure he was dried and warmed. Edwin retorted that there were plenty more where Hobby came from, which cheered neither me nor Hobby. But I think Edwin did in fact take pity on Hobby, from something he said just now about 'mollycoddling'. I take it he may at least have let the poor kid sit by a fire somewhere.

Talking of fires, I can see the wet black smoke from the fire in Asgrim's quarters gusting and spreading under the downpour. The water must come down his chimney as badly as it comes down mine. I have to build the fire over in one corner of the grate to avoid its being put out completely.

Asgrim did not come out today. I hope it was merely the rain. It was like standing under a waterfall, and cold as the grave out there. But I don't like what Hobby said about him being 'a bit beset'. It sounded as if the disagreements with the guards might have come to a head. If they have, I suspect Asgrim will come off worst – I feel so nervous I can't bear to write more. I'll do Rational Prose for Wolfram instead.

Speak of the devil. Wolfram has been here all afternoon. I shall have to write it tomorrow. Edwin is just coming to light the lamp.

No Hobby this morning. No message. And still pouring. Edwin tells me Hobby is sick, coughing blue murder and feverish. Poor Hobby. I wish I had something good to send him. But it seems that 'over there' was allowed to send him some wine. Asgrim *is* good – the more so as it seems he was very beset indeed these last two days, and indirectly the cause of Wolfram's tedious visit to me.

Hrinkle was here, it seems, going through the affairs of the stronghold with martinet savagery. Two of the soldiers below have been flogged. Wolfram has been hauled over the coals on several counts, and Edwin has been told to bring me less fuel in future – a command that, today at least, he has blandly ignored, remarking, with one of his ponderous leering winks, that I was unlikely to mention the matter, was I? But the bulk of the time Hrinkle spent with Asgrim, without – I think – any particular violence, going into his affairs exhaustively. The guards stated their grievances, it seems. One of them has been replaced. But most of the time, according to Edwin, Hrinkle was checking security, making sure that no messages could get to Asgrim or leave him. I hope to God he had destroyed my note by then, for I hear the place was searched and so was Asgrim himself. For it could have been that Wolfram's visit related to my attempts at philosophy.

But I think not. Wolfram started simply with an enlarged version of the usual interrogation, and then went on – to my considerable alarm – to ask in a lacklustre way, as if he did not really believe in the possibility, how many messages I had sent since I had been a prisoner. I took courage from his lack of conviction and said 'None.' And I stuck to the lie while Wolfram ranged half-heartedly about, suggesting that I threw things out of the window, down the drop, or into the hands of one of the soldiers. It was easy enough to deny that, but I was in a considerable fluster all the same and he may have detected it. I think Wolfram was whipped up here by Hrinkle, who wanted every avenue explored. It does not seem exactly as if anyone thinks that Asgrim has sent me messages, or I to him, but they are making sure all the same. And the reports from me are still unsatisfactory, so Hrinkle told Wolfram to go and have a go at me again. Or that is how I read it, anyway.

Wolfram was rain-spattered, sulkier than usual, and he had a cold too. He is still haggard from his passions over Yule. It was clear to me that he did not want to be here (from which I took courage) and that he regarded the questions he asked as nothing but a bore. He sat in my best chair – the one I packed solid with slips of paper – hogging the fire and annoying me very much. I had spread the cloak there to dry, and I had to move it for Wolfram's benefit, with the result that it is still wet today. When he had done with the questions, Wolfram sighed and asked to see what I had been writing. I gave him my latest Rational Prose, which he smothered a yawn over but set out to read with considerably more concentration than usual. (Reminder to myself: Emily, you must write *more*, or he will want to see *this*.) It was an expanded form of my disquisition on tyranny and people's vitality.

Wolfram said: 'Who's Keyser?'

I told him who Julius Caesar was, and was going on to Augustus and the rest – for I have long ago discovered that I can get rid of Wolfram by boring him, and he bores easily –

when he flapped his knob-knuckled hand at me to be quiet and went back to reading Prose. I had never expected it to receive so much attention, and I was alarmed. Apart from anything else, the gaps in my knowledge are yawning and I had made no secret of them. I had a sudden galvanic horror that I was about to be discovered as an irrelevant foreigner and be turned out free forthwith to starve in the freezing and flooded countryside. As Wolfram read, my face heated and I kept finding that I was shifting anxiously about. What I should do if they turned me out, I just do not know.

At last he lifted his head, stared at the fire and said, in the queer humble, puzzled way he has, that gets him my sympathy even when I least want to give it: 'Why is this all wrong? Is all you know by hearsay?'

He had hit on the heart of the matter, to my terror, yet he was simply puzzled by it. That is Wolfram all over. Humility is so inherent in him that he cannot see when his mind has told him something clear and true. This, though it irritates me profoundly, also touches me deeply. Wolfram, in some ways, is far more deprived and stunted even than Hobby.

I told him hastily that the North was so cut off that we knew generally very little of the rest of the country. He accepted it meekly, and I could have wept for him. I said I had got most of my facts from Edwin, and asked him where they were wrong.

'Oh, everywhere,' he said, rather helplessly. 'The Lowlands are bargaining for peace, you know.' My heart sank at that. 'And you're wrong about Widburn,' he said. 'They took to the fells after the killings, and they cause a deal of airt harrying our men as they go by on the road.' At which my heart lifted a little. Wolfram meanwhile gazed on sadly at the fire. 'And,' he said, 'Gardale's not a patch on Hathriver, not as a place, nor for the people in it. They're lovely people in Hathriver, proud and handsome.' I could see by the fixity of his meditation that he was thinking of Kjarten then. It was clear he was, when he broke out with: 'Hrinkle can go to Markwater. Why can't I?'

I said it didn't seem fair.

'It *isn't* fair!' he said. 'Hrinkle's not one of your great ones yet, whatever he thinks. I have some rights too.' Then, with a frank sort of embarrassment which was, all the same, quite indescribably smug, he said: 'Hrinkle's my brother. Did you know?'

So that's it! I thought. Half-brother, you mean, Wolfram. I see now why he has pull. And I *think* I see why he was kept so far from Kjarten – it would make sense if Hrinkle were equally enamoured. I remember I said, among these thoughts, that I hadn't known, and that certainly Wolfram was entitled to consideration – various vague right things, which Wolfram seemed to appreciate, for he sidled back into my chair and gave me the first moderately friendly look I have had from him. After that he stuck on, and on, mooningly looking at the fire, saying very little, but giving vent every so often to a sighing reminiscence of Kjarten.

'Did you see how bright his hair was?' he said.

I said 'Yes.'

Then, after a while, he said: 'But you can't see his eyes from here.' He seemed to take it for granted that I was in his confidence – I don't know why, except that it reflects the facts, I suppose. It was nearly dark when he left. And he tells me he is coming again today. It looks as if I exchange Edwin for Wolfram in the afternoons, and I'm not sure I like the change.

Hobby is back – much too soon, I should say.

I wonder where Asgrim hid that paper that Hrinkle didn't find it. I have had another note today with two big people fighting on the back of it. Would they be giants, or gods? They are wielding great clubs. Kjarten must have set out to illustrate his whole heathen pantheon. Perhaps it was a pious exercise of some kind, like Scripture lessons in England. The message on the reverse is in a way not inappropriate, for it says: 'Thank you. But what do you say to this? We call on the gods to make our dough rise, but they are gods all the same.' Discuss. Write on one side of the paper only. Oh Asgrim. I was right about that treadmill. As far as I can see, he has just put me the same question the other way round.

Did I leave this under the Rational Prose, or on top? I wish to heaven I could remember. It was underneath when I came in from the courtyard. Let us hope it was underneath when I went out. Oh it *must* have been. I would surely not be fool enough to leave it where Wolfram could see it – but Wolfram himself is so damn devious that it would be just like him to put it underneath when he had read it so that I should suspect nothing. If *only* I could remember. The fact is, I have got so used to getting messages and writing my thoughts in safety that I'm growing careless. I must take a grip on myself. And I think I had better warn Asgrim.

I didn't write much, you see, because I was too busy thinking of the question Asgrim set me – *posed*, Emily, not *set*: I'm sure he didn't intend to sound like an Examining Board. They don't have them here, as far as I know. Then, as it was time to see him, I went out as usual, into a fine, itching drizzle, against which Asgrim had turned up his hood for once – usually he goes bare-headed. In spite of the drizzle, he did not seem nearly so miserable today. He smiled, and looked as much as to say 'You got my message?' And I nodded. Then, I suppose to explain it, he went into a bit of a droll pantomime, hand-spreading, shoulder-humping and so on, which I think was meant to show me the way your mind goes round and round on these questions once you start, and perhaps by way of apology for asking me about them too. He made me laugh, I must confess, and himself too by the end. And all this was in the face of the guards, who were humped up in the background looking my way because of the drizzle, and who appeared quite unconcerned. One of them was the swart one, by the way. I had rather been hoping he was the one Hrinkle replaced, but it looks as if it was one of the other ones, more's the pity. Anyway, neither he, nor the other, made any objection to Asgrim's miming, and for nearly half an hour we were very cordial and carefree with one another – almost in the way we were when Kjarten was here. I suppose Asgrim must be heartily glad that he had come off so well from Hrinkle's visit. He's a brave man, I know, but it must have been a hideous strain and he must be most relieved that nothing incriminating was found. I know what I go through – am going through.

Because Wolfram came slouching out about five minutes before Asgrim went in and told me rudely to come in out of the wet at once. I protested. I know Wolfram fairly well by now and I have never known him be really firm yet. And he told me to shut up. At least, they say 'Shut your mouth' here, which sounds even ruder. No – now I come to think of it, I remember Wolfram said: 'Shut *thy* mouth,' which alarms me more than ever, even though the way he said it was just plain peevish. But, as far as I can gather, you only *thee* and *thou* a person here to show contempt. Edwin *thous* Hobby all the time, and tended to do it to me too, in the beginning, when he thought I was no lady.

At the time, this was lost on me, because I was watching Asgrim move away circumspectly to the back wall, with the guards turning reluctantly after him into the force of the drizzle, and I simply did not want to leave. I said: 'Oh, please, Wolfram!'

'Well, then, stay,' he said, very surly.

So I stayed. Not that it did much good. Asgrim looked over once or twice from the far wall to see if Wolfram was still there. And of course he was. I didn't like the way he looked at Asgrim at all. There was a sort of fixity of malice to it, made none the better to see by the way the rain plastered Wolfram's dingy hair down and dripped off the end of his nose. I know, looking at him, I thought: 'My God, Wolfram's got it in for Asgrim!' I suppose it was the row over Kjarten that did it. But it was not until I got indoors and Wolfram slunk away downstairs that I began to wonder what was the immediate cause of that look. Oh, I do pray it was not my stupid, stupid negligence.

Of course, it may not be that bad. If Wolfram made no secret of his feelings for Kjarten in front of me, then I was nearly as indiscreet in front of him. It may simply have occurred to him to make use of his knowledge – in which case, I should fear for myself, especially after that *thy*. But, somehow, from that look, I get the feeling that Wolfram is after Asgrim, not me, and that he's not going to rest until he's got something concrete on him. I must warn Asgrim – and hide this writing in future. No. I daren't. Even if I burn it, that is tantamount to admitting it was incriminating. Wolfram – oh, speak of the devil.

What an afternoon! I had a notion that if Wolfram came in the morning, he would not pay me the promised visit in the afternoon as well. And I – Now here is Edwin coming upstairs. There's no peace in this prison.

This morning I have managed to get rid of Edwin by sitting with my p

Wolfram alarms me. I have no idea what he thinks he's up to. When he came in so suddenly, I pulled a sheet of Rational Prose over what I had just put down and hoped for the best. He didn't ask to see it. That's what makes me feel he knows what is in it. Yes, I know he would much rather *not* see my writing, but it is such a contrast to his manner of the day before yesterday when he insisted on reading whole pages. This time he just threw himself sulkily down in my one-time rickety chair and, after staring at the fire a while, began on Kjarten. Even that was half-hearted, as if he felt he had to say something. But he warmed to his task fairly quickly and treated me to some pretty ripe sentimentalities about the whiteness of Kjarten's neck and the peachy ripeness of his cheeks. He quite sickened me. Real his feelings may be, but his expression of them is not. So, desperate for a change of subject, I thought to myself: 'I'll try a little fishing for what's really on your mind, my lad.' And, while we were at it, since he had prevented me thinking about Asgrim's question, I thought he might as well help me discuss it. After all, he claims to be educated.

So, via the difference in my Northern beliefs, I led him round to the gods.

'The gods,' says Wolfram. 'Oh, the gods. I don't bother much with them. They don't bother much with men, thou knows.'

I said we thought differently in the North. 'Do you mean to say,' I remember asking, 'that you don't see the gods as holy – you know, something which makes life better, makes all the dull ordinary things worthwhile, I mean? Don't the gods seem splendid to you at all?'

'I suppose they're fine enough,' Wolfram conceded. 'But they're nothing to do with me.' Then he thought for a bit and added: 'Woden's men think otherwise, mind – at least, those that worship do. Some call themselves Woden's men so they

needn't keep their word. Woden's a great liar, thou knows.'
And he cackled a bit at the idea.

I am quite ready to believe that many people, particularly
Wolfram's kind, are very cynical about these gods of theirs.
They can't have much to offer Wolfram. So I tried to get at
the matter another way, and asked him rather insistently
whether there was not *something* he regarded as holy, or at
least something that struck him as grander than the
common.

He did not seem to mind my asking. He just shrugged and
answered: 'No, I think not,' to every way I could find of
putting the question, and went on staring at the fire.

'You're educated,' I said, in exasperation. 'What have you
been taught to believe in?'

And he shrugged again and said: 'The gods,' without even
apparently seeing his answer as funny. And he did not seem
conscious that I was fishing for something, or even surprised
that I should ask so. When I laughed at that last answer, he
looked at me for a moment, I think to find out whether I was
laughing *at* him or not. I was not. It would have been too
mean. People have laughed and jeered at Wolfram most of
his life, I am sure. And I am sure too that Wolfram saw I was
not laughing at him, because he smiled. That is why I am
fairly sure that what he said next had no malice in it at all,
which makes it all the odder.

'It may sound funny,' he said, 'but we're all taught to
believe. The thralls pray to the gods. Even some highborn do.
But we know the gods are busy with their own things.
There's the saying "We call on the gods shoeing a horse, but
they are the gods all the same." Thou must know that. Don't
they say that in the North?'

'No,' I said, blank as my next clean sheet, and that paper
set up on one edge would have felt more secure than I did.
What I felt was beyond horror, into a kind of wasteland of

conviction behind. I just thought: 'He *has* read my writing,' and was quite calm about it. 'If the gods don't help,' I said, 'who does then?' just as if nothing whatsoever of importance had happened.

Wolfram said, exactly in his usual manner, rather drearily: 'We help ourselves, I suppose,' and went on looking at the fire.

The obvious conclusion is that he was fishing, or hinting too. But I really don't think that was the case. He had not a scrap of malice beforehand, nor triumph after he said it. Yet I don't think it was an accident either. Wolfram, I think, has that kind of suggestible mind. He had seen the proverb once that day, connected with me, and it occurred to him again when our conversation suggested it. Only, being the snob he is, he said 'shoeing a horse' where Asgrim said 'make our dough rise'. I was dying to ask him which was the most common form of it, but I had not the courage. I could not have done it naturally. So I had to sit and let him tell me, in a random kind of way, about the various beliefs connected with the gods: Thor strength, Frey fertility – just as one might expect, and Wolfram is not the man to make that interesting. And while he talked, I suppose because he had given my mind such a jolt, my thoughts fairly roared, like a fire when you poke it.

It seemed to me very significant that Asgrim chose bread. As if he were connecting the leaven that raises the lumpish dough with the action of his great thoughts, which elevate trivia, and both these with the distant, separate grandeur of the gods themselves. He might have said 'they work large, they work small' – or that these were the same thing. But that is surely only another way of connecting your impressions. I still think he asked me the same thing in another way.

As for Wolfram, I cannot think why, instead of calling

soldiers, summoning Hrinkle and having my rooms searched, he sat in front of my fire telling me about the gods. While I thought and he talked, I noticed, in the same quiet, beyond-despairing way, that every so often he called me *thee* or *thou*. It struck me as so ominous that, by way of forcing the issue, I decided to ask him about it.

'Tell me,' I said. 'In the North we say *thee* and *thou* to those beneath us and those we think ill of. Is it the same here?'

Wolfram thought about it. He thought so strenuously that I am sure no one had asked him to consider the rationale of it before. 'I don't think so,' he said. 'No. I think not. You call your friends and fellows' (he meant equals, I think) '*thou*. And those you love. I would give anything to be calling Kjarten *thou*.'

That was odd again. I had to let him go on about Kjarten some more while I thought it out in my turn. It looks as if they use it like the French use *tu*. In which case, I suppose I am to consider myself on easy terms with Wolfram. Then, in heaven's name, what does he intend? I have spent most of the night worrying. This morning I wrote to Asgrim: 'Your saying is good, since it gathers small and great into one, all needing leaven. But you still asked the same question twice. You should leave that and go on to other things. And take more care. Wolfram would give his eyes to harm you.'

Now I think that in my effort to put my ideas into what I know of his dialect, I have contrived to sound bossy and peevish, not to speak of melodramatic about Wolfram. But what could I do? Short of calling him *thou*, which would be both presumptuous and unnatural, there is no way of squashing friendship into a small strip of paper.

He was pensive again today. It was raining hard, and the guards irritably ordered him in. Edwin tells me the rivers are flooding all over. The civil war is held up for the moment. I must ask Wolfram what is really going on.

Bother Wolfram. He takes up time so. But I did find out from him that Edwin's account is substantially true. There is a stasis at present. People of Hathriver and Widburn are carrying on sporadic guerrilla warfare. Hilda and Hugh are toying with peace and have sent envoys to Regan. The only active person is their mother, who, it seems, has installed herself in this Widfell place and talks of resisting to the death. Hrinkle has done some fairly nasty purging in Gardale, which Wolfram seems to regret mildly. But he has no sympathy with my horror. He claims that, beside the dead lord of Gardale, Hrinkle is as gentle as a child. In a glum way, he seems to see his side as in the right, but he has no convictions about it. He has no convictions about anything. I could shake him.

Now here has nearly a week of rain gone by and I have been too disheartened to write much at anything. There was nothing to say. Edwin and Wolfram between them would depress Pangloss, and Hobby has been off duty with another bout of flu. Poor Hobby. He looked so ill this morning that I wished I had something to give him. But I had nothing. He brought me another message too, bless him. That was a relief. I have not seen Asgrim all this time. The rain was too heavy. I only went out for short intervals, and if Asgrim was out too I must have missed him. But he is all right, though it is plain the old treadmill has been working just the same. 'True,' he says. 'I asked twice. But this of leaven was a new thought. Tell me, if truth is this leaven through all things, is it the same as the laws of a kingdom?' The picture on the back might be a tree, with some sort of a man who might be climbing it, or hanging from it somehow. I don't know what it is supposed to be. This makes half of at least four pictures. He must have four more in hand to put his problems on. I wish he had said something about Wolfram, or at least promised to be careful.

In England the answer would be easy. I would say No, it's the spirit behind the laws. But I have been looking through what I have written in my Rational Prose about the laws here (and I shall ask Wolfram this afternoon) and I am not sure the spirit of the law here is what Asgrim or I would regard as the truth. They seem to have some rather savage customs. For instance, if a man or woman is killed, they have a monetary value. The killer seems to have to pay a certain sum either to a relative (if the victim is yeoman or highborn) or to the overlord (if the victim was a thrall). And if the killer cannot or will not pay, Edwin tells me he is outlawed. Outlawry seems a poor way (and dangerous) to beg the question. You must end up with a band of cutthroats. And, on first thoughts, it seemed to me that to price a body at so much was plain barbarous. People are not *things*.

Then I had second thoughts, to some extent. We certainly object to a state of mind in which everything has its exact equivalent in money – you end up costing inspiration, art and morality. Yet, in England, this is what we do, more and more. A symphony or a picture comes to be regarded as being worth so much, or so much. And this valuing seems to entail a curious tenderness about people – a man is a human, he carries insurance, he has precious rights; so that if anyone kills him, or he kills anyone, we either demand his life in return or, nowadays, with a tender sort of barbarity, we demand *part* of his life and require that he lives some years of life in death in a jail. Believe you me, that is no joke.

The laws here seem to imply an opposite state of mind, in which most objects in life are without price, but men are held to be of limited value once they are corpses – as if, once dead, they had indeed become *things*. You do not destroy one man for destroying another. Life looks to the living. They pay, and are at liberty to recompense society if they can. To go on living is a way to help your fellows, after all. In a way, this manner of thinking has more hope to it than ours. The only trouble is that this does not make much of a deterrent against killing – but this may be merely my insular point of view.

I asked Wolfram. He droned out his disjected phrases for an hour, as I was afraid he would. He does know about law, no question. It seems I have the substance right. The administration of the system varies from place to place. Wolfram repeatedly cited Hathriver, where, it seems, justice is traditionally administered humanely and progressively. Asgrim evidently had local history behind him, but in his hands, Wolfram admits, the system flourished as never before. The decisions of Hathriver are still followed by the rest of the country. Well. Now I see what I shall reply. It will have to be the spirit behind the law at Hathriver.

I said that this morning. The answer came with the afternoon fuel. Hobby, still white and poorly, hauls it out of his boot with a respectful grin. I no longer feel quite such a fraud, and I grinned back. For, in a way, Hobby is right to think of these messages as important to him. I see where Asgrim is tending. He is, as I thought, one of those who need to rest their decisions on some kind of philosophical basis, and it looks as if the leaven-idea was something of a breakthrough for him. There is a goddess on the back of this one, which says: 'You have done me a great kindness. Tell me then how you would like to see this kingdom ruled.' Tall order, for one slip of paper, but I will do my best. We were out together briefly this morning, and it was good to see him.

He looked pale, but not unhappy. The roofs were black with the wet, and it came on to pour after a minute or so. But the sight of him has heartened me to try to give him his difficult answer.

It was not easy to answer Asgrim at the best of times. Now, with all that has been going on, I have hardly had a moment to think of modes of government – let alone set them down on a strip of paper. And even if I do, it is possible that there will be no Hobby to take it in the morning. All the same, I am crouching here in my chair, wrapped in cloak and blanket, with this absurd little tiny lamp actually on my paper, so that my pen splutters ink on it, trying to sort out my thoughts before the fire dies completely. I can scarcely think for hope and dejection and doubt.

Let me tell it in order.

Wolfram arrived soon after I had laid down my pen to think what I should answer. He was in an odd agitated mood. He sat in the usual chair and stared at the fire. The wood was damp, so that it smoked heavily and, every so often, flared to a fizzling spurt and steamed; and Wolfram's conversation, I swear, was exactly represented by that fire.

He sat and glowered for a while, and then suddenly burst out with: 'I hate Mark!' I said I agreed, from what I'd seen of the place. I asked him what the town was like, but he had gone damp again and said: 'Oh, all right.' Then, after a little, he flared out again and said he wished he could go and live in the mountains by Widmark, not in this dreary town where no one knew anything and no one cared anyway. I asked him what was so good about the mountains, and he said he didn't know. Then he began to fizzle out a few more remarks, from which I gathered that he had once been on holiday there when he was a boy. He had these wonderful, golden, idyllic memories of the place that you do get from your childhood.

I thought this was a sign of grace. I tried to tell him that this was the kind of grand and holy thing one could live by. Maybe I was crass. Anyhow, Wolfram went all mulish and said that was not what he meant at all. It seems, from what he said, that his excitement had been due to a contrivance like an Alpine railway. He had ridden in a seat dangling from a hawser and had so arrived at the place where some kind of engine worked the lift. It was the engine he had loved. They did not have engines in Mark – this seemed to be his complaint.

Somehow, I was rather surprised to hear they had engines at all. I have been thinking of the place as totally pre-industrial – quite wrongly, I now know. Wolfram, in his dampest, dreariest manner, tells me that there are contrivances of many kinds: the Lowlands use steam pumps, Gardale has a mechanical funfair, they mine coal in Widburn on what I should call a large commercial scale, except that most of this coal seems to go to drive a bank of steam-organs in Hathriver, which are accounted one of the wonders of the place. But no one appears to use a machine where a man would do. Wolfram was rather outraged that I should think of such a thing. Machines are either grossly serviceable or plain fun. Then I said What about using a machine to provide light? But it seems they do that too, almost everywhere except Mark. Each place organizes its own supply, and only Mark is backward in this.

'Thou sees why I think it's a hole?' Wolfram said. I did. I was about to ask if they used machines in warfare, when Wolfram broke out into a tirade against Mark for being a hole and a dump and a place with no future. It is not even one of the major lordships, to hear Wolfram. Hrinkle is an upstart – the uncreative kind, a grabber of good things from other places, with no concern to better his own holding. According to Wolfram, Hrinkle quite cynically made use of the outcry over the freeing of the thralls for his own ends. I had not realized that Wolfram hated him so. But then, again, I am not sure that Wolfram does hate him. Some trouble lies behind this outburst. Wolfram is upset and depressed, and I wish I could be sure of the reason. I can't help remembering that he didn't mention Kjarten once this afternoon.

Kjarten is the trouble, you see. Edwin came rolling and reeking in at suppertime, with a great fuss and importance of winks and leers and 'Shall I tell you, or shall I not?' It was plain he was bursting with news, but he wanted me to ask him. He wanted to get me so curious that I would come off my high horse and ask him. Hobby seemed equally excited. His face was bright pink and his eyes glistened.

So I began on a sort of parley with Edwin, as if we were a couple of diplomats: I would climb down a peg or so, if Edwin would tell me a fact – only, of course, we neither of us said so in so many words. And while we parleyed, Hobby went dutifully about, venting every minute a most startlingly hoarse and hollow cough. Before long, it occurred to me that Hobby was badly ill. When I looked closely, I could see his eyes were standing out and fixed, so that you could really see the eyeball as half an orb, and the light catching the iris as it stared. The flush was pure fever. I could feel the heat off him whenever he came near. I grew so troubled about him that I lost patience with Edwin's manoeuvring entirely. I told him to stop it and just to tell me, please. He was delighted, but, I think, a little disappointed in his easy triumph. But he told me, and Hobby came near to listen too. I get the feeling that Hobby had been itching to hear it told. Maybe he had dragged himself up here on purpose, for he is not always on duty at supper.

There is a rumour that Kjarten has escaped. I dare put it no higher than that. Edwin has chapter and verse for it, but, since I have been talking to Wolfram, I have come to know that Edwin has chapter and verse for a number of things which are entirely untrue. Or, as far as I know, untrue. I wish I dared believe this. According to Edwin, Kjarten escaped from Markwater two days ago disguised as a maidservant. It seems that this disguise and his transport were both arranged for from outside and somehow smuggled in to him. There has been hue and cry after him ever since, but, Edwin says, he has gone to ground very thoroughly and Hrinkle can find no trace of him at all. There is no question that Edwin thinks the whole thing a very pretty piece of organization and rather admires whoever managed it. So would I, if only I knew it were true. I was forced to enact a little hearty delight for Edwin's benefit – I felt I owed him that – before I asked him how he knew. His source is not very satisfactory. He 'heard say in Mark.'

Then I am afraid I turned to the matter of poor Hobby and tried to impress on Edwin (and on Hobby himself) that Hobby is really ill. Hobby looked glassily sheepish and said he 'would do' – accompanying his assertion with another reverberant cough which seemed to me to contradict it flatly. Edwin claimed that if Hobby said he would do, then he *would* do, and I could get no further until Edwin came to lock up. Then I think I impressed him – not with pity – with my own concern. I went right up to the old horror and even took hold of his greasy and splattered coat, and I begged and implored him to see that Hobby went to bed and, if possible, had a doctor. I said I didn't want to see him in this state (that is the kind of selfish statement Edwin understands) and ended by hinting that if Edwin cared about me at all he would do what I asked. I flattered him and I pleaded – oh, it was a disgraceful exhibition, but if it does Hobby any good, I don't mind. I'd do it again. Edwin grudgingly agreed that he would 'look to it.' That was all I could wring from him. I suspect I have given him a sense of power by twice grovelling to him in one evening, and he is not one to make concessions in his turn. He is going to lord it over me tomorrow, I know he is.

Oh dear, I have trimmed the lamp and it still flickers. But I *must* go on. This rumour bothers me so. If it were true, it's marvellous: Kjarten free, with a chance to grow up pleasant, and a weight off Asgrim's mind. Hope for Hathriver, too, since Kjarten at least is a figurehead for them. This ought to stiffen resistance and prolong the mopping-up by years – unless (Lord! what a ghastly thought) Hrinkle offers to kill Asgrim unless Kjarten is returned. Let's hope he dare not. But I see it's not all roses, even if it is true. And how do I know it *is* true? I am oppressed by Wolfram's strange behaviour. I have come to see, dreadfully clearly, what a closed circuit my sources of information might be. Neither Wolfram nor Edwin have any reason to tell me the truth: I am supposed to be their enemy. And if Edwin believes this rumour and tells me it in good faith, it may only be that Wolfram has put it about, knowing Edwin will tell me. If he did, then it must be with a view to tempting me or Asgrim to some indiscretion – giving us enough rope to hang ourselves. Then what? I am certain that the rumour, true or false, will be studiously kept from Asgrim – if true, to ensure his continued good behaviour; if false, so that I might tell him, upon which he might make some move he has not hitherto dared make, thus convicting us both. But then Hobby   Now the lamp.

The lamp died on me. I have been thinking all night in the dark. Now the sun is just up – and a fine day for the moment, at least – and I shall set my conclusions down. I must tell Asgrim about Kjarten. It seems only right, since it is possible no one else will, but I shall make it clear that I have no confirmation of it. I shall have to risk his taking action of some kind – I know enough of him to believe he will – but in these dark watches I have seen that I have put myself at risk for months now, with this writing. What is one more risk in a good cause?

So much for that. Now, his question. I think he is thinking along these sort of lines: 'If I ever get out of here, should I seize power and make myself king, relying on my good intentions to constitute a "truth" running through the whole?' And he has asked me if I should like to see it. But to do this is to be another Hrinkle, with the best will in the world. And his successor might not be so right-minded.

Now I know that there is no political set-up ever invented that is not open to abuse in the wrong hands, *but* – in the light of Asgrim's own notion of 'truth', which one can take to be a kind of informing genius – I have been studying to grasp the present system here. Even in the throes of civil war, seen through Edwin's strong-coloured inaccuracies and Wolfram's drabber discourse, it comes out rather well. The country is divided into regions called *marks* – each with highly individual characteristics and each largely self-governing. These, in turn, are grouped into larger units under the twelve overlords. It almost seems as if the 'truth' of Dalemark is in this apparent diversity with its kind of ramshackle overall unity.

What is to prevent the twelve overlords being brought into a closer unity, in a council, say, with one of their number presiding and – in times of stress only – being given more absolute power? That seems to suit the genius of the country, and in the right hands it might work. I think, too (having been brought up in a democracy), that the lower orders should have their say in the business of the marks, and that the thralls should most certainly be freed and join the rest of the lower ranks as equals. How to say this on one strip of paper? I have used three already, and have them hidden ready to burn. Now to try again.

'The truth is in the marks. I would see them kept, and their overlords brought together into one council, with one among them to have the last word and, in times of trouble only, to hold the rank of king. The thralls should be freed and all lesser men given a say in the doings of the marks. Then the truth of Hathriver might leaven the whole. I have heard it said Kjarten escaped three days ago, but this may be false. Emily.' Well, that will have to do. I think I hear Edwin. And I am a fool. What shall I do if Hobby has been sent to bed again?

Hobby was there, pale and damp. His teeth kept chattering, poor boy, and when I touched his wrist it felt icy. But he swore he felt better. Edwin swore he *was* better and stumped off to open the doors. So I gave Hobby my note, feeling strong compunction at asking this of him when he was not well. The worst of it is, if the rumour is an attempt to incriminate us, Hobby will suffer as much as anyone. Let's hope he is old campaigner enough to look out for himself if the worst happens.

I could not resist kneeling down beside him on the hearth – that was when I touched his wrist – and saying: 'Hobby, you will take care of yourself, won't you?'

A double-entendre which I believe Hobby understood. He grinned a little. He said: 'I'll do,' and produced his nasty cough again.

'Please do,' I said, and then Edwin stumps in and finds me kneeling there. He was so peevish about it that I could swear he was jealous, childishly jealous, that I was concerned about Hobby and yet turned not a hair at the thought of Edwin's poor feet, rarely so painful. Rarely so fiddlestick. But I had to butter him up a bit for fear he would revenge himself on Hobby. The last twelve hours have really put me under

Edwin's thumb, good and proper. At this rate, I shall be licking his boots tomorrow.

Oh ye gods! Oh ye gods! The fat is in the fire now, properly. And not at all in the way I expected. If my God has no power in this strange place, I shall pray to the ones who have. But I don't think these strange gods know mercy. Mercy is what I need. Matters are out of my hands now. And to think that only half an hour ago I was walking in the brisk Spring sunshine smiling over at Asgrim and he at me. I was wondering what he would make of my prescription for the government of his country, and he, by the looks of it, was in a state of pleasant anticipation, enjoying the bright new weather.

Then out comes Wolfram, all pinched and glowering, and kicks the wall beside me, really viciously, looking broodingly over at Asgrim.

I felt fairly secure this time. My writing was on a shelf in the bedroom, with some of my hairs threaded between the pages, so that I should *know* at least if someone examined it. (No one did. There was no need.) 'What's the matter?' I said to Wolfram, and he kicked the wall again. 'Well, what is it?' I said.

Wolfram began to swear. The way they swear here makes my gorge rise. I simply can't write it down – and I thought *I* could be fairly foul-mouthed. Wolfram took Asgrim and Asgrim's mother and the gods to pieces with the utmost obscenity – and assembled them again back to front – before he stopped. Then I said again what was the matter. He said: 'Come inside. I don't want him to hear,' jabbing a knuckle over Asgrim's way – Asgrim was watching us rather carefully, and I don't blame him.

'But he can't hear from here,' I said.

'I don't care,' says Wolfram, and stumps off indoors. I felt I had to follow, because I didn't like to leave him alone to read my writing. I waved to Asgrim, who waved soberly back, and went in to find Wolfram stuck across the usual chair with his legs stretched out and his toes turned in, the picture of sulky fury.

'That talk,' he said. 'It's true.'

'What talk?' I said, very careful. I could have danced to think it was true. I actually thanked my stars I had told Asgrim.

'Oh, didn't thou know?' said Wolfram. 'Kjarten. Yesterday everyone was saying Kjarten had got away, and I tried not to believe it. But it's true. He's gone. Three days ago. Hrinkle came here this morning raving mad about it. And it's all right for him. He's been seeing Kjarten almost once a week, but what about *me*?'

I hope I never have to listen again to such a childish whining tirade as that. Wolfram threw himself about in his chair, railing at his bad luck, Hrinkle's unfair good luck, shedding tears, squalling that nobody loved him. Then he wiped his nose on the back of his hand, sat forward and began on Asgrim. He seems convinced that Asgrim organized Kjarten's escape somehow – though I don't see how he could have done – and swore that Asgrim did it to keep Kjarten away from him, and that he would be even yet. Oh, on and on. Then he went on to his lovely lost Kjarten. And it was on the tip of my tongue to say that Wolfram had just as much chance of having Kjarten now as he ever had, when he was off on Hrinkle again, clawing and picking at the chair in his misery, jerking out things about blood and birth and let Hrinkle wait and see, until I suddenly realized – and so did Wolfram – that he had one of my strips of paper in his hand. He must have pulled it out of the chair in his clawings. He held it in both hands and stared at it in a puzzled way. He kept on, meanwhile, with his tirade, but the phrases came out slower and slower and with less conviction as he became more and more preoccupied with the strip of paper.

At length, he looked over at me to see if I could explain the mystery. I looked back, without any particular feeling that I know of. I remember thinking: 'You work it out for yourself, my lad. You don't expect me to help you, do you?' But I didn't feel derision, or defiance, or even apprehension. It was as if everything was in abeyance, waiting for Wolfram's mind to bite on the problem.

He stopped talking after a while and thought about it, pulling the paper backwards and forwards, and wrapping it round his knuckly left forefinger. Then it seemed to occur to him to look for more where this came from. He turned round and searched, down by the arm of the chair, and turned back holding the six or so strips that remained there. These he spread out in a fan and contemplated in turn, bending the tops, noticing, I think, where I had dirtied the edges to prevent them showing. It seemed to me that he thought about them for hours and hours and, looking back, I suppose it was the oddest thing. Both of us sat calmly there, and Wolfram never said a word. Nor did I. Once, Wolfram turned to me and seemed to be going to say something. But he thought better of it, shut his mouth, and bent over the papers again. After a while, he began to flap them softly against the palm of his hand, staring into the fire and whistling a little between his teeth. I just have not the faintest idea what was going on in his head.

Then he left, still not having said a word. He just got up, put the paper in his pocket, and, shooting me a funny dubious look, simply went out. The moment the bolt went home outside the door I began to shake all over. My teeth chattered. I know tears were pouring down my face as I went flying out into the court to see if, by any blessed chance,

Asgrim was still there. He was not, of course. I had been too long indoors watching Wolfram's mind work.

Oh God, don't let them harm Hobby! Let no one connect this with Asgrim. I hope I shall be brave enough not to tell.

Edwin's late with lunch. I can tell by the sun. What does that mean? I'm jumping at the slightest noise. No, here he comes.

In a bad mood. Feet killing him and he can't find Hobby. That must mean the worst. I hope Hobby made off and hasn't been caught. Edwin asked why I had such a high colour. I nearly told him Fear. Haven't been able to eat. Each time I hear a noise, I jump away from my incriminating writing and end up, quite involuntarily, in the courtyard. Wonder if I mean to throw myself off when they come. You can't talk of meaning. I have no intentions and no will.

I think Wolfram is right. The gods here are pitiless. They offer nothing to humans but retribution – no kindness, no morality, nothing. My punishment seems to be total isolation. I have seen no one but Edwin for a week now. I have had no heart to write before this. It was all too painful.

Soon after Edwin left, I heard Wolfram's voice, distantly, from over the way. I was in the courtyard after the first syllable, dreading to see what I saw. Asgrim was out there, standing between two guards. He never once looked at me. And Wolfram was there, gesturing overbearingly at the other four guards, who were in and out of the door I can't see, carrying things and throwing them in a heap in the yard. There were bits of chairs, tables, portions of beds, bedding, carpets – every conceivable kind of furnishing, and all of it ripped to pieces.

Asgrim watched each piece as it came, so totally without expression that he seemed to have lost all his personal characteristics. I remember no privacy or integrity about him at all – nothing that was not just generally human. I think that was the worst thing I saw. He simply stood there, as blank as a new house or an empty landscape. I suppose he knew discovery was inevitable.

That came when they struggled out with two halves of a big oak table. Wolfram held up a hand, yapping at them to wait, and pounced. I saw him work like a terrier at its underneath. A leg came off and he threw it aside; and finally he stood up triumphantly with two sheets of paper. Even from here I could see they were singed and scrawled upon. But I think there was writing on the back of one. Asgrim shrugged as Wolfram turned it over and scanned it and then ran shouting to the doorway. Hrinkle came out then. I could just see his head, and his hand snatching the paper from Wolfram. And I heard the great roar of laughter he gave. He clapped Wolfram on the back, and Wolfram looked odiously, smirkingly pleased. Then Hrinkle beckoned to the guards to bring Asgrim inside again, and they all crowded in after him, leaving nothing but the great heap of broken furniture in the yard.

That was all. The rest happened indoors. I was out there most of the day, and that was all I saw, but even if I had not heard Edwin, it would be clear to me that it is not merely an order for close confinement that keeps Asgrim out of the yard. Hrinkle wanted to know all about those messages, and he can no longer use Kjarten as a threat. Hrinkle has gone today, thank God. Edwin tells me that the old lady of the Lowlands is marching, despite the floods, to join the folk of Widburn.

Oh but Edwin claims to know all about it. He can't let the matter drop. Edwin has had a field day, indescribably horrible, of tender curiosity, veiled sadism, malignant revelation of hard fact, and howling glee once he discovered that his claim to know all about it had me hanging on his words. I think the tender curiosity is worst. He tries to plumb my feelings, and Asgrim's, with a sort of gentle, ardent prurience. Asgrim's sufferings appall him, genuinely, in every nasty detail. They trouble him deliciously. He is like someone with a skin disease, scratching. He seems quite aware that Wolfram discovered Asgrim's hoard of paper after talking to me, and he wants to know how and why, oh desperately. I can't stop him probing. I am too sick with myself. Sick!

It might be said that I could not have prevented it, but I know I could have done. I let Wolfram's queer assumption of friendship take me in utterly. How completely sickens me. I knew what Wolfram is – devious, out for his own advantage as strongly and instinctively as the flea I caught from Edwin just now, capable of using his own genuine feelings to his main end – and I took his camaraderie at face value. Instead of boring him out of my prison, I encouraged him. And of course the longer he sat in that chair, the more likely it was he would discover what I had packed it with. Oh fool. Fool. And Asgrim must be a fool too if he does not realize that I somehow gave him away. He must have seen me in the courtyard, watching, with my stupid, evident anxiety, and he could have seen I was unharmed. He must think I bargained his safety for mine, particularly as I think he did not get my last message. Oh, round and round. I have been over how much he must despise me so many times in my head. I prayed that Wolfram might set Hrinkle on me too, but he never did, and now Hrinkle has gone. Why he never did I can't quite see, but I suspect the reason is that Wolfram always had a fairly just estimate of my irrelevance. Under his gaucheness and his stupidity, Wolfram has this terrible flea-like instinct for what is important.

So I am condemned to safety. And Asgrim – The worst is – I must get myself to write it – If I see him again, he will not be the same. Edwin tells me Hrinkle broke him. He says Asgrim screamed and cried and begged Hrinkle to stop. He was reduced, violated, childish, blubbering, not a person any longer. God, I find it so appalling that I keep trying not to believe it! Edwin says Hrinkle had Asgrim kiss his foot. My head goes blank on that. For a moment I think none of it is true. But of course it is. My spirit is not proof against pain. Why should his be?

And Hobby is dead. Poor Hobby. It is a condemnation of me that whenever I think of Hobby my first regret is that he does not seem to have delivered my last note. Not that I know. It has not, so far as I know, been found on Hobby, but probably nobody looked. Why should they? Nobody, not even Edwin, seems to have suspected Hobby of any part in this. And Hobby seems to have bravely toiled about his duties in the stronghold until some time on the day Wolfram discovered the paper. Then, being unable to go on, he curled up at the corner of some stairway and died. They did not find him until the evening. Edwin told me that night, in the midst of all the other news, and thought no more of it than that it was very inconvenient of Hobby to go and die just then without giving anyone notice of his intention. I keep shocking myself by thinking the same callous thing in another way. Poor Hobby. He deserves better of me at least. Deluded he may have been, but his reliability and sang-froid amaze me now when I think of him. It is very bad not to accord him consideration in death, if not in life. Very bad. And yet, poor boy, he was one of those born not to be considered. I do not mean that he was a thrall (which Edwin tells me was indeed the case), I mean that he was simply humble and unlovely, as useful as a saw or a hammer – and just as you are irritated if the handle is loose on either of these, so you were irritated if Hobby showed any personal feelings about anything. Not fair. Not fair at all. I keep reminding myself that Hobby was a human being too.

Dear, how the days pass! I think Spring is here. The air is smooth and mild now. Edwin tells me the floods are abating. Hrinkle is preparing to be very vigorous in the Lowlands. But nothing has happened. I do not like this new boy of Edwin's. He is a knowing little beast, as nasty-minded as Edwin and as self-seeking as Wolfram. Ye gods, I miss Hobby. Every day that passes I miss him more. I had not realized what stoic values he quietly represented. Hobby gave me a faith in human nature that I find hard to hold to now.

Human nature? Faith? I don't know. I am in a stupid flutter, compounded of the wrong and the right reasons. What am I to make of this?

There were Edwin's steps on the stairs just now, and others, heavy and ringing, which I did not know. Then the door opens and Edwin appears, backwards, saying: 'This here's the one. Two minutes, mind. My time's not my own.' Then he lets edge in round him an enormous, soldierly man, and whisks away again, locking the door behind him.

The huge man stood there, staring round the room and at me, in a brisk, matter-of-fact way, and then gave me a nodding kind of bow – which is possibly customary here. He was very dark, as well as very big, and I must say I have seldom seen anyone with such firm, clean, kindly good looks. There was an air of cheerfulness and sanity about him which disconcerted me utterly – feeling, as I do, the opposite of both these days. Besides, it is such an age since I have been near a personable man – or a kindly one – that I seem to have forgotten how to behave. I blushed, ludicrously. It was ludicrous because, throughout our interview, the man was most tidily respectful and did not, quite evidently, find me interesting as a female. You know how you can tell. In my bad and fluttered state of mind, I have been looking earnestly in the mirror to see why. I can't. I do not look as dingy as I feel. Perhaps I am not his type. Such a pity – he was a regular charmer.

Anyway, fluttering apart, I had a distinct impression that I had seen the man before, but I could not imagine where. You would think him impossible to miss. 'Please, who are you?' I said.

'You may have seen me, lady,' he said. 'Guard on Asgrim, over the way there.'

And I said: 'Oh yes, of *course*!' He is the one I think of as Swart-one. He gives quite a different impression over the way – or gave it. Asgrim's personality always eclipsed his guards – or did. Maybe not now – but I don't want to think of it.

Then he said – Swart-one: I still don't know his name – a little awkwardly and pompously, as people like him do when they are delivering a message: 'He – prisoner in our charge – anxious to know if you are in health and asked me to do the errand.'

I was touched by that. It dawned on me that Asgrim, far from despising me, had no means of knowing that Wolfram had not turned on me later that day. I asked Swart-one to assure him that I was perfectly all right and, as I said, I wished I was not. For he is bound to despise me now, if he didn't before. How can he fail to? It looks so bad that I am left unharmed – I wonder if Wolfram meant it to, curse him. But, at the time, that was only a passing thought. I was much more anxious to know how Asgrim was. Yet I was so afraid of hearing terrible things, and so put out by Swart-one's clean cheerful presence, that I stammered out the enquiry in the most reluctant and guilty way. I hope Swart-one does not report in detail – but I think he won't: he didn't strike me as someone who was good at describing things.

He said reticently: 'Things have been bad over there.' I stammered out that I realized that. So he said, kindly: 'They're bettering. He's on his feet again now. We do our best for him, you know. You mustn't think too ill of us for what we did under orders.' He had such a monumental neutrality about him that I found myself looking down vistas of physical horror and felt quite ill. I said wretchedly that I quite understood, and that made him kinder than ever. 'I always do what I can for him,' he assured me. 'He's a man you have to look up to.'

'Even when he's insulting you?' I said. There was that scene in the yard. I remember clearly that Swart-one nearly hit Asgrim. But I'm afraid I said it out of pure desire to flatter Swart-one – or nearly pure: I didn't believe he was sincere in what he said.

And he grinned a loyal and affectionate grin – about this and other incidents, I suppose. 'Things he says, lady. He has a tongue like no one else – and we've had a deal of it lately, I can tell you. But, seeing how things are, we bear with it.'

It was altogether schoolboyish, the way he said that, in its genuine admiration. And I think the forbearance is genuine too. Asgrim is not so badly off as he might be. Swart-one said quite a bit more – all in his short stilted sentences and his odd clipped accent, which is Markwater speech, according to Edwin – both about his admiration and about the various comforts and small illicit freedoms he and his fellows have given Asgrim lately. It seems as if he and his fellows are prepared to do anything within reason for him. Or they are now. Much as I wished to think Swart-one sincere in all this, I couldn't help wondering how much of what he said had its origins in guilt. They helped reduce Asgrim to this state, after all. As to that state, it came through the clipped discourse rather clearly that Asgrim is sick and querulous

and behaving near-on as childishly as Kjarten. Nothing will
possess him to show gratitude. This is what Swart-one
principally admires him for. It doesn't strike me as admir-
able, but then think of the cause. He probably hates their
guts.

'And now nothing will please him,' says Swart-one, 'but
that one of us should bring you the writing. I said it should
be me. But have the goodness to say I brought you nothing
but word of mouth, lady.'

Of course I promised. He pulled this paper from his pocket
and gave it me. Then he knocked at the door and Edwin let
him out before I could find out whether Asgrim had written
it recently or long ago – I'm sure he hardly stayed the two
minutes Edwin specified. It is odd how such a short space can
bulk so large. I keep dwelling on his visit as if it had lasted
two hours. But I wish he had stayed long enough to tell me
when this verse was written. It is so hard to tell – except that
I doubt if Asgrim has paper these days. From its looks, it
could be the sheet Wolfram got out of the table. It is the
other half of the last drawing – curious: the only other half I
have had – of the man in the tree. Woden, of course. He
hanged himself on the world-tree in search of knowledge. I
have the rest of the Ash, the ravens, the well at its foot, and
the noose from which the god stiffly dangles. I shall put the
verse down shortly, once I have decided how and why it
came now.

No. It came openly, or nearly openly. It has the air of ends
tied up after the recent nasty mess. And it would not have
come if anyone thought it important. I can only conclude
that Asgrim told Hrinkle of his correspondence with me. I see
I have known he must have done, ever since Edwin told me,
but to find out this way is so shaming, is what I'm trying to
say; and in having my privacy in this burst apart, I see how
shamefully they burst his. I feel laid bare like a frog on a

board, so what must he feel? How *could* they? What can there be left? No. I think this must have been written long ago.

> But truth, which is another thing
> Aside from laws or words or time,
> Has strangely entered space,
> Lifting the clod from under
> Moving men from men asunder
> And only leaves us dying.
> Truth is the fire that fetches thunder,
> Kindled of itself, and only mine
> In the heart that had its fashioning.

I wish I knew what the hell it means. I get the feeling that it refers to a complete argument of which I am ignorant – terms, conclusions and all. Or it could be the private vision of a sick mind, which has meaning only for the sufferer – in which case it was written recently. But, in either case, what did he intend to tell me? It's important, I'm sure. I am certain he is trying to tell me what he found out on the treadmill – it has an air of finality, almost triumphant, which I would share if I could. But I can't understand. All I know is that it has brought hard before me Asgrim, grey and vivisected, trying to pull his mind together and come to terms with his captivity again. It moves me to a compassion so wretched that it hurts – a different order of feeling, utterly, than the flutters I keep feeling over Swart-one. How I can have the two feelings simultaneously beats me.

Something happened last night. I have been awake ever since, wondering. I wish Edwin would come, but it's only half an hour after sunrise. I shall have to wait an hour or so more to find out what it was. It's unbearable.

There was gunfire for an hour or more. I could see lights out of all three windows, and hear shouting. After a bit, a bell began to ring, insanely. Whoever rang it did not wait for the clapper to return to the centre of the bell, but went on wildly tugging away at the rope so that it banged back and forth, jangling, sometimes striking the bell, sometimes off balance and silent, and then hitting the bell again in a stutter of unresonating bangs. An alarm of some sort. It was clear the whole stronghold was aroused, from the lights and the yelling. Then those guns began. Ye gods! Is Mark besieged, or what? Things are quiet now. They fell quiet after a couple of hours of bedlam. There was a further burst of activity a little before dawn, nothing so loud as the first, and now silence. A cold, pink, silent dawn. Come quickly, Edwin, you garrulous old fool. I must know what has happened.

I can hardly believe it. Asgrim has escaped. I can't tell whether to call it desolate joy or splendid misery. He got away last night in that confusion, and it sounds as if it was all very carefully planned. How, I cannot think. And Edwin's narrative is so muddled – he was beside himself with excitement, and that wretched child Albert, his new help, muddled things further by telling me repeatedly how it was he who had rung the alarm bell.

'First thing I thought to do,' he kept saying. 'I was up there in my shirt, nothing but my shirt on, pulling away. Did you hear the great noise I made?'

I told him I did and to shut up, but he is not the child to shut up when he has something to boast of. So I had to listen to Edwin through his inane clamour, and I doubt if I have got Edwin's facts straight, let alone the truth of the matter.

I gather he laid out a guard and got out of a window, and thence over the roofs of the fortress to the town. Somebody helped him over the walls of the stronghold, because there was a rope-ladder found later. But, meanwhile, as soon as he was on his way, a man called Harold appeared in front of the town and launched some kind of attack on it. This was the first part of the noise. I suppose the idea was a diversion. Naturally, this aroused the remaining guards and Asgrim's escape was discovered. They assumed he had gone to join this man Harold and went racing off in the wrong direction. Edwin says everything was in frantic confusion for a couple of hours, until Harold was beaten off and chased northwards by the defending militia. And I gather it was a narrow squeak. Harold nearly took the town. Then, just before dawn, they found the rope-ladder on the other side of the stronghold, and there was a further pursuit, this time east-wards, in the right direction. But it seems Asgrim had by then got clear away. It sounds to have been a night of rare confusion. Edwin says Hrinkle has taken most of the troops away south with him, which accounts for Harold's near-success.

Lord, I am thankful Asgrim made it. When I consider what I have heard of the state of his mind and body, I can only call it miraculous. Edwin agrees with me. He persists in under-standing it even less than I do. It seems Wolfram is about to interrogate the five remaining guards – the sixth died this morning – and perhaps something will emerge from that.

Yes, something has emerged all right. I feel a bit rueful. Edwin is all scathing indignation spiced with covert ap-plause, and I must say it was cool of Asgrim. He obviously has not his reputation for nothing. It is now certain that he was not as badly hurt as he made everyone believe. He put on quite a performance of weakness, fretfulness and disorder of mind. He complained of obscure pains, and insisted that he had received some kind of internal injury – medicine, it seems, is not Mark's strong suit – and they swallowed it. The guards gave him their half-guilty sympathy and, if Swart-one is anything to go by, a good deal of admiration for his colourful grumbling. I am afraid they were truly taken in. It looks as if the arrangements for this escape were made through their innocent connivance. Edwin has not got the details yet, but he tells me that one of them actually procured him a file. They took messages, obligingly, which seemed innocuous but are now thought to have had a double meaning (I wish I knew what the one I got means). And they actually stood by while Asgrim exercised to ensure that he would be able to hoist himself on to the roof. Asgrim, it seems, would arise, grumbling and fretting, complaining of terrible stiffness and shooting pains in his side, and would declare that the only thing which eased it was to hang by his hands from a beam in one of the rooms. So they let him, appalled, so Edwin tells me, at the way the effort of it would send the sweat soaking through his clothes and filling his hair, and never guessing why it was done. It is such a splendid piece of opportunism that you would almost think Hrinkle did Asgrim a favour, injuring him. I could laugh. Though I wish it had not been Swart-one that Asgrim killed.

No news of Asgrim yet. But this Harold, whom I now find to be lord of Widburn where the massacres were, has gathered more troops and seems to be on his way east to Gardale. Hrinkle is hurrying back, but has not got here yet. And Wolfram today hanged a wretched tradesman – a baker, I believe – for sending Asgrim a cake by one of the guards, which is thought to have held the file.

No news today, either. There is another stasis. Hrinkle did not come here. He is posted between the old lady of the Lowlands and her other potential allies. Regan is after Harold before he can join Asgrim, but no one knows where Asgrim has got to.

Blight on everything. Wolfram has been here. He is a strange creature. I swear he came to be comforted – and how he has the gall to expect me to be social after— But I could see he was not at all sure of his welcome. He fidgeted and stood just inside the door and asked drearily how I was getting on – he was in his dreariest mood. And I was more than a little curt with him at first, until he became so unutterably hang-dog that I took pity on him.

We held stilted, semi-cordial conversation. He sat on a different chair, rather self-consciously, and said he thought it was all up with him as soon as Hrinkle came back. Hrinkle would never forgive him for Asgrim's escape, not in a thousand years, even though, he claims, he has acted with great firmness and decision. The firmness, I discovered, was the hanging of the unfortunate baker. And it became increasingly clear that it was the hangings that were upsetting Wolfram. He had hanged the baker and two of his apprentices, since none admitted to the file and each accused the others, and Wolfram, because he is now Governor of the town and stronghold (as a reward for his discovery of the paper), had had to be present at the execution. It had revolted him. He went away and was sick. Then he could not get it out of his mind. He stood it for two days and then came, if you please, to see if I could help him. It makes me wonder what the hell Wolfram thinks our relationship is. Perhaps he doesn't know either.

Anyway, there he was twisting his warty hands and

fidgeting his great limp legs and asking me to help him forget it. How could I? He has killed three people in cold blood and will have to take the consequences. All I could say was that perhaps he would think twice before he ordered another hanging. And he said fervently that he would.

Then we got on to the cause of the hangings and, as usual, Wolfram has made the vivid thing commonplace and given plain facts a dreary oddity. He has made Asgrim sound so cynical, so calculating. 'I suppose,' says Wolfram, 'he must have thought it worth all those lives. Hrinkle will hang the five guards, thou knows, and one is dead already. Then there's the three bakers, twenty or so helpers we've not found yet, and all Harold's folk if we had caught them. He must be sure of his worth, don't thou think?'

I said something about the organization involved. Wolfram said it was luck, and ruthlessness. We had something of an argument. Wolfram agreed that Harold's attack was pre-arranged and said, in a numb kind of way, that Asgrim must have been able to get more messages out than people had realized. But not, he said, after he and Hrinkle found the paper. He assures me that the famous messages Edwin thought the guards carried were entirely to ask for essential things from the town, all of them quite innocent, such as fresh clothes and new shoes. The cake was the only thing which was not what it seemed.

'No,' he said. 'It was all planned long ago. And, if you ask me, he was lucky to get away with it. Very lucky. The way I read it, the time was fixed around Yule or thereabouts, and when it came he had to up and go, or lose all, whatever shape he was in.'

'He was in bad shape, then?' I said.

'Oh yes,' said Wolfram. 'Very bad shape. Hrinkle did him a deal of harm over the three days.'

My stomach turns over to think of the dull calm way

Wolfram talked of that. But it was not like the hangings. He didn't see it. Hrinkle sent him away and he only heard about it afterwards. I asked him, and he admitted, with shamed shiftings, that Hrinkle knew he would never stand it. I was furious, all the same, and I was going to tell him so if he had not forestalled me by being indignant on his own account.

'Asgrim makes me sick,' he said. 'All that false confession and cringing and whimpering – play-acting not to get hurt so that he'd be fit to climb when the time came. I'd be ashamed. And what makes me so angry, rarely so angry, is that for all he knew Hrinkle would kill Kjarten as soon as he was gone. *He* didn't know Kjarten was free. You can be sure we kept that from him.'

I wish now I had told Wolfram of my last message. I wish I had pretended I knew for certain Asgrim had got it. I would do anything rather than think so badly of Asgrim, or have Wolfram think it. If he got that message, then it was almost as if I gave him the all-clear and of course he was free to escape. That's how I hope it was. Or Hobby could have told him. But I wish I knew. I can't help thinking that the man who could quietly bash Swart-one's head in might well be quite as ruthless over Kjarten. Oh no. I am convinced that Kjarten's escape was Stage-One in a plan they probably settled over Yule, and that Stage-Two depended on Asgrim hearing, somehow, of Kjarten's safety. And perhaps that had nothing to do with me either.

But I do think Wolfram is right about the rest, the more I consider it. Asgrim, far from using his injuries to get the sympathy of the guards, was nearly prevented by Wolfram's discovery from following out the plans of some months. He has been lucky, and I can only hope he is not suffering too much. But the evidence is clear enough. The fact that I had just half of so many different pictures suggests that many more messages went (perhaps through Hobby) than ever came to me. And the nature of his messages to me suggests that his mind was turning to what he could do once he got out of Mark. I fancy that the quarrels he used to pick with Swart-one and the other guards were part of the scheme. Maybe they were to end up by knocking him down – and then guiltily playing the part they actually played for other reasons. How shall I ever know?

But I wish Wolfram had not been and put all this into my head. It leaves a bad taste. I feel hurt, bitterly and unreasonably, that Asgrim should have been thinking of so many things beside me. I feel afraid, because I don't know how far he is ruthless and how far lucky. I would give the earth to know just a little more.

Just a little more! Ye gods! This last week we have heard nothing but Asgrim. Life here is as changed as it is in the rest of the country.

The day after Wolfram came to see me, the country went mad. Asgrim was in Gardale, and Kjarten with him, and they were appealing for all who wore alvery to come to their side. All who wore it came and, Edwin says, many more besides. A large number of people went from Mark and all the remaining soldiers deserted. The North climbed off its fence at last and marched down to aid Asgrim. Wolfram says that at least three-quarters of the population is mustering to Hathriver. Hrinkle was beaten in a battle here – or quite near here – yesterday, before he had time to throw himself into the stronghold, and rumour has it that Asgrim cut his throat in person in the course of it. Now it is the merest mopping up – a much simpler business than Hrinkle had of it.

We in Mark are in a very strange position. For three days, Wolfram was preparing to stand a siege and let Hrinkle in as soon as he got here. Then, on the fourth day, Hrinkle sent

word that he would fight on the plains to the south-west, so
the preparations relaxed a little. But the old lady of the
Lowlands, and Hilda's lot, sallied out from west and south
and forced Hrinkle northwards into the arms of the people
mustering at Hathriver. The next news we had was that
Hrinkle had turned back and was flying for his life here to
Mark, with Asgrim, Harold and the main man from the
North all hard on his heels. People jumped into action here
again. But, as I said, they caught Hrinkle. There is only Regan
to account for now. The whole emphasis of the operation has
shifted north and west, and Mark seems to have been
bypassed. We seem to have lost all our significance. We
huddle in this backwater, waiting, and nothing happens.

I see I have written 'We' all the time. Quite in Wolfram's
manner of accepting without comment the true state of
affairs. We are in this together, the people in this fortress and
I. All of us forgotten, hushed and hopeless. I don't know why
I go on writing this, except out of habit. There is no longer
any need to defy or outwit the powers that be.

Wolfram was here this morning. He came just after Edwin
had been and told me about Hrinkle's defeat, with Albert
chirpily and obsequiously butting in all through.

Edwin was scared, but in a twitter of excitement all the
same. 'Mark's finished,' he kept saying. 'I don't know where
I shall turn. We shall all be dead this time next week, as soon
as Asgrim gets here.' He was farting and belching, I think
with sheer apprehension, and ashamed of it for once. He said
troubles always made him bilious, and actually apologized.
Then he reiterated that he knew not where to turn, and the
rest. But I cut in and said Couldn't he run away? 'Nowhere
to run to,' he said. 'Countryside's against us. Mark's against
us. We must wait for our weird.'

'There's no quarter for us Hrinkle's men,' says Albert
smugly. 'We're all dead men now.'

Trust Albert to swank about even this, cocksure little devil.
I don't suppose for a moment Albert has visualized himself
actually dying. He'd sing another tune if he had. Edwin has
visualized it, vividly. He is scared stiff, but it adds wonderfully to his notion of poor old ill-treated Edwin.

Wolfram, to do him justice, is a good deal more dignified.
He came in very quietly and wandered about the room a
little. After a while, he remarked: 'Hrinkle's dead. Did they
tell thee?'

I said, rather awkwardly, that Edwin had said so and that it
was hard on Wolfram.

'Oh,' he said, 'not really. I'd been expecting it. And I never
liked him much.' Then he wandered a little more and said:
'There's nothing to do now but wait.'

'For Asgrim to come?' I said – and when I think of the
vibrating hope with which I asked that question I can hardly
credit it, even now. The hope I have lived in this week shakes
me still, like a great machine, and it will not stop although it
is driving nothing.

Wolfram said thoughtfully, neutrally: 'No. Asgrim won't
come here. He has bigger things to see to. We've no troops to
speak of and we can't harm him, thou sees.'

I said, and I do not know how I managed to enunciate it:
'Are you sure?'

'Quite sure,' he said. 'Why should he come? He has the
rest of the land to settle first. After that, he may deal out
justice to such as remain in Mark. We shall have to wait for
that.'

How could I have not jumped up and screamed at him for
his patience? All I did was sit there like a stuffed thing,
saying: 'Is there really nothing to be done?'

'Nothing,' says Wolfram. 'We've lost, Emily. Thou knows
that.'

We neither of us said anything for a while. I have been

thinking about that strange, quiet space. Wolfram stood by
the hearth and I sat in the chair, and we were both quite
aware of the true state of affairs. It was in Wolfram's most
characteristic manner. He knew how I felt and I knew how
he felt, and neither of us had struggled for the knowledge.
Wolfram had just let me know it was there, because it was
there, and I know it never occurred to him to dissemble.
Wolfram never dissembles – this is the odd thing about him.
He has called me *thou* and now by my true name, because he
feels genuinely friendly towards me. I see now that he did
not set Hrinkle on me too, not to injure me with Asgrim, but
because it never occurred to him to harm me. I am his friend.
And of course he is quite right. I may struggle fretfully to
deny it, but I feel just the same towards Wolfram. I could
have harmed him over Kjarten, but I never dreamt of doing
so. He is my friend. What a weird and comfortless thing to
know. But it is plain truth, like the other.

We have both lost. He's right. But he did not get it really
home to me until he was, rather aimlessly, leaving the room.
Then he stopped, with the door half open, and said: 'Does
thou want to come down? There's no need for thee to be
locked up now, thou knows.'

I couldn't go. I couldn't face it just then. It was too much. I
thanked him and asked if I might come out later.

'When thou likes,' he said, and went off, leaving the door
ajar. I have been sitting in the draught from it all this time,
trying to muster courage to go through it.

I did it. I have been out and around the castle these last two
days. It is the strangest feeling to be this much free, and quite
exhausting. I have had to retreat back here from time to
time, as if it were home, away from the overwhelming size
and barrenness of the place. There is scarcely anyone here.

The few of us who are left tend to gather in the kitchens, where there is a fire, a certain amount of food, and an ill-tempered cook. I eat there now and watch Edwin picking sickeningly at his teeth, Albert guzzling, and Wolfram drearily munching. Supplies are short, even for our small number. I suppose we shall starve in the end.

The rest of the castle is nothing but acres of stone floors, passages, stairs and rooms. People have left belongings here and there as they fled. I came across a purse full of gold coins in the soldiers' quarters yesterday, but nobody wants it. As Edwin said, what good is it to us? They are Hrinkle's currency, and even if the townspeople would deal with us, it is not legal tender any more. Currency is being made in all the other provinces now, and you have to use that. Albert says they would rather have a Northern penny or a Hathriver farthing than this whole purse of Mark gold.

Wolfram says there are rumours that Regan has been defeated somewhere in the north-west.

Yes, the rumours are confirmed today. Asgrim is moving south again. The vibrations of my unquelled hope have driven me to a desperate exploration. I have been to visit his prison. I wish I had not gone. The truth hurts so.

Asgrim had a prison entirely appropriate to him. He knew what was fitting, what was due to himself. I found a suite of rooms, three or four times the size of mine, grandiose with vaulted ceilings and great arched fireplaces. They have put back most of the furniture and roughly reassembled it, so that the rooms give an empty impression of what they were like when he was there. They are rich and comfortable. Except for the bars on the windows, you would think you were in a section of some Stately Home. I wandered about, feeling Asgrim's personality forcibly – more forcibly, I think, than ever before. I could see him writing at the big table, glancing at the guards, and seizing his chance to slip his charred paper into its framework. I could see him sitting on the couch, standing by the fireplace, washing in the ornate bowl outside his bedroom. I could see Kjarten screwing up drawings and tossing them into that wide, cold grate, and Asgrim, I think, rescuing them unobtrusively with the heel of his shoe, keeping up a heavy, decorous calmness while he did it.

'Decorous' is a word that comes in well here. I think it was the *decorum* of those rooms which oppressed me most. There was nothing that was not somehow fitting for the home of a great man, from the patterned carpets to the sombre embroidered covers of his large square bed. It is all right, proper, noble, and nothing to do with me. The guards had camp-beds in his bedroom and just outside it. The one in the bedroom was very near Asgrim's bed. It must have been an easy matter to lean out and smash the iron bar down on Swart-one's head. I could see the space where he took the bar out of the window too. Economically done. Cool, courageous and lucky. The guards outside swore they heard nothing until it was too late.

Yes, for all these rooms had seen miseries and horrors, what they show you is austere grandeur. There is little joy and no kindness in them. You feel the pressure of Asgrim's overriding purpose there. He meant to free first his son and then himself, and then to take his revenge. He did so. And nothing would possess him to come back. You feel that too. There was no sign that he was happy – indeed, it is certain he never could have been, not more than momentarily – and no sign that he was ever doubtful. I begin to see that the impression he gave of inviolate strength was due to the very certainty of his intentions. Oh, these rooms are cold and grand and hard in a way that makes me shudder. And if this is what he is like, whatever possessed him to trifle with me?

The door to the courtyard was unlocked. I went out there for a minute. It is much bigger than I realized. Asgrim had to walk in a very small portion of it if he was to see me. I looked over to my place. It seems somewhat above his, inadequate and insecure. My door is low and lopsided, what I can see of it, and anyone walking in my court must look as if they are treading the edge of a precipice. It is very cheerless. No wonder he pitied me – for I think he did. You can see the apple-tree much more clearly from his court. It is all bursting pale green buds, with the blossom getting pink between just now. But I am a fool to believe Edwin. It can't be a pippin: you have to graft them. It is nothing more than a meagre little crab-apple, seeded by some bird.

This week is hell. Hell. Edwin goes in hourly expectation of hearing Asgrim is crowned king. Even Wolfram admits it is likely.

No news of a coronation yet, but a council has been set up of those lordships who survived the fighting, or their heirs, and the aldermen of every town except Mark. Aldorman is like Mayor. The marks are all being restored and reinstated, under further lords and councils. Wolfram shakes his head and says glumly that Asgrim is trying to put the clock back and that it won't do. He says that after all the upheaval you can't put things back to what they were two generations ago, especially now all the thralls are freed. I don't know. It looks to me as if Asgrim is trying to do what I suggested in my last note. But I can't believe it. I can't, not with Mark itself abandoned like this, almost as if town and citadel were left to die. We are almost the only people in the area now. Edwin gets news by going out on the main road and accosting travellers.

And I still hope. This is such stupidity. I cannot believe that

a man with Asgrim's regard for integrity would do this to me,
even though I know he has done it. I have been severe with
myself. I have gone through my writing, and I have seen I
never wrote him anything that was not cautious and a little
cold. He must think I never cared. Perhaps he thinks I
betrayed him to Wolfram. But I believe it does not matter to
him what I think, for the more I consider it, the clearer it is to
me that I was just an object, out beyond his prison, on which
he hung some of the feelings he had no other outlet for. Is
this always the way things are? Do we never know anyone
better than this? The gods alone know.

But I think it was not quite like that. I suspect that my
ignorance of the country and its language has led me to be
taken in by a nice play – a sort of courtly love. I am sure of it.
Asgrim never once called me *thou*. It was all ceremonious
and respectful and distant. And the verses he wrote made it
clear, from the start, that what he wanted to feel was a
something-else, metaphysical, large and abstract, that only
ever, at the most, included me along with the rest of his
world. The last one he sent says as much:

> '. . . the fire that fetches thunder,
> Kindled of itself . . .'

Which is as much as to say: 'I have induced in myself all the
feelings I had about you, although you may be a nice girl,
and you have certainly taught me one or two things I shall go
away and use to advantage.' Or is that too cynical?

I think he never meant to be dishonest. I'm sure he
imagined I knew the conventions. But all this talk of Truth.
Even in this land it means more than one thing – reality,
fidelity, integrity, knowledge of your ideal – but then they
only have the one word for all these things. Did Asgrim
know, for a moment, that he was playing with this word? I
think I knew, but I hid it from myself. I thought he meant

fidelity, but now I see it was the only thing he didn't mean. He used Truth for all the others, impartially. And I understood him to that extent, but wouldn't see it.

Yet I believe he cared. I *know* he cared. He took risks enough to make that obvious. Even though we could never get near one another, he felt something. He may have decided it was impossible and unreal – as I see now it was – but then what is possible, what is real, what is true? This was a terrible waste of feeling.

They tell me Asgrim married Hilda yesterday. Did he need to do that? Edwin says he wishes him joy of it – Hilda is supposed to be in love with her brother. I think, from what I saw, that may be true. A bad end to a wretched business. I have no heart to write any more today.

Other Vista Fantasy titles include

Lady in Gil Rebecca Bradley   0 575 60190 6

Golden Witchbreed Mary Gentle   0 575 60033 0

Ancient Light Mary Gentle   0 575 60112 4

The Tough Guide to Fantasyland Diana Wynne Jones
0 575 60106 X

A Sudden Wild Magic Diana Wynne Jones   0 575 60197 3

The Blue Manor Jenny Jones   0 575 60010 1

Hawkwood's Voyage Paul Kearney   0 575 60034 9

The Heretic Kings Paul Kearney   0 575 60186 8

Terry Pratchett's Discworld Quizbook
David Langford   0 575 60000 4

A Land Fit for Heroes vol 3: The Dragon Wakes
Phillip Mann   0 575 60012 8

A Land Fit for Heroes vol 4: The Burning Forest
Phillip Mann   0 575 60070 5

Eric Terry Pratchett   0 575 60001 2

The Discworld Companion Terry Pratchett and
Stephen Briggs   0 575 60030 6

The Gates of Noon Michael Scott Rohan   0 575 60032 2

Cloud Castles Michael Scott Rohan   0 575 60023 3

The Lord of Middle Air Michael Scott Rohan   0 575 60234 1

VISTA books are available from all good bookshops or from:
Cassell C.S.
Book Service By Post
PO Box 29, Douglas I-O-M
IM99 1BQ
telephone: 01624 675137, fax: 01624 670923

VISTA